No one loved Ame~~~
more than Mack Bola~~

No one cherished the ideals on which she was founded more than he did. "The land of the free and the home of the brave" was more than a catchphrase. It was an ideal by which he lived. To him freedom was everything and defending it wasn't just a right, but the basic responsibility of every citizen.

Bolan knew sacrifice was called for. The defense of liberty came with a cost, and he had given up more than most.

He had no illusions about war. It was a deadly, dirty business. Those who glorified it were usually those who had never been in uniform. Warfare didn't deserve to be extolled. Rather, it was the selfless service of the men and women who willingly gave their lives for their country that should be glorified. They were the genuine heroes, one and all.

Don Pendleton's Mack
Bolan®
Age of War

A GOLD EAGLE BOOK FROM
WORLDWIDE®

TORONTO • NEW YORK • LONDON
AMSTERDAM • PARIS • SYDNEY • HAMBURG
STOCKHOLM • ATHENS • TOKYO • MILAN
MADRID • WARSAW • BUDAPEST • AUCKLAND

First edition May 2003

ISBN 0-373-61490-X

Special thanks and acknowledgment to
David Robbins for his contribution to this work.

AGE OF WAR

Thus, what is of supreme importance in war is to attack the enemy's strategy.

—Sun Tzu,
The Art of War

I have to outthink as well as outfight those who would destroy our freedom. If I don't stay one step ahead of them, I've lost before the battle begins.

—Mack Bolan

PROLOGUE

Pakistan

Malik Sharik enjoyed killing Americans. Killing smug Britishers and those arrogant French brought some degree of satisfaction. Killing Israelis, the bitter enemies of his people, was always a treat. But there was something about killing Americans that brought a special sort of pleasure. When he killed an American, it was as if he inflicted a wound on Satan himself. For after all, wasn't America the Great Satan? The nation through which the Evil One was trying to gain mastery of the world?

Unfortunately, to date, Sharik hadn't been able to indulge his passion as often as he liked. His tally stood at four British, three French, twenty-one Israelis and two Americans. But all that was about to change. He was about to help kill several more, and he couldn't be happier.

Twilight was falling on Islamabad, Pakistan. Its narrow streets were choked with pedestrians and vehicles. From Sharik's vantage point on the roof of an apartment building that overlooked the opulent home of the finance minister, a river of humanity flowed for as far as the eye could see.

Malik checked his wristwatch. It was a little past six. The banquet was slated to begin at seven, so he could expect the guests to start arriving shortly. Time to verify everyone was in position. Reaching down, he tweaked the volume control on the Audionic walkie-talkie clipped to his belt. The latest model, it had a squelch feature that completely eliminated background noise and a transceiver that automatically switched between the send and receive modes. Al-Jabbar's deep pockets had its benefits.

"Report," Malik said.

"Tac One, ready," Hakim said from his position at the rear of the walled grounds. "No guards visible."

"Tac Two, ready," announced Thabit, who was on the balcony of an apartment on a side street. "Two guards visible on a patio. Another at a second floor window."

"Tac Three, ready," Bahira reported from her post directly across from the front gate. "Four guards at the gate. Two more along the drive. They aren't paying any attention to me."

Looking due south, Malik could see Thabit, the young Egyptian, prone on the balcony, a blanket pulled over him and the Vektor R-4 assault rifle he was armed with. Only Thabit's nose and part of his face showed.

Malik could also see Bahira, off to his right. She was dressed in traditional attire, in a burqa complete with a veil and headpiece, and had set up a fig display across from the front gate. To all intents and purposes she was a typical street vendor. No one would suspect that in one of those barrels of figs was a Beretta AR 70/90. He had given her the post of honor, as it was called. It was her job to kill the American ambassador.

Sharik was north of the minister's home. That way they had all four points of the compass covered. In the unlikely event Bahira failed, he and Thabit both had clear lines of fire and could finish what she started.

Frankly Sharik would much rather have placed a bomb in one of the fig barrels or in the house itself, but he had his orders. And it wouldn't be wise to defy the will of Aban Abbas. Not if he wanted to go on breathing.

Strange, Sharik thought, how he could both admire and fear a man at the same time. He had the highest respect for the founder of Al-Jabbar. Abbas was a great man. His vision of a world ruled by Islam, a world without infidels, was dear to Sharik's heart. He hated the false religion of the Western nations as much as Abbas did. They were brothers of the spirit in that regard.

Yet kindred spirits or no, Sharik was under no delusions. If he inadvertently angered Abbas, the consequences would be swift and severe. He had to always be careful what he said and what he did. Their leader didn't tolerate incompetence, laziness or failure. Or anything that smacked of heresy or blasphemy.

He remembered all too vividly the fate of the Syrian, Haji, whose fondness for nightclubs and women did not sit well with the great man. Sharik had tried to warn Haji, discreetly, of course, that he had to be more diligent in his prayers and devotions. But Haji couldn't be bothered.

One night the Syrian had the supreme stupidity to return to the compound well after midnight with a loose woman in tow. Aban Abbas was furious. He had the woman forcibly removed, then called Haji into his office. Sharik had been there, along with the other lieutenants. The others had no idea what was going to occur, but Sharik did. He had been with Abbas the longest. He knew the man as well as he knew himself.

Abbas had smiled and bid Haji take a seat. In polite, reserved tones he told the younger man how disappointed he was. How he had hoped Haji could control his baser impulses and become a credit to their "family of dedicated brothers and sisters willing to sacrifice themselves for the greater good of the cause." Then Aban walked around the desk, talking all the while as a father might to a wayward son. Never once raising his voice, never once appearing to be angry.

Haji, the fool, had laughed. He said that while he wanted to stamp out the Great Satan as much as the next man, there were certain things in life just as important. Certain needs that had to be met.

Abbas smiled, clapped Haji on the shoulder and said, "We all do what we must, my brother." And just like that, Abbas drew a dagger from under his sleeve and slit Haji's throat from ear to ear.

It had taken them half the next day to clean the blood.

No, Sharik would sooner leap into a blazing furnace than anger Aban Abbas. So if the man insisted on "the personal touch," as he so often phrased it, rather than use bombs or chemical weapons, who was Sharik to argue?

The growl of an engine intruded on his reverie. Raising his head above the coping, he saw the first limousine approach the gate. It bore the flag of the Spanish ambassador. "This isn't the one," he said into his earphone mouthpiece.

"Do you think I don't know that?" Bahira's voice crackled in his ear.

Malik frowned. He never had understood why Abbas permitted women in the organization. Their place was in the home, raising children and tending to their husbands' needs. But Abbas insisted that anyone willing to martyr themselves was welcome. Male or female, young or old and any nationality under the sun.

Bahira was Afghan. Her brother, a member of the Taliban, had been killed along with more than a dozen others when an American cruise missile struck their headquarters. Ever since, Bahira's sole purpose in life was to destroy as many Americans as she could. She had asked Abbas for the honor of eliminating the ambassador, and their leader consented.

Sharik wouldn't have. Not that he thought she couldn't do the job. Bahira had already proven herself willing and capable. Six months ago in Bombay she sprayed a nightclub with autofire, killing nine American servicemen. Prior to that, she had been involved in the assassination of several prominent American businessmen in Saudi Arabia.

Sharik had no problem with her commitment. It was her personality. Bahira grated on him like sandpaper on metal. She was always carping, criticizing, arguing. Other members of Al-Jabbar were of the opinion her bitterness was the result of her brother's death. Sharik believed it was her natural disposition. She had been born a shrew and never saw fit to change.

Another limousine was crawling up the jammed street. This one brought the British ambassador.

Sharik shifted his legs to relieve a cramp. He had been sitting cross-legged for almost an hour, his Ameli machine gun hidden under a blanket beside him. It would stay covered until their target arrived. Otherwise someone might spot it and call the police.

The apartment building was eight stories high, tall by Islamabad standards. But a couple of blocks to the north was another building twenty stories high. To the northeast sat a mosque, to the southeast reared a hill covered with the homes of the poorer class. They all overlooked the apartment building, and Sharik.

A third limo rounded an intersection several blocks away. From the antenna fluttered a small American flag.

"Here he comes," Malik said into the microphone. "May God be with us." Lifting the blanket so he could slide partly under it, he adjusted the Ameli's bipod. Of Spanish manufacture, it had the reputation of being one of the best light machine guns on the market. He had used it several times during the past year, and it never let him down. With a cyclic rate of 1200 rounds a minute, low recoil and accurate inbuilt sights, it was ideal for tactical situations like this.

"I have our quarry spotted," Bahira said. Rising from her stool, she bent over the fig barrel containing the autorifle and pretended to rummage through the figs.

To the south Thabit had sat up.

Sharik thought of the headlines that would blare across the globe the following day: American Ambassador Slain by Terrorists, and grinned. It was yet another blow against the Great Satan that defiled every Arab nation through its unending manipulation of governments and events. Yet another clear message to the evil elite who would rule the earth that the holy warriors of Islam were wise to their wickedness and would oppose them at every turn.

The American ambassador's limo was only two blocks off.

Sharik lived for the day when Muslims everywhere would awaken to the peril they were in. To the day when a Jihad against the United States was launched, not by a lone provincial government, as in the Taliban's case, but by every Arab government in the world. An irresistible tide of righteousness that would not only bring the Great Satan to its knees, but wipe it from existence.

One more block and the limo would be there. The gate was open wide, guards flanking either side.

Bahira plunged her right arm into the fig barrel. Her back was to the gate, and the guards didn't notice.

Sharik centered the Ameli on the men at the gate. They were his responsibility. Bahira's was the ambassador and whoever was in the limo with him. Thabit was backup, should it be needed. As for Hakim, as soon as he heard shots he was to get to their vehicle and be ready to race for the airport the instant they joined him.

The limo turned into the driveway and braked. The driver's window started to lower, no doubt so he could show the appropriate credentials.

As he always did on the cusp of a kill, Sharik tingled from head to toe. Another few seconds and all their careful planning would pay off. The people on the street had no inkling of what was about to unfold. Men, women and children were going about their daily routines oblivious to the angel of death hovering over them. Malik knew innocent bystanders might be slain in the cross fire, but their lives were of no consequence when balanced in the scales against the goals of Al-Jabbar.

Bahira pulled the Beretta AR 70/90 from the fig barrel. The bipod and carrying handle had been removed and the stock shortened to make it more compact and easier to use. Holding it close against the folds of her loose-fitting dress, she swiveled toward the limo and started briskly across the street.

One of the guards had bent toward the limo's open window. It was the moment Bahira had been waiting for. Snapping the Beretta into firing postion, she ran toward the vehicle. Or started to. For she had barely taken two steps when the top of her head exploded in a shower of gore and brains and she was slammed off her feet by the impact of a heavy-caliber slug.

Sharik couldn't say what made him do what he did next. Throwing off the blanket, he threw himself to the left and scrambled toward the roof access door. It saved his life. Glancing back, he saw the blanket buck into the air as if plucked by invisible hands, and heard the *thwip* of a slug. He reached the door and rose into a crouch before the sniper could fire again.

One fact was apparent. Whoever shot Bahira and tried to shoot him was north of their positions, and higher up than he was. Which told him there was only one spot the shots could come from—the twenty-story building due north of him.

Shouts and screams rose from the street. Pedestrians were milling about in fear, and two of the guards were rushing toward Bahira.

Sharik glanced to the south. Thabit had jumped to his feet and was aiming at the limousine. Suddenly Thabit stumbled against the wall as if he had tripped. He looked around wildly, staggered back to the rail and raised his assault rifle once more. A second round stiffened him like a board. The Vektor fell from his limp fingers and clattered over the rail. A moment later he pitched after it.

Belatedly Sharik realized he hadn't heard any of the shots. The sniper had to be using a sound suppressor. Exercising extreme caution, he put his left eye to the edge of the door casing. He saw nothing to indicate where the sniper might be. Ducking back, he slid to the other side and tried again.

For a fleeting moment a figure was silhouetted on the roof of the twenty-story building. Sharik couldn't tell much other than the sniper had dark hair and was wearing a long black coat. The man disappeared, and he took that as his cue to do the same. Sirens were wailing in the distance. Soon the area would swarm with police.

Dashing to the blanket, Malik wrapped the Ameli in it and turned to flee. A crowd had gathered around Bahira, and a policeman was directing traffic past her body. As much as he disliked the shrew, Sharik never wanted anything like this to happen.

Bahira and Thabit, both. He shuddered to think how their leader would react. Aban Abbas didn't take it well when his followers were slain or imprisoned. The last time it happened, when the Jordanians had the audacity to arrest an Al-Jabbar member implicated in the bombing of an American attaché, Abbas had the four men who took him into custody assassinated.

Sharik barreled down six of the eight flights, then abruptly slowed. An older man and woman were descending the stairs ahead of him, and he didn't care to arouse suspicion by barging past them. Chafing at the delay, he followed them to the lobby, then hurried past and out the front door.

Moving left, into an alley, Sharik broke into a run. There was still a chance. The sniper wouldn't want to draw attention to himself, either, and it was possible the man hadn't reached ground level yet.

The terrorist was still half a block away when he saw the tall man in the trench coat step from a side entrance, walk to a brown sedan and climb in. In the sniper's right hand was a long green duffel bag. The man gunned the engine and drove off.

Again Sharik had only a glimpse. But this time it was enough to establish that the sniper was a big man with hard features, and from the looks of him, a foreigner. Sharik slid his cellular phone from his jacket and pressed Send. There was no use in delaying. Abbas had to be told.

Whoever the sniper was, he had better be on his guard. Because Al-Jabbar avenged its own. They wouldn't rest until they tracked the man down and repaid blood for blood.

CHAPTER ONE

Greece

The Executioner wasn't in the best of moods.

Mack Bolan didn't mind when the Feds wanted to whisk him to Greece on short notice. They had reliable intel pointing to a hit on the vice-president by the terrorist organization known as Al-Jabbar, which Bolan had been out to shut down for some time now. He was glad to have another crack at them. The last time had been in Islamabad, Pakistan, when he thwarted an attempt to kill the American ambassador. The attempted hit did go down, but Bolan had been able to kill two of the terrorists and scatter the others. The vice-president had been unscathed.

But Bolan did mind when an operation was botched. Hal Brognola, director of the covert Sensitive Operations Group, had told him the Greek military would see to it none of the terrorists escaped. Roadblocks were supposed to be thrown up and the villa cordoned off the moment Bolan told them to, which the Executioner did the instant he spotted the four terrorists coming over the hill south of the vineyards. But the Greek liaison officer waiting in the villa, the one who was to relay the word to nearby military units, claimed he never received the message.

Bolan wasn't prone to show his anger, but he came awful close when he heard the news. He'd been assured complete cooperation. The liaison, a colonel in the Greek army, had seemed sincere and competent. Colonel Haralambos met him at the Athens airport and drove him to the villa where they made plans to lay their trap. The President had already been in contact with the vice-president and instructed him and his entourage to vacate the premises until further notice.

It was Colonel Haralambos who supplied Bolan with a handheld military radio to contact him at the appropriate moment. At the Executioner's request, they even tested the radios to be sure they worked.

So what could have gone wrong? That was what Bolan wondered until he checked the officer's radio and discovered the batteries had gone dead. The colonel apologized profusely, but the harm had been done. Two of the terrorists made good their escape, much to Bolan's disappointment.

Now the soldier was on his way back to his hotel, his fingers wrapped around the steering wheel and his mind trying to wrap itself around the problem of Al-Jabbar. The organization had been in existence only about a decade and had a remarkable string of assassinations to its credit. As best the Feds could determine, the total stood at forty-one with maybe a dozen unconfirmed possibles.

No one could say for sure because Al-Jabbar never claimed credit for their kills. They were a secretive group, their leader's identity unknown, their membership roster a complete mystery. Intel suggested they had a headquarters, but the Feds couldn't pinpoint its location.

Bolan considered them the most dangerous group of terrorists out there. They weren't as high profile as some; they didn't go in for publicity. And they had the dubious distinction of never targeting civilians. But all that only showed they were all business, pros who went about their lethal trade quietly and efficiently.

Some U.S. government officials downplayed the threat Al-Jabbar posed. In their eyes, since the group never blew up buildings or indulged in bio terror, they weren't to be taken quite as seriously. As an undersecretary at the Defense Department was quoted in a magazine as saying, "These are second-rate gunmen. They go around shooting people. It's not as if anyone should lose any sleep over them."

In Bolan's estimation the undersecretary had it backward. It was precisely because they selectively targeted important individuals—and never failed—that they *were* a force to be reckoned with. At least, they hadn't failed until Bolan put himself on their scent. Twice now he had foiled them. But it wasn't enough. He wanted to track them to their lair and put them out of business permanently.

The Stadium Hotel overlooked the magnificent sports stadium Athens boasted. Bolan's room was on the seventh floor. He threw his duffel on the bed, tossed his trench coat over a chair and went into the bathroom.

He was unzipping his shaving kit when there was a knock on the door. Setting the kit on the sink, he drew his Beretta 93-R from its holster under his left arm. From a slender pocket in his combat blacksuit he slid a sound suppressor and quickly threaded it onto the barrel. Cat-footing over to the door, he leaned against the jamb.

The knock was repeated.

"Who is it?" Bolan demanded. He wasn't expecting anyone and it always paid to take precautions.

"Mr. Belasko?"

Belasko was the cover name Bolan was using for this mission. He recognized the voice but could think of no conceivable reason for the man to be there.

"Mr. Belasko? It is I, Colonel Haralambos. I need to speak with you, if you please."

Bolan twisted the lock, gripped the knob and slowly eased the door open an inch. "This is unexpected."

"My apologies, but I have news of the utmost urgency. Maybe I come in?"

"By all means." Bolan pushed the door wide and let the colonel walk past. He scanned the hall before closing the door to verify the Greek was alone.

Haralambos was a short, stocky man in the twilight of his career. He had an olive complexion, beefy cheeks and bushy eyebrows. His uniform was immaculate and neatly pressed. The overhead light glistened on his balding pate when he removed his hat and stood at attention.

"What can I do for you, Colonel?" Bolan prodded when the man just stood there.

Haralambos glanced at the Beretta, then coughed to clear his throat. "I would like to atone for my negligence. It was remiss of me not to check the batteries before taking those units into the field."

"Mistakes happen," Bolan said to be polite. Although in this case the mistake bordered on out-and-out stupidity.

"You are too charitable. Because of me, two seasoned terrorists got away. Every life they take from this day on will be on my conscience. I would rather not live with that burden if it can be helped."

Bolan folded his arms across his chest. "You mentioned something about news?"

"Yes. Not two minutes after you left the villa, I received a call. My people have uncovered a lead. We might know where the two terrorists are right this minute. If you'd like, I will take you there."

Warning bells jangled in Bolan's mind. After the radio fiasco he had no reason to trust Haralambos and every reason to suspect he might be on the take. Terrorists sometimes paid military officers and police large sums of money to look the other way. It could be the colonel was leading him into a trap. "Take me where?"

"To a warehouse in Piraeus. It is believed two of the terrorists might be there awaiting transportation out of the country. My superiors instructed me to take a detachment and surround the place, but I thought perhaps you would rather handle this instead."

Bolan's suspicions climbed. It seemed strange the man would defy orders in so blatant a fashion. "Why me?" he demanded bluntly.

"Several reasons. First, as I said, to atone for my mistake. Second, to spare lives. The terrorists are not likely to give up without a fight, and I would rather avoid a battle in the middle of a major city if I can help it. Third, I remembered you telling me how you would very much like to meet up with them again and finish what you'd started. Here is your chance." Haralambos grinned. "What do you say, Mr. Belasko? Are you interested?"

Bolan had to admit the colonel's rationale was plausible. "It would be the two of us?"

"And my driver. I will instruct him to stay in our vehicle and be ready to call for backup should we need it."

"Very well." Bolan slipped into his trench coat and slid the strap to his duffel over his shoulder. He tended to believe Haralambos was sincere. But even if he were wrong and it was a trap, the terrorists might be there to spring it themselves, and that suited him just fine. Turnabout, as the old saying had it, was fair play.

A military jeep was waiting at the curb. A sergeant saluted and opened the door for them, and said something in Greek to the officer.

"My driver says I am to contact General Mylonas right away."

Bolan eased into the back seat and placed the duffel beside him. Haralambos sat in the front on the passenger side. As the driver wheeled into traffic, the colonel removed a mike from a clip on the dash and contacted his headquarters.

The Executioner's Greek was sketchy. He knew a few phrases and could wrestle with a menu but that was about it. He had to wait for Haralambos to translate.

"General Mylonas has just informed me that all airports, bus terminals and railroad stations were sealed off in time. The general is convinced the two terrorists must still be in country."

"You never explained why you believe they're at this warehouse," Bolan mentioned.

"Our people have established that two of the terrorists registered at the Aegean Hotel yesterday under assumed identities." Haralambos pointed at an intersection and snapped directions at the driver, who promptly took a right. "We've also learned they rented a car from a local agency. A car that paid the warehouse in question a visit last evening."

"And how exactly would you know that?"

"My apologies. About two weeks ago the warehouse came under police suspicion as a drop point for smugglers. Since then, the police have had it under continuous surveillance. They have secretly videotaped all the comings and goings and kept a record of every vehicle and boat that has stopped there." Haralambos glanced back and smiled. "One of those vehicles was the rental car used by the two terrorists."

"What makes you think the terrorists are there now?" Bolan inquired.

The officer's smile widened. "Because the car is there. We instructed the police to let us know the minute it returned."

Once again, Bolan reflected, it was all plausible. And an incredible stroke of luck. It could be the terrorists were waiting for a ship and were lying low at the warehouse until it arrived.

"I should let you know that General Mylonas does not entirely agree with my decision. He would rather send in troops. I had to remind him the prime minister stressed we must accord you every courtesy and do whatever you request."

Reading between the lines, Bolan understood the colonel had gone out on a limb for his sake. "I'm grateful for your help."

"Just so we do not let them get away. The general will not be so forgiving a second time. He was furious when I explained about the radios."

"So your butt is in the slinger."

"Pardon?" Haralambos said, then laughed. "Oh. An American figure of speech. Yes, indeed, my butt is most definitely in the slinger. If I let these two slip through my fingers again, my career will be ruined. I will either be demoted to the rank of lieutenant or sent to a remote outpost in the northern mountains where I will languish for the rest of my days." Haralambos scowled. "The general made that quite plain."

Bolan didn't like the gamble the colonel was taking. "Maybe you should call in troops after all. Or at least more police."

"I should? I thought you preferred to go in alone?"

"I do. But it wouldn't hurt to have police surround the place so the terrorists can't slip past us like they did at the villa."

"Ah. Yes. Consider it done." Haralambos picked up the mike and made a call.

Piraeus was a major harbor. Thousands of seaworthy vessels and smaller ships and boats sailed in and out of port every year. Textiles, food and machinery were the three most common legal cargoes. Drugs and guns were the most common illegal variety. Smuggling was widespread, and although Greek authorities did their best to stem the tide, Piraeus had a reputation as a smuggler's mecca.

The warehouse district was busy twenty-four hours a day. The particular warehouse Haralambos had referred to, however, was as dark as pitch and gave every appearance of being deserted.

The jeep pulled into the parking lot of a dry cleaner's across the street. In an unmarked van parked in the shadows were three police officers. The colonel consulted with them and came back to the jeep to report, "The car is still there." He pointed at a late-model sedan barely visible near the warehouse entrance. "They say that two men went inside and never came back out."

"Has anyone been there since?" Bolan wondered. He had climbed out to survey the vicinity.

"No. They have an officer over on the wharf the warehouse fronts, keeping watch for boats. But so far it has been as quiet as a cemetery." Haralambos gazed down the street. "The extra police should be here in fifteen minutes, at the most. We can go in then."

"We?"

"I know you want to do it alone. And trust me, were it my decision, I would gladly let you. I have never been in combat, Mr. Belasko, and I have no romantic notions of pitting myself against hardened terrorists. But General Mylonas gave me a direct order. He insists I accompany you inside."

Bolan wished it were otherwise. A kill zone was no place for an amateur. The last thing he needed was to have to watch Haralambos's back and his own at the same time. "Maybe we can work something out—" he began.

The colonel raised a hand, palm out. "Please. Do not try to talk me out of it. As much as I would gladly stay out here, I cannot disobey my superior. Not in this. If nothing else, I have always been a good soldier."

Bolan let it drop. "I'd better get ready," he said, climbing back into the jeep. Opening the duffel, he rummaged inside. The Weatherby Mark V he had used at the villa was broken down and in its special case, but he wouldn't use it here. He needed something smaller. Something better suited to close confines.

Something with bells and whistles for night use. And he had just the thing.

In recent years the Heckler & Koch MP-5 submachine gun had become popular with law-enforcement agencies around the world. With good reason. Compact and versatile, the MP-5 delivered dependable firepower and could be modified for various combat applications.

The version Bolan had brought along was an MP-5 SD. It varied from the standard model in several regards. Instead of a buttstock, the end of the receiver was closed by a cap, which shortened the overall length by more than six inches. A night scope and laser sight could be mounted on top, and Bolan pulled out his tool kit to do just that.

The MP-5 SD was also the silenced version of the line. A special casing was attached to the short barrel, serving as an inbuilt suppressor. Divided into two chambers, it reduced the SMG's noise level to a whisper.

Bolan's had another modification. He had asked that a front grip be added between the suppressor and the receiver to provide better control and balance, a lot like the front grip on his Beretta 93-R. And since the majority of MP-5s came with only full-auto or single-shot capability, he had specifically requested a model with a 3-round burst capability, as well.

The MP-5 also came fitted with a sling, which Bolan slid over his right shoulder. He already had the Beretta snug in its holster. Now he strapped a holstered Desert Eagle on his right hip, attached a boot knife and sheath to his right ankle, and slipped a few grenades and other tools of his trade into the pockets of his blacksuit for good measure.

Colonel Haralambos had been talking to one of the policemen. He hurried over and pointed down street. "Your timing is perfect. Here they come."

A military-style troop transport was rumbling toward them. It swung into the parking lot and a police captain hopped out of the cab. Haralambos stepped to meet him. A minute later the flap at the back of the truck rose and out spilled two dozen police officers. They formed into three rows and stood at attention while the captain relayed their orders.

Bolan was chafing to enter the warehouse. Every second of delay increased the likelihood the terrorists would get away. If they hadn't already. A golden opportunity to capture an Al-Jabbar member alive was being squandered. It had never been done before, and Bolan knew the Feds would give anything to get their hands on a living, breathing, potential treasure trove of intel. If he could take one of the terrorists alive, and if the Feds could persuade their prisoner to talk, they could put Al-Jabbar out of operation that much sooner. A couple of big ifs, to be sure, but he rated the reward worth the risks.

The police started to deploy, efficiently, quietly, keeping well back from the warehouse so as not to alert those inside. Once the captain received word on his walkie-talkie that his men were in position, Haralambos looked at Bolan and smiled.

"Now it is up to us, my friend. Or should I say, up to you? I am completely at your service. You are the expert in these matters, not I."

The officer's candor was refreshing. Too many times in the past, Bolan had to contend with arrogant know-it-alls who resented being forced to work with an outsider. "Stay behind me and do exactly as I do."

"Without fail," Haralambos promised. "I have four grandchildren who I am extremely fond of. I very much desire to see them again."

Bolan headed across the street. Not a single vehicle other than the truck had come by since they arrived, and now police were stationed at both ends of the block to insure civilians didn't stray into the fire zone.

The soldier activated the Starlight scope and raised the MP-5 to eye level. The darkness seemed to magically dissolve. He could see the front of the warehouse almost as well as if it were daylight, albeit tinted a slight shade of green. Two windows overlooked the parking area but there was no movement in, either. He padded to the rental car, verified it was empty and stepped to the front door.

Haralambos was breathing much too heavily. The man was understandably nervous, and Bolan hoped that wouldn't make him careless. The colonel was armed with a MAT 49 and held it clutched to his chest as if afraid he might drop it.

Bolan tried the doorknob. He expected it to be locked and was glad to be proved wrong. He eased the door open wide enough for a look inside. Crates were stacked to the ceiling, mountains of them on either side. A narrow aisle led from the entrance into the building's bowels. No lights were on; the place was as quiet as a mausoleum.

Braced for an outcry or a welcome of lead, Bolan slipped inside. If there was an office, he reflected, it had to be at the other end, close to the docks. A hand tugged at his sleeve, and he stopped.

"I cannot see a thing, Mr. Belasko," Haralambos whispered.

Bolan frowned. One of the cardinal rules of clandestine ops was to maintain silence at all costs. Especially at moments like this when their enemies might be close at hand. But the harm had been done, so he responded, "Stay here. I'll go on alone." Which was how he wanted it to be, anyway.

"But I have my orders," Haralambos objected.

"You're inside. You've done as the general wanted," Bolan whispered. "Now it's up to me. Wait for me to give you the all clear."

"I don't know—"

"Think of those grandkids of yours." Bolan moved on before the colonel could argue, his back to the left-hand crates, his forefinger curled around the MP-5's trigger. Thanks to the scope he could see well enough to distinguish gaps between the stacks. He peered into each before sidling by. Once he thought he heard a noise and he stopped and listened, but it wasn't repeated.

A glow appeared at the far end, on the right. Bolan sprinted to the crates on the other side and moved along them until he came to an open area. A small office lay just beyond. Light streamed from the open door, but no sounds issued from within.

Bolan switched off the night-vision scope. It operated on the principle of magnifying ambient light. In the dark and near dark it worked fine, but when near a light source, it was prone to severe scope glare. Or the unit might shut itself off to prevent internal damage. For the moment, at least, he was better off relying on his own sight.

To the right of the office door lay a crate, opened and empty. Bolan had to go around it, into the light, to reach the office. As he did so he heard a scraping noise from across the way, followed by the unmistakable ratchet of a weapon's bolt being thrown. He threw himself back into the darkness a millisecond before an SMG fitted with a sound suppressor coughed discreetly.

Bolan dropped flat as slugs buzzed above him. He couldn't see the terrorist but he had a fair idea where the man was and he responded in kind.

A second SMG joined the fray. This one wasn't silenced, and its staccato chatter echoed loudly off the galvanized tin roof.

Bolan saw a flash, triggered a 3-round burst and instantly rolled to the left. Slugs bit into the floor, missing him by a whisker. Heaving up, he ran to the nearest stack of crates and squatted.

The terrorists were over in the far left corner. To reach them Bolan needed to cross thirty feet of open space. They would cut him down before he made it halfway.

But not if he temporarily blinded them.

Bolan removed an Mk1 illumination grenade from a side pocket on his blacksuit. Filled with a magnesium-based mixture, the bomb would emit 55,000 candlepower for about half a minute after it was detonated. As he started to pull the pin, he heard footsteps patter in the central aisle. It had to be Haralambos. Bolan hoped the Greek had the good sense not to say anything or do anything that would give him away.

Suddenly the terrorist with the silenced SMG triggered a long burst. He wasn't firing at Bolan, though. He was shooting toward the center aisle. Haralambos's MAT 49 burped in answer, and the second terrorist opened up.

Yanking the pin from the Mk1, Bolan rose to throw it but had to duck when stray rounds peppered the crates he was behind. The moment the firing stopped, he flung the grenade in an overhand arc, dropped back down and buried his face in his forearms, simultaneously shouting, "Colonel! Cover your eyes!"

Brilliant light flared, light so bright that even with his face pressed to his sleeve, to Bolan it seemed as if the sun had gone nova. He ticked off the seconds in his head, and when he reached twenty-five he was up and racing around the crates toward the corner. As he passed the aisle, he discovered his worry had been justified.

His ally was down.

CHAPTER TWO

The Executioner also discovered that the corner of the warehouse was empty. The two terrorists had vanished. Bolan's first priority was to investigate and find out where they had gone, but he rushed to the stricken officer and sank to one knee.

Haralambos was in bad shape. He had taken multiple rounds full in the chest, and dark stains were spreading across his uniform. "I'm sorry," he rasped. "I heard the shots and thought you could use my help."

Bolan saw blood bubble from a corner of the man's mouth. His gut balling into a knot, he scanned the warehouse but still saw no trace of the terrorists.

"Did you get them?"

The soldier shook his head.

"Then don't waste time with me. After them. I'll call for help." Grunting, Haralambos painfully lowered an arm toward his belt.

Bolan unclipped the radio for him, shoved it into the colonel's hand and rose. He checked behind the crates on the right side before moving toward the corner. The light from the grenade was almost gone, but enough remained for him to notice lines in the floor where there shouldn't be any. Lines, and a thin recessed metal ring.

It was a trapdoor. Bending, Bolan gripped the ring, leaned backed so his body wasn't exposed to potentially deadly autofire and pulled. The door rose easily on well-oiled hinges. Through the opening wafted the dank scent of salt water.

Bolan cautiously looked over the edge. Buttressed by thick concrete pylons, the end of the warehouse jutted over the water. Fifty feet below, small waves lapped at a hidden dock reached by a ladder from the trapdoor. Tied to the dock were two speedboats, sleek outboard cruisers able to outrun most anything on the water. There was room for a third. Lying flat, Bolan dipped his head lower and spotted it moving off quietly so as not to draw the attention of the police. Two men were on it, one at the wheel, the other at the stern, paddling.

The man wielding the paddle saw Bolan. Dropping it, he leveled a sound-suppressed SMG.

Bolan barely jerked back in time. Slugs thudded into the floorboards and zinged through the opening. He heard the motor rev to life, then yells from several directions. Slinging the MP-5, he dropped down the ladder three rungs at a time. The terrorists were speeding rapidly away. He undid the mooring line and sprang onto the second boat. It was too much to expect to find the key in the ignition, but jump-starting a boat wasn't much different from jump-starting cars, and thanks to his Ka-bar knife and quick fingers, within ninety seconds he had turned the motor over and opened the throttle to give chase.

As the speedboat swept out from under the warehouse, gunfire crackled and rounds bit into the cockpit.

Bolan realized the police were firing at him in the mistaken notion he was another terrorist. Tucking at the knees, he weathered the hailstorm and sped for the open harbor.

The speedboat responded to the throttle and wheel like a thoroughbred to the touch of the reins. There was no need to inspect the motor to know it was souped to the max. A typical smuggler's craft, proving the police had been right to place the warehouse under surveillance.

The terrorists were rocketing westward at a reckless clip. Ships large and small filled the harbor, to say nothing of dozens of boats of every type and size, from fishing prams to yachts to schooners.

Whoever souped up Bolan's craft had done a superb job. At over forty knots the soldier flew parallel to his quarry's wake, a fine spray wetting his hair and dampening his face. He had to overtake them soon, or they were liable to slip away in the maze of ships that clogged the port.

Sparking bullets abruptly speckled the stern of the other craft. The soldier instinctively dropped low as leaden rain bit into the foredeck and five or six rounds punched holes in the windshield. He didn't bother returning fire. At that distance, and with the water as choppy as it was, scoring a hit would be more luck than skill. He concentrated on narrowing the gap.

Off in the night the lights of an ocean-going freighter appeared, creeping slowly into port guided by a tug. Most craft would sensibly give it a wide berth, but the terrorists were making straight for it. They had to be up to something, but exactly what, Bolan couldn't begin to guess.

Then a new element intruded itself. A spotlight

splashed across the water, courtesy of a helicopter streaking in fast and low from landward. By its markings it was a police chopper, and the officers inside now made the same mistake the police on the dock had made. The spotlight impaled his craft, and someone began shouting at him in Greek over a megaphone. Ordering him to stop, Bolan figured.

The speedboat was equipped with a radio. Thinking to use it to let the authorities know he was one of the good guys, Bolan flicked the power switch on and studied the digital display. He had no idea which frequency the police monitored. To find it, he'd have to go up and down the entire dial. He reached for the microphone, then jerked back as sparks erupted from the control panel, narrowly missing his face and eyes. One or more of the slugs fired at him from the dock had torn through the radio's vitals.

The chopper was almost on top of him. It banked lower, the beat of its rotor blades audible above the roar of the speedboat. A side door opened, and the business end of a machine gun was trained on Bolan's craft. Again someone shouted at him in Greek, this time adding in English, "We repeat! This is the Piraeus Port Authority! Turn off your motor and raise your hands in the air! A launch is on its way and will board you shortly!"

So it wasn't the regular police, Bolan realized. That complicated things. To his knowledge, Colonel Haralambos hadn't contacted them about the terrorists, or about him. They didn't know he was in Greece with the tacit approval of the Greek government. To the men in the copter he was a possible smuggler and would be treated accordingly.

As if to emphasize the point, the machine gun cut

loose, stitching the water to starboard with a short burst of rounds.

Warning shots, Bolan assumed, and glanced back. The chopper was a variation on the French-made Alouette. Equipped with floats and incorporating a slightly longer fuselage, it was ideal for patrolling over water. Outrunning it was out of the question, but Bolan couldn't just throttle down and let the real terrorists escape.

Maybe there was another option. Suddenly slowing to a crawl, Bolan elevated his arms. He wagged them back and forth, pointing to the west at the other speedboat. The chopper settled lower, the prop wash buffeting him like a gale in a hurricane. He kept pointing, hoping they would take the hint. To the east a siren wailed and lights flashed, a sign the launch would soon arrive. Bolan jabbed his fingers harder. Suddenly the spotlight swiveled, spiking across the water to catch the other speedboat in its glare.

The pilot did exactly as Bolan hoped. Like a great bird of prey, it swooped up over him and flashed toward the terrorists.

Several hundreds yards to the east the launch was closing fast.

Gripping the throttle, Bolan opened her up again and the speedboat hurtled forward, the bow practically leaping out of the water. He saw the copter gain swiftly on the other craft. One terrorist was bent over the wheel. The second appeared to be trying to work the bolt of an assault rifle.

The pair was as good as caught. A strategically placed burst from the copter's machine gun would stop their speedboat dead in the water. They might be willing to go out in a blaze of misguided glory, or to commit suicide. But if Bolan could get close enough, he could wing either or both and cover them until the launch arrived.

Then the second terrorist straightened and pressed his weapon to his shoulder. With a start, Bolan saw it was fitted with a grenade launcher. The man hadn't been working the bolt; he had been feeding in a grenade.

The Greek chopper was much too low and much too close to the other speedboat. Belatedly the pilot realized his mistake, and the copter tilted and started to rise. But it hadn't risen ten feet when the grenade launcher chugged. The terrorist at the wheel promptly swerved sharply to the right.

Bolan cut back on the throttle not two seconds before the grenade went off. The *crump* of the blast was but a prelude for a much larger one as the helicopter itself went up in a blaze of light and sound. A huge fireball engulfed the aircraft, reducing the fuselage to so much twisted, charred metal. The chopper canted, its damaged blades still crookedly spinning, and plunged cockpit-first into the sea.

The terrorists were back on their original heading, bearing directly toward the tug and freighter. Bolan opened up the throttle again. To his rear the launch slowed and moved toward the flaming debris slowly sinking from sight. Looking for survivors, no doubt. And destined to be disappointed.

The gap between the two speedboats had widened, but Bolan was confident the killers couldn't shake him. He had to remember to keep his eyes on the man with the grenade launcher or court the same fate as the chopper.

Crewmen were running about on the tug's bow and

pointing toward where it went down. A light started flashing above the tug's cabin, and a small spotlight was switched on and trained on the oncoming speedboat.

The terrorists didn't seem to mind. They sped past the tug with hardly a glance and angled toward the freighter. The man with the grenade launcher again tucked the weapon to his shoulder.

Cold rage knifed through Bolan. He knew what they were about to do, what they had intended to do all along, and he was powerless to prevent it. They weren't close enough for him to use the MP-5. He wouldn't be able to prevent the tragedy about to unfold.

The other speedboat was broadside to the giant freighter. Holding his assault rifle almost vertical, the terrorist fired a grenade high against the hull. Fingers flying, with no wasted movement whatsoever, he quickly loaded another and fired again. Loaded a third and fired it. All so fast, the third was in the air before the first detonated.

Bolan veered to the right. The hull of a ship that size should be thick enough to withstand the blast of an ordinary grenade with minimal damage. The terrorists were bound to know that, too, and had to have used high-explosive, armor-piercing grenades instead. Probably with a fuse delay.

A blast rocked the night. Then another and one more. But they were minor compared to the one that occurred on their heels, as, with a tremendous explosion, part of the freighter's side spewed outward like an erupting volcano. Great spouts of flame shot across the water. Debris showered like rain.

A roiling red-and-orange wall rushed toward Bolan.

He pressed on the throttle, but it was already as far as it would go. Blistering heat enveloped him, and for a few harrowing moments he thought the speedboat would be engulfed. Then the heat subsided, and a glance showed the fireball coalescing in on itself and the ship. Thick clouds of smoke poured from the freighter and swiftly spread. Klaxons had gone off. Up at the rail, people were scurrying about and pointing at a cavity in the vessel's side.

Bolan swung to the left to take up the chase, but the other speedboat had been swallowed by the smoke and was nowhere in sight. Slowing, he steered directly into it and cast about for some sign. The smoke, though, grew thicker by the minute, and it was soon so bad he had to cover his mouth and nose with one hand in order to keep from coughing. Faced with the futility of locating them, not to mention the danger of colliding with the freighter, he spun the wheel, reversing direction.

Bedlam ran rampant on the ship. Yells and screams were mixed with the grating wail of the Klaxons and the muffled popping sounds of other explosions taking place inside the freighter.

Bolan emerged into starlight and fresh air. Drinking it deep into his lungs, he headed east in a wide loop. His sweep took half an hour, and at the end he had to concede they had given him the slip. He made for shore.

The warehouse was awash in light. Dozens of police and emergency vehicles with flashing lights surrounded it, and police were all over the place, like agitated bees over a hive. Nine or ten were on the main dock. As Bolan brought the speedboat in, they trained their hardware on him and snapped commands in

Greek. He elevated his arms to demonstrate he wasn't a threat and called out the colonel's name. One of the policemen ran into the warehouse. The others swarmed onto the boat, relieved him of the MP-5, the Beretta and the Desert Eagle, and roughly hauled him out.

For a minute Bolan thought he would be dragged to police headquarters and thrown into a cell. Then the policeman who had gone off returned, and with him was the captain who had spoken with Colonel Haralambos earlier. At his command, Bolan was released and his weapons returned.

"My apologies, sir," the captain said in heavily accented English. "These men had no way of knowing who you are."

"But you do?" Bolan asked as he slung the MP-5.

"Colonel Haralambos informed me of your—how shall I put this?—special status. He did not say a lot. But enough for me to know you have official sanction at the highest levels."

That was Hal Brognola's doing. Whenever and wherever possible, the big Fed smoothed things over for Bolan so he could get the job done with a minimum of hassles. Contacts, official liaisons, safe houses, transportation, Brognola took care of them all. The trick was to do it without drawing too much attention to Bolan.

Bolan hurried toward the front of the warehouse. "How is the colonel? Have they taken him to the hospital yet?"

"They are just about to," the captain answered, "but it does not look good. He's stopped breathing once already, and the paramedics barely revived him."

An ambulance was parked near the entrance, the

rear doors open, and a pair of husky paramedics were about to lift the colonel in. Haralambos was strapped to a gurney, a respirator over his mouth. His eyes were open, and when he saw Bolan, he weakly lifted one hand and said something to the medics, who reluctantly paused. "Did you get them, Mr. Belasko?" Haralambos wheezed.

Bolan shook his head.

"I was so hoping you would." Haralambos coughed, his face clouding. "I did not want to die in vain." He smiled wanly. "I guess I will never see those sweet grandchildren of mine ever again, eh?"

"You should not be talking, sir," the captain interrupted. "We must get you into surgery without delay."

"It is too late, I am afraid," Haralambos said, and in the blink of an eye, he was gone. His body deflated like a punctured balloon and went completely limp as blood bubbled over his lower lip and down his chin.

Bolan stepped back, giving the paramedics room. They were professionals, these two, and they frantically sought to revive their patient. They tried everything they could but to no avail. A blanket was draped over the body, and it was slid inside the ambulance. Both doors were slammed shut. The flashing lights were turned off and the ambulance silently pulled out.

Bolan stood and watched until it was out of sight. He couldn't say exactly why, given he hardly knew the man, but the Greek's passing affected him. Haralambos had been a decent, considerate human being. He deserved better. He deserved to grow old and be there for those grandkids of his. Not to be coldly gunned down by people who snuffed human life as casually as most people would crush a fly.

"My men and I are at your disposal," the captain volunteered. "If we can be of any help, all you have to do is ask."

Bolan just wanted to get to his hotel. The jeep was still in the parking lot across the street, and he trudged toward it.

The police captain kept pace. "Is there anything you can tell me about the men who killed Colonel Haralambos? Their identifies, perhaps? He mentioned they were terrorists but nothing more."

"They are members of Al-Jabbar," Bolan revealed.

"*Those* devils? I have heard of them. What were they doing in Greece?"

"They tried to assassinate the American vice-president."

"Ah. And you stopped them?"

Bolan had already said enough. More than he should. Brognola didn't want the attempt to become common knowledge. It was part of the reason the Fed had asked his help instead of simply letting the Secret Service handle it.

The sergeant had the passenger door open. His expression told Bolan he knew about the colonel, and the soldier slid in without comment.

The captain bent down. "When I file my report, what do I say about you?"

"I was never here. You never saw me. You never talked to me."

"Highly irregular, sir. But I will honor the colonel's request and do as you want." The captain opened his mouth, then paused, as if unsure to say what was on his mind.

"Yes?" Bolan prompted.

"These pigs who killed the colonel. I would hate to

think they will get away with it. Justice demands an accounting. I hope your government will not rest until they have been paid back in kind.''

"Count on it,'' the Executioner vowed. More than ever, he wanted to track Al-Jabbar to their lair and end their vicious spree.

"That is good." The captain patted the door. "I will detain you no longer. Good day.''

Bolan nodded at the driver, who pulled out, then eyed him quizzically. "My hotel,'' Bolan said. Twisting, he slid the duffel from the back seat onto the floor between his feet. One by one he replaced everything except the Beretta, then shrugged into his trench coat. By that time they were halfway to Athens, and the sergeant hadn't uttered a word. "I'm sorry about your colonel,'' Bolan offered.

The soldier's English wasn't as fluent as his superior's. "Much good man,'' he agreed. "Much kind man. Family much cry.''

That was all they said the entire ride.

Bolan thanked the noncom and took the elevator to his room. He had barely set down the duffel when the phone rang. He had a hunch who it would be, and he was right.

"I hear it didn't go so well, Striker," Hal Brognola said without preliminaries.

"To hell in a handbasket is how I would describe it,'' Bolan said. Propping a pillow against the headboard, he sank onto his back. "Everything that could go wrong, did.''

"Murphy's Law strikes again. My contact in the prime minister's office informs me the liaison was killed. And something about a freighter nearly being sunk.''

Briefly Bolan filled him in, concluding with, "So we're no closer to eliminating Al-Jabbar than we were two days ago. They have more lives than a cat."

"The Greeks have taken charge of the bodies at the vineyards and are trying to identify them. Maybe something will turn up." Brognola's exasperation was audible. "In the meantime, I've booked you on the afternoon flight out of Athens tomorrow. There's nothing on the burner at Stony Man at the moment, so I thought you would like a leisurely flight home."

"Cancel my reservation," Bolan said.

"You're staying over?"

"Al-Jabbar has become my number-one priority. I'll wait to see if the Greeks hit pay dirt, and if they do, take it from there."

"Far be it from me to criticize, but that's a long shot. Those two terrorists you shot in Islamabad were never identified. We ran their fingerprints through every national and international database we have access to and came up empty-handed."

Bolan could tell his friend didn't like the idea of him staying on. But it might save him flying all the way back if the Greeks uncovered valuable intelligence. "Sooner or later they'll slip up. They all do, eventually."

"Want me to send Jack over to keep you company?"

Jack Grimaldi was another of Bolan's closest friends, an ace pilot who spent most of his time shuttling Stony Man Farm personnel to hot spots around the world. "I'll handle this one solo."

"There's no harm in asking for help. The last report we had, Al-Jabbar has upward of thirty members. As good as you are, a little assistance will go a long way toward evening the odds.''

"No.''

"I see.'' The big Fed was quiet for a moment. "Is there something I'm missing here? Something you're not telling me?''

"I want to take down Al-Jabbar. It's as simple as that.''

"Who are you kidding?'' Brognola quipped. "Nothing is ever simple with you. But if this is how you want it, we'll play it your way.''

Bolan had an afterthought. "Before you go, there's one thing. Can you have a new liaison assigned?'' To cut through the red tape, if nothing else.

"I'll contact the prime minister's undersecretary and arrange to have someone assigned. And this time I'll stress how grateful we would be if they let you handle things your way.''

The soldier didn't bother to point out they had stressed it the first time but the general had overridden their wishes. That was the trouble with trying to circumvent chains of command in a foreign country; there was always someone, somewhere, who thought he knew better.

"One last item and I'll let you get your beauty sleep,'' Brognola said. "The President mentioned how grateful he was for our intervention on the Veep's behalf. He asked me to relay his thanks to whoever was responsible.'' Brognola chuckled. "So thanks.''

"You didn't tell him it was me?''

"I thought it best not to spoil his mood. You know as well as I do he has serious reservations about the wisdom of relying on the services of a someone who once operated outside the government's official purview.''

Bolan gazed out the window at Athens's skyline. It was another reminder, as if any were needed, that his working relationship with Uncle Sam rested on the thinnest of ice. They needed his expertise, his skill, but they were wary of being found out. Of the public learning, in newspaper parlance, that the government was in bed with a former lone wolf who had long worked outside the law. A revelation like that was every politician's worst nightmare.

"You take care, Striker, you hear?" Brognola said.

"Always." The dial tone hummed in Bolan's ear and he hung up. It had been a while since the big Fed brought up his unofficial status, and it made him wonder if there was more to the comment than Brognola let on. Shrugging, he walked into the bathroom and stripped off his shirt. He wouldn't lose any sleep over it.

Bolan had more important matters to occupy him. Al-Jabbar, for starters. If the Greeks came up empty he was back to square one. Which was to say, nowhere. He could use a lucky break right about now but he had been at this business too long to expect miracles.

Still, a little one wouldn't hurt.

CHAPTER THREE

It had been a slow news day. The kind Mort Collins hated.

Mort was *Newstime* magazine's Athens bureau chief. He had held the post for eight years and hated every minute of it. He hated Greece. He hated the food. He hated the climate. He hated the mountains. He hated the ocean. In fact, it was common knowledge among everyone who knew Mort that he hated everything in life except Mort Collins. And New York City.

Collins's dream was to snag a transfer to the Big Apple. He had been born and raised there, and his sole ambition in life was to get back where he belonged. He'd never wanted to come to Athens. His bosses at *Newstime* had insisted. They claimed he was the right man and sent him there anyway.

It was his misfortune to be born into a wealthy family, and to have a mother and father who gave him the finest education money could buy. They sent him to a prestigious private school where students were required to take three years of one of half a dozen foreign languages offered. Collins chose Greek, only because the woman who taught it gave him many a pleasant daydream. He had the further misfortune to become so fluent in it, he could speak it like a native.

So here he was, in the prime of his career, stuck at a post he despised. But Collins hadn't given up hope. All he needed was to break a major story, to show his employers what he was capable of, and he was confident they would bend over backward to reassign him anywhere he wanted. Goodbye Athens, hello New York City.

Sadly, Athens wasn't a hotbed of major news. Collins covered political squabbles, an occasional bank robbery, the Mafia's ongoing shenanigans, the Greek-Turkish conflict, and interviewed Greece's shakers and movers. Which to him was about as stimulating as watching moss grow.

But a call came into the office from a stringer in Piraeus. A ship was on fire, the guy said. And there were police all over the place. Since the only other person in the office was the Greek cleaning lady, Collins decided to swing out to the harbor on his way home and get the lowdown. He wasn't expecting much of a story, but when he arrived and saw the scene for himself, his interest was piqued.

The harbor was abuzz with activity. The freighter had been anchored well out from shore so it wouldn't pose a danger and was being sprayed with fire-retardant foam by a pair of tugs. Half a dozen helicopters were zipping back and forth, their searchlights sweeping the water. And as the caller claimed, police were everywhere. Collins guessed that every cop within fifty miles had been brought in. He also saw military transports and regular Army troops moving about.

Something was up. Something big. A large crowd had gathered to witness the spectacle, and Collins had to wend his way through it to get close enough for a good look at the freighter. Several policemen were keeping the people from pressing to close to the water's edge. Collins showed his credentials to one and asked if the guy knew what had happened.

"I am sorry, sir, I do not," the man politely answered. "We have been told it is none of our business, and to let them handle it."

"Them?" Max asked.

"The military, sir. They are in charge of things."

Collins's interest soared. He noticed a warehouse to his left that had been cordoned off by police. A lot of soldiers were moving about, and military vehicles filled the parking area. Plastering a smile on his face, he ambled over and flashed his ID to a policeman who held out an arm to bar his way.

"I'm with *Newstime*," Collins said. "I'd like to see what is going on over there."

"You can go no farther, sir. My orders are not to let anyone past this point."

"Is there someone I can talk to?" Collins persisted. He saw soldiers carrying crates from the warehouse and loading them into a truck. "Your superior, perhaps?"

For once luck was with him. Another policeman approached. "I am Captain Dimitrakopoulus. Perhaps I may be of help."

Collins showed his press credentials again. "I'd appreciate any information you can share."

The captain motioned him to one side and said in a voice low enough not to be overheard, "Will this be strictly off the record? Between the two of us?"

"Of course," Collins assured him. "I received a report of an explosion. Is that a military vessel out there? Is it carrying munitions and they're afraid the whole ship will go up?''

"Oh, no, sir, nothing like that." Lowering his voice even more, the captain said, "Terrorists were to blame."

Collins scribbled the word on his notepad. This was getting better and better by the second. "You know this for sure, do you?"

Captain Dimitrakopoulus straightened. "I will have you know I was one of the first on the scene. My men and I were ordered to surround the warehouse, and I heard and saw much of what happened. I was there when the ambulance took away the army officer the terrorists killed."

"Do you know this officer's name?" Collins asked, scribbling furiously.

"That I cannot divulge, sorry. You need to contact their public-relations officer."

Collins absently nodded. "What about these terrorists? How many were there?"

"Two, I believe."

"Only two?"

"That is more than enough when they are members of Al-Jabbar. You have heard of it, have you not?"

Collins's fingers froze. Al-Jabbar had been featured in a recent *Newstime* article on terrorist organizations. Any story about them was bound to make the next issue. He could hardly wait to file his report. "I wonder what they were doing here?" he absently commented.

"Trying to escape, I should think, after their attempt on your vice-president's life failed."

An electric tingle shot down Collins's spine. Struggling to keep his voice calm, he said, "Do I understand you correctly? Al-Jabbar terrorists tried to assassinate the vice-president of the United States?"

"That is what I was told, yes."

Collins let the full significance sink in. He had stumbled on a beaut. An honest-to-God headliner. The cover story for the next *Newstime*. One that could finally bring about his cherished dream. But he had to be careful not to get ahead of himself. He needed sources, corroboration, supporting facts. "Who told you this, Captain?"

Dimitrakopoulus was about to say something but caught himself. "I am sorry, Mr. Collins. I was instructed to keep the information confidential. You will have to find out on your own, if you can."

"Can you at least tell me where the assassination attempt took place?"

"That I do not know, sorry."

Collins shoved the notepad into his pocket. He had learned as much as he was going to here. "I thank you for your invaluable help. Rest assured your name will never be mentioned in my article."

Collins's mind was in a whirl all the way back to Athens. He had to jump on the story before someone else did. His biggest fear was another journalist would beat him to the punch. As soon as he reached his office, he snatched his little black book of contacts from his desk drawer and began placing calls.

He had scores of names and numbers. At one time or another he had interviewed everyone of influence, from military leaders to heads of state. He knew people at every government agency and in every branch of law enforcement. All the years he had spent suffering were finally paying off.

It took only an hour. By then Collins had confirmed

that there was indeed an assassination attempt, that it occurred at the villa of Constantine Panopoulis, that two terrorists had been slain and two others escaped, and there had been a running firefight at the harbor that resulted in the deaths of an army colonel, three police officers in a helicopter and five crewmen on board the freighter.

A couple of puzzling aspects arose. For one thing, Collins established that the Secret Service whisked the vice-president from the villa well before the attempt was made. The Secret Service agent he spoke to was adamant in insisting the Secret Service had nothing to do with the deaths of the two terrorists. And reliable sources in the Greek military and police claimed they weren't involved, either. Leaving Collins to wonder who was.

The other puzzling aspect had to do with how the U.S. government learned of the plot beforehand. From all indications Collins was convinced they had. He phoned the vice-president's press secretary. He talked to an assistant to the Greek prime minister. Neither would help. Then he thought of an American professor at Athens University. A mild-mannered, scholarly sort who also happened to be in the employ of the CIA. The newsman had uncovered that choice tidbit at a cocktail party at the U.S. Embassy. He occasionally called the man, Fred Schoenfield, to have information verified or refuted.

"This is all news to me, Mr. Collins," Schoenfield said. "I'm even more in the dark than you are. Maybe an informant forewarned our side. Maybe a wiretap uncovered the plan. There are a host of possibilities."

"I thought as much," Collins replied. He could get

by without the information although it would be nice to have.

"Although," the unlikely spy said thoughtfully, "if I was a betting man, I'd lay money they gleaned the intel from our global surveillance system. It's reached the point where they can eavesdrop on practically anyone, anywhere, anytime."

"Which system is this?" Collins asked.

"Don't tell me you've never heard of Echelon?"

THE AFTERNOON after Mack Bolan spoke to Hal Brognola there was a rap on his door. He answered it to find a tall, gray-haired Greek in an expensive brown suit and tie, holding a briefcase.

"Mr. Belasko? Permit me to introduce myself. Dimitri Kastorian, at your service." The man gave a slight bow. "I am your new liaison with my government."

"No army officer this time?" Bolan said, motioning for his visitor to enter.

"Mr. Brognola felt it best if your new contact had direct access to the prime minister. I am on his personal staff, and can ring him any hour of the day or night." Kastorian set his briefcase on the table and removed a manila folder. "My first order of business is to inform you we have identified one of the terrorists slain at the villa."

The file consisted of a single sheet. Under a photo of Narmer, taken when he was younger, was the pertinent bio, such as it was. "Sahura Narmer," Bolan read aloud. "Egyptian. Age, twenty-four. Place of birth, Cairo. Worked as a file clerk until two years ago when he disappeared. No criminal record." Bolan glanced at Kastorian. "How did your people identify him so fast?"

"Dental records were one factor. His family turned them over to Egyptian authorities when they reported him missing. The other was his fingertip." Kastorian wriggled the little finger on his left hand. "Narmer lost the end of his when he was ten. His father was cutting weeds with a scythe and Narmer came up behind him without saying anything. The boy was lucky he did not lose his head instead."

"Is that all we know so far?" Bolan had hoped for more, a lot more.

"We have established that Narmer and another terrorist registered at the Acropolis Hotel under forged identities. The police have gone over their rooms and obtained fingerprints, but it could be weeks before a match is found, if ever. To be honest, identifying Narmer so quickly was a surprise."

So there it was. Bolan was left with nothing to go on. Brognola had been right. Staying on was a waste of time.

"There is more news," Kastorian said. "Narmer and his accomplice rented a car. In it we found a cellular phone. The serial number is being traced even as we speak. By this time tomorrow we should know where Narmer obtained it. And, more importantly, his service provider."

Which in turn, Bolan knew, might result in a complete record of every phone call Narmer ever made or received. A treasure trove of intel that could point them in the direction of Al-Jabbar's base of operations. So waiting around hadn't been a waste of time, after all.

"I am sorry we cannot get the information sooner."

"No problem at all," Bolan said.

Kastorian reached into the briefcase for something else. "I will pass on our findings to Mr. Brognola as soon as I receive them, and to you, if you are still here in Athens."

"Why wouldn't I be?" Bolan asked. With the prospect of a major break looming, he wasn't inclined to go anywhere.

The Greek unfolded a map and placed it on the table. "Because it is my understanding you are eager to catch the terrorists who killed Colonel Haralambos. And we think we know where they are."

Bolan was all interest. He bent over the map and noticed a tiny island in the Aegean Sea had been circled in red. "What do you have?"

"Initially we thought the terrorists had rendezvoused with a ship and were halfway across the Mediterranean by now. But then a high-altitude reconnaissance plane took some interesting photos." Kastorian plucked a packet of photographs from the briefcase and spread them out alongside the map. "It was a routine flight over disputed waters in the Aegean. We claim the area as ours. The Turks claim it as theirs."

The soldier was well aware of the long-standing dispute between the two nations.

"See this?" Kastorian tapped the first photo. On it was a tiny silvery dot, also circled in red. "And these others?"

Bolan nodded. On all the photos except one was a similar dot. The last was a blowup, but not much could be discerned other than it was a small, sleek, slender craft, and judging from the wake, moving like a bat out of hell. "You think it's the speedboat the terrorists escaped in?"

"That is our supposition, yes. The boats hidden under the warehouse were retrofitted with extra gas tanks, extending their range by hundreds of kilometers. Granted, there are almost as many boats in Greece as there are cars, but we find it highly interesting where this particular speedboat was bound."

Bolan bent over the map and read the name of the island. "Thenas?"

"An uninhabited speck far from anywhere," Kastorian revealed. "Reefs offshore make it supremely treacherous to shipping and boaters. No one ever goes there. Yet this speedboat did. It arrived about noon today, and to the best of our knowledge it has not left."

"The terrorists are still there?"

"Unless they sprouted wings, yes. We have taken high-altitude photos of the island and the surrounding sea every half hour, and no ship or boat has gone anywhere near it. We suspect they are waiting to be picked up under cover of darkness." Kastorian leaned on the table. "And before you ask, yes, we debated sending in our navy. But as I mentioned, Thenas is in disputed waters. The prime minister is afraid the Turkish government would construe it as an act of aggression."

"So you'd like me to go in and flush them out? Is that what this is leading up to?"

"If you have no objections, yes. We can have you there inside of ninety minutes. One of the fastest helicopters in the Hellenic Army Aviation Force is fueled and waiting to go."

The soldier could hardly object to having another crack at the elusive pair. "Let me grab my duffel and we're out of here." He collected the few items he had in the bathroom, pulled on his trench coat and was ready.

Sixteen minutes later Bolan was streaking eastward toward the Gulf of Evvoia. The copter was an American-made AH-1 Cobra, one of eight, the young pilot mentioned, sold to Greece as part of an arms-package deal. It had a top airspeed at sea level of more than 140 miles per hour and a maximum range of 315 miles. It seated two.

Lieutenant Dienekes was from Sparta. A cocky hot-shot, he handled the Cobra with a level of skill Jack Grimaldi would admire. He pointed out the plain at Marathon where a famous battle was fought against the Persians and offhandedly mentioned he could trace his family's lineage back to the illustrious three hundred who fought to the death beside Leonidas.

They crossed the gulf, which was sprinkled with fishermen and pleasure craft, and shot over the rolling mountains and verdant valleys of picturesque Evvoia. Beyond lay the pristine Aegean and a host of islands, large and small.

Bolan, seated in the gunner's seat in the nose, frequently consulted his watch and glanced over his shoulder to gauge how long it would be until sunset. They had to reach Thenas by then. Not only was that when the terrorists were likely to picked up, but landing in the dark would be a dicey proposition. According to Dimitri Kastorian, there wasn't a flat spot on the island. It was an outcropping of volcanic rock about half a mile in diameter, its surface so twisted and pitted and rent with ravines and fissures that finding a spot to set down would be like finding the venerable needle in a haystack. At night it would be impossible.

"These men you are after," said Dienekes. "I spit on them and their cowardice. To kill people from ambush is not the way of a true warrior."

Bolan thought of his tour as a military sniper. Of the severe toll he wreaked on the other side by taking out their officers and select troops. "Sometimes that's necessary."

"Is blowing up innocent women and children necessary? Is killing infants the act of a warrior? I can not believe you are defending them, Mr. Belasko."

Neither could Bolan. Terrorism under any guise was an evil that had to be expunged. The pilot's voice crackled in his helmet again.

"Do not get me wrong. I admire the work you do. To go where your country needs you, to kill vermin like these, to know you are making the world a safer place in which to live. It must be very rewarding, eh?"

"It has to be done."

"But surely it gives you a good feeling inside? All the lives you must save? Your country will honor you with its highest medals."

As if that would ever happen, Bolan reflected. More than likely, one day Uncle Sam would decide he was more of a political liability than an asset and he would find himself the hunted rather than the hunter. Talk about ironies. No one loved America more than he did. No one cherished the ideals on which she was founded more than him. "The land of the free and the home of the brave" was more than a catchphrase. It was an ideal by which he lived. To him freedom was everything, and defending it was not just a right but the basic responsibility of every citizen.

Bolan knew sacrifice was called for. The defense of liberty came with a cost, and he had given up more than most. He would never have a wife to lie beside him at night, never have children to bounce on his knee, never know the exquisite joy of a family and a home. Loneliness came with the territory.

"I envy you, Mr. Belasko," the lieutenant was saying. "I am a warrior from a family with a fine tradition of warriors. But my country has not been at war in many years, and I sometimes think I will grow old and retire without ever firing a round in combat."

Maybe Dienekes was the lucky one, Bolan thought, but he didn't say so aloud. He had no illusions about war. It was a deadly, dirty business. Those who glorified it were usually those who had never been in uniform. Warfare didn't deserve to be extolled. Rather, it was the selfless service of the men and women who willingly gave their lives for their country who should be glorified. They were genuine heroes, one and all.

Bolan shifted his legs so he was more comfortable. He was dressed in his blacksuit and rigged for combat. Wedged in front of him was his duffel. He had decided to take it with him since there was no telling how long he would be on Thenas or where he would go from there. His weapons, his night-vision scope, his maps, his food rations, his cell phone, he might need any and all of them before this was done.

For a Spartan, young Dienekes wasn't very laconic. "I miss the days of my ancestors, Mr. Belasko. The days when battles were fought man against man. Where is the honor in dropping bombs from so high up the planes that drop them cannot been seen with the naked eye? Or firing a cruise missile from a thousand miles away? The old ways were better, I think. Purer. Nobler. Were it up to me, that is how war would be fought today."

"Were it up to me," Bolan said, "there would be no war at all."

"Strange words coming from someone like yourself. You kill for a living. Is that not true?"

"I do what needs to be done."

"You said the same before. Is that all this is to you, then? You are performing your duty and nothing more?"

"Duty is only part of the equation," Bolan answered. "I see it as an eternal war between good and evil. Between those who believe in freedom and those who want to remake the world in their image and are willing to exterminate anyone who doesn't see it their way. A war that's been taking place since the dawn of time. But now the threat to freedom is greater than ever because modern technology has made evil that much more powerful."

"I have never thought of it in quite that way," Dienekes admitted.

"Evil never rests and neither can we. There has never been a day in recorded human history where there wasn't a war taking place somewhere. We must be vigilant in freedom's defense, or evil will finally win out." Bolan hadn't meant to climb on a soapbox, but the pilot's comments had struck a nerve.

"So to you, what you do is more than duty. It is a calling."

"I don't know as I'd go that far."

"You have given me much to contemplate, and for that I thank you." Dienekes chuckled. "Who would have thought a warrior would be so deep a thinker?"

To Bolan they went hand in hand. Settling back, he gazed out over the glimmering expanse of the Aegean. The farther they went, the fewer ships and boats they encountered. Soon there were none at all, just the sea and now and then a small island. Most appeared to be uninhabited.

"ETA in five minutes," Dienekes announced.

At last. Bolan opened the duffel and took out the M-16, which he had broken down into the upper and lower receiver groups, and began to reassemble it. He was surprised to hear Dienekes swear.

"Mr. Belasko, I think we have a problem. I am picking up a blip on my radar. It's a jet fighter."

"Why is that a problem?"

"It's a Turkish fighter, and it has a fix on us."

CHAPTER FOUR

Greece and Turkey had a long history of boundary disputes. Their long-standing rivalry over Cyprus was common knowledge. Less newsworthy were the dozens of times each year one side accused the other of unauthorized excursions into their airspace.

Greece and Turkey were also U.S. allies. For decades the U.S. government had walked a tactful tightrope in order not to antagonize one side or the other. Arms and munitions had been sold to both nations. So it was that Mack Bolan found himself in a U.S.-made Cobra helicopter whisking low over the Aegean Sea as toward them streaked a U.S.-made F-16 jet fighter.

The Turkish pilot came in fast and steep. At over Mach 1 the jet flashed past the chopper, the roar of its Pratt & Whitney turbofan drowning out the sound of the Cobra's Avco Lycoming engine. Bolan caught a fleeting glimpse of the pilot and then the jet was past them and climbing.

In a dogfight the Cobra would be at a severe disadvantage. It was armed with an M-197 cannon, TOW antitank missiles and a pair of short-range Sidewinder air-to-air missiles. But the F-16 had cannon and missiles of its own, as well as Westinghouse AN/ALQ-119 and AN/ALQ-131 ECM pods and other advanced electronic countermeasure components that would effectively neutralize the Sidewinders.

Lieutenant Dienekes, though, didn't change his heading. He was on the radio, reporting the incident to his superiors.

Again the F-16 roared past. This time the pilot did the last thing Bolan expected; he grinned and waved. The silver war bird arced up and away, performing a crisp aerial loop, and within seconds it was flying back the way it had come, toward Turkish soil.

Dienekes swore again, adding, "Those crazy Turks! Do you see what we have to put up with? They do that all the time. To them it is some kind of grand game."

"Would you rather he shot us down?"

"Of course not. But mark my words, Mr. Belasko. One of these days, one of their pilots or one of ours will forget himself and make a mistake that will plunge both our countries into all-out war."

"I would hate to see that happen," Bolan mentioned. The wonder of it was that it hadn't happened already. The threat was always there. If not over Cyprus, then over airspace violations.

"One minute to drop," the lieutenant reported.

Bolan closed the duffel and peered out the cockpit. They had dipped so low they were nearly skimming the waves. Dienekes angled around to approach the island from the north. A precaution based on the fact the reconnaissance photos showed the speedboat had done so from the south.

The Cobra was rapidly losing airspeed. Ahead, Bolan spied the island, and it was every bit as bleak and desolate as the Greeks led him to believe. A great, knotted mound of ancient gnarled rock jutting skyward like an angry fist. There wasn't a plant anywhere. Not so much as a blade of grass.

In seconds Thenas was under them. Lieutenant Dienekes banked right and left, seeking a safe site to touch down. Flat spots were extremely few and far between. Much of the surface rolled and dipped like the Aegean's waves, broken by large holes and wide depressions. Stony knobs and rocky spikes bristled like quills on a porcupine.

"There!" Dienekes declared suddenly.

Like a hummingbird swooping onto a feeder, the Cobra dropped onto a level area no longer than the copter's landing skids.

Bolan raised the upward-hinged side door, gripped the M-16 in one hand, the duffel in the other and rose. "Thanks for the ride, Lieutenant." Careful to keep an eye on the spinning rotor blades, he climbed from the cockpit. Then, bent at the waist, he ran a dozen yards and turned.

The Cobra was already rising. Dienekes smiled and gave him a thumbs-up. For a moment the chopper hovered, then it rocketed off across the sea to the northwest.

Bolan didn't linger. There was always a chance the terrorists had spotted the Cobra and might be converging on him that very minute. He hurried south, moving as fast as the inhospitable terrain allowed. He had never seen volcanic strata quite like this. Many of the rocks were sharp enough to cut exposed flesh.

A basin three feet wide and two feet deep afforded Bolan the perfect place to ditch the duffel for the time being, which he did after taking out the cell phone. Twilight was descending, but it would be awhile before darkness claimed the Aegean. The only signs of life were gulls circling to the southeast. He cat-footed from outcropping to outcropping, only showing himself when he had no other choice.

Mingled with the distant cries of the gulls and the pounding of the waves was the constant low whistle of the wind. Thirty knots, at least, and according to the Greeks, at night it was worse.

The soldier had traveled approximately two hundred yards when the wind shifted. It came at him from out of the southeast and brought with it not only the moist scent of the sea, but the faint odor of cooked food. So the terrorists *were* still there. And if they were busy eating, they had no idea anyone else was on the island.

Bolan worked his way toward the southeast shoreline. There was no evidence of a fire, but they would be smart enough to hide it. He covered another two hundred yards. The aroma of food was so strong his mouth was watering. But he had yet to spot anyone. A moment later, without warning, the rock surface sloped away, and there, twenty yards off, was a brown tent. Beyond it, pulled almost entirely out of the water, was the same speedboat he had chased in Athens.

Dropping flat, Bolan scooted back until his eyes were above the rim. He heard low voices speaking in Arabic. It would be ridiculously easy to cut them down. A sustained burst from the autorifle or a fragmentation grenade fired into the tent was all it would take. But Bolan had other plans. The two terrorists were unwitting bait. Logic dictated that if they were being picked up, it would be by some of their own kind, either other Al-Jabbar members or sympathizers. Bolan wanted them all in his crosshairs. He was perfectly content to lie there and wait for whoever was going to show.

The flap rustled and out strode a muscular man with icy features, carrying an unusual slender case. Squatting, he set it in front of him, undid a latch and opened it. From where Bolan lay, he could see the inside of the lid was actually a computer screen. A laptop of some kind, he guessed. But then the Arab removed a small satellite dish from a recessed compartment. The dish wasn't more than ten inches in diameter and had tiny telescoping legs. Unrolling a short cable, the terrorist connected it between the base of the dish and the main unit. Next, he slid a pencil-thin headphone over his left ear and plugged the jack into the proper input.

Bolan had never seen a com link unit quite like it. It was as state-of-the-art as they came, the best current technology had to offer, rivaling anything the U.S. military used.

The Arab pressed a button and the unit hummed to life. After he tapped a few keys the small dish slowly began rotating. There was a sustained beep. The terrorist typed rapidly, there was another beep, then the man began to talk into the headset.

Bolan was impressed. In all the intel gathered on Al-Jabbar there wasn't a whisper they were so high-tech. The Feds regarded them as another run-of-the-mill fanatical organization, no smarter or more sophisticated than any other. But here was proof to the contrary. It took a lot of know-how, and a lot of money, to acquire and use a unit like that.

The flap parted again. Out stepped a younger man with curly black hair and a cleft chin. He had a tin bowl in his hand, and as he stood there ladling soup into his mouth, he gazed eastward toward the Turkish coast, which was only a third as far away as Greece.

Were Bolan a betting man, he'd wager that whoever came to pick them up was bound from Turkey. The young terrorist spoke to his comrade, who was listening on the headset and gestured for silence. Annoyed, the younger man scowled, turned and walked toward high ground.

Toward the exact spot where Bolan was lying.

MALIK SHARIK WAS uneasy. He didn't like being stuck on a speck of rock in the empty vastness of sea. He didn't like having barely enough fuel in the speedboat to go ten kilometers. Nor did he like having only a two-day supply of food and water. If something went wrong, if the individual they were counting on to rescue them failed to show, they would be stranded. Without fresh water they wouldn't last the week. Their rotting bodies would lie unclaimed and unhonored, to eventually be consumed by crabs and the incessantly noisy gulls. It wasn't how a holy warrior should die.

The Saudi was talking to their Turkish contact. Sharik gathered there would be a delay of some kind, which didn't sit well with him. He tried to ask for details, but Rakin hushed him as if he were a wayward child. The man's arrogance was insufferable.

Sharik almost stalked off to be by himself. He took a few steps toward the low rise that overlooked their camp, then remembered how treacherous the terrain was and changed his mind. Their campsite was the one spot on the whole wretched island where a man could move about without the damnable rocks cutting into his shoes, his clothes, his very flesh.

Wheeling, Sharik stared eastward and spooned the last of his soup into his mouth. The packet boasted it was as delicious as homemade, but the broth was tastless and the lumps that passed for noodles had the consistency of wet clay.

He had much to be unhappy about. High on his list was the debacle in Athens. It was bad enough they failed to kill the American vice-president. It was bad enough they lost two of their own. Then, to be forced to put their emergency contingency plan into effect and flee for their very lives was the ultimate indignity. And all because of *him*, the one Sharik had seen in Islamabad, the dark-haired demon with the hard face who showed up everywhere they did. Somehow he found out they were awaiting transport at the warehouse and snuck to within a dozen yards of where they were before they realized it. His shots came so close, one nicked Sharik's left ear.

The mystery man raised so many questions. Who was he? How did he always know where they were?

Aban Abbas would be furious. Sharik wasn't looking forward to making his report. He was looking forward, though, to getting off that miserable island. So when their uplink beeped and Rakin removed the headset, he asked, "Well, don't keep it secret. What did he say?"

"The Turks have stepped up their military patrols along the coast. Hassan cannot leave until midnight. He says to expect him about two in the morning."

"Good. The sooner we are off this dung heap, the happier I will be."

"A word to the wise. You must learn to cultivate patience and a deeper faith in the beneficence of God."

Sharik's temper flared. He would tolerate a lot of things, but not having his faith questioned. "I am as dedicated as any member of Al-Jabbar. I have complete faith that God will see us safe and sound back to our base.''

''Then how do you explain how nervous and irritable you have been? A true holy warrior stays calm when beset by adversity.''

Sharik would dearly have loved to kill the Saudi then and there. But Abbas needed Rakin's money for their great cause, which came before all else. ''Instead of nitpicking my faults, you would do better to dwell on how our leader will judge your performance. Your first mission was a dismal failure.''

''Through no fault of mine,'' Rakin said. ''There must be a traitor in our midst. How else could the Americans have learned of our plan?''

Sharik hadn't thought of that. How else, indeed? Three times now the American sniper had foiled them. Once could be considered a coincidence. Two times could be construed as an extraordinary fluke. But three times definitely pointed to foreknowledge.

''I have confidence Abbas will learn the traitor's identity,'' Rakin commented. ''After all, only a handful knew about the Athens mission, and two of them are now dead.'' Rakin's thin lips curled in his customary smirk. ''Interesting, is it not, that this makes the second mission you have been on where we lost brothers in arms?''

''Are you saying I am the traitor?'' Sharik snapped, and started toward the other with his right fist clenched.

''I offered only an observation,'' Rakin responded, casually placing his hand on the 9 mm Makarov pistol tucked under his belt. ''Make of it what you will.''

Sharik regained control and stopped. He wouldn't put it past the Saudi to use that pistol if provoked, and his own weapons were in the tent. "I have been with Abbas as long as anyone. And I have been on more missions than most. Missions, need I remind you, that succeeded? Were I a traitor, it would have been apparent long before now."

"Maybe so," Rakin said. "But it is not for me to pass judgment. It is Abbas, and God, you must answer to."

Sharik had taken all the veiled insults he was going to. He stormed into the tent, set the tin dish next to the propane stove and slung the Ameli over his right shoulder. It was a sad state of affairs, he mused, when waging a holy war depended on men like Rakin. Men so petty they were an insult to their exalted cause. He pushed on the flap and went back out. As he straightened, his gaze happened to sweep the rise and drift across it to the sea. Belatedly an image stamped itself on his mind, an image of something he had just seen. But it couldn't be.

Casually strolling toward the water, Sharik watched the rise out of the corner of one eye. There it was again. Movement. So quick, had he blinked he'd have missed it. As impossible as it seemed, his eyes hadn't deceived him. Someone was up there. Someone was spying on them.

Sharik turned and walked toward Rakin. He pretended to be interested in the darkening sky, in the Aegean, in a flock of gulls, in everything except the rise. The Saudi was studying the monitor and didn't look up. "Do you think fishermen ever visit this island?" Sharik inquired.

"I doubt it. Their boats are too big to make it over the reefs."

"And no one lives here."

"Look around you. Did you ever see a place less fit for human habitation? There is no fresh water, no vegetation of any kind. A person might as well live on the moon."

"I wonder how Abbas learned of Thenas."

"Weren't you the one who told me he has contacts all over the Middle East and Mediterranean? Maybe he asked his smuggler friends to suggest somewhere we could escape to in an emergency, and this was it." Rakin tore his eyes from the digital readout. "Why are you bringing all this up?"

"Because we are not alone. I saw someone watching us." He hastily added, "Do not look around or he might suspect we know."

Skepticism oozed from Rakin. "You were seeing things. It was a trick of the shadows and nothing more."

"I tell you I saw someone."

Rakin's brow knit. "Where?"

"On the rim to the north."

"All right. I will humor you." Rakin stood. "I need my submachine gun. Watch for my signal and we will rush it together. You go right, I will go left. If someone is up there we will catch them between us."

"Someone *is* there," Malik insisted.

"A mermaid perhaps, or a cyclops," Rakin mocked him. "I hear the Greeks claim these waters were once haunted by all manner of strange creatures." Laughing, he walked toward the tent.

Sharik shifted to the south so the lurker on the rise wouldn't suspect what they were up to. Stars were blossoming. Soon it would be too dark to see much of anything. From out on the water came a strange sound, an almost humanlike cry, similar to that a baby might make. A dolphin, perhaps, Sharik thought, although he didn't really know enough about sea life to say. He was a child of the high desert. All the more reason for him to look forward to their return to the compound.

The Saudi was taking too long. Sharik glanced at the tent and heard the ratchet of the HK-53's cocking handle being pulled. He hoped whoever was spying on them hadn't heard it, too.

Rakin stepped out, the SMG close to his right leg. He looked over and nodded.

In concert, their weapons leveled, they sprinted toward the rise.

THE EXECUTIONER was a keen student of body posture. Long ago he had learned it gave him an edge at crucial moments. Like when he had to penetrate enemy lines and needed to know if a guard was alert or could easily be taken down. Or when he was up against a bevy of gunners and needed to know which was most apt to fire first. Or simply for telling whether someone was being honest or not.

Body posture spoke volumes.

When the Palestinian scanned the rise, Bolan ducked down, waited a few seconds, then raised his head again. The Palestinian was looking away, but there was a certain tenseness to his posture that hadn't been there before. The man turned as if staring out to sea, but Bolan wasn't fooled. He flattened again, then began crawling backward. When he had gone far enough so neither of them would spot him, he rose and loped to the north. He didn't know how much time he had, and when he came to a waist-deep hollow, he jumped into it and knelt with his back to the pitted rock.

They took longer than Bolan thought they would. But then he saw them, rushing up over the rim, the young Palestinian to the east, the other to the west. They swept their SMGs back and forth, primed to kill. A minute elapsed, and the hawk-faced Arab smirked, lowered his HK-53 and made a comment that provoked an angry reply from the Palestinian.

Bolan didn't need to speak Arabic to tell that the older man didn't believe the other terrorist had seen him. An argument broke out. It ended when the older man flicked a hand in disgust and went back down.

His cheeks reddening, the Palestinian glared and muttered under his breath. He surveyed the island from end to end. Then he, too, pivoted on his heel and descended.

Bolan stayed put as night's mantle deepened. Soon he could move about freely. Until then there was no need to press his luck. He would hear if a boat approached, and take appropriate action.

Relaxing, the soldier propped the M-16 beside him. Now was as good a time as any to find out if the cell phone worked. He slid it from its pocket, pressed the on button, and when the display lit up, extended the antenna and tapped in a special number. Ideally it would link him with the embassy in Athens, and from there his call would be relayed to Brognola. On the third ring a woman answered, but the signal was so weak and there was so much static Bolan couldn't make sense of what she was saying. He rang off. He would try again later.

A million stars filled the heavens but no moon. In that regard Bolan lucked out. A wraith among shadows, he crept toward the camp but this time circled wide to the east.

Lit by a lantern on a stub of rock, the older Arab was at the com link, typing on the keyboard. The Palestinian was over by the west shore, pacing like an angry leopard.

Bolan eased onto his stomach. For more than an hour he watched and waited, ignoring infrequent growls of hunger from his stomach.

More time passed. The Palestinian went into the tent, and another lantern soon glowed within. The other terrorist stayed busy sending and receiving messages until almost midnight, at which point he removed the headset, stood and called to his companion. A brief exchange resulted in the latter climbing into the speedboat. He emerged carrying a canvas pouch from which he took four cylindrical objects.

Flares, Bolan realized. The Palestinian laid them on the ground but didn't ignite them. Plainly, the pair was getting ready to signal someone. He hoped it would be soon, but the older man sat down and resumed typing, and the Palestinian went back into the tent.

Another hour passed.

By the soldier's watch it was quarter past two when the older man switched off the uplink, replaced the dish and the headset and closed the case. Soon after, the Palestinian reappeared, and both searched the sky to the east.

Bolan pricked his ears for the throb of a boat's motor, but all he heard was the whistle of the wind. Then, quite distant, came a metallic growl. He made sure the M-16's selector lever was set on semi and tucked the stock to his shoulder.

The Palestinian shouted excitedly. Dashing to the

flares, he ignited them one by one and deposited them at ten-yard intervals from south to north.

The growl grew in volume. The sound of a plane, not a boat. And since there wasn't a safe spot anywhere on Thenas for one to land, Bolan suspected it was a seaplane, a favorite of smugglers throughout the region. It should be close enough to spot, but he couldn't locate it, which hinted it was flying without its running lights in violation of international law.

A whoop went up from the Palestinian, and he pointed at a star where there hadn't been one a second ago. The star resolved into several lights on a heading that would bring them directly over the island.

Bolan wouldn't make his presence known until the aircraft landed. A few well-placed shots should guarantee it didn't go anywhere while he dealt with its occupants and the terrorists.

The plane went into a dive. As it soared overhead, Bolan saw pontoons on the bottom.

The Palestinian was showing more teeth than a used car salesman who had just made a sale, and even his companion appeared happy their deliverance had arrived. Grasping the case, he stepped to the water's edge.

The seaplane made a second pass. When it was only forty yards out, a spotlight speared the night, the wide beam impaling Bolan like a laser. He had no time to hide. The beam swept over him, and he was up and running, but the harm had been done. Autofire bracketed him, slugs ricocheting on either side. He threw himself behind a gnarled spine and hugged rock as more rounds whined and zinged overhead.

Heaving onto his knees, Bolan returned fire. But the

terrorists had sought cover, and the best he could do was momentarily pin them down.

The seaplane was executing a tight circle to approach Thenas head-on from the south.

There was a distinct cough, the kind a grenade launcher made when a grenade was fired. Bent at the waist, Bolan raced to the north. He had gone only about fifteen yards when a hole yawned before him. He was too close to avoid it. Throwing his arms in front of him, he fell four or five feet, doing a belly flop that jarred the breath from his lungs. Then the grenade went off, the blast like thunder, and stinging chunks of rock rained like hail. His ears rang, and a sharp pang lanced his left eardrum.

It took only a minute for the ringing to subside enough for Bolan to stand. He brought up the M-16, thinking the terrorists had to be almost on top of him. But they had vanished.

The growl of the speedboat explained their absence. Bolan levered up out of the hole and sprinted toward the camp. He reached the rise to discover the boat racing out to meet the seaplane. They weren't quite out of range, but the speedboat was black as pitch and he couldn't see, either. He banged off a few rounds anyway. Predictably, they had no effect. Soon the boat was too far out. He had to look on in simmering frustration as the speedboat pulled alongside the seaplane and the terrorists climbed into it. Wasting no time, the pilot immediately took off.

Bolan swore. Twice now those two had gotten away from him. Next time, he silently vowed, it would be different.

CHAPTER FIVE

Somalia

Aban Abbas was a troubled man. If he didn't know better he would think God had forsaken him. A passage from the Book gave him great comfort, one that said The truth came from God, and among men there should not be doubters. And if there was one thing Abbas knew with complete certainty, it was that he was doing God's will.

Why then, Abbas kept asking himself, did the last two missions fail? An hour ago he had received word from Sharik and Rakin, and since then had been sequestered in his office, trying to make sense of things. He wondered if the fault were his. If maybe there had been a flaw in his plan. Over and over Abbas reviewed it, and over and over he came to the same conclusion. The fault lay somewhere else. But exactly where eluded him.

Dawn would soon break. Yawning, he picked up the remote control to the television and turned it on. There might be something on the news about Athens. The best source of information on anything pertaining to America and Americans was CNN's European feed, and he switched right to it.

Geographically, Al-Jabbar's fortress hideaway was isolated from the rest of the world. To the west and south were hundreds of kilometers of unforgiving desert. To the east, perhaps a hundred kilometers, was the Indian Ocean. To the north lay the Gulf of Aden. Abbas had chosen the site, after much deliberation, due to two factors. First, it was centrally located, allowing his warriors to reach any given spot in the Middle East relatively quickly. Second, the host government was a hotbed of corruption. As long as he made regular monthly payments to a few important officials, he could operate as he pleased without interference.

There were no landlines into the fortress. No phone lines that could be traced. Abbas didn't need them. It was a testament to the marvels of modern technology that he could maintain contact with the outside world without them. And, too, keep abreast of current developments through the latest in satellite TV.

A portly newsman was going on about an IRA bombing in London. Abbas couldn't care less. Unbelievers all, as far as he was concerned. He was glad to see them kill off one another.

A woman came on to talk about the weather. The dress she wore was much too tight, and her shoulders, neck and face were as bare and sleek as that of any street whore. Abbas frowned in disgust. Infidel women had the morals of alley cats. He couldn't wait for the day when the whole world was under Muslim sway, and women everywhere were required to cover themselves in public, as was proper.

Commercials were next. Drivel for the brain, was how Abbas thought of them. Yet they always fascinated him, for they gave insight into the Western world, into the things unbelievers considered important. Cars, clothes and credit cards were the big three. Never any mention of God or the Prophet.

Not a day went by that Abbas failed to thank God he had been born into the one true faith. Some of his fondest childhood memories were of the countless days spent reciting verses in school. Learning the Book by rote until he could recite it Sura by Sura.

Abbas reverently ran his hand over the cover of the Koran. To him, as the Christians would say, the Koran was the holy of holies. His every act was based on its teachings. His every thought steeped in its wisdom. His childhood ambition had been to spread its greatness and its glory to all the world. Not by force of arms, but as a teacher of righteousness.

Then came that fateful day when Abbas was twelve years old, and he journeyed to Lebanon with his father, a highly successful businessman. His father always hoped Abbas would follow in his footsteps, but the world of trade and finance paled beside the true faith.

There, Abbas first encountered unbelievers. Specifically, American sailors on shore leave. How vividly he remembered the shock of seeing those big, coarse men parade down the street, laughing and swearing and acting as if the street were theirs. In their arms were loose women. In their hands, liquor bottles. In broad daylight they did this, in full sight of decent people.

Abbas's father told him to avert his eyes, and Abbas tried but couldn't resist looking. As the Americans strolled by, his father had commented in English, "You should all be ashamed of yourselves." His father was fluent in the language and had insisted he learn it, as well.

Abbas's heart had leaped into his throat when the

Americans halted and one of them, the biggest and coarsest of the bunch, swaggered over to his father.

"Were you talking to us?" the American demanded. His eyes were bloodshot, and his breath reeked of alcohol.

"You are making a spectacle," his father said. "You and your friends would do well to go indoors."

"Or what? You'll report us to Shore Patrol? Go ahead. See if we give a damn. This is our first port of call in eight months, and we're out to have some fun." The man turned to go. "Besides, we're not doing anything we wouldn't do in our own country."

"But this is not America. You insult every devout Muslim with your blatant debauchery."

Abbas thought for a second the sailor would hit his father. But the man did something worse. Something Abbas never forgot. Every word, every gesture, was indelibly seared into his memory, and was the catalyst that set him on the road he had taken.

"Big words, pal. But who the hell are you to judge us? Your beliefs don't mean squat to me or my friends." The big man had poked Abbas's father in the chest. "We piss on you, and we piss on your religion. We have the right to do as we damn well please so long as we don't break any laws."

"There are higher laws than those of man."

At that, the American laughed and slapped his thigh. "Oh, I get it now! You're one of those holier-than-thou types. I've met assholes like you in my own country. Walking around with their noses in the air, thinking they're better than everyone else." He poked Abbas's father again. "Well, I've got news for you. You stink when you sweat, just like the rest of us."

Abbas hadn't understood that last remark until later.

He had watched the big American swagger back to his companions and listened to their taunts and rough mirth, his ears burning with the slight done his father and his heart burning with rage at the slight to their faith. He had yearned for his father to strike them down, but his father merely shook his head and muttered, "Unbelievers!"

The incident gave Abbas much to think about. Until that moment he hadn't been interested in other lands, other cultures. They had seemed so remote, so alien. In his innocence and naïveté he thought they had no bearing on his life or his people. But he was wrong, so very wrong.

Abbas studied the ways of the West with a keen intensity his father found alarming. But Abbas was only after knowledge. He wanted to understand why Americans and those like them were the way they were. Why everything about them was so different. Why they studied a different Book and worshiped a different prophet. Why they deported themselves like animals and let their women run around half dressed.

The answer eluded Abbas until, in his confusion and bewilderment, he went to ask the one person who would surely know—his teacher. He remembered to this day the kindly smile the venerable old man bestowed, and how, after stroking his long white beard, the teacher shared an insight that forever after impacted Abbas's life.

"It is no wonder you cannot find the answer, for he who is to blame goes to great lengths to hide it. The master deceiver does not want his handiwork recognized. He delights in hiding the truth from earnest seekers and in befuddling fools." The teacher had paused. "Americans are not like you and I. They are not children of God. Satan rules their lives, and through them, seeks to pervert us.''

The Koran contained many mentions of Satan. The faithful were encouraged to resist his wicked guile and live upright lives. But it had never occurred to Abbas there might be entire countries under Satan's sway. His whole worldview was altered in that one brief instant. ''Do they know this?''

''Of course not,'' his teacher replied. ''They believe they follow in the steps of God. But that does not make them any less evil.''

''What are we to do about them?'' Abbas asked, and was answered with a quote from the Book.

''Fight you therefore against the friends of Satan.''

The foundation was laid. Abbas grew to resent any and all adverse influences on Muslim culture. He learned there were many who shared his view. But to his dismay, few were willing to do anything about it. Few were willing to oppose those in Satan's thrall. They would do the great struggle lip service, and that was all.

Not Abbas. Early on, he planned to one day do as his teacher had instructed him and openly fight for the values he held dear. He became a keen student of current affairs, for only through such knowledge could he divine what the enemy was up to and take adequate steps to counter it.

Abbas was twenty-seven when his father died. At last able to do as he pleased, and with enough money to live comfortably, he had traveled extensively, meeting others of a similar bent. He was with the PLF a year an a half. With Hamas two years. With Hezbollah four. And all the while he was learning, adding to his store of knowledge and acquiring the skills that would serve him in good stead when he started his own organization.

Suddenly Abbas heard the word "Athens," and his reverie came to an end. He glanced at the TV. Behind the anchor was a map of Greece, and superimposed over it the words Terrorism Summit. He increased the volume.

"—have learned there was an attempt to kill the vice-president, who is in Greece to address the European summit on behalf of the President. American officials have refused to release details as yet, but we are about to go live with *Newstime*'s Athens bureau chief, Morton Collins, who broke the story. Mr. Collins, can you hear me?"

The image switched to Collins, a balding middle-aged man who smiled nervously into the camera and fussed with his tie. "I can hear you."

"Will you recap what you know so far?"

Collins fidgeted and coughed. "Four terrorists tried to kill the vice-president yesterday. Two were killed, although by whom is not exactly clear yet—"

"Is it true the terrorists were members of the organization known as Al-Jabbar?"

Aban Abbas felt the blood drain from his face.

"According to my sources, yes." Collins smiled thinly. "Al-Jabbar is sort of second-rate, as terrorists go, and never attempted anything this big before. Their last known activity was in Pakistan, you might recall, where they tried to murder the American ambassador, and failed."

Abbas gripped the Koran so tightly his fingers hurt. The whole world would now think of them as incompetent bumblers.

Collins was gaining confidence and prattled on.

"Al-Jabbar was out of their league here. The two who escaped barely got away with their lives after a running gun battle in the harbor. Greek authorities deserve to be complimented for how swiftly they responded to the threat." He added, almost offhandedly, "Although, to be fair, the terrorists never really had a chance. Our side knew about the attempt well in advance."

"How's that, Mr. Collins?" the anchor asked.

"I've learned our government intercepted information that forewarned them of the attack. The vice-president has Echelon to thank for saving his life. Perhaps the same can be said of the ambassador in Pakistan."

"Echelon?"

"There have been rumors floating around about it for years. I had no reason to take any of them seriously until I investigated this incident. Echelon is a global surveillance system put in place by the U.S. and some of her allies to intercept telephone, e-mail, fax and telex communications." Collins twisted and held a briefcase up so everyone could see. "In here is my documentation. Some of it is based on classified information so I'm not at liberty to cite my sources."

The anchor was a typically dense sort. "So you're saying our government knew what Al-Jabbar was up to beforehand?"

"Yes, that's exactly what I'm saying. A major Echelon facility is located in the Mediterranean, not far from where I'm standing, in fact. If the terrorists knew where it was, I daresay they would go to any lengths to destroy it."

Out of the mouths of simpletons, Abbas thought, his insides churning. He had never heard of this Echelon before. And if what the buffoon was saying was true, there was only one thing to do.

The anchor thanked Collins and the segment dissolved into a panel discussion with three experts on the state of terrorism in the world today. Abbas clicked off and swiveled his chair toward the door. "Jebel!" he bellowed.

The young Lebanese entered and dutifully bowed. "Sir?"

"Have everyone gather in the courtyard. Ten brothers will be chosen to accompany me on a trip."

"Might I ask to where, great one?" Jebel respectfully inquired.

"Athens."

SOUTHEAST OF Izmir, Turkey, lay arid mountainous country better suited to mountain goats than human habitation. Tire was the largest town of any consequence, located some twenty-five miles inland from the Aegean Sea. On the coast itself was Kildana, a town so small it wasn't found on most maps. The population, according to the last census, stood at sixty-two. And every mother's son of them, according to Hal Brognola, would gladly stick a knife into the back of any government official or foreigner who came snooping around.

Kildana's history was unique. It got its start as a haven for pirates back in the days of Henry Every and Edward England. When the piratical trade died, the inhabitants turned to smuggling, and ever since had made their living on the shady side of the law.

Several times between 1900 and 1950 the Turkish government tried to stamp out the practice, with no more success than trying to stamp out a forest fire with bare feet. Hard evidence was hard to come by. Kildana's residents were as tight-lipped as clams, and their clients were reluctant to talk to prosecutors since those who did invariably disappeared and were never heard from again.

Nowadays, Ankara turned a blind eye to the town. So long as the smugglers didn't commit murder or otherwise draw unwanted attention, they were left to their own illicit devices.

Mack Bolan learned this while onboard a Turkish patrol boat bearing him from Thenas to the Turkish coast. Fortunately for him his cell phone had worked when he tried to contact the big Fed a second time, and Brognola arranged for the Turkish navy to pick him up. It had taken almost ten hours, but now the boat was approaching the coastline, and Bolan relinquished the radio to prepare.

Luck had been with them. A Turkish air force major on patrol had spotted a seaplane cruising landward at sea level in the wee hours of the morning and demanded the aircraft identify itself. The pilot was one Hassan Orgay, Turkish citizen, who claimed he was on his way home from a pleasure jaunt to Crete. The pilot reported it to his superiors, and they ordered him to let the seaplane continue unmolested but to shadow the aircraft to its destination. That turned out to be Kildana.

A flyover an hour earlier established the seaplane was still there, moored to a dock. Satellite surveillance indicated no other planes or boats had left in the intervening hours.

Bolan believed the two Al-Jabbar terrorists were waiting to leave under cover of darkness. It was a long shot, but he might be able to slip in and find them. He had to be careful not to be caught, or the townspeople would see to it he never left their town alive. As he closed the duffel a shadow fell across him.

"Good day." Lieutenant-Commander Pamir smiled. "About ready to depart, I see, Mr. Belasko?" Hands clasped behind his lean back, he surveyed the landmass in the distance. "For your own safety we must let you over the side a kilometer north of Kildana. The sea is rough today, and it will be difficult reaching shore in a raft."

"I'll manage," Bolan said.

Pamir looked him up and down. "Yes, I believe you will. Once you push off, we will continue down the coast to make them think we are on routine patrol. If God smiles on our endeavor, Kildana's inhabitants will be so interested in us, they will not notice you. My orders are to swing back around and be at the retrieval point by 7:00 p.m. Will that give you enough time?"

"It will have to do." Bolan straightened and adjusted his trench coat over his casual shirt and pants.

Pamir's brown eyes twinkled in amusement. "Those are what you are wearing?"

"They're the only clothes I have with me. Why?"

"Kildana is a backward region. Clothes like that would make you—how do you Americans say it?—stand out like a sore thumb. With your consent, I will ask among the crew and see if I can find attire a bit more suitable."

"Go ahead." Bolan appreciated the officer's help. It was best to blend in as much as possible if he was to get in and out of the smugglers' den with a minimum of trouble. Pamir walked off, and Bolan stepped to the front of the bridge and gazed across the forward deck.

The patrol boat was a Yildiz Class FPB 57. Built in Turkey, she had the contours of a pocket destroyer. Four diesels could propel her at up to thirty-seven knots. Her armament included four Harpoon missiles, a 35 mm antiaircraft gun and two 7.62 mm machine guns. The crew complement was forty-five, not counting officers.

At the moment the patrol boat was cruising at twenty knots, her bow pointed landward. Turkey's rugged shoreline stretched the length of the eastern horizon, as yet merely a dark line against the backdrop of blue sky.

In a surprisingly short time, Pamir returned. He had with him a pair of baggy brown pants, a plain beige shirt, Turkish shoes and a coat that had seen better days. "Wear these and you will look just like a native." From one of the coat's pockets he slid a wool cap. "Many men in this region wear these. Pull it low over your ears, keep your chin low and you might be able to pass for a Turk."

Bolan accepted the clothes and headed for the compartment he had been temporarily assigned to change. Since he couldn't very well traipse around Kildana with the M-16 or the MP-5 slung over his shoulder, he had to leave them behind. As well as a lot of other lethal weapons from his duffel.

As the soldier dressed, he mentally reviewed a map Pamir had shown him earlier. North of Kildana were low hills out of which flowed a narrow stream that bordered the town on the east and was its primary source of drinking water. Past the stream lay a narrow plain that wound inland toward a high plateau. To the south were woods broken by deep ravines.

By modern standards Kildana was backward, even primitive. A single main street was hemmed by old buildings packed close against one another. According to Pamir, there were few cars and no streetlights, and modern appliances were as rare as law-abiding citizens.

The people of Kildana were clannish and highly suspicious of strangers. A few years back, the government sent in an undercover operative to try to infiltrate the smuggling fraternity. A month later a sealed barrel showed up on the steps of an Izmir police station. When it was opened, body parts were found inside. Forensics identified the remains as those of the government man.

Bolan examined himself in the mirror. He was taller than the average Turk and had to remember to slouch over while moving about. He also had to avoid eye contact. Blue-eyed Turks weren't unheard-of but it wasn't likely there were many among the smugglers. Buttoning the middle button on his coat, he went out and closed the door.

The dark line on the horizon was now a well-defined coast. Towering mountains were silhouetted in sharp relief inland. The patrol boat was making toward a series of low hills to the southeast, spray hissing over the bow.

Bolan joined Pamir at the starboard rail. Four crewmen were busy inflating a raft. "How much longer?"

"Eight to ten minutes," Pamir answered. "We must let you down on the seaward side in case they have spotters watching from shore. I suggest you lie flat and wait five minutes before you start paddling. By then we will be well away, and they might not notice you.''

''If they do, they do.'' Bolan would rather avoid spilling blood if possible. But if there was no other way, he wouldn't hesitate to do so.

Pamir glanced at him. ''I wonder if you truly realize what you are getting yourself into. They are not normal people, these Kildanaians. They are throwbacks to long ago, to a time when violence was a daily way of life. A psychologist would say they are not in their right minds.''

''I have a job to do.''

''I admire your sense of duty. I just hope it does not get you killed.'' Pamir leaned on the rail. ''I would not do what you are doing, my friend, and I have a much better chance of succeeding because I am Turkish. You don't even speak our language.''

Bolan shrugged. He didn't speak Chinese or Pakistani or Kurdish or dozens of other languages, but that had never stopped him from achieving his objective.

''A few words to the wise. Do not stare at any of the women. Their men will take it as a slight and kill you on the spot. There are no police in Kildana, so you cannot expect help from that quarter. There is no mosque, either, which gives you some idea of how religious the people are.''

The raft was almost ready. Pamir shook Bolan's hand in parting and excused himself to go to the bridge. Soon the patrol boat reduced speed and changed its heading to a more southerly course. They were running parallel to the coast but far enough out that anyone watching through binoculars wouldn't be able to tell what was taking place on deck.

The seamen dragged the inflatable to the rail. Ropes were attached, the paddles placed inside.

Pamir's voice blared from a nearby speaker. The throb of the diesels faded, and the ship came to a dead stop. Again Pamir issued commands, and the four crewmen swiftly lowered the raft over the side and down into the sea.

One of them nodded at Bolan. Grabbing hold of a rope, he slid his legs over the rail and descended hand under hand, his feet braced against the hull. The raft had drifted a few yards out. To reach it, Bolan pushed off and swung lightly down. Kneeling, he untied the ropes at both ends, grasped a paddle and moved another dozen yards off to be well in the clear.

Pamir was on the flying bridge. He gave a crisp salute as the patrol boat's powerful engines chugged to life and the prop churned the water into foam.

Bolan returned it, then lay on his side and twisted his wrist to see his watch. When exactly five minutes had gone by, he rose on his knees and began paddling. The water was calmer than it had been all day, which made paddling easier but also made it easier for anyone on shore to spot him. He didn't like being so exposed, but it couldn't be helped.

A cove ringed partially by bluffs offered a secluded landing spot. Bolan pulled the inflatable in among a cluster of boulders and headed inland. He saw no one. Birds and insects were the only wildlife, although he did spy a few deer tracks. Half a mile in, he came to the stream and followed it south.

Next stop, Kildana.

CHAPTER SIX

A private jet landed at Athens International Airport late in the afternoon. Security was tight, and the eleven passengers were given close scrutiny. They were members of a Somalia trade delegation on their way to Switzerland. Their credentials were in order, and their luggage cleared customs without mishap.

The spokesman for the group was a friendly young woman whose fluency in Greek impressed the officials questioning her. So did her beauty. She could turn heads anywhere, so lovely was her face, so lustrous her hair. The Greeks fawned over her like schoolboys over a first love.

The head of the trade delegation was a big man going gray at the temples. He didn't speak Greek, but he was as friendly as the woman and answered all questions with a candor the customs officials found refreshing. Some of the other members of the delegation seemed a trifle nervous, but that was deemed par for the course. No one liked to be interrogated or have their bags gone through with a fine-tooth comb.

Rented vehicles whisked the delegation to the Acropolis Hotel. They took four adjoining rooms on the same floor, 303 through 306. Leaving their luggage unpacked, all eleven gathered in 303 so the leader could address them.

"Well done, my brothers," Aban Abbas complimented them, then singled out the female member of Al-Jabbar. "Jamilah, you were outstanding, as always. Your aptitude for languages never ceases to amaze me."

His smile was replaced by a look of utmost seriousness. "The next phase must also unfold without a hitch. Jebel, you will drive. Barakah and Yasin, you will come with us. The rest of you will stay in your rooms. Do not answer the phone. Do not answer the door. We will not be more than an hour, I should think."

"What about weapons?' Barakah asked.

"I do not foresee the need."

"Are Malik and Rakin joining us?" asked another.

"No. I contacted them and told them to stay put until they hear from me again. Hassan will fly them anywhere I need them to go." Abbas moved to the door. "Now let us be on our way."

The office building they wanted was in the heart of downtown Athens. On a sign in front the tenants were listed, among them, in large, grand letters: *Newstime, Inc.* Abbas handed Jamilah his cell phone and a slip of paper with the number they wanted, and she punched it in. As they had rehearsed, she knew just what to say.

"Hello? May I speak with Mr. Morton Collins? Tell him it is someone with important information about the recent terrorist attempt on the vice-president's life." Jamilah covered the phone and winked at Abbas. "Mr. Collins? I saw you on the news. Are you perhaps interested in information the Greek govern-

ment has uncovered about the identities of the two
terrorists who got away? You are?''

Abbas had picked a lure the journalist couldn't resist. Now all Jamilah had to do was reel him in.

''I hear that sometimes news organizations pay for
such information. How much is this worth for you?''
Jamilah listened a bit. ''Yes, that is a fair amount. But
no, I would prefer not to meet your at your office.
There is a restaurant one block east of where you
work. Would that be satisfactory?''

Abbas grinned. They could see the restaurant from
where they were.

''Yes, that's the one. Can you meet me there in,
say, five minutes? You can? Thank you. I promise you
will not be disappointed in what I have.'' Jamilah rang
off and gave the phone back to Abbas.

In Arabic she said, ''The simpleton offered me five
hundred dollars. He will have it with him.''

''It is not money we are after,'' Abbas noted, glancing into the back seat at Barakah and Yasin. ''I will
roll down my window and distract him. Get him into
the car as quickly as you can. Once inside, he is ours.''

They watched the wide bronze-gilded double doors
to the building's lobby. Not two minutes went by, and
out bustled the person Abbas had seen on CNN, shrugging into a jacket. He had a briefcase with him.
Quickly Abbas rolled down his window. As the journalists came alongside the car, he smiled and said in
English, ''Mr. Collins? We would very much like a
word with you.''

In Arabic, to Barakah and Yasin, he said, ''Now.''

Mort Collins stopped and peered into the vehicle in
confusion. ''Who are you?'' he asked.

Jamilah leaned forward so Collins could see her and

beamed her sweetest smile. "I'm the one who just talked to you on the phone. I've changed my mind about the restaurant. Please get in and I will explain."

By then Barakah and Yasin were on either side of him. They took an arm to guide him into the back seat between them, and if he suspected, he didn't give any sign of it.

"I must say. This is most irregular," Collins said, placing the briefcase on his knees. "Why the cloak-and-dagger silliness?"

Abbas snapped his fingers at Jebel, and the young Lebanese pulled from the curb. The terrorist leader had instructed him to obey the speed limit and not do anything that would spark police interest.

"Where are you taking me?" Collins asked Jamilah. "And perhaps you would introduce me to your friends."

Shifting in the front seat, Abbas said, "Introductions are not necessary except in my case. I am Aban Abbas, the head of Al-Jabbar. Perhaps you have heard of it?"

Collins's brow furrowed and he looked at each of them, then back at Abbas. Suddenly his eyes grew as wide as walnuts. He visibly paled, and the knuckles of his fingers wrapped around the briefcase handle grew white. "This can't be! What would an organization like Al-Jabbar want with me? I'm no one of any consequence."

"You underrate your worth. I have traveled a considerable distance to make your acquaintance."

"It can't be," Collins repeated, with a lot less conviction. The tip of his tongue rimmed his lips, and his throat bobbed. "What can I do for you?"

"All in due course," Abbas said. "A friend of ours

has rented a house on the outskirts of the city. Once we arrive everything will be made clear."

"You don't mean to harm me, do you?"

It was more a plea than a question. "Of course not," Abbas lied. "Since when do we kill journalists? All we want is information."

Collins was quiet after that, but he constantly gnawed on his lower lip and glanced repeatedly at the back doors as if considering whether to make a break for freedom. He never did, and when they pulled into the gravel drive to a small brick house that sat well back from the road amid tall trees, it was too late. They ushered him inside. Sheets covered most of the furniture, and a layer of dust showed the house hadn't been occupied in months.

"Is this one of your safe houses?" Collins asked nervously.

"We have never been here before," Abbas said, "and once our business is concluded, we will never come here again." He yanked a sheet off a chair. "Make yourself comfortable, American. This should not take too long."

At the word "American," Collins flinched as if he had been slapped. Clutching the briefcase with both hands, he slowly sat. "I give you my word I will never tell the authorities about this place, or about your being in Greece."

"Of that I am positive." Abbas removed the sheet from another chair and swung it around so it faced the other. Sinking down, he said, "Before we begin, I want to impress on you the need for your complete cooperation."

To Barakah and Yasin, who were on either side of

the journalist, he said, "Break the little finger on his left hand."

Bending, the pair pinned Collins's arms. The newsman was so startled, he dropped the briefcase and tried to wrench free but his strength was no match for theirs. "What are you doing?" he squawked.

Barakah gripped the designated finger. At the last instant Collins divined their intent and cried, "No! Please!"

The crack of the finger breaking was like the snap of a dry twig. Collins screeched and thrashed and went all red in the face.

"Calm down, American," Abbas said, "or I will have them break another one."

Blubbering like an infant, Collins sagged and mewed, "Why? In God's name, tell me why?"

"In God's name, as in everything we do," Abbas said. "It was an object lesson. Answer my questions truthfully or have a finger broken each time I suspect you of lying. The choice is yours."

"Why single me out for this treatment? What have I done to deserve this?"

"I saw your interview on CNN," Abbas mentioned. "And I would learn more about this Echelon you spoke of."

"Is that all?" Rising anger eclipsed the journalist's fear. "Hell, you could have gone on the Internet and learned just about all there is to know. There's no need to put me through this torture."

Abbas gestured at Yasin. "Break the little finger on the insolent fool's other hand."

Yasin went to grab it, but Collins wasn't the complete coward Abbas had supposed. The journalist butted his forehead against Yasin's temple, dazing him, and almost caused Yasin to lose his hold. Collins fought fiercely to rise. Yasin and Barakah were hard pressed to hold him down.

Abbas had witnessed enough. Rising, he calmly walked over, gripped the finger he had chosen, and with a sharp twist of his wrist, broke it cleanly at the knuckle.

Throwing back his head, Collins screamed and shook from side to side. Spittle dribbled over his lower lip and down his chin. "No more! Please!" he wailed as soon as he found his voice. "Anything you want, I'll do!"

Abbas reclaimed his seat. "Very well. We will try again. But I warn you, my patience is at an end. If breaking your fingers is not inducement enough, there are other means of persuading you. Infinitely worse means," he stressed.

"I'll behave! I promise! Ask away."

"You mentioned in the interview that you had gained access to classified information about Echelon."

"That's true," Collins verified.

"Where did you obtain this information?"

Collins hesitated, but only for a second. "From several sources. An American CIA operative, a Greek general and a highly placed official at the American Embassy with contacts at the Department of Defense."

"So in your estimation the information is valid?"

Tears were forming in the corners of the journalist's eyes. Bobbing his fleshy chin, he responded, "In my opinion, yes. But bear in mind I never received corroboration from my government."

Abbas smirked. "They would hardly confirm secrets they did not want revealed."

To Jamilah he said in Arabic, "Hand me the cur's suitcase." When she deposited it on his lap, he pressed the appropriate buttons to release the two latches but nothing happened.

He noticed the lock beside each latch. "Do you have the key?"

"On a key ring in my right front pants pocket."

Abbas instructed Yasin to bring it to him, then switched to English again. "In that same interview you mentioned an Echelon site located somewhere in the Mediterranean. Where exactly would that be?"

"Cyprus," Collins disclosed.

"I said 'exactly.'"

"Ayios Nikolaos, Cyprus," Collins clarified. "It's all there in the briefcase. In the manila folder on the top."

And so it was. Abbas thumbed through dozens of neatly typed pages complete with maps and diagrams. The Cyprus installation was but one of many around the globe. A paragraph caught Abbas's eye, and he read aloud, "The Cyprus site is of special importance because of its proximity to the Middle East and northern Africa, and because it is ideally situated to intercept transmissions from numerous satellites serving those regions as well as Europe."

"So I was told, yes," Collins said. "What else would you like to know? Anything my file doesn't cover, I'm sure I can get for you."

Abbas found the man's eagerness to please pathetic. "There is one thing."

He hefted the file. "Where is Echelon based? There must be a headquarters. Somewhere the other sites report to. Someplace the American government collects all the information.''

"Fort George Meade, Maryland.'' Collins had to be in intense pain, but his curiosity momentarily overrode it. "If you don't mind my asking, why all this interest? Your organization's specialty has always been assassination. What do you care about a bunch of eavesdropping equipment?''

"I care a great deal when that equipment was used to thwart two of my operations,'' Abbas said. "And when it cost me the lives of four holy warriors.''

"There's not much you can do. No one can get near an Echelon site. They're as well protected as Fort Knox.''

For a moment the allusion puzzled Abbas, until he remembered the American gold repository. "Even Fort Knox can be destroyed if one is clever enough.'' Closing the briefcase, he placed it beside his chair, then stood. "I thank you for the information you have provided. And for showing me the grave mistake I made.''

"Mistake?''

"It was wrong of me to limit our targets to individuals. I see now we should devote our energies to crippling the Great Satan in other ways. Such as crippling your country's ability to spy on the rest of the world.''

"You can't be serious.''

"I have never been more serious about anything in my life.'' Abbas undid his belt buckle and began to remove his leather belt.

"What in the world are you doing?'' Collins asked, more amused than anything else.

"Your usefulness is at an end, I'm afraid.'' Bin Abbas wrapped one end of the belt around his left hand

and the other end around his right, then snapped it several times. "Hold him down," he commanded in Arabic.

Barakah and Yasin pressed in close against the chair and bore down on the American with all their weight.

"Wait!" Collins squealed. "What are you up to?"

Abbas moved around behind him. "It should be obvious, even to someone as lacking in intellect as you."

"God, no!" Collins pleaded. He sought to rise but couldn't. "There's no need! I told you I'll keep quiet!"

"That you will," Abbas agreed. In a fluid motion, he slipped the belt over the journalist's head and clamped it around his neck. Collins screamed, or tried to. Crossing both wrists, Abbas constricted the leather and wrenched.

The journalist bucked upward, his arms nearly rising off the chair. For a second it appeared he would shake off Barakah and Yasin. But only for a second. Wheezing and sputtering, he sank down. His face grew so red, his flesh was practically the same color as blood. Making one last attempt to save himself, he jerked violently to the right, then to the left. The tip of his tongue jutted between his lips, and his eyes began to bulge. His movements grew weaker and weaker. A final convulsion, and the deed was done.

Abbas unwrapped his belt and motioned for Barakah and Yasin to let go. "Our work here is done."

"Malik will be sorry he missed this," Yasin commented. "He loves to kill Americans."

"Soon he will get his chance."

MALIK SHARIK PACED the dock at Kildana as he had paced the rocky shore of Thenas. He was anxious to hear from Aban Abbas so he and Rakin could get out of there. The town wasn't to his liking. It had a sinister air about it that grated on his nerves, a gloomy atmosphere that had more to do with its inhabitants than the few clouds scuttling overhead.

Sharik tried telling himself he was imagining things. He gazed across the sunlit Aegean and up at the blue sky, and all seemed right with the world. Then he turned and was confronted by the cold stares of the dozen or so Turks lining the shore. Many had guns, and all had sheaths to wicked curved daggers wedged under their belts.

"Relax, will you?" Rakin said. He was seated on a crate, completely at ease. "Abbas will contact us when he is ready."

"It's not that," Sharik said, and would have elaborated, but Hassan Orgay chose that moment to stride onto the dock. "You were gone long enough," Sharik complained in English, the one language they both spoke. He didn't much like Orgay, either. A greasy slab of a man with a moon face and yellow teeth, Orgay was only slightly less hostile than the rest of Kildana's populace.

"Food does not grow on trees." Orgay held a bulging paper sack aloft. *"Lakerda, midye dolmasi, sigara boregi."*

"You know I don't speak Turkish," Sharik said, certain the smuggler was deliberately trying to annoy him.

"Salted fish strips, stuffed mussels and pastries," Orgay translated, then stiffened and stared out to sea.

Sharik spun. Icy fingers clawed his chest at the sight of a Turkish patrol boat. His panic subsided when he realized it was bearing from north to south, and he let out a breath he hadn't known he was holding.

"Strange," Orgay said. "The next routine patrol is not due to pass by until tomorrow afternoon."

"The navy lets you know their schedule, do they?" Sharik couldn't resist taunting him.

"We have our sources, Palestinian. How else did you think we elude their boats so easily?" Orgay scratched the stubble dotting his chin. "This one is not on patrol. It is up to something else."

"Maybe your government suspects we are here."

"Were that the case, the patrol boat would be steaming toward this dock." Orgay tossed the sack to Rakin, who had to drop the stick he was whittling on to catch it. "Fill your bellies while I go talk with my people."

"Wait," Sharik declared. "What if our leader calls while you are gone and wants us to fly out right away?"

"You did not mind my leaving to fetch food," Orgay responded. "And this is much more important. We must post sentries and send a man with binoculars to the top of the nearest hill."

"All because a patrol boat went by?"

"My people have not lasted as long as they have by taking our enemies lightly. If the government is up to something, if they try to infiltrate us as they have in the past, whoever they send will regret it. We will chop him into pieces and feed him to our dogs."

CHAPTER SEVEN

The Executioner followed the ribbon of a stream south until he came to the last of the low hills. The afternoon was hot, the air humid. Sweat trickled from under the woolen cap Lieutenant-Commander Pamir had lent him as he hiked toward the top to study the layout of Kildana. Halfway up, a pungent odor brought him to a halt.

Crouching, Bolan scoured the crest and saw puffs of smoke rising on the sluggish breeze. He crept higher, his right hand on the Beretta. Soon he came to a gully that effectively hid him until he reached the top.

A sentry had been posted, an old man whose hair and beard were flecked with gray. He was seated on a flat boulder, a Turkish-made 9 mm Rexim-Favor SMG across his lap. As best Bolan could remember, it was a hybrid model based on a French design. Although the Turkish army used them for a number of years, the Rexim-Favor never saw widespread use because the firing mechanism was considered too complicated.

The old Turk was puffing contentedly on a pipe while scrutinizing the countryside to the northwest.

A rock the size of Bolan's fist was perfect for his

purpose. Clutching it in his right hand, he stalked out of the gully. A glance to his left showed the tops of buildings and a few people moving along the dusty main street. He had to stay low or someone in Kildana might spot him.

Moving with stealth born of long experience, the soldier came within an arm's length of the old Turk and raised the rock to strike.

The sentry chose that moment to take the pipe from his mouth and elevate his arms to stretch. In doing so, he turned his head a fraction, just enough to spot Bolan. Instantly the soldier swung, but displaying surprising agility for someone his age, the Turk dodged the blow and vaulted to his feet as if fired from a cannon, grabbing the Rexim-Favor as he rose.

Suddenly Bolan found himself staring down the muzzle of the SMG. He slammed the rock against the barrel, swatting the weapon aside at the exact split second the old man squeezed the trigger, and sprang to the right to avoid the spray of lead sure to tear up the hilltop. But no shots rang out. In his haste, the Turk had neglected to flick the fire selector switch. The SMG was still on safety.

Realizing his mistake, the old man clawed at the switch to remedy it.

Bolan was faster. Stepping in close, he smashed the rock against the Rexim-Favor's wooden pistol grip, knocking the subgun from the Turk's grasp, then pivoted and delivered a backhand swipe at the man's temple.

The Turk ducked. Before Bolan could swing again, he flourished a wicked curved dagger. The blade gleamed in the sunlight as the old man streaked it from its sheath in a glittering arc meant to disembowel.

Bolan sprang back, saving himself. He grabbed for the Beretta, but another swing of the dagger thwarted him, nearly taking off several fingers in the process.

The old Turk was wily enough to know he had to press hard if he was to prevail, and that was exactly what he did. Weaving a tapestry of cold steel, he didn't give Bolan a moment's respite.

The Executioner couldn't dodge forever. The Beretta was his best bet, but its sound suppressor wasn't attached. The shots would be heard in Kildana, bringing more smugglers on the run.

But Bolan was nothing if not adaptable. Skipping to the left to avoid a thrust at his ribs, he threw the rock with all his strength at the old Turk's right knee. It struck with an audible snap, and the old man doubled over in agony. Before he could straighten, Bolan delivered an uppercut that caught the Turk flush on the tip of his jaw and lifted him clear off his feet. The dagger went flying from bony fingers gone limp as the old man smacked to the ground, unconscious.

Squatting, Bolan cut strips from the Turk's loose-fitting shirt, bound the man's wrists and ankles and applied a gag. Ejecting the Rexim-Favor's magazine, he tossed the SMG down the slope, and a few seconds later sent the dagger skittering after it. Then, on his belly, he crawled to where he could he could look out over the den of iniquity harboring the terrorists.

Kildana was everything Pamir claimed. Ancient, shadowy, ominous, a pall of quiet hung over the town. Most of the houses were boxlike affairs with flat roofs and small windows, built so close together there was barely room to walk between them. A lone Jeep parked a block from the dock was the only transportation in evidence other than the seaplane and several boats. The dock itself was deserted.

Bolan saw two women walking along a narrow side street. Although many Turkish women had long since adopted Western attire, these two wore old-fashioned burqas and were carrying buckets. At the junction with the main street they turned toward the stream.

Sliding backward until it was safe to stand, Bolan headed down the north side of the hill. As he passed the old Turk, the man groaned. Once at the bottom, he worked around to the west until he was in sight of the long dock—and the seaplane. It was a tactical mistake for the terrorists to leave their most valuable link to the outside world unattended, and he wasn't one to let an opportunity to sabotage the aircraft slip by.

Several shacks were situated at the near end. Shoving his hands into his pockets and tucking his chin to his chest so no one could get a good look at his face, Bolan brazenly strode into the open. Although his natural impulse was to run, he resisted the urge. Should anyone be watching, it might arouse suspicion.

Bolan had just reached the first shack when the door to a large building fifty yards away opened, and out filed over a dozen stern-faced Turks. They were tough-looking, rough-hewn men, two-legged predators like those Bolan had encountered time and time again in countless other countries, other climes, hardmen who would give no quarter and ask for none. Each carried an autorifle or an SMG. Paring off, they spread out and moved into Kildana as if beginning a search-and-destroy mission.

Bolan didn't know what to make of it. They couldn't know he was there, so the logical conclusion had to be they were after someone else.

One pair walked to the seaplane to stand guard.

He drew the Beretta, reached into his coat pocket for the sound suppressor and threaded it onto the barrel. Folding down the grip in front of the trigger guard, he adopted a two-handed stance and was on the verge of banging off a 3-round burst when the door to the same building opened again, and out came three stragglers. One was a Turk with a craggy moon face that would give children nightmares. The others were more familiar; the young Palestinian and the older man from Thenas. Bolan tried to take aim, but they turned the far corner and were gone before he could fire.

Moments later the Jeep's engine cranked over. Bolan wondered if the terrorists were waiting for the cover of dark to fly out. Maybe they intended to travel overland to Izmir or Ankara and book passage on a conventional flight.

Bolan couldn't let them get away, not a third time. Lowering the Beretta, he held it under his coat and walked toward the rear of the buildings on the north side of town. Neither of the Turks by the seaplane noticed. One was gazing out to the sea, the other engrossed in a cigarette.

The Jeep's horn blared; someone hollered in Turkish.

Bolan darted into a gap barely wider than his shoulders and sprinted to the front. The Jeep was across the street. A Turk was at the wheel. Another was climbing in. The terrorists weren't anywhere around.

The driver pulled out, heading east, and Bolan looked around the corner to satisfy himself it didn't stop to pick up the terrorists. Rattling across the wooden bridge over the stream, it sped inland in a cloud of dust.

The terrorists still had to be somewhere in Kildana. All Bolan had to do was find them without being caught. He began to retrace his steps, then drew up short. A heavyset woman was at the far end, peering in at him. Thanks to her veil, Bolan couldn't see her face. He braced for an outcry but after staring a few moments she waddled off. Perhaps to inform some of the men she had seen a stranger.

Bolan hurried to the opening. The smart thing was to leave, but voices gave him pause. He looked out and saw the heavyset woman talking to two others. She was gesturing excitedly at the gap. The next instant they started toward it.

Whirling, Bolan hastened to the main street. He ducked around the corner before the women could spot him and slid into a recessed doorway. Farther down was a pair of stone-faced Turks, their backs to him. Across the way another duo was going from building to building. He glanced toward the dock and saw four more by the boats.

The soldier figured he would stay where he was until the coast was clear, but fate had other ideas. A man's voice came from the other side of the door, and with it approaching footsteps. Pulling his hat low, he walked eastward. His skin prickled as he heard the door open and then more footsteps, but they moved away from him.

Bolan was almost abreast of a window when without warning a swarthy hand gripping a meat cleaver poked out. A veiled head followed it. The woman gazed toward the men across the street, muttered something in Turkish and drew back. Amazingly she hadn't noticed him. As he strode past the window, loud squawking erupted, and he looked in to see her bent over a table, the meat cleaver in one hand, a struggling chicken in the other. As he looked on, the cleaver descended with a loud thunk.

Up ahead a side street appeared. Bolan had to pass several doorways to reach it, and as he came to the second, a startled cry greeted him. The door was open, and two small girls and a boy were playing inside. He had come on them so quietly, he'd spooked them.

Bolan kept on walking. One more dwelling and he would reach the side street where there were fewer people.

Suddenly a feeling he was being watched came over him. Bolan glanced back, but no one was behind him. Nor were the men down the street looking in his direction. He was about to chalk it up to his imagination when movement in a window across the street alerted him to a woman in a dark blue burqa. Her face was hidden by a veil, but there was no doubt she had taken an undue interest in what he was up to.

To his rear, feet scuffed the ground. The boy had stepped outside and was studying him intently.

It took every iota of willpower Bolan possessed to continue to stroll along as if he had every right to be there. Without warning, another women stepped from the next doorway. She was the first female he had seen whose face wasn't covered. In her eighties, she had leathery skin seamed with lines and cracks. Her thin lips curled in a perpetual frown, she turned toward him and stopped dead in surprise.

Bolan went to go around her, but the crone gripped his sleeve and addressed him in Turkish. Smiling, he tugged loose and continued on, but the harm had been done. Her dark eyes narrowed. A gnarled finger rose to point accusingly. And from her wizened mouth keened a sound the likes of which Bolan had never heard a human throat utter—a high-pitched trilling that rapidly swelled in volume to become an ear-splitting shriek.

It was a warning cry, one taken up by the woman in the window across the street. Leaning out, she pointed at Bolan and vented a trilling screech louder than the crone's.

Every man within earshot had spun. Others rushed from buildings, bringing guns to bear.

"Damn." Bolan whipped out the Beretta. Adopting a two-handed grip, he fired 3-round bursts into a pair of Turks on his side of the street and shifted to do the same to a pair on the other side, but they were already seeking cover. Starting toward the intersection, he felt a stinging pain in his right shoulder.

The crone was trying to kill him. She had drawn one of those curved daggers the Turks were so fond of from under the folds of her baggy dress, but her first swing merely nicked him. Now she came at him with a vengeance, thrusting and slashing and trilling all the while.

Bolan backpedaled, staying barely a half step ahead of her flashing blade. He didn't want to hurt the old woman if he could help it, but she left him no choice. Inadvertently he backed against the house, and she was on him before he could skip aside, her dagger thirsting for his throat. He shot her between the eyes.

More women were leaning from windows or had dashed from doorways to point and trill in inhuman chorus. Some of the men began to fire on the fly, their slugs zinging dangerously close. And as if that weren't enough, the boy he'd seen earlier flew at him, a sharpened stick hiked overhead to stab.

The short hairs at the warrior's nape tingled as he realized it wasn't just the men he had to contend with. Every last person in Kildana, including every woman and child, was now out to kill him.

Bolan sidestepped the boy's rush and kicked him in the gut. It dropped the kid in his tracks, and he fell to his knees. But then, pointing fiercely at Bolan, he opened his mouth and trilled like the women were doing.

Boots drummed. Into the side street charged a burly Turk leveling an Uzi. Bolan chopped him down with a burst from the Beretta, rotated on the balls of his feet and headed for the hills. But the three women he had seen earlier, the heavyset one and her friends, were at the other end of the side street, brandishing daggers. Spreading out at arm's length so he couldn't get past them, they swept toward him, trilling at the top of their lungs.

From the main street rose the shouts of more approaching men.

A narrow doorway appeared on Bolan's right. Without breaking stride he slammed his right shoulder against it, and the ancient wood buckled under the impact like a plank with dry-rot. He found himself in a musty room with a low ceiling, empty except for a rickety chair and a bench. Straight ahead was a short, narrow hall. He raced down it into a kitchen area and turned to go through a doorway on the right.

A woman abruptly filled it. Clasped in her left arm was an infant swaddled in a blanket. She took one look at Bolan, threw back her head and trilled. Behind her other women materialized, several producing daggers.

The soldier would never risk endangering a baby. Wheeling, he ran to the front of the house. The front door was already open. As he raced into the afternoon sunlight, he recognized it as the same doorway the old crone had emerged from. Armed men were streaming into the side street and hadn't noticed him.

Bolan spun to the right, hoping to reach the dock. But women were all over, and on spying him, they pointed, trilled and swarmed like angry wasps, their daggers glinting in the sunlight. He shot two who got too close, shot another trying to stab him from the side. The others momentarily slowed, but the four men who had been by the boats were bounding up the street to cut him off, each unlimbering an SMG or an autorifle.

The soldier veered toward the buildings on the south side of the street. The op had gone to hell. It was kill or be killed. Eliminating the terrorists had become secondary to making it out of Kildana alive. And at the moment that prospect was exceedingly slim. Shifting from right to left, he fired at those posing the greatest threat. A man aiming an AK-47 toppled with his brain cored. Another with a Sola Super pitched forward with a slug through an eye.

Guns were blasting on all sides. Leaden hornets buzzed Bolan's head. Miniature geysers sprouted near his feet. One of the Turks from the dock cut loose with a Portuguese FBP but aimed too low. Bolan's aim was better.

More than two dozen townspeople were converging on him. Bullet after bullet pockmarked the building he was racing toward. A young woman who rushed out of the front door was turned into a sieve by withering fire from her own people.

Miraculously, Bolan reached the entrance unscathed and rushed inside. Crouching against the wall, he ejected the Beretta's magazine, slapped home another and flipped the fire selector to single shot. Then, drawing the Desert Eagle, he rose with a gun in each hand and backed into a shadowed corner. Trying to flee was pointless. There were too many, and they were too close. He had to make a stand.

Caught up in a frenzy of raw savagery, Turks poured into the house after him.

Bolan triggered shots as fast as targets presented themselves. The first five through the doorway spilled to the floor, partially blocking it, forcing those who came through after them to scramble over the bodies.

With ambidextrous precision Bolan squeezed off round after round, the boom of the .44 Magnum Desert Eagle eclipsing the crisper bark of the Beretta. Ten bodies filled the doorway, and still the smugglers and their women fought to break through.

The soldier had a major tactical edge. The Turks were charging from bright sunlight into a murky room, and it took their eyes several seconds to adjust. Seconds he denied them. In addition, they had no idea exactly where he was. Those with guns sprayed lead wildly as they burst in, and the slugs came nowhere near him.

A smuggler with an MP-5 was typical. He heaved out of the throng and snapped off half a dozen rounds from the hip, swinging his weapon from right to left while squinting to try to pinpoint Bolan's position. He never got the chance. Bolan sighted down the Eagle and blew off the top of the Turk's skull.

Another man scrambled over the top of the pile. Bolan dropped him in place with a shot from the 93-R.

Suddenly the attack ceased. The bedlam died.

Outside, someone began to speak in a low, commanding tone.

Bolan reloaded both weapons. Ten feet from him lay a woman in a spreading scarlet pool. Her veil had come partially undone, revealing a young, attractive face, so serene in death it lent the illusion she was asleep. A twinge of conscience spiked him. Even though he learned long ago the female of the human species was as deadly as the male, he rarely had to kill women, and there was a part of him, deep down inside, that regretted doing so. He had to remind himself that if any of them got close enough, they would gladly slit his throat.

Now the Turks were whispering. Maybe they thought he understood Turkish and didn't want him to hear what they were up to. Furtive rustling and the patter of footsteps ensued.

Bolan crept toward a front window and cautiously peered out. The street was deserted. He looked toward the dock and as far to the east as he could, but the mob had dispersed. They were up to something, and it would be foolish to stay there until they carried it out. He turned toward the front door, then froze.

Four men were emerging from a building down the street. One had a rocket launcher over a shoulder.

Whirling, Bolan ran deeper into the house. The next room was the kitchen. Beyond was a narrow hall leading to a pair of small bedrooms. But there was no back door. Reasoning there had to be another way out, he returned to the kitchen and pushed aside a tapestry covering the left-hand wall. And found a side door. He was about to open it when whispering came from the other side.

They were out there, some of them, waiting for him to show himself.

Bolan was trapped. Any moment now the men in the main street would fire the rocket launcher. It had appeared to be an old German-made PZF44. The Panzerfaust, Bolan recalled, used a shaped-charge warhead, 80 mm or larger, capable of reducing much of the house to rubble. If he retreated to the bedrooms, he would be spared the brunt of the blast but the roof or one of the walls still might come crashing down on top of him. Better, he believed, to take his chances with the Turks waiting outside.

With the thought came action. Using one finger, Bolan yanked the door wide open. His abrupt appearance surprised the four men and two women in the gap between the buildings. Three died in half as many seconds. He slammed the Desert Eagle against the temple of a woman wielding a knife, shifted and sent a round into the forehead of a man with an AK-47, shifted again and dispatched the last man. All done so fast, not one got off a shot.

Bolan raced toward the rear. The men in the main street were bound to have heard, and sure enough, when he reached the corner and glanced back, they were at the other end. The Turk with the PZF44 was sighting down the launcher tube. Extending the Desert Eagle, Bolan fired twice into the man's sternum. The Turk staggered back, the launcher's muzzle dipping at the very instant the trigger mechanism was squeezed.

Bolan dived past the corner as artificial thunder rocked Kildana. He landed hard on his stomach and protectively threw his hands over his head. Debris pelted down, chunks and bits of building and clods of dirt, along with grisly pieces of flesh and body parts.

The rocket had struck in the midst of the group between the buildings.

Something thudded heavily against Bolan's back and bounced off. He stayed flat until the unnatural rain ended, then rose to his knees. Beside him lay half a human arm. A few feet away were several toes attached to a pulpy strand of flesh.

Heaving upright, Bolan jogged toward the sea. He had several blocks to go. At any second he expected more Turks to come rushing after him, but none did. Nor did he hear any voices.

Then a new sound broke the stillness, one that spurred the soldier into running full out. He came to a side street and leveled his weapons, but the street was empty.

The distinct growl of a prop engine was growing louder.

Another fifty yards and Bolan would reach the dock. A veiled face appeared at a rear window, and he took hasty aim, but it was withdrawn. He skirted a wire pen that containing noisy chickens, vaulted an old wooden cart and covered the remaining distance.

The growl had changed pitch. Bolan knew what he would see when he cleared the last building, and he fought down a rising tide of frustration. The seaplane was heading out into the Aegean, gaining speed rapidly. It was already out of range. All he could do was stand and watch as the pontoons lifted into the air and the aircraft banked to the south.

"Damn."

The terrorists had gotten away again.

Bolan hoped the Turkish air force tracked the seaplane to its destination. His back to the wall of the last house, he sidled to the main street. It was still deserted.

So was the dock. Somewhere a child began to bawl, but her cry was smothered, perhaps by a parental hand.

For Bolan to remain in Kildana was pointless. It was hours to the rendezvous, and he would rather wait out on the sea than here, where every hand was turned against him. Accordingly, he sidestepped toward the boats.

A lean figure was momentarily silhouetted on a nearby roof but ducked from sight before Bolan could tell whether it was a man or a woman. Another Turk appeared in a doorway farther down the street, spotted him and melted into the shadows.

Of the three boats, the one Bolan liked most was a souped-up powerboat fitted with a twin diesel. It was also equipped with sonar and a variety of other high-tech hardware useful for eluding detection. The key was missing, but that didn't stop him. Prudently keeping any eye on the town, he soon turned over the engine and moved to cast off.

Suddenly the figure on the roof reappeared. It was a woman, holding a small child to her bosom. She shook a fist, raised her head to the heavens and cried out, as if appealing to God to strike him dead.

Bolan removed the mooring lines, gripped the wheel and carefully edged the powerboat from the dock. Once in the clear he opened the throttle. He thought maybe some of the smugglers would rush out of hiding, hop in the other boats and give chase, but they didn't. His last sight of Kildana was of its corpse-littered street.

CHAPTER EIGHT

Cyprus

Cyprus hadn't changed much since Aban Abbas was there last.

Located forty miles south of Turkey, the island was famed for it rugged mountains, picturesque beaches and old hilltop castles. It was also noted for the long-festering dispute between the Turks and the Greeks over who should exercise control.

Not so widely known was the fact a third party had a vested interest in Cyprus. Until 1960 the island had been part of the British Empire. When the Britons signed the treaty that created the Republic of Cyprus, they shrewdly insisted on a provision granting them perpetual sovereignty over two key military installations.

The Sovereign Base Areas, as they became known, were a strategic link to the Mideast and Africa. One was in eastern Cyprus and called, fittingly enough, the Eastern Sovereign Base Area. The other, the Western Sovereign Base Area, including the garrison at Episkopi, interested Abbas more. According to information unearthed by the late Mort Collins, hidden behind the facility's high walls was the Echelon station responsible for two of Al-Jabbar's holy missions going awry.

Operated under the purview of the National Security Agency, the site was considered part of the Joint Signal Service Unit and protected around the clock by British soldiers. Penetrating their security would be a challenge, but Abbas was supremely confident he could do anything he put his mind to.

Playing the part of a typical tourist, Abbas had Jamilah rent a car. With Barakah and Yasin along, they made a circuit of the base perimeter. At one point the road came within three hundred yards of the wall. Beyond it were three huge white radomes, spherical covers used to conceal large parabolic antennae, along with an open array of rod antennae and rhombic-shaped antennae.

"There is what we want," Abbas said, pointing at a two-story building midway between the radomes. "The Echelon command center." Closing the briefcase he had taken from Collins, he scoured the brush-covered ground between the road and the high wall. "We will hit it tonight—2:00 a.m. should do."

"The ten of us against an entire miliary base?" Jamilah said. "You know I would follow you to the gates of hell, but this—"

"The barracks are at the other end, and most of the soldiers will be asleep. All that need concern us are a few guards and the Echelon staff." Abbas went to stroke her hair but remembered Barakah and Yasin were in the car, and placed his hand on the seat between them. He had an example to set. It wasn't fitting for a leader to show he was subject to the same earthly desires as other men.

"Your pardon, sir," Yasin said, "but shouldn't we

take the time to plan this out to the smallest detail, as you always advise us?"

"Time is our enemy," Abbas pointed out. "By now the American journalist has been reported missing. Those he worked with will know of his interest in Echelon. The American government might place this facility on high alert."

Barakah stirred. "There is little chance of that, I should think. We buried the pig in the basement of the house and covered the grave with fresh concrete. No evidence exists linking us to him."

"Not specifically, but never underestimate our enemies. Americans are evil and arrogant, but they are not stupid." Abbas stared at the radomes. "So we strike tonight. Now drive me into town. I must meet with my contact and confirm he can supply the arms and explosives we'll need."

"Explosives." Jamilah made the word sound equivalent to the plague. "We have never worked with them before."

"I have," Abbas corrected her. "During my time with Hamas I was taught by an expert. I am versed in the use of all kinds, and I will teach the rest of you. By morning those domes will be rubble." A newfound sense of excitement coursed through him. Al-Jabbar was entering into a new arena of activity bound to boost their prestige in the Muslim world. The following day, headlines everywhere would announce the site's destruction. And by making a few discreet phone calls, he would insure his organization received due credit.

What then? Abbas wondered. Simple assassinations paled by comparison. Al-Jabbar had to expand its horizons, move on to bigger, more spectacular targets.

"Master," Yasin said politely, "how soon will it take them to rebuild?"

"Rebuild?" Abbas repeated, his mind preoccupied with what they could do to top themselves.

"Those domes. How long will the facility be shut down? Six months? A year? It is too bad we cannot put it out of operation permanently."

A physical blow couldn't have jarred Abbas more. All the effort they were going to, and the Americans would have the site up and running again in another six months or so. It diminished their accomplishment. But he wasn't about to cancel the mission. It wouldn't look good were he to back out after Yasin's comment. The others might think he hadn't thought the mission through.

Reluctantly Abbas admitted to himself that he had let his thirst for vengeance get the better of his judgment. Destroying Echelon was a grand goal, but the only way to shut it down completely was to strike at the heart of the global network, not at one lone site.

The heart of the network. The phrase rang in Abbas's mind like the pealing of a bell. An idea sprouted, an idea so sensational, so intoxicating in its sheer brilliance, he was amazed no one had thought of it before.

"Are you all right?" Jamilah asked. "You have the most unusual expression."

"I have never felt better." Impulsively Abbas gave her elbow an affectionate squeeze none of the others noticed. "God has graced me with new wisdom. I know my purpose for being, and the cusp of my life is in the balance."

"I am not sure I understand."

"Nor I," Barakah said.

"All you need know for now is that all we have

done to this point is but a minor prelude to an achievement that will put Al-Jabbar on the tongue of every person on the planet. Praise God for his guidance! We are His sword, and our blade will bite deeper into Satan than any before us.''

A chorus of ''Praise God!'' filled the car.

Aban Abbas laughed with delight.

THE YILDIZ-CLASS FPB 57 cleaved the Aegean Sea like a giant knife. Alone near the bow, dressed once again in his own clothes, Mack Bolan leaned on the rail and let the fine spray moisten his face and hair. To the west a blazing red sun was being slowly devoured. To the east lay the Turkish shoreline and a flock of squawking gulls.

''You are a remarkable man, Mr. Belasko,'' Lieutenant-Commander Pamir remarked.

Bolan turned. He hadn't heard the officer approach over the hiss of water and the seagulls. The patrol boat had retrieved him an hour ago and was steaming south along the coast. ''No more so than most,'' he responded.

''You are too modest.'' The Turkish officer took a pack of cigarettes from his shirt pocket and offered one to Bolan, but the soldier shook his head. ''The men I sent ashore have radioed an update. They found twenty-seven bodies and the parts of five or six more. Single-handedly, you wiped out over half of Kildana's population.''

''They brought it on themselves.'' Bolan faced the sea. He had already shut the firefight from his memory and didn't care to have it brought up.

Pamir lit the cigarette and tossed the match over the

side. "In one afternoon you have done what my government couldn't do in a hundred years."

"Don't make more of what happened than there is."

The officer arched an eyebrow. "You crippled their smuggling operation. It will be years before they are as active as they have been, if ever. Surely that merits praise?"

"The terrorists got away."

"Ah." Pamir puffed a few times, then blew a smoke ring. "Hassan Orgay is a fine pilot. And a clever one. We didn't spot him on our way north to rendezvous with you, nor did his aircraft show up on our radar. My guess is he headed inland, at treetop level. He could be anywhere by now."

"Wasn't your air force supposed to have some jets in the area?"

"The fighters were a couple of miles out so the smugglers wouldn't spot them. Keeping a low profile, as you might say, so as not to arouse their suspicions and put you in danger."

Bolan stared at the briny water below. He was back to square one. No new intel, no solid leads pointing him toward Al-Jabbar's base of operations. He might as well head to the States.

"I am sorry, Mr. Belakso," Pamir said. "We did what we thought best. If it is any consolation, my government scrambled a dozen more aircraft to scour the southeast coast and its adjacent waters. They might yet turn up something."

"They might," Bolan said without much conviction. The way his luck had been running, the two terrorists had made a clean getaway and were free to go on killing as long their fanatical hearts desired.

"I put in a call to your superior in Washington, as you requested. But it will be awhile before we hear back, I am told." Pamir blew a larger smoke ring. "Disgusting habit, I know, but I have not been able to stop. The only thing worse than nicotine addiction is being addicted to chocolate." He chuckled.

Bolan wasn't in the mood for small talk. He preferred to be by himself, but it would be a breach of professional etiquette to give the officer the cold shoulder. The man was only being friendly.

"These thugs you are after, this Al-Jabbar, I hope you do to them as you did to the smugglers. Their kind give Muslims everywhere a bad name." Pamir looked at the cigarette, grimaced and flicked it into the sea. "I would not blame your countrymen if they believed all followers of Islam are lunatics."

"There are always a few too blinded by their prejudice to see the truth," Bolan commented. "But most Americans realize not all Muslims are our enemies."

"Most Turks are Muslim. But I guess you already know that. We have a much more modern outlook than fundamentalists like Al-Jabbar, who see the world as Satan's playground and believe they are doing the will of God when they slay innocent women and children." Pamir leaned on the rail. "But then, every religion has a fundamentalist element, do they not? Those who believe only they will go to heaven or paradise, and everyone else will burn in the pit."

Bolan said nothing. If history had taught humanity anything, it was that there were always those who thought they were right and everyone else was wrong. Fanatics who had no qualms about snuffing out the lives of those they looked down their noses on.

"Ironic, is it not?"

"What?"

"Almost all the religions of the world preach love and brotherhood, but their followers can never seem to live together in peace. Which, I suppose, is just as well. Or men like you and I would be out of work."

Human nature being what it was, Bolan couldn't see his personal war ever ending. His one hope was that there would always be warriors willing to make the ultimate sacrifice to preserve the values free men everywhere held dear.

Just then the squawk box blared in Turkish, and Pamir straightened. "Our presence is required on the bridge. Your Mr. Brognola very much desires to speak with you."

Yildiz Class vessels were equipped with state-of-the-art communications and navigation equipment. The communications officer handed Bolan a headset, and after adjusting it, the soldier stepped to one side. "Hal? Can you hear me?"

"Loud and clear, Striker," was the big Fed's reply. He sounded as if he were in the next compartment. "It's taken a bit longer than I anticipated to get back to you. We've had a major break, and I needed to confirm the intel before committing resources to ferry you where you need to go."

"And that would be?"

"Sunny Somalia. The land where warlords are a dime a dozen. Where there are more corrupt politicians than you can shake a Ka-bar at. And where terrorist training camps are a thriving industry in themselves."

"You've located an Al-Jabbar training camp?"

"If our intel is on the money, it's a combo deal. Two for the price of one. Training camp and base of operations, rolled into one." Brognola paused. "Whoever the leader of Al-Jabbar is, he's kept us on the ropes until today. He obtains all his arms and provisions through shell companies and has a complicated network of e-mail accounts and phone numbers under a dozen false identities. Trying to track him down has been like trying to peel an onion. We've had to take it one layer at a time and pray we eventually hit pay dirt.''

"Are you deliberately keeping me in suspense?"

Brognola laughed. "For a man who can lie motionless for hours waiting for a perfect shot, you sure don't have much patience, do you? Very well. Our Echelon site at Ayios Nikolaos intercepted a message about an hour and a half ago. Your friends in the seaplane made the mistake of radioing Somalia direct. We were able to triangulate and have the location pegged to a ten-square-mile area in northern Somalia.''

"That's still a lot of ground to cover."

"O ye of little faith. By the time you reach Kyrenia, our satellites will have the actual site nailed, complete with high-resolution photos.''

"Kyrenia? Then I'm heading for Cyprus?''

"The Turkish Republic of Northern Cyprus, to be exact. Very hush-hush, you understand, since officially our government hasn't recognized the TRNC and we don't want the Greeks mad at us. The Turks have agreed to supply a car and a driver to take you to the Western Sovereign Base Area, where the British will get you on a military jet and ferry you to northern Somalia.''

"What's my ETA in Cyprus?''

"Your should reach Kyrenia about five or six in the a.m. I wish it were sooner, but it's the best I can do, given the logistics. We don't have any of our ships or flyboys anywhere near you at the moment. Use the time to catch up on your sleep.''

"I'll try, Mother.''

"Don't use that tone with me,'' Brognola bantered. "If you knew all the strings I've had to pull to pull this off—'' He stopped. "Come to think of it, when you get to Ayios Nikolaos, stop by the Echelon facility. I'll have the satellite photos relayed there, and you can pick them up and study them on the flight to Somalia.''

"Once again you've covered all the angles.''

"It's why they pay me the big bucks.'' Brognola grew pensive. "You know, it wouldn't hurt to have backup on this one. Phoenix Force is in Southeast Asia at the moment, but I could have them join you in Somalia in, say, twenty-four to thirty-six hours, depending on how soon they can wrap up their op.''

"I won't need them,'' Bolan said.

"Really? We're talking maybe thirty or more terrorists, at a presumably heavily fortified location. You're the best, granted, but you don't fly around in tights with a big red S on your chest.''

"And?''

"No one is invincible. I'm sure David and his boys wouldn't mind swinging by to help you kick a little terrorist booty on their way home.''

Bolan didn't doubt that one bit. David McCarter hated terrorists with a fiery passion. But he didn't think much of the idea of having to wait another whole day. Once he hit Somalia, he wanted to get in and out as quickly as possible. "Thanks, but no thanks.''

"Okay. Give me a ring when you reach Cyprus. I expect to camp out in my office until this is over with.''

The link went dead. Bolan removed the headset and handed it to the communications officer, then joined Pamir at a forward window. ''It looks like you're stuck with me a while yet.''

''So I have been informed by the admiral. If you're hungry, I can have food brought to your compartment. And if you would like some company, I can bring my chess set. An American serviceman stationed in Ankara taught me how to play years ago. I have been in his debt ever since. I love the game.''

Bolan indulged in a smile. ''Just don't hold it against me when I win.''

IT HAS BEEN SAID that catching an enemy napping is half the battle. In that case, Al-Jabbar had its strike against the Echelon facility on Cyrpus won before the terrorists went over the perimeter wall.

At 2:00 a.m. the surrounding streets were largely empty, the surrounding homes and businesses dark. A stray dog roving the brush-covered ground between the wall and the nearest road was the only living creature to observe eleven camouflage-clad figures stalk toward the base with all the stealth of a pack of wolves closing in on prey.

Aban Abbas spotted the mongrel and raised his French-made FAMAS but didn't fire. Even though it was fitted with a sound suppressor, the SMG would make some noise. Noise a sharp-eared sentry might hear. As long as the animal didn't bark, he would let it go.

The others had slowed when Abbas did, and now he waved them on. It had been years since he was personally involved in a mission like this, and it was great to feel the old, familiar sense of excitement pulse through his veins. Abbas had forgotten how thrilling it was. Coming to a shallow gully, he hopped into it and dropped onto his stomach on the other side. The others imitated his example.

Jamilah was on his right, her features hidden by a black ski mask. Her teeth gleamed white in the darkness.

Barakah was on the left. "No sign of guards yet," he whispered.

"They will be inside the wall," was Abbas's guess. A hundred feet to the north was a spotlight, a hundred feet to the south another. But at the point where he intended to go over, it was as black as pitch. The lights didn't overlap, as they should. He expected better of the British; lax security was more typical of American installations.

A final sprint, and Abbas was at the base of the wall. He pointed at Yasin, the undisputed strongest member of Al-Jabbar. Yasin slung his submachine gun, cupped his hands and braced himself.

By prior arrangement, Barakah was first to place a foot in Yasin's hands and be hurled upward as if fired from a cannon. Catching hold of the top with both hands, Barakah checked the other side, nodded to let them know the coast was clear and swung up and over.

Jamilah was next, Jebel third, Abbas fourth. He remembered to bend his knees as he landed to better absorb the shock, then scooted into a patch of inky shadow to crouch and wait for the others. Three more had joined them when Jebel tugged at his sleeve and motioned to the south.

A pair of British soldiers was approaching. They were still a fair way off, so Abbas was safe in whispering loud enough for Yasin to hear, "Guards are coming! Stop until I give you the word."

To those with him he said softly, "Stay down. I will take them myself, when they are right on top of us."

The young guards, members of the Royal Military Police, weren't expecting trouble. Their Sterlings were slung, and they were talking about England and how much they missed it.

Abbas grinned as he curled his finger around the FAMAS's trigger. He had almost forgotten how exquisitely invigorating it was to kill an enemy. Years spent organizing the group's missions had dulled his sensibilities. The compact autorifle was already on automatic. He pressed a button that limited each burst to three rounds and sighted on the chest of one of the Britons. When they were only a stone's throw off, he stroked the trigger, shifted the sights to the chest of the second guard and stroked the trigger a second time. Both homesick soldiers crumpled without a sound.

"Send over the rest!" Abbas commanded Yasin. He then ordered Jamilah and those on the near side to spread out so they would be in position to provide cover fire should things go wrong. But God favored them. And when all eleven were over, the terrorist leader gestured and led them at a trot past the nearest radome to the command center. Isolated from other base buildings, it was a ripe fig waiting to be plucked.

Amazingly, no guards were posted at the entrance. Even more incredibly, when Abbas tried the doorknob, it turned without resistance. Someone had either inadvertently left the door unlocked or the Echelon personnel, composed mainly of Americans, had too much confidence in their British protectors.

Across a circular lobby sat a man in uniform, dozing at his desk. Abbas nodded at Jamilah, and she put a slug through the man's brain.

Two narrow halls branched into the interior. Abbas took Jamilah and four others to the right. Barakah went to the left with the rest.

Abbas was disappointed. He had imagined the facility would be abuzz with activity, but it was as still as a tomb. They passed a number of small unoccupied offices and came to a spacious room with glass walls. Inside, four technicians were scattered at various computer terminals and electronic monitors, doing whatever their work entailed. Judging by the number of empty chairs at other work posts, during the day the workforce was many times larger.

The leader of Al-Jabbar glided to a glass door and eased it open. Two more technicians were at a coffee machine, drinking and chatting. On the other side of the command center was another glass door, Barakah framed in the opening. Abbas signaled to let the other know the slackers by the coffee machine weren't to be touched just yet, then he stepped aside so his people could file in.

It was a magnificent slaughter. Ten silenced SMGs and autorifles chugged in unison, reducing the workers in their chairs to perforated sieves.

Abbas didn't take part. He was advancing on the bewildered pair by the coffee machine, his subgun leveled meaningfully. "Good evening," he said amiably, amused by their shock. One had dropped a paper cup, spilling coffee all over his shoes. The other's mouth was open wide enough to swallow a melon. "My friends and I do not have much time, so I will come straight to the point. I need to learn all you can tell me about Echelon's headquarters in America." He swung the muzzle from one to the other. "Which of you is interested in living the longest?"

Defiance flared in the eyes of the man who had dropped the coffee, and Abbas shot him through the heart.

The other technician was a puny broomstick who began quaking so badly, his legs almost buckled.

Abbas glanced over his shoulders. Jamilah, Jebel, Barakah and Yasin were setting charges of C-4 exactly as he had instructed while the rest were busy gathering every manual, file and disk in sight and stuffing them into their backpacks. Facing the terrified tech, he smiled and said, "Now then. Care to start, or would you rather stop breathing?"

The man began to talk.

CHAPTER NINE

Somalia

Rimmed by mountains along the Gulf of Aden, northern Somalia jutted into the Indian Ocean like the tip of a giant spear. It had the distinction of being some of the most inhospitable terrain on the face of the planet and was so arid, some parts barely received an inch of rain a year. Desert wasteland and vast rocky areas defied all man's attempts to gain more than the most meager of footholds. Scorpions and snakes thrived.

So did terrorists.

As the Executioner had long ago learned, evil flourished not only in the dark corners of the human mind, but also in the dark corners of the earth. In northern Somalia terrorist organizations found a safe haven from the prying eyes of the Western countries they yearned to topple.

Local interference was minimal. For a substantial fee, Somali officials were willing to give the terrorists free reign.

More than a dozen terrorist training camps were currently active—that the Feds knew of. Most consisted of tents pitched in the middle of nowhere, and were it not for the daily rattle of gunfire and frequent explosions as the terrorists honed their deadly skills, the camps might be mistaken for those of wandering nomads.

Bolan's parachute came down approximately seven miles northeast of the site believed to be Al-Jabbar's base of operations. The first thing he did was stash the chute in a ravine, then check his gear. He was dressed in desert camo and armed to the gills. The backpack he had brought contained enough food and water to last three days, as well as his sole link to the outside world—a radio.

Bolan wore dark glasses to shield his eyes from the sun's relentless glare. All around was a sea of rock sprinkled with boulders. He consulted his map and verified his heading by his wrist compass. Then, slinging his M-16, he began the long hike ahead.

The soldier hadn't taken ten steps when a puff adder sunning itself hissed at him, baring inch-long fangs, and slithered under a flat boulder. Bolan was wearing combat boots but he still had to be careful where he stepped.

The heat was relentless; it baked a man alive. Waves of it rippled in the air, distorting distant objects. Bolan became caked with sweat. His throat became parched, but he refused to touch his water so soon. He had to ration his supply. There was no telling when he would find more.

Folded in Bolan's shirt pocket was the latest satellite photo of his destination. The image showed a high hill or bluff with buildings perched on top. A few more structures were visible in the shadows at its base. From the air it didn't look like much, no different from other isolated Somali outposts. A casual observer would never suspect the truth, that it was where the fanatical seed of Al-Jabbar had taken root. A seed Bolan intended to dig out and destroy.

As he hiked along, the soldier thought about his brief visit to Cyprus. About Ayios Nikolaos and the charred debris was what remained of the Echelon facility. When he arrived, the Western Sovereign Base Area had been swarming with soldiers. Military police were everywhere, and the high brass were barking orders right and left. A bevy of Greek officials were on hand to inspect the damage. His liaison, a Major Fawcett, sadly relayed the news two Royal Military Police had been slain and seven people inside the facility were missing and presumed killed in the blast.

Echelon had been crippled. The Cyprus site had been instrumental in monitoring telephone, radio and satellite communications from the Middle East and northern Africa, prime regions for terrorist activity.

An anonymous caller to a local newspaper claimed Al-Jabbar was responsible. The caller also promised more death and destruction were to follow.

It gave Bolan more reason than ever to want to bring them down. Al-Jabbar was shifting focus. From assassinating ambassadors and politicians it had graduated to surgical strikes against critical targets. The organization had entered the big leagues in a major way and had to be stopped before they struck again.

Bolan had talked to Hal Brognola, and the big Fed was fit to be tied.

"Striker, there was no forewarning, no inkling of what they were up to. And now that they've had a taste of major success, they're bound to pull a similar stunt before too long. The next time the death toll could be astronomically higher."

"I'll shut them down," Bolan had vowed.

"The people we lost were dedicated to their jobs, to their country. They deserved better than to be snuffed out by madmen. And now our intelligence-gathering capability has been severely impaired. Once words gets out, terrorists everywhere will be celebrating and singing Al-Jabbar's praises."

But the celebration wouldn't last long. Not if Bolan could help it.

Brognola believed, and the Executioner tended to agree, that those responsible for the attack had headed straight for their Somalian base afterward and were there now, reveling in their victory. If so, he stood an excellent chance of catching them off guard.

A piercing shriek high in the sky drew the warrior's gaze to an eagle circling in search of prey. Suddenly the eagle tucked its wings to its sides and hurtled groundward. Whatever the eagle was after was on the other side of a low rise. Bolan was halfway up it when the great bird reappeared, a small animal grasped in its iron talons. What it was, exactly, he couldn't quite tell.

The afternoon sun continued to climb. Bolan repeatedly mopped at his brow but couldn't stop the steady trickle of stinging sweat into his eyes. Twice he took binoculars from his backpack, but all he saw ahead was the same bleak landscape.

By his reckoning Bolan had gone about four miles when he came to a cluster of boulders in the shade of a hill and halted. Taking a seat, he propped the M-16 beside him and indulged himself with several sips of water. Not much, just enough to moisten his mouth and relieve his dry throat.

It shouldn't be long, Bolan mused, before he spied

the base, but he'd have to wait for dark to go in. Screwing the cap on the canteen, he slipped it into the backpack, placed the backpack on the ground and leaned back.

Something brushed against Bolan's right hand. He glanced down to find a hairy brown spider as big and thick as a grenade. It was waving its front forelegs in the air and had its other legs coiled to pounce. Eight tiny eyes were fixed on his fingers, and its large fangs were opening and closing reflexively.

Bolan had never seen this particular type of spider before, but he had a strong hunch it was poisonous. And that if he moved, it would strike. He thought that by sitting perfectly still, he would cause it to soon lose interest and go elsewhere. But it showed no such inclination.

One of the forelegs brushed the edge of Bolan's hand, and the spider came nearer, its fangs now a string's width from his skin.

Bolan began to bend his left foot back toward his left hand. He had to move slowly or invite an attack, and it seemed to take forever for his ankle to rise high enough for him to reach the Ka-bar combat knife strapped to it. Unfastening the snap, he palmed the hilt and eased the blade free.

The spider placed its forelegs on his second and third fingers and ran them back and forth.

Only then did it dawn on Bolan the arachnid was trying to determine what he was. It was possible the thing had mistaken his hand for another spider but now wasn't so sure. Its multiple eyes bent closer. Suddenly it sprang back, scrambled down the boulder and darted off with amazing speed.

Bolan grinned and replaced the knife. Enough rest.

Shrugging into the backpack, he grabbed the M-16 and climbed to the top of the hill. And promptly flattened.

Outlined in stark relief against the southern horizon was a steep, rocky crag hundreds of feet high. The top had to be fifteen to twenty acres in extent. Stone walls bordered it, built long ago by whoever built the towering fortress the walls were part of. It resembled a castle, with ramparts and towers and a wide wooden gate that opened onto a dirt road that wound down to a small village at the bottom of the crag.

Bolan started to reach into his backpack for his binoculars. Off to his right a tiny bell jingled, and around a knoll thirty yards away a goat appeared. Four others followed it, nipping at random clumps of dry grass. A girl of thirteen or fourteen trailed after them. She wore a long skirt and sandals, and despite the heat, a shawl over her head and shoulders. She was humming to herself and wagging a stick at the goats to herd them along.

Bolan scowled. Civilians always complicated matters. The girl had to be from the village, and she and her people might be on friendly terms with the terrorists. They might not take too kindly to someone wanting to wipe out the terrorists.

The goats were ambling toward the hill.

Not caring to be spotted, Bolan began to slide down. He turned, started to stand and received a jolt of surprise.

Another girl had come unnoticed around the side and was calmly studying him. Only ten years old or so, her dark eyes alive with interest.

Bolan slowly slung the M-16. When she smiled and raised her hand in a gesture of greeting, he returned it. She spoke to him in Somali and pointed toward the rocky crag. "Do you speak English?" he asked.

The girl held her fingers close to her ears and wriggled them. Again she pointed at the crag and repeated whatever she had said.

By her inflection and expression, Bolan could tell she was asking a question. Maybe she wanted to know if he were a member of Al-Jabbar. The people in the village had to be accustomed to encountering the terrorists now and then, which explained why she wasn't scared of him. He decided a little fib wouldn't hurt. Pointing to the fortress, he nodded and smiled and said, "Al-Jabbar."

Around the hill came the older girl. A sister, perhaps. She said a few words to the younger one, then spied Bolan and stopped dead. Her attitude was nowhere near as friendly. Snapping at the younger one, she beckoned.

The smaller girl reluctantly went over. Indicating Bolan, she said something that included, "Al-Jabbar."

At that the older girl gripped the younger's wrist and hauled her out of there. The tinkle of bells rapidly receded.

Bolan walked up the hill. Urging the goats ahead of them, the pair was hurrying toward the village. The younger one glanced back and smiled, and was roundly cuffed on the head by her sibling.

To linger invited discovery. The girls were bound to tell their parents, who might see fit to come find him. Or, worse, make mention of him to a member of Al-Jabbar. Bolan jogged to a dry wash that meandered in the general direction of the crag. It was also overrun with scorpions, and he could hardly take five steps without stepping on one. Most scuttled off, but a few came at him with their tails upraised and their large pinchers waving wildly. Evading them was simple enough but time-consuming.

It took Bolan an hour and a half to travel to within a hundred yards of the village. He counted nine thatched-roof dwellings, each with its own small corral that held goats and donkeys. Seven men were seated under a tree, smoking, while a group of women gathered by a stone well, large clay vessels balanced on their heads.

It was like turning back a page of history to an earlier era, to the Somalia that existed a century or more ago. Truth to tell, though, much of the world was the same. Those living in modern nations, with their host of modern appliances and never-ending parade of luxuries, tended to forget that many people worldwide still lived as their ancestors had. From rural China to the remote Amazon, from the exotic islands of the South Pacific to the hinterlands of the Canadian Arctic, life was conducted much as it had always been.

Bolan had seen a lot more of the world than most. In his travels he had learned poverty was the norm, not the exception, and electricity the greatest boon to civilization since the invention of the wheel.

The two girls came out of a dwelling. They had reached the village long before him, and the goats they had been tending were in a corral. Walking over to the women, they squatted near the one who had to be their mother. Neither showed any interest in the hill where they had seen him, which he construed as a good sign.

Suddenly every villager in sight looked up at the fortress. Bolan heard it, too—the mechanical growl of an engine. A brown flatbed truck barreled out the gate and roared down the dirt road, raising a cloud of dust in its wake. Two camouflage-clad terrorists were in the cab, four more in the open bed. The driver took the turns much too fast, and it was a wonder the truck didn't careen out of control.

The Somalis under the tree rose. The women were hustling toward their homes, shooing children who didn't move fast enough. By the time the truck reached the bottom, only the men were left, waiting in a silent, sullen knot.

It didn't take any great leap of logic to figure out the villagers weren't fond of the outsiders.

The truck slewed to a stop, and out hopped the man on the passenger side of the cab. A swarthy, brutish character of Middle East extraction, he swaggered over to the Somalis and growled at them in their own language. When no one answered him, he gripped the oldest by the arm and shook him.

Other Somalis made as if to intervene but stopped when the terrorists on the truck bed jumped down and leveled their weapons.

A heated dispute arose between the oldest Somali and the swarthy leader.

What it was about, Bolan couldn't say. It was tempting to drop the terrorists where they stood, but it would alert their fellow fanatics up above. And he couldn't have that. So he had to content himself with lying low for the time being.

The dispute ended. Some of the Somalis went to various corrals and returned leading four goats by short ropes. The terrorists loaded the animals onto the truck, the driver executed a U-turn and the vehicle rumbled up the bluff.

Angrily shaking their fists, the Somalis blistered the

air with curses. Their fury was understandable. To families barely eking out a living, the loss of an animal they relied on for milk, meat and clothing could be catastrophic.

Something told Bolan it wasn't the first time this had happened, but were it up to the Somalis, it would be the last.

Singly and in pairs their wives and children emerged. A woman broke into tears, wailing as if she had lost her best friend. Her husband tried to console her, but she cried all the harder.

The way of the world, Bolan reflected. Since the dawn of time the strong had always preyed on the weak and the helpless. It was the natural order of things except in countries where there were men and women of high moral principle willing to defy the strong on the weak's behalf.

The truck was passing through the gate. Bolan trained his binoculars on the fortress and adjusted the magnification. Two guards were lazily pacing the ramparts. Nowhere near enough for a fortification that size. The terrorists had become complacent, and complacency was always a prelude to carelessness, and defeat.

At the east end of the fortress, sticking a few feet above the wall, was part of a rotor capped by helicopter blades. Bolan assumed the terrorists had used the chopper to travel to Cyprus and back, and he put it at the top of his list for making intimate acquaintance with some plastic explosive.

Rolling onto his back, the soldier cupped his hands behind his head. He had a few hours until nightfall and might as well relax.

Bolan mopped a sleeve across his forehead. The

heat was stifling, but he had experienced worse. At least it wasn't as humid as the jungle of Southeast Asia or the Amazon. Twisting, he double-checked the village. The men were still under the tree, the women gathered at the well, the children playing. Life was back to normal. But occasional angry glances were cast at the ancient fortress that loomed over their primitive homes like some great predator waiting to pounce.

Drowsiness set in. Bolan had only caught a few hours sleep the night before. He could use a few more. But now wasn't the right time or place. Shaking himself, he sat up. Nothing stirred in the wash or the surrounding desert until close to sunset when a rodent of some kind came out of a hole on the other side, took one look at Bolan, chittered like crazy and scampered back into its burrow.

The soldier was glad when the last vestige of the blazing sun sank below the horizon. He adjusted the straps to his backpack, blew dust off the M-16 and crouched below the rim. Almost all the villagers had gone in. A few stragglers were taking their sweet time, and he was forced to wait another ten minutes before it was safe to leave the wash and double-time toward the dirt road.

Until he was past the village Bolan had adequate cover. But the lower part of the slope was as wide open as a Kansas prairie. Some men might have risked it. Bolan hunkered behind a boulder and bided his time. Bit by bit the sky darkened, miring the desert in gloom. When he couldn't see his hand at arm's length, he jogged to the road and started up.

Light filled a few fortress windows. Shadows occasionally flicked across the casements, and a man's head and shoulders showed above the parapet.

The Executioner was a third of the way there when the stillness was broken by the purr of an engine. But it didn't come from inside the fortress; it was borne to him from out of the desert to the southwest. A pair of headlights pierced the night, the size of peas at that distance.

Bolan hadn't seen a road beyond the crag, but there had to be one because the vehicle was moving much too fast to be traveling cross-country across broken, boulder-ridden terrain. He continued to climb. The vehicle was miles off yet and would take a while getting there. On his right a line of boulders materialized, and he moved closer to be that much nearer to cover. It was well he did, for not five seconds later a gruff shout came from the fortress, and on its heels a spotlight lanced down the road toward him.

Dropping to his knees behind a boulder, Bolan prepared for a firefight. He thought the terrorists had spotted him, but there were no additional outcries. Nor was there movement on the ramparts. It was either routine procedure for them to turn on the spotlight at night as a standard security precaution, or else they had done it for the sake of their soon-to-arrive guests.

Staying well shy of the lit area, Bolan glided higher. In a way the spotlight helped. The human eye wasn't designed to simultaneously see with equal clarity into patches of light and dark. The pupils in the eyes needed time to adjust. The spotlight would hamper the sentries' ability to spot him.

The purr became a sustained snarl.

Bolan had been around enough military vehicles to know a jeep when he heard it. The driver was shifting

gears with practiced skill and drove as if he were trying to qualify for the Indy 500. The vehicle reached
the bottom of the crag and roared upward.

The soldier ducked to avoid the sweep of headlights. When he looked out again, three terrorists had
appeared. One was the bull-chested brute who had demanded goats from the villagers. His brawny hands on
his hips, an insolent sneer on his lips, he planted himself in the middle of the gate.

The jeep braked, and out hopped a Somali officer
in full uniform. According to his insignia, he was a
general. A big man with a prominent hooked nose and
a pointed chin, he strode to the brutish terrorist in
charge and offered his hand.

The man shook, but did not seem particulary
pleased by the visit.

Bolan had no clue what was going down. The pair
swapped gruff greetings, then the leader motioned for
the jeep to precede them into the fortress. The two
men entered, their posture suggesting neither was all
that comfortable with the other.

Whoever the Somali was, he had to be high in the
government. There weren't more than eight or nine
generals in the whole Somali army, which hinted this
was an official visit.

The last thing Bolan needed was another complication. Brognola wouldn't take it too well if he killed
a Somali officer. The U.S. wasn't on the best of terms
with the Somali government as it was. Ideally, he
should wait for the general to leave, but that might not
be until morning.

The other two terrorists were going in. Someone
yelled, and a chain clanked and rattled.

The gate began to swing shut. Bolan could make it

through, but the spotlight would impale him before he went ten feet. He had to find another way in. Angling to the right, he sprinted for the high fortress wall. Once in its shadow, he prowled in search of a door or a window low enough for him to reach.

The west, south and east sides of the crag were sheer cliffs, and at several points the fortress wall came perilously close to the edge. Deliberately so, Bolan guessed, to render the stronghold virtually impregnable. He came to a spot where there was barely a foot of earth between the wall and a drop of hundreds of feet, and cautiously extended his foot to what he thought was a firm place. He shifted most of his weight to it and eased forward, his hands pressed against the wall. Unexpectedly, the earth under his right foot gave way. Gripping the wall harder, Bolan tried to shift his weight onto his left foot, but gravity, and the added weight of his backpack, pitched him forward.

Bolan's right leg went over the side. Lunging upward, he grabbed a protrusion on one of the rough-hewn stones and stopped his fall, but only for a moment. Suddenly the ground under his left foot cascaded from under him like so much sand. His hold on the stone only delayed the inevitable for a split second.

Then down he plummeted.

CHAPTER TEN

The Executioner's reflexes were second to none. As his legs dropped out from under him and he started to drop like a stone, he clutched at the rock wall for all he was worth. Gouging his fingers into cracks between the stones, he rammed the steel tips of his boots into the cliff face, digging them into the dirt as far as they would go.

It worked. Bolan stopped falling, but he was half over the cliff, clinging like a fly to a glass pane, with nothing to grab to pull himself to safety nor a foothold worthy of the name. And as if that were not enough, at that moment voices drifted from above.

A pair of sentries was on the rampart. Craning his neck, Bolan saw the glow of a cigarette and heard low laughter. He dared not move. More dirt and rocks would cascade over the precipice, and the terrorists were bound to hear. Unable to defend himself, he wouldn't last two seconds. He had to wait for them to go.

Bolan held on, his fingers and toes strained to their limit, his shoulders and calves protesting. He had slung the M-16 over his left shoulder before he made that last step, and it slid lower, toward his elbow, threatening to unbalance him, with potentially disastrous consequences.

The soldier glanced up. The tip of the cigarette was fire red. Whoever was smoking it was leaning on the parapet. All he had to do was look down and he'd spot him.

The man at the parapet suddenly tossed the cigarette over the side. Like a lone firefly tumbling end over end, it dropped toward Bolan. Half a foot overhead it struck the wall and bounced off, showering him with tiny sparks.

The voices dwindled.

Gritting his teeth, Bolan pushed upward. Or tried to. His fingers and toes didn't have enough of a hold to lever his full two-hundred-plus pounds high enough. Worse, the added pressure caused more earth to rain from under his left foot, weakening his hold drastically.

Bolan's fingers and shoulders would soon tire. There was only one way to save himself. Abruptly letting go, he flung himself as high and as far to the right as he could, his legs serving as twin fulcrums to gain added height. Twisting his back to the precipice, he dug his fingers into the cracks, nearly ripping off several fingernails.

It almost wasn't enough. Bolan felt himself start to go over the side and flung his left leg along the bottom of the wall to better distribute his weight. It worked. For a minute he lay still. Then, wary of the ground crumbling out from under him again, he slowly pulled himself onto his knees and crawled five or six yards to firmer footing.

Bolan didn't waste time congratulating himself on

his narrow escape. Rising, he moved on, treading as light as a feather.

The fortress wasn't square like a castle. The builders had matched its shape to that of the bluff, which was roughly oval. There were no corners, no right angles, just a continuous curving expanse of wall. He passed under four narrow windows, all too high to reach, and came to a fifth.

Bolan stopped. It was only about fifteen feet up. He might be able to reach the sill, but should he slip, jagged boulders were waiting at the bottom to dash him to pieces.

Sitting, the soldier removed his combat boots and socks. He stuffed his socks into the boots, then tied the laces together and slung the boots around his neck so they lay across the top of his backpack. Next, he tightened the sling on the M-16 so it had no slack whatsoever and slung it over his right shoulder. Loosening his belt, he slid the buttstock underneath, partway down his pant leg, then fastened the belt again. He tested whether the rifle would shift by pushing against the hand guard. It was tucked tight.

Bolan wedged the toes of his right foot into the cracks, reached up and began to climb. The hand- and footholds were tenuous at best. He had to grope and feel for each one. Six feet off the ground the cracks thinned. Smaller stones had been used from that point on up, with only a hairline space between them. If he so much as sneezed, he would lose his grip.

The wind didn't help any. It had grown a lot stronger since sunset. Invisible hands pushed against his backpack, but he had it strapped too securely to be dislodged. Or so he thought. Eight feet up, and a gust buffeted him so strongly, his fingers slipped. Exerting every sinew in his forearms, he maintained his perch until the wind slackened and he could go on.

At a height of twelve feet Bolan slowly raised his right hand and caught hold of the stone sill. Gingerly placing his left hand next to his right, he performed a chin-up and pulled himself high enough to hook his elbows over the edge. A musty scent assailed him. The room was as black as coal.

Getting inside would be a feat in itself. The windows weren't more than a foot and a half wide.

Bolan slipped his hands in, one on either side, and raised himself high enough to sit on the sill. There was hardly enough room for a bird, let alone a grown man, but he managed, his left arm wrapped fast. Sliding his boots from around his neck, he dropped them inside. Then, carefully loosening the straps to his backpack, he slowly slid it off, shoved it through ahead of him and let it follow his boots.

Unslinging the M-16, the soldier held the autorifle by the muzzle and lowered it as far as he could. He had to drop it the final few feet. The clatter it made was much too loud, and tensing, he listened but heard nothing to show the terrorists had overheard.

Shifting, Bolan slid his shoulders into the opening. It was a tight fit, but by wriggling and pushing against the inner wall, he squeezed in. Something brushed against his face, something sticky that clung to his cheeks and chin. Spiderwebs, he imagined. Pushing harder, he slid his legs in and balanced on the sill. From a shirt pocket he produced a pencil flashlight and switched it on. He was in a storage room. In one corner were old benches and a broken table, stacked haphazardly. In another was a pile of rolled-up rugs, of all things. Other odds and ends, mostly furnishings, covered much of the stone floor, all of it covered with the dust of disuse.

Pointing the flashlight straight down, Bolan took note of where the M-16 and the backpack lay. Then, swinging his feet under him, he released his hold. He landed in a crouch and trained the flashlight on the ceiling. He had been right about the spiderwebs. They covered it from wall to wall.

Bolan swiftly donned his socks and shoes. He slipped his arms into the backpack, reclaimed the M-16 and stepped to a stout wooden door. A metal latch tarnished with rust had to be pressed. Although he only swung the heavy door inward a crack, the hinges creaked loud enough to be heard in Cyprus.

Quickly Bolan opened the door all the way and ran to his left down a narrow stone corridor. If anyone had heard, it would take them a bit to investigate. He had time to do a little exploring.

Dust swirled in the flashlight's beam. More spiderwebs glittered like spun silk. Another door appeared out of the gloom, and Bolan pressed an ear to it. He heard nothing to indicate anyone was on the other side. He opened it and slipped through, finding himself in a long, empty corridor lit by lanterns at both ends.

Six doorways, three on either side, begged investigation. The M-16 on semiauto, Bolan moved to the first. This time the hinges didn't make a sound. He'd stumbled on another storage room, but this one was crammed with enough ammunition to supply an army. Most was for 7.62 mm and 5.56 mm weapons.

Once more shrugging out of the backpack, Bolan removed a packet of C-4 already rigged with a timer and det cord. He set the timer for forty minutes, hid the packet behind a crate at the rear and moved on to the next chamber. He was on a roll. This one contained rocket launchers and rockets, sixty mines and kegs of conventional black powder. He hid another packet of C-4 after setting the timer to coincide with the first.

Bazookas and machine guns were stored in the next room. Bolan didn't plant C-4 this time. He had three packets left, and he needed to scatter them about the fortress to maximize the collateral damage. Slipping out, he hurried to the next room and was reaching for the latch when voices sounded at the far end of the hall.

Instantly Bolan ducked into yet another munitions-crammed chamber. He left the door open enough to see two people move past the junction. One was the brutish terrorist, the other the Somali general.

"—wish he were here," the general was saying in English. "He has a lot of explaining to do."

"Present your complaint and I will relay it to him," the terrorist said. "He left me in command so I…" Their voices trailed off.

His curiosity piqued, Bolan sped to the junction. The pair was entering a room farther down the corridor. He verified no one else was in the corridor and quick-stepped to the doorway.

A large circular table dominated a spacious room. To one side chairs were arranged in long rows. The two men were taking seats at the table and were so intent on each other, neither noticed Bolan drop into a crouch, dart between two of the rows and sink to his knees.

"We are alone and can speak freely, Aykut," the general began. "So perhaps you will be good enough to explain?"

"If I knew what you were talking about, I would."

"Can it truly be you do not know?" the Somali asked skeptically. "It has been on all the news channels. Our president heard about it on the radio, of all things, and sent for me right away. I am here at his personal order."

"What is it he heard, General Nbibi?"

"Al-Jabbar is claiming credit for the destruction of an Echelon facility jointly run by the United States and the British, in Cyprus. Since your leader is not present, I gather he must be personally involved."

"I would not know," Aykut said. "He did not confide his destination when he left several days ago."

Nbibi drummed his fingers on the table. "My government is extremely displeased. Our arrangement specifically requires your leader to inform us of undertakings of this magnitude."

Aykut leaned back and scratched at stubble sprinkling his double chin. "I do not understand. Your government has never complained before."

"We never had cause to. We were always kept abreast of developments." Nbibi oozed resentment. "But now, thanks to your leader's willful oversight, our country has been put in a highly compromising position."

"Your government had nothing to do with it."

"We know that and you know that, but the Americans and British do not. Have you forgotten Afghanistan? My government does not want our skies darkened by American bombers and our cities invaded by American troops."

Aykut chortled. "Let them come. Somalia is not Afghanistan. Your people will rise up and drive the arrogant spawn of Satan out. Have you forgotten how the Americans were humiliated in Mogadishu in 1993?''

''Have you been listening to American media propaganda? It was not the American military that suffered humiliation in Mogadishu. We did. One hundred and fifty of their Delta Force and Rangers killed almost a thousand Somali fighters. The American media never reported the true story, or those men would be enshrined as heroes.''

''You almost sound as if you admire them.''

The general squared his shoulders. ''I am a professional soldier. I admire bravery wherever I encounter it. Even when it is displayed by my enemies.''

''The only true bravery is in service to God.''

Nbibi pushed his chair back from the table and stood. ''This is getting me nowhere. Inform Abbas when he returns that he must contact me immediately or Al-Jabbar will be expelled from Somalia.''

Aykut also rose, glowering. ''He will not like being threatened. We are not your servants to be bossed around on a whim.''

The Somali's fist struck the table with a resounding thump. ''I do not care what any of you like! Where do you think you are? This is Somalia, not Syria. Al-Jabbar will abide by the restrictions my government has imposed, or I will return with a full regiment and enough artillery to reduce this fortress to rubble.''

''Please, General.'' Aykut backpedaled. ''I meant no disrespect. I am sure Abbas will explain everything to your satisfaction.''

''He had better.'' The officer consulted his wristwatch. ''It is too late for me to start back now. Can you put my driver and I up for the night?''

''Of course. You can stay in the same room as the

last time. I will have food and drink brought, and whatever else you require.''

Bolan watched them walk toward the corridor. The general was in the lead. They were only a few yards away when the officer halted and gazed quizzically at the doorway, then at the rows of chairs.

Bolan shot a quick glance in the same direction. Another terrorist had shown up and was staring right at him in blatant surprise. The man had a Czech-made Skorpion on a shoulder sling, and as Bolan looked over, he grabbed it and swung it up to fire. The Executioner beat him by a hair, triggering a burst that stitched the terrorist's chest and flung him back against the wall.

Even as he fired, Bolan started to pivot toward Nbibi and Aykut. The brutish terrorist was clutching an autopistol in a holster. He never cleared leather. Bolan shot him in the face, then swiveled to cover the general, who was frozen in temporary shock. And was clearly unarmed.

''You would be wise to get in your jeep and leave,'' Bolan said. Sliding a short, black grenade from a pocket, he fed it into the 40 mm M-203 grenade launcher attached to the underside of the M-16.

''Who are you?'' Nbibi blurted.

''Payback.'' Bolan gestured for the Somali to walk in front of him to the doorway. There was a commotion from somewhere nearby; shouts and the stomp of booted feet.

''You are an American, aren't you? Part of an elite strike force sent to wipe out Al-Jabbar for their attack on the Echelon installation?'' Nbibi shook his head in amazement. ''But how did you find their sanctuary so soon?''

Bolan couldn't resist. "We have our ways." The commotion was growing louder by the second. "Unless you want to be caught in a cross fire I suggest you take my advice and make yourself scarce."

The general didn't share the sense of urgency. "Before I go, there is something I do not understand. Why are you letting me live?"

"Would you rather I didn't? Pick up a gun and point it at me."

The general nodded. "So. A man of honor. You will forgive me if I am not overly eager to die. You impress me as being a most formidable individual." He took a step, then paused. "You will need to be. The odds are eighteen to one against you."

"They were just as high for our boys in Mogadishu," Bolan reminded him.

The commotion was an uproar, coming from the right. The general gave a little wave and turned to the left. And stepped smack into a hail of lead that turned him into a crimson-spattered sieve in the blink of an eye. He died on his feet, astonishment his last emotion, and oozed soundlessly to the floor.

Leaning into the corridor, Bolan spied the pair of trigger-happy terrorists responsible. They were at a junction, SMGs to their shoulders. Accidentally killing the general had rooted them in disbelief, giving him the edge he needed. He chopped both in two with a sustained burst.

More yells erupted beyond the bend, and five men swept into view. The sight of their fallen companions slowed them a bit, and it was then, when their attention was on the floor, that Bolan let fly with the M-576 buckshot grenade and ducked back into the room.

Designed for jungle use and other close quarters, the M-576 had a higher muzzle velocity than most grenades. It struck the stone floor slightly in front of the quintet and detonated with a thunderous blast. A scream rose in anguish and was abruptly smothered. When the rumbling died and the dust began to settle, Bolan warily stepped out.

The effect of buckshot was devastating. In a shotgun, at close range, it shredded human flesh and could blow a hole in a man big enough to stick a fist through. The effect of a buckshot grenade, or the Multiple-protectile Canister, as the military formally referred to it, was a lot worse. In a confined space the M-576 literally tore its targets to pieces.

The five terrorists were no exception.

A glance was enough to assure Bolan they no longer posed a threat. Turning to the left, he hurried to another junction, listened a moment, then took the left fork. In the space of a minute he had reduced the odds to eleven to one.

More shouts rose from various points in the fortress.

A closed door was ahead, and Bolan slowed to try the latch. From floor to ceiling the chamber was crammed with munitions, more than all the previous rooms combined. He set a timer so it, too, would go off at the same time, placed the packet where no one would find it unless they searched hard and long, and moved to the door.

Four terrorists were jogging down the corridor toward him. One had a walkie-talkie to his ear and was talking excitedly in Arabic.

Bolan let them go by. Now that he had learned the true leader of Al-Jabbar wasn't at the fortress, he would like to find out where the man had gone. And there was something else. Brognola had told him the Feds estimated Al-Jabbar's strength at thirty-strong. Yet Nbibi claimed only eighteen were present. Where were the others? With Abbas? If so, what were they up to? Questions he might be able to answer if he could locate a command center or a communications post.

For the next fifteen minutes Bolan played a deadly game of hide-and-seek. The terrorists made so much noise in their search that eluding them was no great feat, but several times he barely found a hiding place in time. And all the while, the minutes were ticking down to when the packets would go off.

Yet another corridor brought the soldier to an archway that opened onto a courtyard. At the moment it was empty. Not so the ramparts. Two sentries were near the gate, one on either side. They didn't spot him.

A third terrorist rushed from a doorway across the way, shouted up to them, and on hearing their answer, dashed inside.

Lanterns hung from pegs on all four sides of the courtyard, too faint to illuminate it. Dappled by shadow, Bolan sidled along the wall to another archway. Whenever one of the terrorists happened to glance in his direction, he froze until the man looked away.

The first door in the next corridor was different than the rest. It was newer, a modern door with a knob instead of a latch, and it was locked. Bolan was handy with a lock pick, but that took time. He could shoot the door open, but the sentries and anyone else in the vicinity would hear. Unless the autofire was drowned out by a louder noise.

Returning to the arch, Bolan fed another grenade

into the M-203. This time it was an ordinary M-406 high-explosive round. He pried up the sight leaf mount. The distance was about a hundred meters, only a third of the M-203's maximum effective range. Aiming above the gate, midway between the sentries, he fired, then spun and raced toward the closed door.

The grenade went off before he reached it, but the reverberations were echoing throughout the fortress when he emptied the M-16's magazine into the wood around the knob, chewing it to bits. One kick, and the door swung inward.

Someone had gone to a lot of expense to turn the drab stone chamber into a comfortable office. Wood paneling hugged the walls; a rug covered the floor. A large oak desk and an easy chair sat near some shelves stacked high with magazines. On the right wall was a calendar with a photo of a mosque, on the left wall a plaque with Arabic lettering.

Bolan shut the door, replaced the spent magazine with a fresh one and moved around the desk. None of the drawers was locked. In one he found a notebook nearly filled with Arabic writing and diagrams. In another a leather binder with lists of what might be names and phone numbers. In a third were passports from nine different countries, all showing the same man with his features slightly altered. Fakes, Bolan guessed, and placed them in a side pocket in his backpack along with the rest.

He added one last item. A gold watch. Whoever it belonged to was bound to have left his fingerprints.

Out in the courtyard, voices were lifted in anger.

Bolan rigged another packet of C-4 under the desk and stepped to the door. Time to wrap it up. There should be nine terrorists left, and he wasn't leaving until he had accounted for as many as he could. He headed for the courtyard, and from under the arch spied three terrorists over by the shattered gate. The two sentries lay sprawled in pools of blood.

Sighting down the autorifle, Bolan squeezed the trigger three times in swift succession. At each burst a terrorist dropped.

Six to go, and the job was done.

Bolan took a couple of strides, then jerked back as the archway was peppered by lead from somewhere to his right. A terrorist began to shout, no doubt alerting the rest who were left to his location.

Backing away, Bolan turned and ran to a junction. He took the left fork, followed it to another junction and again turned left. He slowed, the M-16 at his waist. Another archway was at the end, and a terrorist with an AK-47 crouched under it, the weapon trained on where he had just been. Slinking forward on silent soles, the soldier centered his sights on the back of the man's skull and blew it to pieces.

Running to the archway, Bolan straddled the dead fanatic and glanced out. The courtyard was deserted except for bodies. He began to turn and suddenly sensed he wasn't alone. Thinking the man he had shot wasn't dead, he leaped to one side.

Cold steel flashed, and something struck the autorifle a resounding blow. A blow so powerful, the M-16 was torn from his grasp and clattered to the floor.

Bolan whirled.

Confronting him was another Somali in uniform. A sergeant. It had to be the general's driver. He was a mountain of a man whose muscles bulged like cords of wood and who wielded a glittering machete. He said something in Somali, and when Bolan didn't respond, he switched to English. "You must be the bastard who killed General Nbibi! For that, I will cut you to pieces."

Bolan wasn't given the chance to explain the terrorists were responsible. For hardly were the words out of the soldier's mouth than he attacked.

CHAPTER ELEVEN

The Executioner stepped back and felt air fan his neck. The machete had missed by a hair's width. He grabbed for the Beretta, but as he swept it from his shoulder rig, the flat of the machete's wide blade struck it hard enough to tear it from his fingers and send it skittering across the floor.

Wearing a look of fierce resolve, the Somali sergeant hefted his weapon and declared, "I liked General Nbibi. He treated me decent. This is for him!" Lunging, he cleaved the tempered steel in a tremendous stroke.

Bolan flung himself to the right. Again the machete missed, again not by much. He dropped his hand toward the Desert Eagle but had to snatch it up when the sergeant swung at his wrist. To slow the Somali he snapped a kick at the soldier's knee and connected. Most men would have buckled. The sergeant uttered a feral growl and redoubled his effort to land a killing blow.

Dodging right, dodging left, ducking and weaving, Bolan evaded his adversary. Once more he tried for the Desert Eagle and almost lost several fingers.

Bolan took a long bound back. The Somali lunged, overextending himself, and the soldier quickly seized his adversary's wrist and elbow and drove his knee into the man's arm. That should have been enough to force the Somali to drop the machete, but he wrenched loose and whipped it overhead.

In combat there was no such thing as fair play. Bolan did what he had to in order to survive. As the gleaming blade rose, he smashed his right fist into the Somali's groin. The sergeant staggered. Leaping into the air, the Executioner rammed the tip of his right boot into the man's neck.

The big Somali sputtered, dropped the machete and clutched at his throat. His legs swayed but he didn't go down. Instead, flinging his arms wide, he roared like a lion and pounced.

Bolan tried to twist aside, in vain. Bands of steel encircled him, pinning his arms to his sides, and he was lifted off the floor. Like a grizzly applying a bear hug, the Somali squeezed and squeezed.

It was like being caught in the coils of a python. Bolan thrashed and kicked and strained, but the pressure on his rib cage continued to build. His ribs were on fire. Any second they would cave in. He pounded his forehead against the other man's face, but it only made the Somali mad.

Blood trickling from his nose, the sergeant lowered his shoulders and hurled himself at the wall. Bolan bore the brunt, and for a second he thought his spine had been shattered. Breath whooshed from his lungs, and the corridor spun. Before the soldier could try again to crush him, he tore his hands free and smashed his fists against the sergeant's ears.

Hurt anew, the Somali tottered.

Bolan strained to break loose and had almost succeeded when his opponent roared, swiveled at the hips and threw him bodily against the other wall. His left shoulder hit so hard his entire side went numb, and it took a few seconds for him to prop his right hand under him and rise. Seconds the Somali used to step in close and kick him in the stomach.

Knocked onto his back, Bolan saw the sergeant raise the same boot to stomp him on the head. He reacted instinctively. His right hand closed on the Desert Eagle, and he pointed it at the only part of the sergeant's body he could see—between the Somali's legs. He stroked the trigger twice.

Rocked onto his heels, the sergeant windmilled his arms to maintain his balance but couldn't. A red geyser spewed from his mouth and nostrils as he melted to the floor, his huge muscles twitching as he died.

Bolan was slow in standing. Flexing and unflexing his left fingers, he pumped his arm up and down to try to alleviate the numbness. It worked to a degree. Moving to the M-16, he picked it up and was about to head for the courtyard when a pair of terrorists appeared in the archway. The instant they saw him they opened fire.

To Bolan's right was the doorway to the office. Hurling himself through it, he rolled into a crouch, reversed direction and hurled himself right back out. The terrorists were caught flatfooted. They weren't expecting him to reappear so soon and had started forward. Firing from the hip, he nailed both before they could get off more rounds.

Only four terrorists were left, but they could be anywhere. Pumping another M-406 explosive grenade into the launcher, Bolan crept to the courtyard. No terrorists there. Nor on the rampart. He edged to the left, his back to the wall, intending to make a complete circuit and listen at each archway for some sign of exactly where the remaining terrorists were.

Then the unexpected intruded.

Figures materialized at the front gate. Bolan immediately took aim and just as promptly lowered the autorifle. Somalis from the village, five men and two women, were nervously glancing all about. Appalled at the carnage and destruction, they halted just inside and whispered among themselves.

The rest of the terrorists might show up at any moment. Bolan doubted they would be glad to see the Somalis. They might, in fact, gun them down out of sheer spite. Stepping into the open, he caught the Somalis' attention. They fearfully clustered closer together. He motioned for them to leave, but they were either misunderstood or too scared to budge.

Suddenly a lanky, bearded terrorist came darting out of an archway across the courtyard. Without hesitation he opened up with an Uzi on the villagers. Only the fact he rushed his initial burst saved their lives.

Bolan, on the other hand, took the fraction of a second needed to settle the M-16's sights on the center of the terrorist's torso. When next he glanced at the Somalis, they were in full flight down the road.

And now there were three.

The soldier continued his circuit. When he was near the west wall he spied General Nbibi's jeep parked in an alcove on the north side. Suddenly slugs pinged off the wall above him. Dropping flat, he saw two gunners on the east rampart. From their vantage point they had clear shots, but they were poor marksmen. They expended their magazines, peppering the walls and the ground.

As soon as the firing stopped, Bolan was up and

racing across the courtyard. He reached a corner a heartbeat ahead of more lead. Temporarily safe, he resorted to the grenade launcher. The trajectory had to be just right. With the rim of a cartridge he loosened the screw at the base of the sight leaf and made the appropriate adjustment.

The pair was still up there, waiting for him to show himself. Bolan poked his head out and drew it right back again, drawing their fire. When they stopped, he popped out and launched the grenade.

They saw it coming and panicked. One ran left, the other right, but neither raced far enough to escape the blast radius. Both were blown off their feet and catapulted head over heels to the courtyard.

One to go. Bolan checked his watch. There was still time to set another packet of C-4. He considered making a sweep of the rooms on the north side to find somewhere conducive to secondary explosions. Another room filled with munitions would be just the thing.

Or a jeep with a tankful of gas.

The soldier had to remove his pack, lie on his back and shimmy underneath to attach the packet. In twelve minutes the fortress would go up like a giant Roman candle. From the alcove he sprinted to what was left of the gate and stepped through.

The villagers were almost to the bottom of the crag. One had lit a torch and was herding the rest ahead.

Bolan headed down. There were any number of spots to lie in wait for the last terrorist but he didn't stop until he heard someone attempting to crank over the jeep's engine. The starter grinded like a defective buzz saw.

It had to be the last terrorist. The man was unaware

of the C-4, and if he got the jeep running and came speeding down the road...

Bolan ran. Only a minute or two, and the fireworks would begin. The villagers had spotted him and stopped. They were safe enough, but he was still much too close.

A few seconds passed, and the jeep's engine roared to life. Gears clashed. Bolan glanced back and saw a terrorist in fatigues about to nose the jeep through the ragged opening in the gate made by his grenade. The opening wasn't quite wide enough, and only the grille had made it through when the jeep became stuck.

Undaunted, the terrorist tromped on the gas pedal. Tires spun fiercely, churning dirt into the air. A cloud of dust enveloped the vehicle and its occupant, growing thicker by the moment.

Bolan checked his wristwatch and ran faster. With a sound reminiscent of two tin cans rubbing together, the jeep began to force its way through. But once again it became stuck. The driver threw the transmission into reverse and with a violent lurch backed up nine or ten yards. He shifted and revved the engine.

On the left were some boulders. Bolan veered toward them, but he had yards to go when the driver popped the tranny into drive and zoomed toward the gate like the jeep was rocket propelled.

The C-4 underneath it went off, the explosion magnified by the simultaneous blasts of the other packets. A roiling fireball engulfed the gate, and sheets of flame spouted from the south and east sections of the fortress.

A wave of blistering heat struck Bolan, along with enough concussive force to nearly knock him off his feet. Gaining the boulders, he hunkered.

Now the munitions were exploding, one room after another, a chain reaction of thunderous proportions. A dazzling pyrotechnic display lit up the sky. Fiery meteors streamed over the walls in a deluge of molten rain. The heat became so intense, Bolan's skin felt as if it were melting. Rising, he hurried lower, holding one arm across his face to protect it.

Villagers were sleepily shuffling from their dwellings to witness the spectacle. Some held candles; a few had oil lamps. Soon the entire population was gawking in awestruck astonishment to a collective refrain of oohs and ahs.

Bolan slung the M-16. He had done what he set out to do, but his work was nowhere near done. Destroying Al-Jabbar's base hadn't destroyed the terrorist group. Abbas and at least ten others were still out there, somewhere, plotting new assaults on America and the freedoms she extolled.

With their headquarters gone, where would Al-Jabbar retreat to? Bolan wondered. It was the million-dollar question, one it might take the Feds weeks, if not months, to answer. He thought of the items in his backpack and reached around to give it a pat. Maybe, just maybe, valuable intel would be gleaned, intel that would help him close the book on Al-Jabbar once and for all.

Bolan looked back one last time. Flames fifty feet high were eating at the stronghold, and a broad section of roof had collapsed. It would take days for the fire to burn itself out. All the king's horses and all the king's men, as the nursery rhyme had it, wouldn't be able to restore the fortress to its former state.

Several villagers were moving toward the road. Once a few did, the rest saw fit to follow, and as Bolan approached the bottom he was greeted by a nervous knot of men, women and children. "I mean you no harm," he assured them.

The little girl who had stumbled on him out in the desert shouldered past her elders and grinned, only to be snatched back by her mother.

Bolan bore to the left to go around them, but the old man who had argued with Aykut stepped forward, palm extended, signifying he should stop. The old man said something in Somali, smiled warmly, then clapped his hands.

Two women ran off and shortly came hurrying back, and they weren't alone.

The soldier realized the villagers wanted to thank him for ridding them of the terrorists. And to properly show the depth of their gratitude, they were giving him one of their most prized possessions.

But what in the world was he going to do with a goat?

ABAN ABBAS HAD SAID it many times before and he would say it again—Americans were their own worst enemies. Unbelievably naive, they committed blunders no security-conscious Israeli or South Korean would ever be guilty of.

For instance, shortly after the World Trade Center attacks, Abbas had been watching the news and reveling in the death and destruction when a segment piqued his interest. A reporter was interviewing an American politician about the things that needed to be done to make America's shores safe. The politician mentioned that one of their top priorities should be increasing the budgets and manpower of the Coast Guard and major port authorities.

"Foreign vessels could smuggle in terrorists by the shipload and we wouldn't know it," the politician intoned ominously. "They could even bring in a nuclear bomb and transport it by truck anywhere in the country."

"Is it really that serious a problem?" the newsman had asked.

Then came the part that made Abbas sit up and take notice.

"Look around you," the politician said, sweeping his arm at a bustling harbor in the background. "This is the port of New York. Each day over a hundred ships dock here. Yet it's a rare day if as many as fifteen are boarded and searched. We don't have the manpower. We don't have the necessary screening procedures in place. Steps must be taken to correct our oversight and—"

The politician babbled on, but Abbas hadn't listened. He was extrapolating the numbers in his head. Eighty-five percent of inbound vessels went unsearched. He would have thought it was more like ten to fifteen percent. It meant the odds of being able to smuggle something into America were almost five times higher than the odds of being caught.

To call the revelation astounding didn't do it justice. It was an abominable weakness no one in other countries would be naive enough to admit to.

Abbas never forgot that newscast. He'd filed the statistic in the back of his mind, and now, en route to America, he was glad he had. The freighter they were on would dock at Spain in a couple of days, and there they would transfer to an oceangoing tanker bound for New York City.

He was seated on a cot in a forward compartment

once used as a gaming room. Other cots and sleeping bags took up most of the available space. Conditions were cramped, and some of his followers were less than pleased.

Jebel was one. "I do not see why we could not have cabins," the young Lebanese groused.

"For one thing," Abbas responded, "this is a freighter, not a luxury ship. It has few cabins and they are occupied. For another, we must keep to ourselves as much as we can. The fewer who see us, the better."

"I do not mind the inconvenience," Jamilah said from her cot beside Abbas's. "What is a little sacrifice in the war against the Great Satan?"

Abbas smiled. At moments like these, he wished he could take her in his arms and crush her to his chest. "Exactly. The rest of you would do well to adopt her attitude. Our accommodations in the tanker will not be much better. And on the last leg of our journey, when we are almost to New York, we must hide in a false hold in case the tanker is boarded and inspected."

"America!" Yasin said eagerly. "I have never been there before. Just think! To stand on the shores of the Great Satan itself!"

"Do not let yourself be influenced by what you see," Abbas warned. "In many respects Americans will not seem much different than our own people. Many will smile and treat you kindly. But do not be deceived. Their acts, their very thoughts, are steeped in Satan's lies. Never forget they are your enemies."

Barakah nodded. "Our master speaks true. Every hand will be against us. We must be as clever as foxes in all we do."

Abbas shifted toward the pair who had joined them

only minutes before the freighter set out from Cyprus. "And what say you, Malik? Rakin? The two of you have been unusually quiet since we were reunited."

"I am troubled, great one," Sharik said. "I worry that when we reach America, *he* will be there. The one who thwarted our attempt on the vice-president. The one who nearly caught us in Athens, and again on Thenas. The same one who later showed up in Kildana."

"You worry too much, my brother."

"With all due respect, you did not see him. He is a devil, this one. He always knows exactly where to find us."

"Do not make him out to be more than he is," Abbas scolded. "There is a logical explanation. Through Echelon, the American government intercepted our calls. Of course he always showed up. They knew where to find you. But now we have destroyed their installation on Cyprus, and soon we will deal the entire Echelon network a crippling blow." Abbas took a box of raisins from a pocket and popped a handful into his mouth.

"Even so, I hope we have seen the last of him," Sharik said. "Those Turkish smugglers tried to stop him and couldn't. An entire town, and he brought it to its knees."

Rakin rose onto an elbow and swore. "You are too timid. He is a man, and nothing more. He can be killed like any other. If he shows up again, I will prove it to you by slaying him myself."

Abbas changed the subject. "Your focus now must be on America." Reaching under his cot, he lifted a briefcase and set it in front of him. "In here is information worth its weight in gold. With it, our success is guaranteed.''

"Are those the files the American at the Cyprus facility showed you?" Sharik asked. "The ones Barakah was telling me about?"

"They are," Abbas stated. He now knew the location of every Echelon site in the world. Not only that, he could access secret government files from any computer terminal with the aid of a special disk. Code words, encryption protocols, he had it all.

"Where will we go once we reach New York?" Jebel inquired.

"I will tell you when the right time comes," Abbas answered. "The less you know in advance, the less you can reveal if you are arrested."

Yasin rested his chin on his forearms. "What I want to know is how you prepared our passage on such short notice."

"A smart leader thinks ahead and has every contingency covered," Abbas replied. "That is why I insist each of you keep several passports from different countries on hand. And why all of us with dark hair and beards will dye our hair a lighter shade and shave before we reach New York."

Barakah put a hand to his bushy beard. "I have never taken a razor to my skin in my life. The same as my father, and my father's father. You ask too much, master."

"I ask only what is necessary to accomplish our holy mission," Abbas argued. "If we keep our dark hair and beards, we will stand out. The police, the military, even the American public are on the lookout for Arabs or anyone who remotely looks like an Arab.

A few alterations to our appearance, and we can avoid unnecessary trouble.''

"My father will never forgive me if I cut off my beard,'' Barakah persisted.

"He will if you do it for the good of Islam. If you want, after we return I will pay him a visit and personally smooth over relations between the two of you.''

"You would do that for me?''

"For you and everyone else,'' Abbas said. "Must I constantly remind you we are brothers in arms? We must always be willing to help one another. By doing so we set an example for those who come after us, and prove to them and the world our calling is holy.''

A respectful silence ensued, broken by the grating of the door. Captain Mustafa Runihara wore a sailor's cap and had his callused hands shoved into his coat's deep pockets. A crusty old salt who had fought for the Palestinian cause when it was in its infancy, he walked over to Abbas with that peculiar rolling gait longtime seamen always had. "I trust everything is to your satisfaction, old friend?''

"You will not hear any complaints,'' Abbas said, pointedly glancing at Jebel. "Has your communications officer been monitoring official channels and newscasts as I requested?''

"We have. Greek authorities believe you are in still in hiding somewhere on the island. The British received an anonymous phone call reporting that you left Cyprus on a fishing boat and are now in Egypt.''

Abbas grinned at Jamilah. "Nicely done.'' He looked at Captain Runihara. "What about the Americans? What do they say?''

"They have been oddly silent. A spokesman for

their embassy issued a short press release announcing they might have substantial news to report in another day or so.'' Runihara clapped Abbas on the back. ''Congratulations. You slipped out right under their noses. Five hours more, and soldiers were going through every ship in port.''

Some of the others laughed and made comments about the intelligence of those searching for them, but Abbas did not join in. The Americans' silence troubled him. It could mean they were on to something. More than the British, more than the Israelis, more than anyone, the Americans were the one adversary the terrorist begrudgingly respected. Their technology was second to none, their training superior to most and their dogged persistence extraordinary.

Runihara was addressing the rest. ''I apologize for confining you to these quarters during daylight hours but I trust you recognize the need. We can not risk having you seen on deck by passing ships or planes overhead.''

''So when do we get to stretch our legs?'' Sharik asked.

''From midnight until 4:00 a.m. the ship operates with a skeleton crew. All are loyal to me, and you are free to go up and enjoy some fresh air. But if another vessel should approach, you must come below until I give you the all clear.''

''Does your crew know who we are?'' This from Rakin.

''A few,'' Runihara admitted. ''Many more suspect. But they will keep their mouths shut.'' He pushed his cap back on his bald head. ''You must keep in mind that crews of ships like this are made up largely of

The Gold Eagle Reader Service™ — Here's how it works:

Accepting your 2 free books and mystery gift places you under no obligation to buy anything. You may keep the books and gift and return the shipping statement marked "cancel." If you do not cancel, about a month later we'll send you 6 additional books and bill you just $29.94* — that's a saving of over 10% off the cover price of all 6 books! And there's no extra charge for shipping! You may cancel at any time, but if you choose to continue, every other month we'll send you 6 more books, which you may either purchase at the discount price or return to us and cancel your subscription.

If offer card is missing write to: Gold Eagle Reader Service, 3010 Walden Ave., P.O. Box 1867, Buffalo, NY 14240-1867

NO POSTAGE
NECESSARY
IF MAILED
IN THE
UNITED STATES

BUSINESS REPLY MAIL

FIRST-CLASS MAIL   PERMIT NO. 717-003   BUFFALO, NY

POSTAGE WILL BE PAID BY ADDRESSEE

GOLD EAGLE READER SERVICE
3010 WALDEN AVE
PO BOX 1867
BUFFALO NY 14240-9952

GET FREE BOOKS and a FREE GIFT WHEN YOU PLAY THE...

SLOT MACHINE GAME!

Just scratch off the silver box with a coin. Then check below to see the gifts you get!

YES! I have scratched off the silver box. Please send me the 2 free Gold Eagle® books and gift for which I qualify. I understand I am under no obligation to purchase any books, as explained on the back of this card.

366 ADL DRSG

166 ADL DRSF
(MB-01/03)

FIRST NAME   LAST NAME

ADDRESS

APT.#   CITY

STATE/PROV.   ZIP/POSTAL CODE

7	7	7	**Worth TWO FREE BOOKS plus a BONUS Mystery Gift!**
🍒	🍒	🍒	**Worth TWO FREE BOOKS!**
♣	♣	♣	**Worth ONE FREE BOOK!**
🔔	🔔	🍒	**TRY AGAIN!**

Visit us online at www.eHarlequin.com

DETACH AND MAIL CARD TODAY!

roughnecks and outcasts, men who have lived outside the law themselves in many cases.''

"They are being well paid for their cooperation,'' Abbas noted. He was expending almost all the reserve funds Al-Jabbar had access to on this enterprise, but the expense was justified if they succeeded. If they failed— No, he refused to so much as entertain the thought of failure.

Runihara squatted by the cot and nudged him with an elbow. "So tell me. Just between old friends. Why are you going to America?''

"You know better,'' Abbas said. No one knew except Jamilah, and she would never share the secret.

"Not even a hint?''

"Not one that will do you any good.'' Besides, the terrorist doubted the old sea dog would believe him. There were moments when it was hard for him to believe it himself. The target he had chosen was a critical cog in American government. Some would call it indispensable. For not only was its headquarters also the headquarters for Echelon, it was the hub from which the Great Satan's evil spread throughout the world. "All I can tell you is that Al-Jabbar is going to plunge a dagger deep into America's heart.''

Aban Abbas planned to destroy the National Security Agency.

CHAPTER TWELVE

To his neighbors he was known as Ben Green. A quiet, unassuming man in his early forties, he owned a large house in a quaint residential section of New Castle, Pennsylvania. He had painted it when he moved in two years ago, and trimmed the overgrown hedgerows. In the summer he mowed his lawn once a week. In the winter he always shoveled his drive and the sidewalk after it snowed. He never held parties. He never blared loud music. In short, he was an ideal neighbor.

Green favored baggy shirts and loose-fitting pants that effectively hid his muscular build. He was an exercise buff, and started every morning, after his prayers to God, with five hundred push-ups. He never went to baseball or football or basketball games, but he did attend local soccer matches and cheered as loudly as everyone else for his favorite teams.

Green worked at the library. He never missed a day of work. He never complained about his schedule. He never became gruff with patrons. In short, in every respect he was an ideal employee.

One day not long after Green had started work, he invited a female co-worker to his house for supper. During the meal she innocently asked how he could afford such a fine house on a librarian's salary, and

Green responded he had used money from an inheritance left to him by a doting aunt to buy the place.

After that, Green never invited another co-worker over.

Green was a voracious reader. He checked out more than a dozen books a week. No one noticed that mixed in with books on American history and politics were a lot of volumes dealing with the Middle East in general and Arab nations in particular.

Every evening when he came home punctually at 6:10 p.m., Green stopped his car at the end of the driveway and got out to open his mailbox and check his mail. Rain or shine, he never neglected the ritual.

On this particular evening, Green braked his Neon, trudged to the mailbox and opened it. He wasn't in the best of moods. He missed his native land and his own people, and dearly yearned to be given permission to go back for a visit, although he knew that was impossible. Once he'd volunteered, the die was cast. There was no going home again.

Green opened the mailbox and pulled out six envelopes. Four contained bills, one was from a credit-card company that wanted him to sign up for their gold card, and the last was a flyer advertising the grand opening of a new store. That was all. Sighing, Green closed the mailbox and drove his car to the garage. Turning off the ignition, he gathered up an armful of books he had checked out that day and entered his house through a side door.

Green set the books on the kitchen counter, tossed the mail into a basket and went to the fridge. There was a small eatery in downtown New Castle that specialized in Arab dishes. The food wasn't the best— nothing could compare to the culinary delights of

Egypt—but they served passable falafel and fool, and their dates were fresh daily.

From the fridge Green took some falafel and made a sandwich. He cut a slab of white cheese and poured a glass of Omar Khayyam wine. Placing it all on a metal tray, he walked into the living room, sat down in his easy chair and used the remote control to turn on the TV.

Hardly had the news come on than the telephone jangled.

Green frowned. The evening meal was one of his favorite times of the day. He didn't like having it interrupted. Carefully setting the tray on the floor, he picked up the receiver on the fourth ring. "Hello?"

A gruff voice said in Egyptian, "Your brothers are coming for a visit." And then the man at the other end hung up.

For a few seconds Green was too stunned to move. It had come! It had finally come! He had known they might use any means, mail, phone, messenger, telegram. But even so, it had been so long that it took a bit for the wonderful reality to sink in.

Laughing giddily, Green hung up. He spun in a circle, leaped into the air and then remembered himself and fell to the floor to bow in thanks to God. Elation coursed through him. Some of his brothers were en route. Whether they were brothers he had met was irrelevant. They were kindred souls, and it would be glorious to be among his own kind again.

Green loathed Americans. They were a shallow, materialistic people, caught up in a mania of self-indulgence that made the hedonistic Romans seem like monks in comparison. Americans were Satan incarnate, and he couldn't wait for the opportunity to strike out at them again, to punish them for their wicked ways.

Green sat down and picked up the tray but left the sandwich untouched. He was too excited to eat. The caller hadn't said how soon the others would arrive, and he had a lot to do before they did.

Taking the tray to the kitchen, Green again opened the refrigerator. He hadn't shopped in a while and was running low. Humming to himself, he left the house, climbed in his car and drove downtown.

The owner of Mezza, Mr. Morgan, was at the cash register and smiled as he entered. "Mr. Green. It has been a few days. I was beginning to think you had switched to hamburgers or fried chicken."

"Not in this life," Green said, smiling as well. For the first time in a long time he was genuinely happy. "I've been busy at work." His English was impeccable, without a trace of accent. But then, he had always been an adept linguist.

"What can we do for you tonight? Are you eating in? Or takeout?"

"I'm throwing a party this weekend and I would like to treat my guests to some authentic Arab cuisine."

The owner's smile widened. "If you can't find what you need here, you can't find it, period. And I must tell you, your attitude is refreshing."

"My attitude?" Green said, puzzled.

"Toward Arab food. I like it because my mother was Jordanian. But many Americans today don't want anything to do with anything that smacks of Arab culture."

"Can you blame them after 9/11?" Green played his part to perfection.

"No, I suppose not," Morgan said. "I was as outraged as everyone else. But I know better than to blame all Muslims for the deeds of a few fanatics." He wiped his hands on his apron and moved toward the deli counter. "For a while there, back then, I was afraid I might go out of business. A lot of my customers stopped coming."

Green couldn't care less, but he nodded as if he were interested and frowned to show he sympathized.

"Now what I can get for you?"

"It's a long list," Green said, and rattled off enough to feed a soccer team. "Do you think you have all that?"

Morgan was studying a case of meats and sundry cheeses. "Most, I think. That's quite a selection. Hardcore Arabic dishes." He turned to another case. "I'm all out of beetroot. And the red fish roe I never have carried. Sorry."

"Do the best you can," Green encouraged him. "While I'm waiting, how about some Egyptian salad and a Tuborg?" His appetite had returned, and he hungrily forked into the mix of tomatoes, cucumbers, watercress, onions, green peppers, parsley and mint leaves while Morgan and a teenage helper busied themselves filling the order. He washed the salad down with the beer and sat back, content.

"All set," Morgan announced in due course. He had placed two full paper bags next to the register and was adding a third.

"How much do I owe you?" Green asked.

Morgan told him, then leaned on the counter and said, "I hope you won't think I'm prying, but I'm curious. Do you have some Arab in your blood, like me? Not that you look Arabic," he added hastily, as if afraid his comment would be construed as an insult. "If I had to guess, I'd say you were Greek. I knew a Greek fella once who had curly sandy hair just like yours. But with a name like Green, that can't be right, can it?"

"I'm more of a mongrel than anything," Green said. He had his Americanisms down pat. "My father had Polish, English and Dutch in him. My mother was a mix of English and Greek." Lies. All lies. Both his parents were Egyptian and could trace their lineage back to the time of the Pharaohs.

"Greek?" Morgan said, grinning. "I was right, then? Well, what do you know. I'm pretty good at guessing that kind of stuff."

"You've sure impressed me." Green paid and carried two of the bags out to his trunk. The teenager brought the third. He tipped the boy, slid behind the wheel and cruised from the parking lot. The rich odor of the white goat's milk cheese and other culinary delights filled the car, bringing back memories of a happier time.

Absorbed in the past, Green turned right onto a secondary road that wound past a golf course. Not many people used it, and he sped up to get home that much sooner. Rounding a curve, he spotted a police car parked on the shoulder on the other side. He braked, but it was too late.

Lights flashing, the police car performed a U-turn and raced after him.

Green fought down fleeting panic, braked and pulled over. The sooner he did, the less apt they were to use their radio. He lowered his window, pulled out his wallet and opened it to his driver's license.

There were two cops, an old one and a young one.

The young one came to the door while the old one hung back, a hand draped near his side arm. A SIG, unless Green was mistaken.

"Good evening, sir," the young cop said. "Were you aware you were going thirty-seven in a twenty-five-mile-per-hour zone?"

Better, Green thought, to play a typical American idiot than give in to his natural urge. "I'm sorry, Officer. I was in a hurry to get home and wasn't paying attention."

The young cop studied the driver's license. "I'm afraid I'll have to write you a ticket, sir. It won't take long."

Green couldn't understand why the policeman was being so polite. He saw the young one glance at the old one and the old one smile and nod. The young one had to be new to the force, Green deduced, and the old one was breaking him in. As long as they stayed away from their vehicle, everything would be fine. The young one began to write the ticket, and Green relaxed.

"Aren't you forgetting something, Charlie?" the old cop prodded.

"Sarge?" the young cop said.

"Wants and warrants. You've got to get into the habit of checking when you pull somebody over or the captain will ream you seven ways from Sunday."

"Sorry, sir." Lowering the clipboard, the young cop walked toward the cruiser.

Green reached under the front seat and wrapped his fingers around the butt of the 9 mm Stechkin he always kept there. A sound suppressor was already threaded onto the barrel, so all he had to do was lean out, fire two swift shots into the back of the young cop's head, shift his arm a few degrees and send two more slugs into the face of the startled older officer.

Climbing out, Green looked both ways. No cars were coming. He opened the Neon's trunk and moved the three bags aside to get at a toolbox. From it he took a pair of gloves, which he slipped on, a coil of wire and a grenade.

The front door on the driver's side of the patrol car was wide open. Green bent and peered inside. He didn't see a video camera but he wasn't leaving anything to chance. Tying one end of the wire to the grenade's pin, he wedged the grenade under the front seat and slowly backed off, unwinding wire as he went. Once in his own car, he unwound another sixty yards or so, let it dangle out the window, and was set to tromp on the gas when he looked into the side mirror and saw the young cop sprawled in the ditch. And the clipboard beside him.

Placing the roll of wire on the seat, Green slid out and retrieved the ticket book. He had almost made an unforgivable blunder. That's what came from not having killed anyone in two years. Tossing the incriminating evidence into the back seat, he climbed in, looped the roll of wire around the steering wheel and accelerated.

The wire rapidly played out. A heartbeat after it went taut, the grenade detonated. The explosion blew out the police car's windows and caused the cruiser's front wheels to buck into the air. It also set off the fuel tank.

The second blast far eclipsed the first. Molten flame wreathed the vehicle as it soared over the ditch like a great ungainly bird. Flipping, it landed on its roof, which crumpled like so much paper. More flames spurted, and from inside came popping and sizzling sounds.

Green didn't stay to admire his handiwork. Raveling the wire, he pushed the speedometer to sixty. At a stop sign he turned right. So far God was smiling on him; he hadn't encountered any other vehicles. At the next intersection he had to wait for the light to change before he could go. Holding to the speed limit, he soon pulled into his driveway and drove into the garage.

Turning the key off, Green killed the headlights and sat in the dark. Those cops had nearly caught him. If the young one had radioed in his license number, their computers would have spit back there was no such person. They would have placed him under arrest and hauled him to their station. When his brothers in arms showed up, he would be languishing behind bars. He couldn't let that happen.

Green slowly raised his hands from the steering wheel. They were shaking. Deeply ashamed at his weakness, he gathered up his groceries and stalked into the house. He was sick to death of America. Sick to death of playing the part of a meek, law-abiding simpleton. He craved action. He prayed that when his brothers arrived, they had a part for him in their mission.

Leaving the kitchen, Green walked down the hall toward his bedroom and came to a full-length mirror on the wall. Stopping, he regarded himself with disdain. His dyed hair and beardless chin were an affront to Islam and to himself.

Then, as if to reassure himself who he truly was, Green said aloud the name he was never supposed to utter. The name given to him by his parents.

"I am Sefu Salim Abbas!"

Reaching out, Sefu touched his reflection and smiled.

Stony Man Farm, Virginia

THE EXECUTIONER was of two minds about downtime. On the one hand he liked being able to hone his marksmanship and other skills. He also liked learning how to handle new weapons and new hardware. He even liked to devote an occasional hour or two to reading a book or watching a movie. But what he definitely didn't like was when the downtime went on for too long. A day here, a day there, he could handle. Three days at a stretch he could live with. Any longer, though, and he began to feel like a tiger cooped in cage.

Now it was the morning of the fourth day since Bolan returned to Stony Man Farm from Somalia, and he was feeling antsy. He wanted to get back out in the world. He kept hoping the Feds would uncover new intel that would set him on Al-Jabbar's trail, but so far their efforts had turned up zilch.

Bolan rose early, as was his custom. He put on a dark blue sweat suit, donned a black headband and headed outside to go jogging.

Situated in the Blue Ridge Mountains of Virginia, to all outward appearances Stony Man Farm seemed no different from the scores of other farms in the region. But looks were deceiving. For hidden behind a facade of ordinary-seeming buildings was a state-of-the-art complex that was the staging ground and ops center for the most elite commandos the U.S. had to offer.

Phoenix Force and Able Team operated out of

Stony Man, as did Mack Bolan when he and the government had a common goal. They were supported by the a cadre of computer and ops experts, the best in their respective fields, along with a number of techs who kept the sophisticated equipment humming.

A golden crown heralded the new dawn when Bolan stepped outside. The morning air was crisp and invigorating, just as he liked it. Breathing deep to oxygenate his lungs, he performed a few warm-up exercises.

The door behind him opened. A whiff of familiar perfume told Bolan who it was before he turned. Barbara Price was the Farm's mission controller. "Morning."

"Mind if I join you?"

Bolan didn't mind at all. Price was more than a friend. On occasion, when either felt the need for companionship, they would get together for an evening. Or a night. "Not at all," he said, grinning. "I just hope you can keep up."

"My, my. Aren't we feeling smug this morning."

They started off running side by side. Occasionally their elbows brushed. Bolan was content to jog, but Price wasn't. She lived for her work. If there was anyone who disliked downtime more than he did, it was her.

"The latest satellite photos show no activity at the Al-Jabbar fortress. We doubt they'll try and rebuild now that it's been compromised."

Bolan settled into an easy rhythm, adjusting his pace to hers.

"Based on the available intel, we think about ten members are unaccounted for. Most if not all were probably involved in the Cyprus escapade. Where they went afterward is anyone's guess."

"Too bad we didn't learn of it beforehand."

"It caught everyone off guard. For years they've been content to specialize in assassinations. Then they go and make a quantum jump into the big leagues." Price paused. "I can't help but wonder what they have up their sleeve next."

"I want first dibs," Bolan told her.

"Don't worry. This is your baby. If intelligence comes up with anything, we'll send you in before we call on Phoenix Force or Able Team."

"They will." Bolan had complete confidence in the intelligence-gathering arm of the U.S. government. Given time, they could ferret out anyone.

"But will we find them in time?" Price responded. She was breathing a little heavier but otherwise ran with the smooth ease of a practiced athlete. "My big worry is that Cyprus wasn't an aberration. That Al-Jabbar has permanently shifted gears into a new phase. It makes them ten times as dangerous."

"Any luck tracking down Abbas?"

"Not yet. The fingerprints we took off the watch and the other items you brought back aren't in any database. We're cross-referencing all our files on every known terrorist who's ever belonged to a terrorist organization, but so far there's no record of anyone by that name. It's one of those worst-case scenarios. A major player who's a complete unknown. We can't even run a psych profile on the guy."

"You should be able to once the journal is translated."

"Which reminds me. I expect to have a hard copy by one. Want to sit in on the briefing? It'll be in the War Room."

"I'll be there," Bolan promised. "What about that

little book with the list of names and phone numbers?''

"We're still working on it. Most are in Middle East countries, where the gears grind exceedingly slow.'' Price slowed a bit. "Say. Any interest in joining me for supper? About sixish? I was thinking chicken Alfredo with maybe a little wine.''

"Make it a beer instead of wine and you have yourself a deal.''

"Fair enough. It's your stomach.''

At sea

THE FREIGHTER WAS only a few hours out of Cadiz, Spain, where the terrorists would transfer to the tanker *Caspian,* when Captain Runihara brought Aban Abbas a radiogram. The message was in a code Abbas had created expressly for his people. To a casual reader it appeared to be from a man to a close friend, updating him on family affairs. To Abbas it was far more, and far worse.

Jamilah, always sensitive to his moods, was first to notice and sat up. "What is wrong? You have gone as pale as a sheet.''

"Our fortress is no more.''

All those within earshot stopped what they were doing. "Did I hear correctly, master?'' Jebel asked.

"How can that be?'' Yasin exclaimed. "What about our brothers we left behind?''

"Only Nassir is left, and he was lucky to escape with his life. The rest are dead.'' Abbas lowered the message and bowed his head. He was devastated, his emotions in upheaval. The work of years, gone. Men he had nurtured like his own children, all slain.

Questions flew fast and furious.

"Was it the Somali army?"

"Was it that local warlord who gave us trouble a while back?"

"Were American bombers responsible?"

Abbas took a deep breath and straightened. He had to be strong, for their sakes if not his own. "Nassir says one man was to blame." In the stunned silenced that followed, he looked at Sharik. "The description he gives is of a big, dark-haired man."

"Him again. I warned you, did I not? Whoever he is, he intends to wipe us from the face of the earth."

Yasin jumped to his feet. "How did this man find our base? We destroyed the Echelon facility that could trace us."

"Perhaps the Americans tracked us down before we blew the building up," Abbas speculated. It was the only logical explanation.

"We have not seen the last of that devil," Sharik predicted.

This time Abbas didn't object to the use of that word. He was inclined to agree. Islamabad. Athens. Thenas. Turkey. Now Somalia. The dark-haired one was always there, like an unwanted shadow. It was entirely possible he would show up in America, too. Something had to be done. Somehow, some way, their pursuer had to be disposed of. If only they could lure him into a trap! Abbas thought. But how, when they had no bait? Then it hit him. They most certainly did have bait. The kind their pursuer couldn't resist: themselves.

Lying down with his hands behind his head, Abbas stared at the bulkhead and turned his mind to the task of turning the tables. The hunted had to become the hunters. After a while a devious smile lit his face. He had just the thing. God willing, not only would Al-Jabbar destroy the NSA and Echelon, but they would also eliminate the dark-haired thorn in their side.

CHAPTER THIRTEEN

Stony Man Farm, Virginia

The War Room was in the basement of the main building at Stony Man Farm. Bolan took the elevator down and found four people already seated. He nodded to Barbara Price and slid into a chair between her and the man at the head of the table.

Hal Brognola had flown in from Washington, D.C., an hour earlier. The big Fed looked as if he hadn't had a good night's sleep in a while, but that was typical. An unlit cigar was clamped in his mouth, and he was chewing on it as if it were a pretzel. That, too, was typical. "Good to see you could make it, Striker," he said, only half in jest. Brognola was a stickler for punctuality, and Bolan was a couple of minutes late.

"The elevator got stuck on the fourteenth floor," Bolan quipped. Actually, the farmhouse had only three levels.

"You had that problem, too?" chimed in a barrel-chested, bearded man who sat in a wheelchair on Brognola's left. Aaron Kurtzman, affectionately dubbed "The Bear," was Stony Man's wizard at intelligence gathering and assimilation, and often advised Brognola on critical matters. He also headed

Stony Man's cybernetic team, which consisted of three exceptionally intelligent and talented individuals, one of whom was next to him, lightly tapping on the table in time to music only he could hear.

Akira Tokaido was the youngest of the mission control team. One would never guess to look at him, clad as he was in a denim jacket and faded jeans, and with the earbuds to a portable CD player firmly implanted in his ears, that he was as brilliant as they came. He had his eyes closed and hadn't heard Bolan arrive.

"I think we can begin," Brognola said to Kurtzman, "provided you can tear your protégé away from his music."

"Kids nowadays," Kurtzman joked, tapping Tokaido on the arm.

Smiling sheepishly, the younger man turned off the CD and placed his hand on a small stack of red binders in front of him. "Sorry. Sometimes I forget myself. Have we started?"

"We'd like to," Brognola said. "What can you tell us about the journal?"

"Translating it posed no problem. It's not in code or anything. Just basic, everyday Arabic. I've developed a special program for translating just about every language on the planet. Took no time at all."

"We double-checked for a hidden code," Kurtzman added, "but the journal is exactly what it appears to be. Namely, the private musings of Aban Abbas, the founder of Al-Jabbar." He nodded at Akira. "You can hand them out now."

The red binders were passed around. Bolan opened his. It was a reproduction, in English, of Abbas's journal. The title was telling. "'The Words and Wisdom of a Humble Holy Warrior of God,'" he read aloud.

"The whole journal is like that," Kurtzman said. "Filled with pious rhetoric about the need to crush the Great Satan. Along with everyday entries that read like a diary."

"You've read the whole thing, I take it?" Brognola said.

"All 102 pages," Kurtzman confirmed, and nodded at Tokaido. "We both have."

"Break it down for us," the big Fed directed.

Kurtzman leaned back in his wheelchair. "In terms of hard intel it's a major disappointment. Abbas is shrewd. He doesn't mention associates by name. He leaves blanks instead."

Brognola made a teepee of his hands under his chin. "Are you telling me we didn't learn anything concrete?"

Kurtzman opened a small notepad beside his binder. "We learned Aban Abbas is Egyptian. Born in a small village south of Cairo. His parents are deceased. He has three brothers and two sisters. One might—and I stress 'might'—be involved in terrorist activity. The others chose normal lives." Kurtzman ran a thick finger down the sheet. "He started the journal about the same time he formed Al-Jabbar. But he never identifies the members except to say where a few are from. Toward the end he goes on and on about a renegade Saudi he has high hopes for as a source of money."

"That's a valuable lead in itself," Barbara Price interjected. "The Saudi government takes a dim view of rogues. With a little political prodding they might be persuaded to ID the guy." She glanced at Hal Brognola.

"I'll do what I can," the big Fed said.

Then, to Kurtzman, "What else?"

"Abbas displays a pathological hatred of the United States. We've seen his kind at work before. But he's more intelligent than your run-of-the-mill fanatic."

Akira Tokaido surprised them by commenting, "He also has a warrior's spirit."

"Where do you get that from?" Brognola demanded.

Tokaido tapped the binder. "From his writings. He says a true warrior should confront an enemy face-to-face. But he realized that isn't always practical in today's world, so he chose assassination as his preferred technique. Two whole pages are devoted to denouncing the World Trade Center attacks as misguided."

"This from the guy responsible for blowing up our Echelon site in Cyprus," Brognola said in disgust. "His philosophy has undergone a sweeping change."

"Maybe, maybe not," Tokaido responded. "In his eyes the site was a legitimate target. Notice he didn't kill civilians."

Brognola snorted. "It's a fine distinction. And I'm willing to bet a year's salary that if civilians had been there, they'd be as dead as the Echelon staff. Don't glorify him. Abbas might see himself as some sort of holy warrior, but when you boil it down, he's nothing but another cold-blooded killer. Correlate what we've gleaned so far and give it to your support staff for further analysis," Brognola told Kurtzman. "Then go through the journal again, and as many times as necessary, to milk it for every bit of intel it has to offer. No reference, however obscure, should be overlooked."

He turned to Price. "What about the list of phone numbers?"

"We're still working on it. So far we've established

a lot are to ordinary businesses and individuals with no overt links to Al-Jabbar.''

"I hope to God it's not another dead end,'' Brognola grumbled.

The door opened, and in came a woman who worked in the communications center. She quietly apologized for interrupting, then handed the big Fed a manila folder. Brognola thanked her and opened it. His eyebrows arched, and suddenly he buried his nose in the folder like a bloodhound taking to new scent. "I'll be damned. Christmas has come early this year."

When the big Fed made no other comment for a bit, Kurtzman said, "Care to share the good news with the rest of us?''

"It seems a couple of police officers in New Castle, Pennsylvania, pulled over a speeder three days ago. They were shot and their patrol car blown up. The culprit thought he got away, but he doesn't know the officers radioed in the make and license number of his vehicle. The police located him, but they didn't move. Some checking revealed everything about the guy is phony.''

"Nothing remarkable there so far,'' Barbara remarked.

"It seems the guy also has an interest in all things Arabic. Since he fit the profile of a potential sleeper, the police notified the FBI.''

Sleepers were terrorists moles who went underground by assuming American identities and living ordinary lives until they were activated. Bolan had encountered more than his fair share.

"This morning the Bureau set up a listening post across the street,'' Brognola continued. "They've got the guy on tape talking to himself in Arabic. So they sent a report up through channels, as required.''

''And what about it has you so excited?'' Kurtzman asked.

Brognola lit up like a Christmas tree. ''A transcript is included. For some reason he's repeated the same two words several times.'' He paused for effect. ''The words are 'Aban Abbas.'''

SPECIAL AGENT IN CHARGE Phil Durkin was playing it by the book. His team was monitoring the suspect around the clock so the man's habits could be established. They had to take him when he least expected, with minimal risk to civilians.

The house the FBI was using was directly across the street and belonged to an industrial engineer by the name of Stuesman, who hadn't objected one bit to staying in a hotel at government expense until it was over.

Late that day Durkin received a phone call from the director. When Agent Frank Hengel wagged the phone and told him who it was, Durkin thought it was a joke. The only time he had ever seen the Bureau's head honcho was at a regional meeting where the director gave a speech on the future of the Bureau in the new millennium.

''Sir?'' Durkin said, placing the receiver to his ear.

''Apprise me of the situation, Agent.''

A swarm of butterflies took flight in Durkin's stomach but he dutifully complied, concluding with, ''I believe we have the situation well in hand.''

''Excellent. We can't blow this. I've received word from higher up. They want this guy alive and unharmed.''

Durkin was dumbfounded by the reference to someone "higher up." So far as he knew, the director answered to one person.

"Agent Durkin?"

"I'm here, sir. We can take him anytime you say."

"Don't rush things. Take as much time as you need. The important thing is not to let him slip through your fingers. Or worse."

Durkin didn't need to ask what "worse" was. He didn't say anything, but he didn't like the idea of treating a potential terrorist with kid gloves. It put those under him at greater risk.

"Once you have the suspect under wraps, call me. No matter what time of day or night. Here's my personal number."

Fishing a pen from his suit, Durkin hastily scribbled it down. "I'll contact you the second we cuff him, sir."

There was a short pause, then, "Agent Durkin, do you know what a career-making moment is?"

Durkin's mouth went as dry as a desert. "Of course, sir."

"This is one of them. Do this right and you're on the fast track to the top."

Left unspoken was what happened if Durkin blew it. Licking his lips, he responded, "You can count on me, sir."

"I hope so. Now take a few deep breaths. Remember, you're a highly trained professional. Use that training. Stick to procedure so if something does go wrong, no one can hold it against you. Understood?"

"Yes, sir." The dial tone hummed in Durkin's ear and he clicked off. That last had been a bit of friendly advice. The director had guessed how nervous he was.

It warmed Durkin to think the man cared about his people.

Giving the phone to Hengel, Durkin walked over to the agent glued to the directional microphone. It was trained on a bedroom window on the second floor. Ben Green, or whatever his real name was, liked to sleep with a window halfway open at night and never bothered to close it all the way in the morning. He tapped Agent James Farouk on the shoulder and Farouk removed his headphones. "Anything new?"

"No, sir. He hasn't made or received any phone calls since he came home from work. And he's not one of those who talk to themselves a lot."

Durkin nodded. Farouk was on loan from the Pittsburgh office. His mother was a Kuwaiti, and Farouk was one of the few FBI agents in all the Northeast fluent in Arabic. Whenever a possible sleeper was uncovered in the Tri-State area, he was flown in to handle the translating.

"The only things he's said in the past hour are, 'I can't wait', and that name he keeps saying every so often, 'Sefu Salim Abbas.'"

"Do you think it's his real name?"

"I can't say, sir. Strange of him to repeat it like he's doing if it is."

Durkin moved to one side of the picture window. The living room was dark, the curtains drawn halfway. The well-kept house across the street, with its neatly trimmed lawn and late-model car in the driveway, seemed so ordinary, so *American*, it was hard to believe it harbored a foreign fanatic bent on America's destruction.

Footsteps sounded on the stairs leading to the second floor, and Agent Wilf Noonan quietly called his name. "We need you upstairs, sir. Something strange is going on."

An agent was posted at each of the upstairs windows facing the target residence. Noonan's post was the master bedroom. He had pulled a chair close enough to see out without being seen, and he motioned for Durkin to take a seat. "Watch the house to the left of Green's and tell me if I'm imagining things."

Durkin looked but saw nothing. A minute elapsed, and he was about to comment to that effect when the drapes on a ground-floor side window parted and a woman appeared. She stared at Green's place for ten seconds or so, then closed the curtains. "What the hell?"

"She's been doing that every couple of minutes for about ten minutes now," Noonan said. "I don't know what to make of it."

Neither did Durkin. She had to be watching the Green place. If she kept it up, Green might notice, and the last thing Durkin needed was for the suspect to become suspicious things weren't as they should be.

"Why would she do such a thing?" Noonan mused. "It's almost as if she knows about Green. But that can't be."

Durkin came out of the chair as if jolted by lightning. "Call the hotel. Ask Mrs. Stuesman if she's phoned any of her friends and told them what we're up to."

"Surely she wouldn't," Noonan said. "I heard you specifically tell them they were not to say a word to anyone."

"Some people just love to gab," Durkin said, and hurried downstairs to Farouk.

"IF YOU HEAR anything unusual, you're to tell me immediately."

"He's watching TV at the moment. *I Dream Of Jeannie*, if you can believe it." Farouk laughed lightly.

Durkin was too concerned about having their surveillance compromised to appreciate the humor. One look at Noonan's expression was enough to have his worst fear confirmed. "Was my hunch right?"

"On the money. The woman in the house next door is Mrs. Agatha Cleary. She's Mrs. Stuesman's best friend. Mrs. Stuesman thought it best to warn her about Green."

Durkin partly blamed himself. When the Stuesmans had asked why the FBI wanted to take over their house for a few days, at the time he'd seen no harm in mentioning Green was a suspected terrorist. Now he wished he'd simply told them it was a matter of national security, and let it go at that.

"Mrs. Stuesman swears she didn't call anyone else," Noonan reported.

Durkin gazed across the street. Procedure dictated that once they were compromised, the suspect should be taken into custody. But Durkin was loath to go barging in. Green was bound to put up a fight, and the orders from above were explicit. The powers that be wanted him alive and unharmed. So they should wait and do it by the numbers. But if Green was on to them, he could fly the coop anytime.

What to do? What do do? Durkin asked himself. All eyes were on him. "Once the sun goes down I want this block cordoned off tighter than a steel drum. We'll wait until an hour or so after he's gone to bed and take him in his sleep."

"And Mrs. Cleary?" Hengel asked.

"Phone her and tell her that if she shows her big nose at that window again, I'll have her charged with interfering with federal agents in the performance of their duty."

"Do you really want me to say that, sir?"

Durkin sighed. "No. Ask her, pretty please, to stay as far from that side of the house as she can until we notify her the coast is clear." No sense in outraging civilians any more than was necessary. Protecting them, after all, was the reason he joined the FBI in the first place. "I just hope our boy isn't on to us."

SEFU ABBAS WAS like a cat on a hot tin roof; he couldn't stay still for more than a few seconds. Although his favorite show was on TV, he couldn't concentrate on it. He kept glancing at the telephone, wishing it would ring, wishing he would find out exactly when his Al-Jabbar brothers were due to arrive. Initially he thought it might be within hours, or possibly the next day. But several had come and gone and he hadn't heard a thing.

Sefu hoped nothing had happened to them. He surfed the news channels every half hour or so, but there had been no mention of Al-Jabbar since the attack on the Echelon facility. Immense pride flooded through him every time he saw video footage of the destruction. And with it, more than a little confusion.

Sefu clearly remembered his older brother saying that to blow up buildings was the act of a coward. True warriors, Aban had proclaimed, fought their enemies face-to-face, man-to-man. Yet Al-Jabbar had blown up the building on Cyrpus. Sefu hoped to learn why when his brothers got there.

The show ended. It was yet another in the endless

stream of pathetic drivel Americans loved to watch.
But this one had certain limited appeal in the shapely
form of the lead actress. With her lustrous hair and
wonderful eyes, she reminded Sefu of a young woman
he knew in Egypt. A woman he had planned to wed.
But then along came the Holy War, and his personal
desires were sacrificed on the altar of his devotion to
God.

Sefu rose and began to pace. He was a bundle of
restless energy, and had been at work, also. Always
on the go. Always having to do something. It was
wrong, he knew. He was supposed to be a model of
self-control. But how could he not be excited after all
this time? He walked into the hall, past the full-length
mirror. As had become his custom the past few days,
he grinned at himself and declared, "I am Sefu Salim
Abbas." It was silly, but it gave him some small degree of petty satisfaction.

Entering the bathroom, Sefu pulled back the shower
curtain. Usually he took his shower a lot later, but he
had nothing else to do until bedtime and the suspense
was eating at him like acid. About to reach for the
knob to turn on the hot water, he changed his mind
and walked out to the living room.

Sefu tried telling himself to calm down. Stepping to
the picture window, he idly gazed up and down the
street. It would be night soon, and the neighborhood
lay quiet under gathering twilight. Lights had come on
all up and down the block. He glanced across the street
and started to turn. Then stopped.

Sefu stared at the home directly across from his.
The Stuesmans lived there. The husband was a football
nut, the wife a chattering simpleton. Their house was
always lit up. Even when they went out, they left the

lights blazing. Typical wasteful Americans. Yet now their house was dark. For the first time since Sefu had moved in, not a single light shone in any of their windows. And yet another oddity; their curtains were partially drawn. Not just downstairs but upstairs as well. They had never done that before.

Sefu walked to his kitchen. One window faced his backyard, another faced his neighbors to the north, the Clearys. Leaving his light off, he peered north just in time to see Mrs. Cleary's face at a ground-floor window. She was gazing at his bedroom. He saw her twist and speak to someone. A hand thrust a phone at her. She talked a moment, then snapped her curtains shut.

Before coming to America Sefu had gone through rigorous training. Part of it had to do with learning to stay alert to changes around him. Every person had their habits, every neighborhood its own rhythms. When those habits and rhythms were broken, it was cause for concern.

Sefu went to his bedroom, yanked on the top drawer to his dresser, tossed the few shirts it contained onto his bed and pried open the secret panel he had installed shortly after he moved in. The wood matched that of the dresser perfectly. No would ever guess there was a hidden compartment. From it he took two passports, a wallet containing a driver's license in the name of Simon LeBeau and other forged papers. He shoved them into a pocket.

Opening his closet, Sefu shrugged into a black jacket and zipped it all the way up. Kneeling, he pulled an old pair of boots from a corner. From one he drew an Astra 300. It was an older-make pistol, and Sefu liked it because it was short and light and had the magazine catch on the heel of the butt, European-style.

The same boot also concealed a sound suppressor, which he threaded on.

From the other boot Sefu removed two magazines, already loaded, and a box of 9 mm shorts. He inserted one of the magazines, pulled back the slide to feed a round into the chamber and tucked the Astra under his belt. The other magazine and the spare ammo went in his jacket.

To reach the basement Sefu had to go through the kitchen. Quietly descending, he crossed to a rear window. A stepladder was beside it, placed there for this very contingency. Climbing it, he peeked out. The backyard was shrouded in darkness. He didn't see anyone along the fence, and the gate was still closed.

He worked the latch and pushed the window open. Squeezing through, he crouched and drew the pistol. The neighborhood was uncommonly quiet. No children were yelling. No dogs were barking. Staying low, he crouch walked to the gate, which was shoulder high. The alley appeared to be empty until someone coughed. A vague figure was at the south end. It took a while to spot another to the north. Policemen, Sefu assumed. They had him boxed in. Or thought they did.

Sefu glided to the south. The policeman on the other side was leaning against the fence, and the top of his head jutted above it. Slowly extending the Astra until the business end almost touched him, Sefu stroked the trigger. The man sank to the ground without a sound.

Catching hold of the top of the fence, Sefu swung up and over. He looked toward the north, but the policeman there hadn't heard the cough of the suppressor. Backing toward the side street, Sefu spied a sedan parked at the curb a dozen feet past the alley. A man in a brown suit was near the front bumper, his hands in his pockets, looking bored.

Sefu rose, held the pistol behind him, lowered his chin and strolled along the sidewalk whistling to himself. From under hooded lids he saw the man stiffen in surprise.

"Excuse me, sir, this block is—"

Sefu shot him between the eyes. Frisking the body, he found the keys to the car and a wallet. He slid in, turned over the engine, performed a sharp U-turn and sped off. A block from the bus station he abandoned it. God was with him, and the next departure was in ten minutes. He didn't care where it was going. He would take it as far as the next town, get off and place a call to a contact in Philadelphia who would arrange for him to reach a safe house.

Since he had nothing better to do, Sefu examined the wallet. He was stunned to discover the man he had shot wasn't a policeman, but an agent of the Federal Bureau of Investigation. The vaunted FBI.

Sefu grinned. Like so much about America, they were vastly overrated.

CHAPTER FOURTEEN

The tanker *Caspian* was twelve nautical miles from the U.S. coast on a direct bearing to New York City when the Coast Guard cutter *Exiter* intercepted her. The newest in the High Endurance Class, the *Exiter* was equipped with a helicopter flight deck, the most sophisticated navigation gear known to man and fixed-mounted machine guns fore and aft.

Captain Mark Wagner ordered the captain of the *Caspian* to bring the tanker to a dead stop in the water and prepare to be boarded.

There was silence on the other end of the radio, then Captain Bruno Tuskindi growled, "Couldn't this wait until we reach port? In a few more hours we'll be there."

"It's not debatable," the Coast Guard officer responded. "Under Section 89 of Title 14 of the United States Code, we are authorized to stop and search any vessel anytime we see fit. So I repeat. You will bring the *Caspian* to a complete stop and prepare to receive a helicopter boarding party on your forward deck."

"We will be ready to receive you," the tanker's captain said, but he didn't sound pleased about it.

Below Wagner's position on the *Exiter*'s bridge, the retractable hangar was being rolled out. The pilot and co-pilot were waiting to board the copter, along with a five-man boarding team. Standard procedure called for a four-man team, but Wagner had orders to make an exception in this case. He stared at the new addition, a big, dark-haired man in a pea coat who had arrived that afternoon at the cutter's berth carrying a duffel bag. They had been told to expect him, and commanded to do whatever he required.

The helicopter being prepared for liftoff was a Sikorsky HH-60J Jayhawk, one of a fleet of forty-two. Fitted with a NAVSTAR Global Positioning System and coupled-doppler hover capability, it was the backbone of the Coast Guard's air arm. Twin T700-GE-401C engines could propel it at a cruising speed of 150 knots for over six hours. Extra fuel capacity enabled it to fly three hundred miles out to sea, stay onsite, hovering for almost an hour, and still have enough fuel left to make it back safely.

The *Caspian* was slowing. Wagner instructed his helmsman to pace her, and craned his neck upward. The tanker dwarfed his vessel. A slight turn to starboard, and the *Caspian* could crush the *Exiter* like so much kindling. But the tanker's captain knew that if he did, he would have the full weight of the United States armed forces down on his head.

A few crewmen were leaning over the rail, staring down. Ordinary swabs who might have no idea the tanker was suspected of harboring terrorists somewhere within its massive superstructure.

Wagner turned and admired his crew's efficiency. They were well-trained, and he would gladly sail with them into the heart of a hurricane, if need be. He barked commands, which were instantly obeyed. Presently, both ships were dead in the water, floating side by side in a choppy sea with slate-gray clouds scuttling overhead.

The latest weather data wasn't promising. A storm was approaching from the west. But it wouldn't arrive before they were done. They had been ordered to wrap up their search in two hours' time, which was hardly enough to do a thorough job. But then, Wagner had to remember their main priority wasn't the interdiction itself, but insuring the dark-haired man in the pea coat got on board the tanker.

Who was he? Wagner wondered one last time, and gave a thumbs-up sign to the pilot about to climb into the chopper.

LIEUTENANT Harve Dickerson had a reputation for being a bit of a cowboy. Which was fitting since he hailed from Oklahoma. After strapping himself into his cockpit seat, he began to run through the standard preflight check with his co-pilot. Hearing voices, Dickerson twisted and saw his boarding team climb into the bay.

The dark-haired man in the pea coat entered last and took a seat at the front.

"Anything special we need to do when we get up there, mister?" Dickerson asked. He didn't quite know what to make of the guy, and he wasn't sure he liked being party to subterfuge. But orders were orders.

"Do what you would ordinarily do," the man said. He had a low, deep voice that suited his commanding presence. "And forget I'm even here."

Dickerson would find that hard to do, but he smiled and nodded and said, "Will do, mister."

"One thing," the man mentioned. "The men I'm after won't hesitate to kill you if you sniff them out.

You and your men have to stay frosty the whole time you're up there.''

"Thanks for the warning, friend," Dickerson said, "but don't worry about us. We're old hands at this. We can take care of ourselves."

Ensign Jake Murphy had overhead. Smirking, he patted his M-16 and declared in his Tennessee drawl, "Hell, mister. If they so much as look at us crosswise, Bess and me will turn 'em into Swiss cheese."

Dickerson forgot about their special "guest" for a while. He had to get the twin T700-GE-401C turbo-shaft engines up to speed and finish the prelim checks. Soon they were good to go, and he radioed as much to the bridge. The captain's voice crackled in his helmet in response.

"You're clear for liftoff, Harve. Be careful up there."

"Roger that," Dickerson acknowledged. Then, over his shoulder to his crew, "Lock and load. Time to get serious." He took her up, whisking off the deck like a hummingbird taking flight, then banked sharply to make the steep vertical climb. He was, in effect, springboarding from one vessel to the other, a move designed to prevent anyone so inclined from getting a lock on them and shooting them down.

Springboarding from one vessel to another required considerable skill, and Dickerson was one of the best. Although he had done it a hundred times or more, he felt his stomach churn slightly and hoped the guy in the pea coat didn't lose his lunch. As the Jayhawk swept up over the tanker, Dickerson had a moment to marvel at its size.

The *Caspian* was a thousand feet long and close to two hundred feet wide, one of the largest in her class.

She was also one of the oldest, and her age showed in the wear and tear her hull had sustained, and the rust no amount of elbow grease could remove. Three crewmen were waiting, the stocky figure of their captain foremost among them.

Dickerson brought the Jayhawk down on the proverbial dime. He landed so close to the reception committee, they had to hold their caps on their heads to keep them from being blown off.

Ensign Murphy yanked the bay door open and deployed his men between the crewmen and the aircraft.

Unstrapping, Dickerson gave control to the copilot. "No one is to step foot in here, you hear?" Taking a clipboard, he crossed the bay. The guy in the pea coat hadn't moved, and it dawned on Dickerson that he had sat in the one spot where he was least likely to be seen from outside. Intentionally, no doubt.

The tanker's captain was a blockhouse on legs. He had a deep scar on his left cheek, and part of his right earlobe was missing. He smiled in greeting but the smile did not touch his beady, glittering eyes. "Welcome aboard. My ship and my crew are at your complete disposal."

"We appreciate that," Dickerson said, although he knew the man didn't meant it. "We'll start aft and work forward."

"May I inquire what you are after?" Tuskindi said. "If it is drugs or arms, I assure you I run a clean ship."

"That's for us to find out," Dickerson answered glibly. It was arrogant of Tuskindi to put on an innocent act when his record showed he was anything but. "Lead the way, if you don't mind."

They started off, and as Dickerson passed the Jayhawk he realized something else. The orders from on high had specified they had to interdict the tanker one hour before sunset, and be done one hour after the sun had gone down. He hadn't thought much of it at the time. But now it hit him that it would give the guy in the pea coat plenty of time to slip unnoticed off the Jayhawk in the dark. And that, too, must be intentional. Who *was* that guy? Dickerson wondered, and then thought no more about him and got down to the business at hand.

MACK BOLAN SAT QUIETLY as the Coast Guardsmen and the reception committee hiked toward the stern. He went on sitting there as the minutes ticked by. Ten, twenty, thirty, and still Bolan didn't move.

A couple of crewmen came along the catwalk toward the Jayhawk, but the co-pilot, a lieutenant junior grade named Gabriel, shooed them away.

Bolan shifted the duffel in his lap. He had another half hour yet. By then it would be dark enough.

The Feds had intercepted several cryptic transmissions to and from the *Caspian* that led them to suspect members of Al-Jabbar were onboard. One had been in code, but there wasn't a code invented that Akira Tokaido and his software couldn't crack. The message hadn't mentioned names, but it warned the recipient that their "castle" had been breached, and they had to meet somewhere else.

It was so amateurish, it was almost childish. The reference to a "castle" had to be New Castle, Pennsylvania. Sefu Abbas was warning those on the tanker not to pay him a visit. Instead, they were to rendezvous "where cats grew trees for whiskers," in the message's own words. The Stony Man staff hadn't figured out where that was yet, but they were working around the clock, and it was only a matter of time.

Brognola didn't know how many terrorists were on-board, but he was determined none would set foot on U.S. soil. To that end, the Coast Guard interdiction had a threefold purpose. As he had put it at Stony Man, "First, there's always a chance the Coast Guard boarding party will find them. Second, the search is a cover for you, Striker, to slip onboard and take up where they leave off if they don't. Third, and most important, by delaying the *Caspian,* I buy time to mobilize an army of federal, state and local authorities who will be on hand to greet the tanker when she arrives in port. If you haven't located them by then, I'll have her gone over from bow to stern. Every bulkhead, every rivet will be inspected."

Bolan had agreed to Brognola's plan. It sounded foolproof, for should option number one and two fail, option three definitely wouldn't.

The sun was sinking below the horizon. Bolan stirred and swiveled in his seat so he could see the length of the tanker. No one was anywhere near.

Gradually the shadows lengthened. By Bolan's watch it had been exactly one hour since Dickerson and company left when he stood, duffel in hand, and stepped to the door. It wasn't his usual bag but a smaller one he had requisitioned expressly for this op.

The Jayhawk had landed between the foremast and the forward deckhouse. Hopping down, Bolan walked around the tail assembly and jogged past the foremast. No one was on the crow's nest. What with all the electronic navigation equipment tankers had to guide them, the crow's nest wasn't used all that often except in northern waters where icebergs posed a continual threat.

Bolan moved around to the far side of the anchor windlass and mooring winch. They were large enough to conceal a car, and wouldn't see use until the ship docked. Ducking behind the winch, he unzipped the duffel and removed an MP-5 K. It was yet another variation on the standard Heckler & Koch short version of the MP-5 subgun, and different from the one he had used in Greece. Among the modifications on this one was a folding butt, which he now extended, and a custom sound suppressor, which he attached. He also attached a laser spot sight. The feature he liked most, though, was a 3-round burst unit. Lastly, his MP-5 K came with a sling, which he looped over his left arm.

Unbuttoning his pea coat, Bolan made sure his grenades were attached to his combat vest. Not explosive grenades. Only a fool would use one on a tanker filled to capacity. These were smoke grenades, and flash illumination grenades that emitted 55,000 candlepower for up to thirty seconds.

The last two items Bolan took from the duffel were a cellular phone he clipped to his belt, and minibinoculars fitted with a strap, which he slid over his head and around his neck. Then he leaned his shoulder against the winch and settled down to wait.

Now and then the soldier saw crewmen cross the huge deck but always at a distance. Once he watched a seaman on a bicycle inspect tank hatches. Another time, a man came down the forward catwalk toward the foremast, but he was only checking a valve, and when he was done, he went back into the deckhouse.

Night fell. The tanker's running lights automatically

came on. Much of the deck was left dark, however, which made Bolan's job that much easier.

The lieutenant in the helicopter switched on the Jayhawk's lights, along with a spotlight that lit up a wide circle around it.

Almost two hours to the minute after the Jayhawk had set down, Lieutenant Dickerson and his team reappeared midway down. Plainly they hadn't found the terrorists. After a short talk between Dickerson and Captain Tuskindi, the Coast Guardsmen climbed into their aircraft, the rotors revved faster and faster, and with a whine of its turbines, the Jayhawk rose and dipped over the starboard rail, bound for its nest on the *Exiter*.

Through the binoculars, Bolan saw Tuskindi flip his middle finger at the copter. The crewmen with him laughed. They had pulled one over on the Coast Guard, and were proud of it. Clapping one another on the back, they turned and ambled into the deckhouse.

It was Bolan's cue. Rising, he climbed onto the catwalk and raced aft. Human nature being what it was, Tuskindi would probably go straight to the terrorists to let them know the coast was clear. Under his feet the throb of the ship's mighty engines began to beat anew. Soon the *Caspian* would be underway.

Bolan was fifty yards from the deckhouse when the same crewman who had checked on the valve a while ago emerged and came down the catwalk toward him. Instantly Bolan gripped the top rail and levered himself over, down onto the deck. He dropped lightly, making little noise thanks to the soft soles of the shoes he had chosen. Cloaked in shadow, he listened to the seaman clomp overhead. As soon as the footsteps faded, he jumped up, caught hold of the bottom rail and clambered back onto the catwalk.

Precious seconds were being squandered. Bolan couldn't afford to lose sight of Tuskindi. He ran to the deckhouse but veered wide of a spotlight and over to a ladder. The deckhouse was built like three boxes stacked on top of one another, each slightly smaller than the one below. He scaled the ladder to the second level, then went up another ladder to the top. Moving past several antennae, he crouched at the aft railing. The corners of his mouth quirked upward.

Tuskindi had gone through the deckhouse and was hurrying along the next section of catwalk toward the stern.

Bolan sprinted to another ladder. Instead of using the rungs, he placed a hand and foot on either side and slid down. He did the same with the next ladder and reached the main deck. By then Tuskindi was nearing the king posts.

Paralleling the catwalk and always keeping to the shadows, Bolan dogged the Russian's steps. According to Bruno Tuskindi's file at Stony Man, he was as shady as they came. He had avoided prison so far only because he was clever enough never to be caught with his hands dirty. The Feds suspected him of drug smuggling and gun running, among other illegal activities. His character was best summed up by the psych profile assessment that he would "do anything for the right price." The terrorists couldn't have chosen a better candidate to sneak them into the country.

The same file contained a flag warning that Tuskindi was prone to fits of incredible violence. Twice in different ports he had been arrested for beating other men so severely, they needed to be hospitalized for weeks.

In each instance Tuskindi claimed self-defense. And since neither victim preferred to press charges, he was released.

Then there was the knife fight that made Tuskindi a legend among cargo ship crews everywhere. In a seedy bar in Lisbon Tuskindi and another captain took a fancy to the same barmaid. After Tuskindi knocked his rival down, the captain and three friends came at him with knives. Tuskindi pulled his own. When it was over, all four were on the floor.

No doubt about it. Bruno Tuskindi was a dangerous man. And most of his crew were cut from the same coarse cloth.

The paragon in question suddenly halted and gazed to the south.

Bolan did likewise. The *Exiter* was circling toward the continental U.S., her flag flying proudly.

The Russian laughed and made another obscene gesture, then lumbered on, muttering to himself.

On the watch for cables, gas-vent lines and hatch covers, Bolan followed. He passed under two huge pipes that bridged the deck from side to side. Once past them, he could see the seven-story wheelhouse astern. Atop it were a towering radar mast and radar antennae, as well as smaller wireless, telegraph and navigation aerials.

Tuskindi reached a point midway between the king posts and the wheelhouse and halted again. Hopping down from the catwalk, he went to a tank hatch on the port side. Bending, he opened the hatch, gazed toward the distant cutter once more and climbed down into the hold.

To reach that hatch, Bolan had to cross over the catwalk. He climbed up the near side and was in the act of hooking his leg over the opposite rail when a door in the wheelhouse opened, spilling a rectangle of light into the night and impaling him in its harsh glare. Vaulting over, he hunkered under the lip.

Footsteps resounded above him.

"I'm not much fond of puttin' my neck in a noose for a bunch of stinkin' camel jockeys," a crewman declared.

"Don't let the captain hear you say that or he'll gut you and feed you to the sharks," another responded.

"He doesn't like having his decisions questioned, that's for sure," added a third.

"I'm not questionin' the captain's right to do as he sees fit," the first man clarified, "but I'd rather be runnin' guns or dope than a pack of fanatics. In case neither of you have been payin' attention to world events, the United States has been crackin' down on terrorists and anyone who has anything to do with them."

"Quit your bellyaching, Eddy. We got through the Coast Guard inspection today okay, didn't we? Another couple of hours and we'll be shed of the camel jockeys for good."

"Good riddance to scum, I say," Eddy declared.

There was more conversation, but their voices were too faint to distinguish the words. Bolan poked his head up and waited until the trio was out of sight, then raced to the open hatch and ducked below.

Descending four rungs, Bolan paused. He was suspended above a catwalk that ran the width of the vessel. A bulkhead was to his left, the hold to his right. Of Tuskindi there was no trace.

The soldier slid silently to the catwalk. What few lights there were did little to alleviate the gloom. He took a step to starboard, then heard a metallic clink from the port side and reversed direction. In seventy-five feet he came to another ladder, this one leading into the tanker's bowels.

Far below a slit of light appeared where there shouldn't be one. Bolan descended faster. He couldn't predict how long Tuskindi would be down there, and it wouldn't do to be caught partway down and have the Russian sound an alarm. His plan was to eliminate the terrorists and slip off the ship when she docked with none of the crew the wiser.

Faint voices wafted upward. Bolan's soles barely touched the rungs, but it seemed as if the ladder went on forever. At last he neared the bottom. Shifting the MP-5 K so he could fire from the hip if he had to, he climbed down the rest of the way and swung toward the light. He found himself in an enclosed space five feet square. A door to a compartment was concealed in the bilgewell, the lowest part of the hold where the ship curved from the keel.

Bruno Tuskindi's gravelly tones reached Bolan's ears as he sidled to the opening, "—wait until the crude has been off-loaded to sneak you ashore. It must be done in the middle of the night, when the docks are least busy."

"I do not like having to stay down here another four or five days," a man with a noticeable accent replied. "That is how long you told us it would take, is it not?"

"Better safe than sorry, eh, Abbas?" the Russian said.

Bolan peeked past the door and saw several Arab men lounging in chairs or sprawled in berths. The captain and the terrorist mastermind, though, were around a corner, and he couldn't get a look at Aban Abbas.

"I believe in taking all due precautions, yes," Abbas agreed. "But a delay that long is unacceptable."

Tuskindi was becoming angry. "Look, you agreed to abide by my terms, no questions asked. Remember?"

It surprised Bolan greatly to hear a woman's voice.

"And do you remember our leader telling you that we would do as you want so long as your actions do not endanger us?"

"How the hell is waiting a few more days going to hurt?" the Russian snapped, then said, "Oh. I get it. You're worried about the Coast Guard. How many times must I repeat myself? They're not about to check us over again after we dock."

"I do not share your confidence," Abbas said. "The fact they stopped the *Caspian* shows the American government suspects something. So I would prefer that my people and I are not onboard when you reach New York City."

"What do you want me to do?" Tuskindi sarcastically asked. "Lower you over the side in a lifeboat when we're half a mile out?"

"That would serve our purpose admirably," Abbas said.

"And how do I explain the missing lifeboat to my superiors?" the Russian argued. "No, you are on my ship and you will do as I instruct you."

One of the terrorists near the door glanced toward it, and Bolan jerked back. He had trouble hearing the next exchange.

"You must have us confused with your crewmen," Aban Abbas stated. "They are at your beck and call.

We are not. We are free to do as we deem best. You will arrange to have us lowered over the side when I give you the word."

Tuskindi's tone became gruffer. "Who the hell do you think you are, bossing me around? All I need do is snap my fingers and two dozen of the meanest sea dogs who ever drew breath will pin you down here until you starve."

"I do not like being threatened."

"That makes two of us, Abbas. The subject is closed."

Bolan heard a rustling sound, then a vivid oath.

"What's this?" the Russian snarled. "You're not letting me leave? Tell these pups of yours to get out of my way or I will slit their stupid throats."

Abbas sounded more amused than anything else as he said, "I have heard of your reputation with a blade, but I've never put much stock in them myself. All things being equal, a man with a knife will lose every time to a man with a gun." The sound of a round being chambered punctuated his comment.

"Now you just hold on!" Tuskindi exclaimed. "You don't want to shoot this close to the tank. You could set off an explosion."

"Do not insult my intelligence, Captain, and I will not insult yours. The *Caspian*'s tanks are made of re-inforced steel. It would take a bazooka to penetrate one. Smalls-arms fire will have no effect at all." Abbas paused. "Malik, check outside to make sure he came here alone. We do not want his crew to find out."

Bolan sprinted toward the ladder, but he hadn't quite reached it when the door swung open and a stupefied terrorist froze in the entryway. Bolan recognized him as one of the pair he had chased from Greece to Turkey.

Sharik screeched in Arabic, and all hell broke loose.

CHAPTER FIFTEEN

The Executioner leveled the MP-5 K and fired a 3-round burst, but quick as he was, Sharik sprang past the corner, out of harm's way. Another Al-Jabbar member a few feet behind him wasn't as fortunate. The rounds cored his chest and flipped him onto his back.

Bolan slammed the door shut but that only bought him a few seconds. He couldn't hold them at bay indefinitely, not when all they had to do was shoot through the door to turn him into a sieve.

Only one recourse was left. Springing to the ladder, Bolan started up swiftly. He didn't take his eyes off the door to the secret compartment, and when it slowly opened, he stopped and palmed a flash grenade. Letting the MP-5 K hang by its sling, he gripped the grenade and yanked the pin.

Several heads appeared in the doorway. The terrorists weren't looking up and didn't see him toss the grenade right down on top of them. Striking one man's shoulder, it bounced into the compartment.

Someone roared a warning in Arabic. Bolan pressed his face against his right forearm and closed his eyes. Even so, when the grenade went off, he had the illusion of staring into a bright white flame. He mentally counted to thirty, opened his eyes again and resumed climbing. Around him brilliant dots danced and swirled, like a swarm of fireflies gone amok.

The terrorists were a lot worse off. Screams and yells of confusion echoed from their hideaway. Two came stumbling through the doorway, their hands clasped to their faces, and one collided with a bulkhead.

It would be several minutes before the effect wore off. In that time, Bolan intended to find a spot on the catwalk where he commanded a clear line of fire at the upper part of the ladder and keep them pinned below until the tanker reached port. A simple enough strategy, but it depended on an element over which he had no control—the crew not interfering.

The soldier had just pulled himself onto the catwalk when Klaxons went off from one end of the giant ship to the other. Boots hammered the deck. Shouts rose from all quarters.

Before too long, Bolan's position might become untenable. There were two hatches into the hold, the one he came through and another to starboard. If crewmen came down both, he could face hostile fire from multiple directions at once.

Another factor had to be considered. The cramped confines of the catwalk weren't to Bolan's liking. They limited his maneuverability, his tactical options. The best place to conduct a firefight was up on deck.

Steps rang on the ladder below him. A burly terrorist was scaling it two rungs at a time. He had an SMG, and when he spotted Bolan, he tried to bring it into play.

The Executioner had already activated the laser sight on his MP-5 K. Fixing a red dot on the center of the terrorist's forehead, he stroked the trigger. The man flopped backward but didn't fall. One leg became entangled in the rungs and the body dangled upside down, great red drops dripping from the entry and exit wounds.

A grating sound to starboard warned Bolan the crew was about to enter the equation. The starboard hatch was a good 125 feet away, and blanketed in darkness. He thought he saw someone drop to the catwalk, and he hurriedly backed into the shadows.

A rifle boomed, the blast amplified by the bulkheads so it resembled a cannon. Simultaneously, a slug caromed off metal a foot above Bolan's head. Triggering a burst, he spun and raced toward the port hatch. Feet pounded overhead, and he realized some of the crew had the same idea. They were trying to reach it to cut him off. If they did, he would be pinned between the hatches and become easy prey.

Bolan ran flat-out.

As if they somehow knew what he was up to, the crewmen overhead ran faster, too, their boots thumping in cadence to his own.

It became a race. Bolan was unable to tell who had the lead but whoever did, it wasn't by much. He reached the ladder and glanced up to see the opening partially blocked by a crewman about to climb down. The man had a revolver, but he was holding it with the barrel pointed up and before he could correct his mistake, Bolan drilled his chest. Screaming, the man fell.

Bolan leaped to one side and felt the catwalk quake with the impact. Stepping back under the hatch, he saw a second crewman poke his head in. He fired, but he didn't think he scored.

"Over here! Over here!" someone bellowed up above. "He's at this end!"

The soldier had to get up on deck before they thought to slam the hatch shut, trapping him down there. Pulling his other flash grenade, he hoped his aim was true, yanked the pin and lobbed it almost straight up. If it struck the rim and bounced back, closing his eyes wouldn't help. He would be temporarily blinded and completely at the mercy of those out to kill him.

But the grenade sailed out the hatch, and the same man who had just hollered, hollered again, in panic.

"A grenade! Run! Run! It's a grenade!"

Bolan flung himself against the bulkhead, one arm over his head. The upper deck shielded him when the grenade detonated, and he was on his way up the ladder barely ten seconds after the glow faded.

A pair of crewmen were staggering as if drunk. One had his hands over his eyes. The other's eyes were wide as saucers and pouring tears.

"I can't see! I can't see!"

Bolan kicked him in the groin, and when that doubled him over, kneed him in the face. The second crewman heard his friend go down and turned, right into an uppercut. One punch was all it took.

Bedlam had seized the *Caspian*. The Klaxons were still wailing into the night, and amid a chorus of cries, crewmen were rushing from the wheelhouse and deckhouse. Several more were clustered by the starboard hatch, and they had seen Bolan emerge. Charging, they opened fire, but most of their rounds were deflected by the catwalk.

Bolan backpedaled toward the port rail. He dropped one crewman, then another. Sustained bursts scattered the rest. By then he was in shadow, and the few shots thrown at him were wide of the mark. Ejecting the empty magazine, he slapped a full one home and pulled back the handle.

There had to be twenty crewmen on deck, with more arriving every second.

Bolan glided toward the bow. Suddenly new firing broke out in the vicinity of the starboard hatch. He dropped low to the deck, then realized none of the rounds was directed at him.

Curses and screams poured from a wild melee of vague forms. Mystified, Bolan tried to make sense of it. Crewmen on his side of the tanker were rushing toward the starboard side, firing as they ran. One took a hit and pitched forward.

A full-fledged battle was taking place.

Someone yelled in Arabic and was in turn drowned out by Bruno Tuskindi. "Give them hell, boys! They want to take over our ship!"

The terrorists were fighting the crew.

Rising, Bolan zigzagged toward the closest cover, a stowed derrick amidships. Several figures had gained the catwalk, but whether they were part of the crew or part of Abbas's bunch was hard to tell until one shouted in Arabic and they began shooting lead fast and furious at the wheelhouse.

Slowing, Bolan placed a red dot on the one in the middle and fired. The others had no idea where the shots came from, and he was aiming at the terrorist on the right when the air near him was blistered by autofire from near the starboard king post. He shot back, aiming at the muzzle-flash, and pumped his legs toward the derrick.

Moist drops splattered Bolan's cheeks. For a moment he thought it was blood but then he smelled the moisture in the air. Clouds filled the sky from horizon to horizon. The storm had arrived, and light rain had begun to fall.

Reaching the derrick, Bolan ducked behind it. The firefight was spreading as more and more crewmen became involved. A clap of thunder momentarily drowned out the conflict, and the next moment the heavens opened, unleashing a deluge. Solid sheets of rain pelted the deck with the hammering cadence of hail. In no time he was drenched.

Visibility was next to zero. Bolan couldn't see his hand at arm's length. An added complication was the wind. It came shrieking out of the northwest, distorting the blasts of gunfire so Bolan had a hard time pinpointing where the shots came from.

The firing tapered but didn't die out entirely. Someone, maybe Tuskindi, was bellowing to be heard above Nature's tantrum, but Bolan couldn't make out what the Russian was saying. Since he wasn't accomplishing anything by squatting there, he moved along the derrick toward the starboard side of the ship.

Without warning, a man appeared out of the downpour. He was only a few feet away, and on seeing Bolan, he snapped a shotgun to his shoulder. The soldier's trigger finger was a shade quicker. Bending over the body, he established it was a crewman of Nordic descent, not a terrorist.

Bolan continued on. It was impossible to hear much of what was going on over the rain, wind and thunder, and there was no telling whether the crew or the terrorists had the upper hand. The storm had thrown a major monkey wrench into the tactical works. He might not be able to eliminate or contain the terrorists before the *Caspian* reached port. In which case he should put in a call to Brognola.

Huddling under the derrick out of the brunt of the downpour, Bolan unclipped his cell phone and punched the red button to activate it. He tapped in the big Fed's cell number, then put the phone to his ear. No ringing, no dial tone, nothing. The storm was to blame. It had cut him off from the outside world. The only way to reach Brognola now was through the ship's radio.

Reattaching the phone to his belt, Bolan crept to the end of the derrick. He thought a vaporous shape flitted across the deck to his right, but he wouldn't swear to it. To his left someone yelled. He continued straight ahead and soon came to the catwalk. Swinging up, he knelt and placed an ear to the metal grid. Faint vibrations alerted him someone was approaching. He spied several forms to stern, slogging through the rain with their shoulders hunched against the elements.

Sliding under the bottom rail on the starboard side, Bolan dropped to the deck. They never spotted him. Once they had disappeared into the watery veil, he started toward the wheelhouse. That was where he would find the ship's communications center.

A few shots pierced the storm. A deadly game of cat and mouse had ensued between the two opposing forces, with Bolan caught in the middle. Several times figures slunk dangerously near, but in each instance he froze and they went on by without spotting him. Another time, he thought he saw a gunner crouched in ambush but it was only a hatch.

The need to move at a snail's pace was vexing. By Bolan's watch it took fifteen minutes to travel what should have taken five. Eventually the dull yellow glow of lights rewarded his patience. He ran the final few yards and moved along a wall to a door. It hung halfway open, and out of it stuck a blood-spattered leg.

Bolan pivoted on the balls of his feet, his finger curled on the MP-5 K's hair trigger, but except for the dead seaman, the passageway was deserted. Picking his way over the body, he went down a short flight of steps. A little farther in he came on another casualty, again a bullet-riddled crewman.

The wheelhouse was the hub of day-to-day operations. Most of the ship's navigation and communications equipment was housed there, as were the captain's quarters, the infirmary and the rec room. The bridge was on the uppermost level, commanding a view of the entire vessel. It was there Bolan was bound, and his approach had to be extremely cautious. Wet footprints showed others had preceded him. From higher in the wheelhouse came a smattering of gunfire, and once a muted explosion. Pausing at a doorway, he heard heavy breathing. Someone was in there, probably with a gun, waiting to blow away any and all enemies who happened by.

Bolan cat-footed back to the last body and hurriedly stripped off the dead man's jacket. He returned to the open compartment, and could still hear the heavy breathing. With a flick of his wrist he tossed the jacket inside to draw fire, then threw himself flat, ready to shoot anything that moved.

It was a reading room or library. Books crammed shelves on all four walls. In the middle lay a young crewman, no more than twenty, a patchwork of holes dotting his torso, a scarlet halo around his body. His lungs labored mightily to draw breath. He was facing the doorway, and on seeing Bolan, he attempted to speak.

Covering him, the soldier walked over. First aid would be of no benefit.

Tears filled the young man's eyes. "Why?" he practically sobbed. "Why? In God's name, why?"

"I'm not one of the terrorists," Bolan whispered.

"I didn't even have a gun. I didn't want any part of it. But they shot me anyway."

"Their kind never need a reason," Bolan said. Blinded by hate, they killed for the sake of killing.

"All I wanted was to see some of the world..." the young man lamented. He exhaled one last time, and his sight-seeing days were over.

Bolan closed the young man's eyes. The Feds had shown him a diagram of the ship before he left Stony Man, and he had the passages and stairwells committed to memory. At the next junction he turned right and started up metal stairs. Almost instantly an SMG barked and slugs ricocheted all around.

Hurrying backward, Bolan craned his neck for a glimpse of the shooter. Whether it was a crewman or terrorist was irrelevant. The man was too well hidden and could drop him before he was halfway up.

There was another stairwell to port. Bolan opted for the path of least resistance and headed to the far side. Occasionally he heard shots and the clomp of booted feet but always from a distance. At the far stairwell he listened, then trained the MP-5 K straight up and took the stairs three at a bound. He had climbed three flights when the wheelhouse shook to the loudest explosion yet, and the most violent. He had to grip the rail to keep his balance. It came from somewhere above.

Proceeding with caution, Bolan gained the top level. He pushed open a pockmarked door. Smoke and dust hung thick in the air, and the passage was littered with debris. A doorway and part of the bulkhead to his left had been ripped apart, and from the ragged cavity poured more smoke.

Whoever was responsible had to be nearby.

Every nerve taut, Bolan inched forward. One glance sufficed to show he wouldn't be radioing the Feds. Explosives had made a shambles of the communications console, sabotage on the part of Al-Jabbar to prevent the crew from requesting help. Two bodies were strewed among the wreckage, one minus its legs, the other in more pieces than a jigsaw puzzle.

Toward the center of the ship was the bridge. Bolan took a few steps, then saw a hand materialize out of a doorway. A spherical object came sailing toward him and hit the floor with a thump. Whirling, he flew to the landing and hurled himself down the stairs. He cleared the first level and was vaulting around the bend when the grenade blew.

Shrapnel zinged and whistled but Bolan was spared. Thankfully the wheelhouse wasn't located near the holding tanks or they would have a catastrophe of the highest magnitude on their hands. He stopped and turned.

Whispered Arabic drifted down the stairwell. Shadows played across the landing. They were after him. Bolan needed a spot to make a stand, and that wasn't it. All they had to do to take him out was drop another grenade.

Firing a burst to slow them, Bolan flew to the bottom and into the passageway that would take him out on deck. Only to find it blocked by a pair of seamen.

They didn't ask who he was. They didn't give him a chance to explain his presence. The moment they laid eyes on him, they jammed bolt-action rifles to their shoulders.

Bolan cut them down where they stood and was out the hatch before his pursuers appeared. It was like plunging into a lake. Rain cascaded over him, soaking him anew. Blinking to clear his vision, he stepped to one side of the opening.

Within seconds several terrorists came stalking around the other end. Well-trained, they advanced in stages, each covering the other.

The Executioner fired. He clipped one, but the others retaliated with a stream of hot lead that whined off the edge of the hatch, forcing him to spring to safety or be perforated. Suddenly he collided with something. Or someone. Spinning, he discovered a crewman who looked as surprised as he was. The man held a pistol but instead of firing it, he uttered an inarticulate cry and bolted through the hatch. A fatal blunder. Autofire impaled him, and shrieking in terror, he withered onto his belly.

Bolan took half a dozen steps from the wheelhouse. The downpour temporarily slackened as lightning rent the sky close to starboard. For a split second the deck was lit up as if by a strobe light, and in the harsh glare he saw armed figures the length and width of the ship, stalking one another. Thunder pealed, a prelude to another firestorm. Simultaneously the rain resumed in all its unbridled fury.

Bolan flattened. So much lead was being thrown, anyone on his feet was at risk. Lunacy at its worst, with neither side liable to emerge a clear-cut victor. Twisting to starboard, he waited for a lull, then crept toward where he hoped the derrick would be. In the deluge it was difficult to gauge, but his instincts served him well.

A small nook under an overhang offered dry haven, and Bolan slid in under it on his haunches. To discover he wasn't alone.

A man lay on his side, facing him, one hand over a wound oozing blood from his stomach. His other hand was empty. "Are you mine or theirs?" the gravel voice of Bruno Tuskindi demanded. "If mine, help me up. If theirs, shoot me, you bastard, and be done with it."

"How about if I'm neither?" Bolan responded, leveling the MP-5 K.

Grunting, Tuskindi rose unsteadily onto his elbow. He was so pale, his skin was stark white against the dark. "Who the hell are you?"

Bolan shifted so he could watch the Russian and the deck both. "I'm hitching a ride into port."

"How the hell—" Tuskindi began, and swore luridly in his native language before switching back to English. "The damned Coast Guard! They brought you, didn't they? You snuck on board when our backs were turned. Am I right?"

"How badly are you hit?" Bolan asked.

"Change the subject, why don't you? See if I give a damn," Tuskindi said bitterly, and leaned against the housing. "What difference does it make? Those stinking fanatics have done me in." He gave a start. "That's why you're here, isn't it? You're after them? Abbas and his loons."

"Where is Abbas now?"

"I wish to hell I knew," Tuskindi snapped. "And I wish to hell I still had my gun so I could walk up to the lying son of a whore and splatter his brains all over the deck." He looked down at himself. "He did this to me, the bastard. I was a fool to think I could ever trust him."

"All this because they didn't want to spend more time down in the hold?" Bolan mentioned.

"How the devil would you—" Again Tuskindi stopped in midsentence. "I get it now. You're the one who was spying on us, the one we thought we had trapped right before the storm broke." A coughing fit racked him, and he doubled over.

"Keep your hands where I can see them," Bolan warned.

"I told you I lost my Uzi," Tuskindi said. When he raised his head, his mouth and chin were dark with blood. "Another couple of minutes and I'll be fit for Davy Jones's locker."

"Did Al-Jabbar bring missiles or rockets with them?" Bolan fished for intel. "Or any crates that could contain biological or chemical weapons?"

"Relax, Fed." The Russian spit. "All they brought were their submachine guns, small arms and a few grenades. Whatever they have planned doesn't involve smuggling anything into your country. Everything they need is already there."

"Abbas said as much?"

"No, but he dropped enough hints." Tuskindi coughed again, his arms wrapped tight around his belly. "It is big, American," he rasped. "He bragged it will make him famous, and that Al-Jabbar will become the most feared terrorist organization on the planet." More blood trickled from a corner of his mouth.

"That's all?"

"What more do you want? Times and dates?" The Russian laughed, but his gruff mirth was strangled by a groan, and he sagged. "You have no idea of the pain."

Bolan switched his weight from one foot to the other. The rain was pounding as hard as ever, and there had to be an inch of water under their shoes. "What goes around, comes around," he remarked.

"You are saying I brought this on myself? Perhaps you have a point. But I make no apologies for how I have lived my life. I have always been my own man. Can you say the same, American?" When Bolan didn't answer, Tuskindi chortled. "I thought as much. Hypocrites, the whole lot of you. For all your talk of freedom, you are dogs on your government's leash."

Bolan wasn't about to dignify the insult with a reply.

"You consider me beneath contempt, no doubt," Tuskindi railed on, "but I only did what I had to in order to survive. In that I am no different than your own politicians, who cut deals your people never hear about to line their own pockets."

"Save your excuses."

"I struck a nerve, did I?" Tuskindi said, and started to laugh. This time it wasn't a groan or coughing fit that cut it short. He stopped of his own accord and abruptly lifted his head. "Did you feel that?"

"Feel what?"

"The movement of the deck. It can only mean one thing. The *Caspian* is changing course."

Bolan was skeptical. What with the driving rain and the lashing wind, a change in heading would go unnoticed.

Tuskindi had to have sensed his disbelief. "I can

feel it, I tell you! I have helmed this ship for seven years, and I know her better than anyone. We are bearing more to the northwest. And since none of my crew would dare change direction without my consent, Abbas must be responsible.''

The soldier remembered how insistent the terrorist leader had been that Al-Jabbar leave the ship before it docked. He began to rise.

Bruno Tuskindi's right hand flashed out from under his left sleeve, his dagger held low for a thrust to the groin. For a man his size he was extremely swift.

So was Bolan. His forefinger twitched, and three rounds chewed the Russian's nose to pulp. As the scourge of the seven seas deflated like a punctured balloon, Bolan finished rising. ''Nice try,'' he said, and barreled out into the storm.

He had to get to the bridge.

CHAPTER SIXTEEN

Stony Man Farm, Virginia

There were times when Hal Brognola would rather smoke his cigars than chew them. This was one of them. With a stogie clamped between his teeth, he paced the floor of his office at Stony Man Farm and glanced repeatedly at the phone. "Come on, Striker, call," he growled.

A light rap at Brognola's door intruded on his funk. "Who is it?" he demanded. He had left specific instructions not to be disturbed unless the President called.

"Barb. I have an update."

"Come on in."

Barbara Price was holding several photographs and wearing a frown. "These are the latest satellite images." She placed them in front of him. "Remember that old saw about anything that can go wrong will go wrong?"

"Murphy's Law." Brognola examined them. All they showed, in marvelous detail, was a nightmare of a storm, a maelstrom of swirling clouds lit by streaks of lightning.

"It's right over the *Caspian*," Price said. "Sustained heavy rain, wind gusts of up to seventy-five miles an hour, localized high seas, the works.''

"Wonderful," Brognola muttered.

"It wasn't this strong when we started tracking it. It picked up strength once it was out over the ocean."

"They usually do." Brognola set the photographs down and sighed. "And now it's pounding the hell out of that tanker. I hope our boy found a cozy dry spot to hole up."

Price nodded at the photos. "This could be why we haven't heard from him. A severe storm like that would smother the signal."

"His cell phone, yes, but not their radio if it's working and he can get to it." Brognola thoughtfully gnawed on his lower lip. "Have the Coast Guard radio the *Caspian* and politely inquire about their status and whether the storm will delay their arrival in port. Monitor and record the call. I want to listen to it."

"Tuskindi might become suspicious."

"Not necessarily. Given the size and intensity of the storm, it's perfectly normal for the Coast Guard to check on ships in the area. Get cracking." Brognola wriggled a finger at the door and she departed. He reached into his jacket for another cigar but left it there and smacked his desk in irritation.

Brognola did *not* want Al-Jabbar making landfall. He did *not* want some of the most vicious terrorists in the world running loose on American soil. He would gladly have sent in a Delta squad or Navy SEALs, but his hands were tied by political constraints. The *Caspian* was sailing under a Liberian flag, and international law didn't allow for the use of overt military force. Then there were the political niceties involved. The President didn't want a military intervention splashed all over the news channels. Discretion was called for. So once again Uncle Sam sent in the one man who had never let them down.

Still, Brognola would dearly have liked to send in backup. Bolan was the best there was at what he did, but he was just one man. And there were times, Brognola suspected, when even Bolan tended to forget that fact. His friend's lone wolf mentality was a plus in certain situations, a detriment in others.

This time around, Brognola had the impression Bolan was taking the whole Al-Jabbar business much too personally. Being thwarted in Greece and Turkey had made Bolan twice as determined to put an end to them, permanently.

Brognola resumed pacing. To an outsider he might seem to be a nervous wreck, but it was actually good for him. It helped him think, and it was also good exercise. Lord knew, he didn't get enough.

Price returned sooner than he anticipated. "Well? What did Tuskindi have to say? Let me hear the tape."

"There isn't one. The Coast Guard couldn't get through."

"Do you mean there was so much electrical interference the *Caspian*'s transmissions were garbled?"

"I mean there were no transmissions, period. The *Caspian* never answered." For a moment Price's usual calm reserve evaporated and she looked as worried as Brognola felt. "The commander offered to send out a boarding party. The *Exiter* is back at her berth, fully manned and ready to go out."

Brognola was sorely tempted. "How much longer until the *Caspian* reaches port?"

"Forty, fifty minutes, depending. The choppy seas

are bound to slow her but not much. Not a ship her size."

"And how long would it take the *Exiter* to interdict her?"

"Twenty minutes, give or take. Less if the storm breaks, which isn't likely at this point. It's fairly stationary."

Brognola did the mental math. Even if all went well, the Coast Guardsmen wouldn't be on board the *Caspian* all that long before the tanker docked. And although going to sea in stormy weather and boarding other vessels under adverse conditions was the kind of thing the Coast Guard specialized in, he would be putting good men and women at extreme risk for questionable cause. It would violate two of the personal rules he lived by. One was that he never put anyone's life in danger needlessly. The other was that he never let personal friendships dictate professional decisions. As much as he valued Bolan's life, as close as they had become, he couldn't, in all conscience, commit to a course of action he wouldn't commit to for others.

"Hal?" Price prompted.

"Tell the Coast Guard thanks, but no thanks. Our original plan is still viable. I have a sixty-man task force waiting for the *Caspian*. If the terrorists are still alive, they'll be taken into custody."

"Okay."

The way Price said it, Brognola felt as if she had jabbed him in the gut with an ice pick. "Mack is a big boy, Barbara. The day we lose faith in him is the day we might as well find new jobs."

LIGHTNING LANCED THE SKY as the Executioner stalked toward the *Caspian*'s wheelhouse. The unrelenting downpour battered him without cease. Underfoot the deck rose and fell. Not enough to make Bolan lose his balance, but enough that he would if he wasn't careful. On either side giant waves crashed against the hull, adding to the din of the raging tempest.

Out of the night came a new exchange of lead. It rose in ferocity and volume until it nearly rivaled the storm. Men screamed and railed. Stray slugs were thrown every which way, and once again Bolan had to drop prone to avoid taking one. The firefight lasted longer than any of the others, and when it was over, low groans could be heard between the howling gusts of wind.

The soldier hadn't gone ten feet when he found the first body. Beyond were more—seven, eight, nine, all crewmen. There had been a concerted effort to retake the wheelhouse and it had failed. Four more bodies were sprawled in front of a passageway heaped high with furniture and whatever else the terrorists could get their hands on.

Bolan didn't get too close. He imagined Al-Jabbar had done the same at every entry, but there had to be a way in. There weren't enough of them to cover all the windows and the roof, too. Recalling the diagram, he hastened to a ladder to port that would take him to the second level. It was close to the side rail, and as he started up, a wave crested, sending a plume of water full into his chest and nearly dislodging him.

No one was on the landing. Bolan tried the door but it was locked. He doubted the terrorists had posted a guard on the other side; they needed every man they had to repel the crew. Sliding a lock pick from his vest, he bent and inserted it. He had to work by feel, a challenging task with the deck tossing and the rain beating down. Soon there was a faint click and the door opened.

Replacing the pick, Bolan sidled inside. He was on the second level of the companionway he had tried to climb a while ago. Glancing up, he saw no one, and made his way higher. He didn't stop until he reached the top. The intervening levels were quiet but that didn't necessarily mean they were deserted.

Bolan cracked the door. The passage wasn't empty, nor did he hear anything. But if Al-Jabbar had indeed taken control, the terrorists could be anywhere. Although his magazine wasn't empty yet, the Executioner inserted a new one, then glided past several open rooms. One was the infirmary, another an office. A third had a lot of charts on the walls. None was occupied.

The next door was shut. BRIDGE was stenciled in bold black letters. Bolan looked both ways, then shoved it open and rushed inside, ready for anything except what he found.

The place was in shambles. The main computer console had been riddled with bullets, and tiny wisps of smoke curled from the holes and cracks. A radar screen had been shattered, a large bank of equipment smashed to useless ruin.

It made no sense to Bolan for the terrorists to have destroyed everything. He picked his way among the litter until flashing red numbers caught his eye. A digital display above the main console was counting down minutes and seconds. To what? He walked to the wheel and gave it a turn. There should be resistance, but there wasn't any. It spun around and around like a roulette wheel, and only stopped when he gripped it again.

The terrorists had disabled the steering control.

Bolan pressed a button on the wall under the words Engine Room but all that came over the squawk box was static. Snipped wires were to blame. He stared out the tinted windows. From this high up he had an unobstructed view of the full unfettered fury of the storm. A charcoal black sky writhed overhead pierced by vivid thunderbolts. Whitecaps roiled the ocean, and high waves were breaking over the distant bow. He saw a lot of bodies but no movement. The crew was either dead, or those still alive had sought cover below. As for the terrorists, he was at a loss. They had gone to all the trouble to seize the bridge, only to destroy and abandon it.

Bolan considered the puzzle from a tactical perspective. With the bridge out of commission no one could control the ship. Not even Al-Jabbar. What possible benefit was that to them? he wondered. Stepping to the bullet-riddled console, he stared at the digital display. Thirty-eight minutes and seven seconds left.

The *Caspian* was an old bucket, but her bridge was modern. She had been retrofitted with a computerized system for controlling her steerage and the engines. Once the coordinates and speed were programmed, the only way to change them was by an override command or by the captain assuming manual control. But the computer and the manual switch had been shot to hell. There was no altering whatever was last fed in.

Bolan glanced out the windows again as chilling insight flooded through him. The terrorists wanted it that way. They had fed in new coordinates and then trashed the bridge so no one could override their commands or take control manually. Bruno Tuskindi had been right about the ship changing course. It was no longer bound for New York City, but for somewhere else, somewhere the terrorists had chosen. And thanks to the storm, the Feds wouldn't realize it until it was too late.

Thirty-seven minutes and ten seconds until they got there.

Bolan tried to reduce speed anyway. He moved the large lever to Full Stop, but the *Caspian* went on plowing through the turbulent seas on its westward course. To stop her now, he had to shut down her power at the source.

The soldier raced from the bridge. The engines were at the stern, the same as the wheelhouse. Once he reached the stairwell, he descended until he came to a metal door labeled Power Plant. It wouldn't open. He tried the pick, but it wouldn't slide into the lock. Peering closer, he saw the keyhole had been fused solid, perhaps by an incendiary strip. Unless he could get his hands on some C-4 or a battering ram, he wasn't getting in there.

Bolan headed back up. He had to hand it to Aban Abbas. The terrorist leader had covered all the bases—almost as if he had it planned in advance, which Bolan wouldn't put past him. Since Al-Jabbar's inception, Abbas had shown a flair for strategy that far exceeded that of the run-of-the-mill terrorist. He was a thinker, one who always stayed a step ahead of everyone else.

At the landing Bolan halted. He had to find the terrorists, but where to start? They weren't on the bridge; they weren't in the engine room. Then he remembered the talk he overheard, and Tuskindi saying, "What do you want me to do? Lower you over the side in a lifeboat when we're half a mile out?" And Abbas had replied, "That would serve our purpose admirably."

Bolan shoved on the door, but the wind shoved back. He had to put his shoulder into it, then slip out before the wind slammed the door shut on him.

The lifeboats were on platforms on either side of the wheelhouse. The Executioner began to climb a ladder to the nearest, and looked up just as an enormous wave curled over the side and slammed into him with the power of a pile driver. Hooking his elbows around the rungs, he clung on with all his strength. The water pulled at him like a living thing, the pressure almost unbearable, and for a few moments he thought he would be torn from his perch. Then the wave dissolved, its energy spent, and he shot to the platform and dashed under the davit.

The lifeboat platform was as deserted as the deck. Bolan had expected as much. No one in his right mind would contemplate lowering a boat in those conditions. But if they weren't there, then where?

UP NEAR THE TANKER'S BOW, Aban Abbas turned from a window to hear Rakin's report. "Yes?"

"All is going according to your plan, master. The deckhouse is secure. Only a few crewmen still live, and they've gone down into the holds to escape us." The Saudi's face lit with sadistic glee. "You have but to command, and we will hunt them down and finish them."

"There is no need," Abbas said. "Soon we will reach land."

"Then there will be no stopping us!" Rakin crowed.

"Confidence is a commendable trait, overconfidence is not," Abbas cautioned. He glanced at Jamilah. "What is the cost of our victory?"

"Three dead, one hurt."

Abbas walked into the next room, where most of the rest were gathered. Ten were left, more than enough to carry out his inspired design. Eleven, once they linked up with Sefu, his brother not only in spirit but in the flesh, as well.

"How are you faring?" he asked Jebel.

The young Lebanese had a deep furrow across his upper arm that was being bandaged by Yasin. "I am fine, great one," he responded cheerfully. "The demon himself could not kill me."

Sharik was in the next chair over. "But he is still out there somewhere. Looking for us, I warrant."

"This is a large ship." Barakah spoke up. "We will be gone long before he finds us, and that will be the last of him."

Abbas could tell Sharik didn't share the same opinion, and to be honest, neither did he. He had been shocked beyond measure when the dark-haired one showed up outside their hiding place in the hold. Abbas wasn't superstitious by nature, but the demon, as they all now referred to him, was enough to make anyone superstitious. Everywhere they went, there he was, an evil genie they couldn't shake, even halfway around the world. It baffled him, and Abbas didn't like things he couldn't understand.

"We have the ropes ready, as you instructed," Barakah was saying. "I just pray the cursed Americans have no means of knowing what we are up to."

"How can you doubt when God had once again come to our aid?" Abbas said. "The storm is a blessing, sent to render our enemies powerless to stop us." He checked his watch. "Nineteen minutes until we hit."

Jebel cleared his throat. "Great one, may I ask you a question?"

"Have I not said my ears are always open? What is it?"

"Did you have all this planned from the beginning? Taking over the *Caspian,* I mean? And programming their computer to do your bidding? If so, truly your wisdom exceeds that of Solomon."

The others perked their ears.

"Do not make more of it than there is," Abbas said, smiling. "We are at war, and in war a competent commander must take every contingency into account. He must ask himself, 'What if this goes wrong?' or 'What if that goes wrong?', and have a backup plan to fall back on. Plans within plans within plans. Only then is success assured."

Abbas moved to the window and stood gazing out with his hands clasped behind his back. "Take Tuskindi and this ship. I would rather have sailed on a different vessel with a different captain, one friendlier to our cause. But we needed to reach America quickly and Tuskindi would sell his soul for the right price. I did not trust him, though, so I made plans to take over should he give us trouble."

"You did an outstanding job, great one," Jebel gushed.

"Others are as worthy of your praise. We could not have done it without Yasin's knowledge of computers and Rakin's experience with ships." Abbas turned. "Or without the beneficence of God, without whom nothing is possible."

Every man there offered a "Praise God" to the ceiling.

"Take heart, my brothers," Abbas encouraged

them. "All has gone well so far. But the biggest challenge yet remains. Once we are on United States soil, we will be among the enemy. We must be as wise as foxes, as deadly as cobras."

Sharik sat up. "How long will we be in America?"

"As short a time as possible. The faster we get in and out, the less chance they have to find us." Abbas pursed his lips. "Besides, we must strike before they can figure out why we are here or all this will have been for nothing."

"May they all burn in eternal fire!" Barakah declared.

Abbas went back into the other room. Only Jamilah was there, staring aft. Walking up close behind her, he breathed deep of the fragrance of her hair. "Anything?"

"No. There is no sign of anyone." Jamilah placed a slender hand on the strap of the SMG slung across her shoulder. "I heard what you said. It is not like you to deceive them."

"How do you mean?" Abbas asked, although he knew perfectly well.

"They are young. They do not see beyond the picture you paint to the reality." Jamilah's reflection in the window became tinged with sadness. "All the planning in the world cannot guarantee we will succeed. The National Security Agency will not throw its doors open and invite us in to destroy it."

"Such pessimism," Abbas scolded.

"Realistic attitude, is more like it. As long as the Americans did not know we were en route to their country, our goal was achievable. Now that they do, the odds drop drastically. If any of us make it out alive, I will be greatly surprised."

"Everyone knew the sacrifice they might be called on to make when they took the oath of brotherhood."

"All well and good, but I fear we are overreaching ourselves this time, Aban."

It was rare for her to call him by his familiar name except when they were alone. Abbas glanced over his shoulder to confirm they were, then gave her shoulder a gentle squeeze. "If we die, we die. God's will be done."

Jamilah faced him to whisper, "The others can perish and I will not shed a tear. But I do not want you to share their fate. I want you to promise me that you will not let yourself be killed."

"It would be foolish. A man has no control over his fate."

"That is not what you told them." Jamilah grasped his left hand in both of hers and pressed it to her chest. "My heart is yours and always will be. As long as breath endures, I will not let harm come to you."

"Be silent." Abbas didn't like to discuss intimate matters where prying ears might overhear.

"Do not be angry with me. A woman in love, even though a warrior, is still a woman in love. And I love you more than you can imagine."

Jamilah titled her head and parted her lips but Abbas pulled away, his emotions in turmoil. Part of him yearned to kiss her. But the other part, his rational self, reminded him this wasn't the right time or place. "Haven't you heard a word I've just said? Control yourself, or I could come to regret ever accepting a woman into Al-Jabbar." Wheeling, he took a step and drew up in consternation.

Sharik was in the doorway. "My pardon, master,"

he said. "I did not mean to intrude." He quickly backed into the other room.

Abbas followed. Sharik went to a corner window, and he walked over next to him. "How much did you see and hear?" he inquired quietly.

"Hardly anything," Sharik said, but he was a terrible liar.

"I hope you will not think less of me. I know I have always taught a true holy warrior does not give in to the enticements this world has to offer. But we are men, and we have needs. So a dalliance now and then is understandable."

"That is not what you told Haji the night he brought that woman to our stronghold," Sharik mentioned. "You slit his throat, if you'll recall."

Abbas resented the other's tone. "There is a crucial difference. He brought a harlot among us. Jamilah loves me."

"If you do not mind my asking, great one, do you love her?"

The question smacked of disrespect, but it also gave Abbas pause. How deeply *did* he care for her? He liked her, yes. He might go so far as to say he was extremely fond of her. But could he honestly say he loved her as she loved him?

"There is no need to answer," Sharik said, sounding disappointed.

"My personal affairs are my own." Abbas grew defensive. "And I would appreciate it if you would not say anything to anyone else."

"Haven't I always done your bidding?" Sharik wouldn't meet Abbas's gaze. "With your consent, I will make a circuit of the deckhouse to make sure the demon is not anywhere near.'' Without waiting for permission he walked out.

Abbas glowered, then caught himself and pretended to be interested in the storm. Sharik had always been among the most loyal of his followers, but something had changed between them. He could feel it.

It worried Abbas to think Sharik might tell some of the others. His leadership depended on their total trust. On their looking up to him for guidance and inspiration. They were bound to think less of him if they learned about Jamilah, and he couldn't permit that to occur. He had to make absolutely certain Sharik never said a word.

Resting his forehead against the glass, Abbas chided himself for being so careless. Like the time in Greece when he squeezed Jamilah's hand in the car. Little lapses like that could cost him dearly.

Maybe Sharik wasn't the only one he had to deal with, Abbas reflected. Maybe, in the words of the West, he should give some thought to killing two birds with one stone.

CHAPTER SEVENTEEN

The storm battered Mack Bolan mercilessly. He had gone from hold to hold, listening at each hatch for signs of the terrorists, and was now approaching the deckhouse. His body bent into the wind, one arm across his forehead to shield his eyes from the worst of the rain, he fought for every yard he gained. The wind never slackened, never gave him a moment's respite. He was tired and wet to the bone, but they were minor discomforts easily ignored.

Bolan's other hand was wrapped around the catwalk rail. He dared not let go. The last time he did, the wind had pushed him back a good dozen steps.

Yet another bolt of lightning seared the sky, crackling so close, Bolan's hair and skin prickled as if to an electric shock. On its heels crashed thunder fit to shatter his eardrums. Trudging on, he mechanically placed one foot in front of the other. Another forty or fifty feet and he would be there.

The soldier had exhausted all other possibilities. Abbas's group wasn't in the wheelhouse, they weren't belowdecks and they hadn't abandoned ship. If he didn't find them in the deckhouse, he might as well admit they had given him the slip. He'd tried to reach Brognola again but his cell phone still wouldn't work.

The only bright spot was that while the wind hadn't slackened, the rain had. Not a lot, but enough that visibility was ten to twelve feet instead of zero. Bolan was about that far from the deckhouse when a figure came along it from the right. Instantly he crouched so as not to be seen, and the figure went in through a door at the end of the catwalk.

The only reason Bolan didn't shoot was because he couldn't say with certainty whether it had been a member of Al-Jabbar or a member of the crew. He stepped nearer and detected movement at a deck-level window. It looked like a woman. Remembering the voice he heard in the hold, he cradled the MP-5 K.

Suddenly the window exploded and the barrel of an SMG protruded. Bolan flung himself to the left as the weapon spat lead. Multiple rounds banged off the catwalk. He tried to grab the bottom rail to arrest his fall but it was too slick, and the next he knew, he tumbled to the deck and landed with a jarring pain to his shoulder.

Bolan rose slowly, his back to the manifold. He had found them at last. But now what? The roll of the deck was worse here than aft, and if he strayed from the catwalk he was liable to wind up on his back. Or else fall prey to the huge waves that clawed at the deck with watery talons.

Another window shattered and a second gunner gave the catwalk a slug shellacking.

Bolan rose and swept the lower windows with a steady burst. As he dropped back down, he felt the *Caspian* shudder. He couldn't account for it; there hadn't been an explosion. Seconds later it happened again, more noticeable than before, and he had the distinct impression the ship was slowing. He wondered if it had anything to do with the digital countdown on the bridge. The glowing hands on his watch revealed there were two minutes and fifty-three seconds left until whatever had been programmed into the *Caspian*'s computers was due to happen.

The tanker shook, a third time. Bolan, glancing up, saw something that explained the *whys* and *wherefores*. To the south, he couldn't say how far, a large beacon probed the night, sweeping back and forth, a beacon so powerful even the rain couldn't dampen its brilliance. It had to be a lighthouse. And if that was the case, the *Caspian* was near to shore. Very near.

A terrible image filled Bolan's mind. With no one at the helm, and with no way to change course or stop, the tanker would soon run aground. Should it break apart, the contents of the holds, hundreds of thousands of gallons of crude, would spill into the ocean. It would result in an environmental disaster the likes of which hadn't been seen since the *Exxon Valdez*. The coastline for hundreds of miles would be impacted, with a devastating loss to marine and bird life. The terrorists had to know the risk. But to them, it was merely another blow struck against the Great Satan. Collateral damage of a whole new sort.

Bolan raised his head above the catwalk but had to duck when several SMGs sought to separate it from his shoulders. He returned their fire, then dropped onto his stomach and snaked forward.

The next second the tanker's bow rose into the air and the *Caspian* lurched as if she had been torpedoed. A raucous grinding, the screech of metal on rock, issued from under the ship, but it didn't last long and the bow sank back down.

It was a good thing Bolan was on his stomach or

he would have been tossed across the deck like a leaf in a gale. As soon as the ship steadied, he continued to crawl. He was close enough for them to spot him but no one opened fire. He decided to make a run for the door, and he was halfway to his feet when the tanker lurched again, worse than the first time. The deck canted to the left. His feet were swept out from under him. There was nothing for him to grab, so he was sent rolling toward the gunwwale. Ordinarily he wouldn't have rolled far but the deck was so wet, so slippery, it was like shooting down a water slide. The soldier was almost to the side rail when the ship again righted itself.

Heaving to his feet, Bolan lunged toward the deckhouse. He had to reach it before something else happened. But he had taken only eight or nine strides when the *Caspian* shook as if in the grip of an earthquake and a new grinding noise rose from under her keel, caterwauling that went on forever, like the rending of an automobile in a junkyard crusher.

Suddenly the tanker came to a stop. One moment it was doing upward of twelve knots, the next it was as motionless as a log. The abrupt change was like being in a car that decelerated from fifty to a dead stop in the blink of an eye.

Bolan was catapulted forward, along with everything else on the deck that wasn't tied down. He threw up his arms to protect himself a fraction of a second before he slammed into the deckhouse like a flesh-and-bone battering ram. He braced for the impact, and for the pain from the bones he was bound to break. But instead of smashing into a solid wall, he struck a window.

Amid a shower of glass shards Bolan thudded onto

his shoulders. Momentum flipped him onto his side, and he lay dazed long enough for anyone who wanted to finish him off to do the job. But no one did.

Marshaling his wits, Bolan pushed onto his knees and hiked his SMG. There wasn't anyone to shoot. The room he had crashed into contained a sofa and some chairs, and that was all.

The terrorists had to be in the next one. Bolan trained his weapon on the doorway, but they didn't come barging in as he figured they would. When half a minute passed and the enemy still didn't show, he scanned the passageway. They weren't there, either. Nor in the next room, or the next.

The thumping of a door banging in the wind served notice on where they had gone. Out toward the bow. Bolan started to go after them, then spied a square object resting on a small table. It was a packet of plastic explosive rigged with a timer, the whole thing overlapped with two-inch-wide electrician's tape. He pried at the tape, enough to realize he couldn't get it off and disconnect the detonator before it was triggered. Only forty-one seconds remained.

With the speed of thought the Executioner grabbed the bombs, then was up and outside. Heedless of the rain and wind, he raced toward the port gunwale.

The packet was large enough to blow a hole in the *Caspian* the size of a tank. To say nothing of the secondary explosions it would trigger. One way or the other, the terrorists were determined to spill the crude. And Bolan was equally determined they wouldn't. A bolt of lightning lit up the deck, revealing a gas vent line directly in his path. He vaulted over it, but as he came down his right heel slipped out from under him and down he went. Unable to stop, he slid clear to the gunwale and stopped himself by thrusting both feet against it.

There wasn't much time left.

Bolan clutched at the rail and straightened. The wind was at his back, sixty to seventy miles an hour of screaming banshee, and when he hurled the packet, the wind caught it and whipped it off into the darkness like an out-of-control kite.

Bolan literally hit the deck and covered his head with both arms. Counting down in his head, he got to seven before the plastic explosives blew with a blast ten times as loud as any thunder. For a few fleeting seconds the foredeck lit up, and the *Caspian* rolled to the right. Metal screeched in protest. But it was short-lived. The thunder faded, the light died and the vessel righted itself and was still.

Leaping to the rail, Bolan peered over the side. As near as he could tell, the hull was intact. No crude was spilling into the sea. But he couldn't see the entire length of the ship, and for all he knew, there might be a break farther down.

The soldier moved to the deckhouse as fast as the rain and wind allowed. It felt great to be someplace dry and out of the elements. He jogged out the door they had left open. Ahead loomed another two hundred feet of storm-battered deck to the foremast. Beyond, another fifty feet or so, was the bow.

Bolan slogged in pursuit. He could make better time now that the deck wasn't rolling and pitching under him, but it was still slick. And the wind was worse than ever. Strong gusts constantly tried to rip him off his feet, and it was all he could do to resist. He kept hoping he would spot the terrorists or hear their voices, but they had too big a lead.

The thought spurred Bolan into tapping into the wellspring of stamina that had always been there when he needed it, and he pushed himself harder. If Al-Jabbar made it off the tanker, finding them in the dark, raging sea would be next to impossible. He'd need a lot of luck, and his had been in short supply of late.

Then, as if to prove Bolan wrong, the storm ended. The rain completely stopped except for a few stray drops, and the wind dropped to half its former intensity. He broke into a run. Visibility was better, but a lot of clouds were still scuttling overhead and it was so dark, he didn't see the huddled figure up in the crow's nest until he was almost abreast of the foremast. Automatically he snapped the MP-5 K into firing posture.

"Don't shoot, mate! God in heaven, please don't shoot!"

"Identify yourself!" Bolan snapped. The voice had a vaguely British accent to it.

"Adam Kentwork, out of Liverpool! When the firing started I came up here to hide. I didn't want any bleeding part of it. I mean, blimey, I didn't hire on this tub to have my arse shot off, now, did I?"

Bolan lowered the SMG. "Did you see anyone go by in the past couple of minutes?"

"I sure did. A whole bunch of blokes. Ten or eleven, I couldn't rightly be sure. And a crumpet, if you can believe it. They were talking all funny-like. Arabic, I reckon. I thank God they didn't spot me or we wouldn't be having—"

Bolan didn't listen to the rest. He sprinted past the anchor windlass and the mooring winch and across open deck to the bow, and when he got there, the worst that could happen had happened.

Al-Jabbar had made it off the ship.

The soldier stepped to the white railing. Four thick ropes had been securely tied to the uppermost and let over the side. He peered down. The tanker had come to ground on a broad, sandy stretch of beach bordered by woodland. Nowhere was there sign of life.

Adjusting the MP-5 K, so it hung across his back, Bolan gripped one of the ropes and climbed over the rail. Like everything else, the rope was soaked. He locked his ankles around it and carefully descended hand-under-hand while scouring the woods for Abbas and his fanatics.

Ten feet from the bottom Bolan unwrapped his legs and let go. The soggy sand cushioned his landing, and after swinging the SMG in front of him, he examined the ground for tracks. Since the terrorists had gone over the side when it was still pouring, the rain had washed away most of their prints. But not all. He found a few, enough to indicate the direction they had taken.

Like a bloodhound hot on the scent of rabid raccoons, the soldier lit out after them. The woods were cloaked in darkness, but he could see well enough to avoid the logs, boulders and thickets that sprouted in front of him.

Bolan wished the cloud cover would disperse so he could get a fix on where he was. The tanker had grounded well north of New York City; that much he knew. How far north was the question.

The soldier slipped a compass from a small pocket in his vest and slowed just enough to read it. The terrorists were bearing to the northwest. Did they have a specific destination in mind, he wondered, or were they running blind, trying to put as much distance as they could between them and the tanker? Pocketing the compass, he poured on the speed.

Suddenly something crashed through the brush to his right. Stopping cold, Bolan pivoted and fixed the laser sight on the first moving thing he saw. A white-tail buck, ears up and nostrils flared, uttered a snort, spun and bolted in great bounds, the white of his tail flashing like a flag.

Bolan bounded off, too, deeper into the forest.

Since everything Aban Abbas did was thought-out well in advance, the soldier had to believe the terrorist chose that area specifically because it was remote and isolated, ideal for a quick getaway. But there had to be human habitation somewhere, and where there were people, there were roads—and the vehicles Abbas needed to spirit his people away.

Moments later several lights appeared. As Bolan drew closer, he saw they were windows in an old house on the side of a hill. Suddenly a scream shattered the night. Autofire ratcheted in response and then it was quiet again.

Fatigue had set in, and Bolan was caked with sweat but he pumped his legs with renewed vigor. He still had more than two hundred yards to go and feared he wouldn't get there in time.

Figures filed from the house to a two-car garage. Some were laughing. One stooped, gripped a handle and swung up the wide door. An overhead light blinked on, bathing an SUV and a sedan. The terrorists climbed into the vehicles and the engines revved to life.

Gritting his teeth in frustration, Bolan tried to get within range. The two vehicles backed out, turned down a gravel drive and sped westward along a narrow dirt road. He bored through a thicket to gain a few precious seconds, but it wasn't enough. He reached the road too late.

Bolan raced up the drive and onto a porch overgrown with ivy. The front door hung ajar, and a few feet inside lay the crumpled form of an elderly man, his body riddled with bullets.

Bolan went through the motions of checking for a pulse. A hallway took him past a living room and a music room containing a piano and a cello to an immaculate kitchen that spoke of loving care. The woman responsible was on the floor by a table. She had white hair done up in a bun and wore an apron that was splotched red. Her eyes were open, and when he entered, she looked at him and her mouth moved but no sounds came out.

Hurrying over, Bolan knelt and gently squeezed her shoulder. "Hang on. I'll call for an ambulance."

Her lips moved again, and Bolan leaned down. "I can't hear you. What are you trying to say?"

"My Harold?" she could barely whisper. "How is he?"

"He's not doing too well," he said gently. "They were terrorists—" Bolan began, but there was no need. She had stiffened, and the light of life fled her eyes. Standing, he unclipped his cell phone and tapped in the special number to Hal Brognola's private office at Stony Man Farm. It was answered on the first ring.

"Mack?"

"I'm here," Bolan said.

"You sound miserable."

Bolan stared at the old woman. "I'm fine."

"You sure? Where are you? More to the point, where the hell is the *Caspian*? The Coast Guard reports it went off radar during the height of the storm. We've been going nuts trying to locate it. Our satellites were useless. We sent a few planes up and they're still out there looking.''

"You'll find it on a beach somewhere north of New York," Bolan said, and filled in the big Fed. Brognola listened in stony silence, not once interrupting, and when Bolan finished, there was a long, drawn-out sigh.

"Damn. They're here, and they're on the loose. Nightmares do become real." The big Fed's tone hardened. "All right. So we deal with it. I'll alert the FBI, have the state police mobilized and get word to every municipal and county law enforcement agency in the Tri-State area. It's a straight-out manhunt now. There's no need for secrecy."

"I want them, Hal."

"Duly noted. We'll advise the other agencies to locate but not apprehend, and relay word immediately."

"You don't understand," Bolan said. "I'm going to take these people down."

"Is it me or is this one getting to you?" Brognola added hastily, "No matter. I'll do all I can short of endangering more lives to give you first crack at them, but don't hold it against me if things don't work out the way we want." Someone said something in the background. It sounded like Barbara Price. "We're getting a fix on your signal. Once I know exactly where you are, I'll send Jack to pick you up. In the meantime, sit tight. Try to get some rest."

"I could use dry clothes."

"Consider it done. Civvies and a blacksuit so you can dress for all occasions."

Bolan cracked a wry grin. "Any word on Sefu Abbas?" The last he had heard, right before he was whisked to the *Exiter,* was that the younger Abbas had given the Feds the slip, killing a couple of FBI agents in the process.

"The one bright spot. Remember that phrase in his message, 'where cats grew trees for whiskers'? We think he was referring to the Catskill Mountains—"

"Which are here in New York," Bolan broke in, spiked by hope.

"It won't surprise me if we find out they're within easy driving distance of where you are."

"That narrows the search area."

"Considerably. The Catskills are about fifty miles long and thirty miles wide. Fifteen hundred square miles is nothing to sneeze at, but it's a hell of a lot better than having to comb the entire state." Brognola paused. "If you ask me, Aban Abbas made the biggest mistake of his life coming here. He's on our turf now, and that gives us the edge."

Bolan hoped so.

THE HUNTING LODGE had seen better days. Decades earlier it had been a hot spot for hunters from as far south as New Jersey. But now most of the bigger bucks had been hunted out, and its prime clientele preferred to travel farther north where there were a lot more trophy racks to be had. The lack of business showed. The buildings were in dire need of a coat of paint, and many of the cabins had cracked windows and roofs in disrepair.

Sefu Abbas came out of one of the cabins he had rented and walked down a winding path flanked by tall pines to the office. The owner, a man in his fifties with a double chin and a belly as big as a clothes basket, looked up from one of the girlie magazines he kept stashed under the counter.

"Howdy, there, young fella. Off into town again tonight, are you?"

"Not tonight, Mr. Lester." Sefu had spent the past several evenings at the small library in the nearby town of Tuttleville. There wasn't much to do at the lodge except listen to the radio and watch a TV with terrible reception.

Mr. Lester ran a pudgy hand across his perspiring brow. "Oh. That's right. Tonight's the big night, ain't it, Mr. LeBeau? Your friends are supposed to get here."

"Before midnight, if they don't lose their way." Sefu found it difficult to contain his excitement. After long months of loneliness he would be reunited with Aban and his friends in Al-Jabbar.

"I'm sorry I ain't got cable and all that fancy jazz the big chains do," Mr. Lester said. "But times have been hard. I'm damn lucky to still be afloat."

Sefu reflected how they couldn't be too hard if Lester ate so well. "That's all right. I don't mind going to the movies." He had become something of a buff since moving to America. All those hours of enforced idleness at night had to be filled some way.

"Where did you say you're from again?"

"New Orleans," Sefu said.

"That's right. Down Louisiana way. I've got to admit, I don't know Creoles from Canadians, but if your friends are as kindly and nice as you, they must be a great bunch of people."

Sefu never failed to be amused by the ignorance of the average American. He couldn't for the life of him understand how they became a superpower. "I am here about the towels. You told me the day I arrived that you would put clean ones in the cabins my friends are to stay in, but you still have not done it.''

''Oh. Damn. My memory ain't what it used to be, son. You'll have to forgive me.'' Lester eased his bulk off a stool and waddled to a closet. ''You don't mind taking 'em yourself, do you? I'm expecting a phone call and I'd hate to miss it.''

Sefu very much doubted the lazy slab of lard was expecting any such thing, but he played along and replied, ''I don't mind at all. Anything to help you out.''

''That's right decent of you.'' Lester brought over an armful of towels and washcloths, then casually remarked, ''That gal from the FBI should be calling anytime now.''

Sefu froze. ''The FBI?''

''Yeah. Some lady agent called about half an hour ago. Wanted to know if I had any foreigners staying here. Can you believe it? The last foreign type I can recall was a fella from Philly. Came up here about a year ago, I think it was, and only stayed a day.''

Sefu knew the man well. He was Syrian, one of Al-Jabbar's network of contacts. Mukhtar was his name, and part of his mission was to keep a list of safe havens in times of emergency, and relay them periodically to Somalia and warriors under cover in America. It was on Mukhtar's advice that Sefu had chosen the lodge in the first place. ''What did you tell the FBI agent?'' he asked.

''I told her the only one I have registered is you, and you're a born-and-bred American. She wanted the registration information, but I couldn't find the damn sheet so she's calling back.'' Lester flourished the sign-in form. ''This time I'm ready for her.''

At that juncture the phone rang.

Sefu reached under his jacket, drew the Astra 300 with the suppressor already threaded on and shot Lester in the temple as his pudgy fingers were wrapping around the receiver. Snatching it up, Sefu said, "Huntsman's Lodge. May I help you?"

"This is Agent Sandra Downing of the FBI. Is Mr. Lester there?"

"I'm sorry. He's left for the evening." Sefu glanced at a framed photo of Lester proudly holding a twelve-pound bass. "He went night fishing with some of his buddies. I'm his brother, George. I'm holding down the fort."

"Did he mention anything to you about a registration slip?"

"No, he sure didn't. He took his six-pack, jumped in his pickup and drove off without hardly a word."

The FBI agent muttered something Sefu couldn't quite hear. "Will you do me a favor, George? Leave word for your brother I'll be calling back tomorrow morning at eight sharp, and he had better have the information I need."

"I sure will. I hope he's not in any trouble," Sefu said, but she had hung up. Grinning at how cleverly he had outwitted her, he stepped to the front door to change the sign from Open to Closed.

Headlights swept into the parking lot and two vehicles pulled in, a sedan and an SUV. Sefu held his breath, hoping against hope, and when he saw the third person to slide from the SUV, he flung the door open and raced down the steps with his arms wide. "Aban! After all this time!"

Brother hugged brother, then Aban gripped Sefu by the shoulders and gleefully asked. "Are you ready to kill Americans?"

"I was born ready."

CHAPTER EIGHTEEN

FBI Agent Sandra Downing didn't know quite what to make of it.

She had relayed her suspicions about the Huntsman's Lodge to the assistant director in charge, per orders. She explained that when she originally talked to Carl Lester, the man had babbled on about everything under the sun and she had a hard time keeping him focused on the issue of the registration slip. At one point, she distinctly remembered him saying that the area up there was great for fishing, and he invited her to come up and try her hand sometime. After she mentioned she didn't fish, Lester commented he used to but he had given it up because of a bad back. How strange, then, Downing thought, when the man who claimed to be his brother said Carl Lester had gone off fishing for the night.

So Downing reported the inconsistency, and thought nothing more of it until she was called into the ADIC's office on the twenty-third floor of 26 Federal Plaza. His window offered a panoramic view of New York City's skyline, but she was only interested in why he had called her in.

"How would you like a crack at the guy who murdered those two agents in New Castle, Pennsylvania?'' Richard Vernon bluntly asked.

For a few seconds Downing had been too surprised to answer. She was only a year out of Quantico, and she hadn't been involved in many apprehensions and arrests. ''Me, sir?''

''The director wants our people in on it, and since you were the one who tipped them to Huntsman's Lodge, he thinks it only fitting you go along.''

''I'm flattered, sir.''

''Stay grounded, Agent. Letting this go to your head can get you killed if you're not careful.'' Vernon swiveled his chair and stepped to a large map of New York State on the wall. ''You and thirty-four other agents are to assemble at a diner in the town of Tuttleville by four-thirty tomorrow morning. Right about here.'' He tapped a spot on the map. ''Go loaded for bear. I'll provide you with detailed directions on how to get there, but it's fairly easy. You take Interstate 84 north and cross over to Highway 28 at Kingston. From there, you take some back roads.''

''I'm sure I can find it, sir. But why so many agents to arrest one terrorist?''

''Because evidently he's not alone. The word is there might be ten or eleven more. All members of Al-Jabbar, the bunch that blew up that Echelon building in Cyprus.''

The surprises kept multiplying. ''How did they all get here?''

''I haven't been privy to that information.'' Vernon took his seat. ''All I know is that after I relayed your report, a plane was sent to overfly the lodge and somehow confirmed the terrorists are there.''

''Will you be in charge of this operation?''

"No, an assistant director from headquarters division is being flown in." Vernon gave her a strange look. "Perhaps it's best if I enlighten on you on certain mitigating factors. Apparently the director had to raise holy hell to get permission for us to go in. He's insisting the Bureau have a hand in nailing the scumbag who killed our boys. But somebody in Washington wanted to send in someone else. So they compromised."

Downing tried to think of who was powerful enough to butt heads with the director. It couldn't be the CIA. A case like this was out of their legal purview. "Did I understand you correctly? They wanted to send in just one guy?"

"So I'm told. And he'll be there tomorrow. Our people are to give him their fullest cooperation. Even the AD."

Downing had never heard of such a thing. Whoever the guy was, he had to have major clout.

"Don't let it affect your focus. Go in, do your job, and things will be fine." Vernon bestowed a rare smile. "You're extremely competent, Agent Downing. I know you're up to this."

Of all the surprises, that had been the greatest. A compliment from ADIC Vernon! Downing had thanked him, and later, on the drive to her apartment, tried to piece together the nuances of their conversation. She didn't quite know what to make of the mystery man they were to work with, but she would find out soon enough.

IT TOOK AN HOUR and ten minutes to reach Tuttleville, as sleepy a hamlet as Sandra Downing ever saw. The diner, appropriately enough, was called Ma's Place, and the "parking lot" ADIC Vernon had mentioned was in reality a dirt lot.

Most of the others involved had already arrived. Downing had to park half a block from the staging area. Her ID in hand, she moved toward a group of agents being addressed by a distinguished-looking gentleman in an expensive suit. She recognized him as Assistant Director Alvin Crampton from headquarters. He was close friends with the director, and rumor had it might have a shot at the position himself some day. She threaded through her fellow agents to hear better, nodding at those she knew.

"—stress enough the crucial nature of this exercise," Crampton was saying. "It is imperative none of the terrorists escape our cordon. Washington fears they plan an atrocity on a par with the World Trade Center disaster, and they want these madmen stopped at all costs."

"You can count on us, sir," an agent at the front declared.

Murmurs of agreement rippled among them. Downing was looking to see how many from her own office were involved when she heard the sound of a helicopter. It flashed in low over the diner and hovered to one side, the two men inside giving them the once-over.

Someone whistled in admiration. "Hey, that's a Cobra. A top military model."

The pilot's lean features creased in a crooked grin. He said something, then laughed and banked the Cobra so sharply, for a second Downing feared it would flip over completely. Across the street was a playground with the usual slide, swings and monkey bars, and nearby was a grassy area barely large enough, in her opinion, for a VW bug. Yet the Cobra's pilot sat the war bird down right on it with breathtaking speed. Gazing over at them, he stuck his thumbs in his ears and scrunched up his face.

"Friendly sort, isn't he?" an agent dryly commented.

"If you ask me, all those hotshot air jockeys are half crazy," another said.

The cockpit opened and out climbed the other man. Once on the ground, he stepped back a safe distance and nodded. The cockpit closed, the pilot wriggled his fingers in parting, and the Cobra whisked off to the south.

The newcomer turned.

A sudden hush descended. Sandra couldn't say why, but she felt it, too. There was something about him. Something she couldn't quite define. A presence, a sense that here was someone extraordinary. Tall, dark and muscular, he moved with the fluid ease of a natural-born athlete. He was undeniably handsome but not in a pretty-boy sort of way. She would describe him as ruggedly good-looking, with a face that bore the stamp of hard experience like a badge of honor.

Over a formfitting black suit the man wore body armor and combat webbing. He was packing plenty of hardware, including an M-16 slung over his left shoulder. The way he carried himself, with his chin high and his shoulders squared, the word that popped into Downing's mind was "soldier."

Assistant Director Crampton hurried to meet him. They shook hands, and Downing was fascinated to see the deference with which the AD treated him. Crampton acted as if he were greeting the President, with a lot of hand-pumping and bobbing of his chin. The soldier absorbed it all in stony silence.

Whoever this guy was, she reflected, he had to have clout at the highest levels. Crampton brought him over, and she heard the AD ask another agent if everyone was present and accounted for. When the agent confirmed that was the case, Crampton cleared his throat.

"May I have your attention? We need to get this show on the road so I'll be brief." Crampton motioned at the soldier. "This is Mr. Belasko. He is sanctioned at the highest level not only to take part in this operation, but to exercise command prerogatives as he sees fit. He has graciously allowed me to handle the details, so here's how we will proceed."

Everyone, Downing included, was all ears.

"Our two SWAT teams will conduct the crux of the operation. The rest of you will primarily be concerned with containment. You'll be divided into four squads, each with a supervisor who will coordinate our deployment and relay instructions in the field." An agent handed Crampton a clipboard and he read four names from a list, appointing them the leaders of Squads A, B, C and D. The same agent then held up a large posterboard with the layout of the Huntsman's Lodge drawn in black magic marker.

Downing edged closer, as did many others.

"When we deploy," Crampton announced, "Squad A will establish a perimeter to the north, B to the east, C to the west, D to the south." As he mentioned each squad, he placed a finger at the appropriate points. "Once we are all in position, at my command our SWAT teams will close in and apprehend the suspects." Crampton glanced at Belasko. "If all this is okay by you, that is."

Bolan nodded, then faced them. "Intel suggests

there could be as many as twelve terrorists. We out-number them but they'll be packing a lot of fire-power." His blue eyes swept them with a penetrating stare. "Get one thing clear here and now and you'll be a lot better off. These are killers, not run-of-the-mill robbery suspects. They won't give up without a fight. So take them down fast and hard."

Crampton said a little too quickly, "Yes, indeed. But be advised that if we can take any alive, we are mandated to do so." He spent the next ten minutes going over the diagram and detailing how events were intended to unfold. "Any questions?" he asked. After answering a few, he consulted the clipboard. "Before I forget, I need to appoint a liaison to work with Mr. Belasko, here. Will Agent Sandra Downing please step forward."

Dumbfounded, Downing had to will her legs to work. She accepted the AD's handshake and mustered her courage to say, "Any special reason you picked me, sir?"

"Any special reason why I shouldn't?" Crampton countered, then added, "You're a qualified marksman, your father was an Army colonel, and you spent your entire childhood living on military bases."

Downing was puzzled as to what all that had to do with her selection but she smiled and said, "I'll do the best I can, sir. What is it, exactly, you want me to do?"

"Pretend you're Mr. Belasko's shadow," Crampton said patronizingly. He introduced her, then moved in among the other agents to dispense further directions.

Left alone by the soldier's side, Downing glanced up at him and tried to quell her nerves. "I guess it's you and me, then, sir."

''Mike.''

''I beg your pardon?''

''You can call me Mike if you want.''

''If you say so, sir.'' Downing had never felt more out of place in her life. ''You just tell me what to do and I'll do it.''

''Have you ever killed before, Agent Downing?''

''No, sir. Can't say as I have. I've never been in a position where I've had to.''

''You're in one now,'' Bolan said, not unkindly. ''If you don't think you can pull the trigger, if you have any doubts whatsoever, stay in the car.'' He grinned. ''I don't like my liaisons gunned down. It spoils my supper.''

Downing chuckled. ''Does it happen often?''

''Too often.''

His earnestness rattled her. She was glad when the order came to gear up because it gave her the opportunity to compose herself. She was a professional. She had a job to do. And she would be damned if she would let Assistant Director Crampton or Mike Belasko or anyone else intimidate her.

The convoy pulled out precisely at five-thirty. To the east the sky was beginning to brighten.

Downing rode in the same car as the AD, in the back seat with Belasko. A Beretta 92-F was in a shoulder holster under her right arm and a Colt M-4 carbine was propped against her leg. Crampton was on the radio, speaking so loudly she almost didn't hear the soldier.

''The AD mentioned you're qualified as a marksman.''

''Yes, sir.'' For some reason Downing felt her cheeks grow warm. ''My goal is to one day be assigned to a Bureau SWAT team. Not many women are, so it will be quite an honor.''

''Your father will be very proud of you.''

Downing looked at him. ''You don't miss a thing, do you?''

''In my line of work I can't afford to. It's the little things that trip us up and put our lives in jeopardy.''

''If it's not out of line, sir, may I ask what exactly it is that you do?'' Downing knew she shouldn't pry, but her curiosity refused to be denied.

''I'm a flyswatter.''

''Come again?''

''When the government needs flies swatted, they call on me. I was all set to go in solo when your director raised such a fuss, the decision came down to make this a joint op.''

''There are no hard feelings, I trust?'' Downing said, and when he nodded and smiled, she leaned back, a lot more at ease. Then the full significance of what he had just said struck home. He had been prepared to take on a dozen terrorists by himself. A person had to either be insane or one of the best soldiers alive to do a thing like that, and he didn't impress her as being a lunatic.

Assistant Director Crampton hooked the mike on the radio and looked over his shoulder. ''With any luck, Mr. Belasko, we'll catch them napping. I plan to stop a quarter of a mile from the lodge and proceed the rest of the way on foot. We'll deploy a hundred yards out and let our SWAT teams move in before we commit ourselves. Is that acceptable?''

''As long as your people do it quietly enough. If you lose the element of surprise, a lot of good agents are going to die.''

"Don't worry, Mr. Belasko. Our people undergo some of the most rigorous training in all of law enforcement. And our SWAT boys are second to none."

Bolan didn't comment, and the AD got on the horn again to tell one of the trailing cars to close formation.

Downing fingered her M-4 and hoped it all went as well as the assistant director seemed to think it would. She remembered her father telling her that in combat nothing was etched in stone. An op could go south fast, and once it started to unravel, sometimes there was no recovering.

Mike Belasko didn't appear the least bit nervous. He was staring eastward, his posture as natural as if he were slumped on a sofa in his living room.

Downing envied him. Her own body was wound as tight as a roll of barbed wire. But as soon as the cars pulled over and everyone climbed out, her nervousness evaporated. Crampton was having everyone line up at the side of the road, the SWAT teams in front.

Belasko didn't wait for them. And since Downing had been told to stay close to him, when he jogged north, she did, too.

The sun was poking above the horizon but much of the countryside was still in shadow. The lodge didn't come into view until they rounded a bend, and then all they could see were the roofs of several cabins.

"On me," Bolan ordered. He crossed a ditch into the woods to their left and bore to the north again.

Downing glued herself to his heels. She was breathing heavily after they had gone a couple of hundred yards, but he wasn't fazed one bit. When he abruptly stopped, she almost ran into him.

The trees thinned ahead and ended at the edge of a field. Past it was a parking lot. Only one vehicle was parked there, a battered old pickup. Bolan, gazing through a small pair of binoculars, scowled. "Damn. I knew I should have gone in alone last night."

"What's wrong?"

"I wish your director hadn't raised such a stink. The delay he caused might end up costing a lot of lives." His jaw muscles twitched, and he looked fit to punch someone. "I'm afraid the terrorists have flown the coop."

Alarmed, Downing asked, "What makes you think so?"

"The two vehicles they stole, an SUV and a sedan, are no longer there. They must have left shortly after the government plane flew over. By now they could be anywhere."

"Maybe only some of them left," she said without much conviction. "And you can't blame the director for wanting the Bureau to have a hand in their apprehension. In case you haven't heard, two of our agents were killed by one of these lowlifes."

"I know all about it." Bolan moved in a crouch toward the field.

About to follow, Downing paused when her headset crackled with Assistant Director Crampton's irritated voice.

"Agent Downing, where the hell are you? I don't like Belasko and you going off by yourselves. You should have told me."

"Do you want me to tell him that, sir?"

"No, no, no. Just keep me informed of your location. We don't want any deaths by friendly fire, now, do we?"

Downing filled the AD in on where they were, then hastened to catch up to the mystery man. "The assistant director says to tell you they're on their—'' Before she could finish, the soldier grabbed her by the shoulder and yanked her down flat beside him. She looked in the direction he was looking, and discovered why.

A man of obvious Arab descent had stepped from a cabin. He was fully dressed, in a short-sleeved shirt and slacks, and was holding a towel. Facing due east, he spread the towel in front of him and got down on his knees.

"What in the world?" Downing whispered.

"His morning prayers," Bolan said.

It stunned her. Even though Downing knew Al-Jabbar was made up of Muslim extremists, she had never given much thought to the religious aspect of their characters. To her they were cold-blooded killers and nothing more.

Two more men came out, one with his own towel, the second carrying a small rug. They knelt on either side of their companion, and all three began bowing and praying.

"Only three out of twelve." Bolan started to crawl.

"That's better than none," Downing said, still miffed by his uncalled-for criticism of the director.

"Shouldn't you tell Crampton?"

"I know my job, thank you," she responded testily. But he was right. She should have reported it the moment the suspects appeared.

"Advise him to stop where he is and keep everyone there until I give the all clear," Belasko ordered. "We don't want the terrorists to spot them if we can help it."

"Will do, sir." Downing stressed the *sir*.

"Also let him know the terrorists are the only guests at the lodge."

"How can you possibly know that?"

"Because those three wouldn't be praying out in the open if anyone else was around. It would draw too much attention."

The agent quietly did as he had instructed. In a bit they came to the field, and the soldier sighted down his M-16. "You wouldn't shoot them when they're unarmed, would you?" she whispered.

"Who says they are?" Bolan retorted, but he lowered the autorifle.

Their prayers lasted longer than Downing would ever have imagined. The sun was almost all the way above the horizon when the trio stood, picked up the towels and rug, and went back inside.

"Now?"

"Now. But remind Crampton the terrorists are wide awake and might have a man posted at the windows."

Downing resented the implication her fellow agents would botch it if they weren't careful, but she smothered her feelings and passed on the message. The soldier snaked into the field, winding sinuously through the high grass, barely disturbing the stems. She tried to do the same, but she lacked his skill. He stopped halfway across.

"This is as close as we dare go."

Excitement rose in Downing. She had never been on a field op this big. Or this dangerous. The soldier, though, was calmness personified. "You do stuff like this all the time, don't you?" she whispered.

"Every day and twice on Sundays."

"How did you ever get involved with whatever you're involved with? Were you tops in your class at

West Point? Or were you a Green Beret or something like that?''

"I killed a lot of people.''

"I get it. That's your way of reminding me it's none of my business. Very well. Lesson learned.''

The soldier had twisted and was staring off to the east. He didn't seem particularly pleased. Downing shifted and discovered why. A line of agents was taking up positions, and although they tried to stick to cover, every now and then she could see one as plain as day. And if she could, so could the terrorists. "They're doing the best they can,'' she whispered.

"Sometimes that's not good enough.''

More agents were spreading out to the north and west. Others formed a line to the south between the field and the woods.

The grass behind Downing rustled, and up beside them crabbed Assistant Director Crampton. He was sweating as if he were in a sauna, and his face was fire-engine red. "We're almost ready,'' he announced proudly.

Belasko didn't say anything so Downing piped up. "I just hope they haven't spotted us, sir.''

"So what if they have? There are three of them and thirty-five of us. They don't stand a snowball's chance in hell should they elect to resist.'' Crampton asked which lodge the terrorists were in, then pressed a hand to his headset. "SWAT One and SWAT Two, are you in position?'' He listened a few moments. "Excellent. We are good to go on cabin number four. I repeat, we are good to go on the fourth cabin.''

Decked out in helmets, armor and camo, the FBI SWAT units closed in, one from the east, the other from the west. Downing admired their military efficiency. How they flitted from spot to spot, always with their weapons at combat ready, one always covering the others.

One day she was going to belong to a Bureau SWAT team, and it would be the happiest of her life.

"I almost hope these fools do fight back," Crampton commented. "It would serve them right."

The teams had honed their coordination to a science. They reached the lodge in question, and while SWAT Two covered all the windows and the door, SWAT One moved in. As yet there was no movement, no sign of life at all, from within the lodge.

"Another few seconds and we'll have them," Crampton boasted. "Like mice in a trap."

SWAT One now had men on either side of the door. At a hand signal from the team leader, two of the agents stepped in front of it to kick it in.

That was when the mice chose to fight back.

CHAPTER NINETEEN

The politics of working with Uncle Sam could be a royal pain. It was the one aspect of Bolan's arrangement with the Feds he liked least. From time to time pressure was brought to bear from outside parties, and Hal Brognola was given no option other than to bend with the prevailing winds.

In this instance, the director of the FBI had complained to the White House that the Bureau deserved a shot at Al-Jabbar. They had lost two of their own to the younger Abbas and had a right to help take him and his associates down. In the interests of fairness, not to mention soothing the ruffled feathers of a staunch supporter, the man in the Oval Office told Brognola to let the FBI play in the sandbox.

So there they were, two FBI SWAT teams, highly trained and supremely competent, about to kick the lid off a can of worms. Bolan's gut instinct was that the can was about to blow up in their faces. Literally. Yet his hands were tied. Even though Brognola had given him the authority to override the AD, the big Fed had also passed on the President's personal request that the FBI be given as much free rein as possible.

In effect, Bolan was there as a glorified observer. He was supposed to offer Crampton the benefit of his expertise and see to it the agents didn't make fatal blunders. But as long as they did everything by the book, all he could do was sit back and hope for the best.

As the two SWAT members prepared to break down the door, autofire from inside churned the door into Swiss cheese and did much the same to them. Their body armor protected them from the worst of the hailstorm, but not from all of it, and down they went.

At the same instant, the door to a cabin catty-corner from the one housing the three terrorists was flung open, revealing a fourth. He had an SMG, and before SWAT One and SWAT Two had any inkling he was there, he cut three of them down with brief but accurate bursts.

"Son of a bitch!" Crampton bawled, then shouted into his headset. "Swanson! Get your wounded out of there! Retreat and regroup! I repeat, retreat and regroup!"

Harder said than done, for now the terrorists in the first cabin were firing through the windows, catching SWAT One and SWAT Two in a withering cross fire. A single SWAT member made it to the corner of another cabin farther down, and he limped badly.

"This can't be happening!" Crampton roared. "This can't be happening!" Then he composed himself to say into his headset, "We have men down! All agents! Converge on the lodge at my command!"

Bolan had lain idly by long enough. He had fulfilled his promise to Brognola, and now it was time to take over. "Cancel that order. I'll handle it alone."

"Like hell! Those are our people on the ground, and we'll get them out of there!"

"Remember what the director told you," Bolan

said. "I have the authority to assume command at any time."

The assistant director hesitated. He nodded a couple of times, his reason asserting itself over his outrage. But then one of the terrorists fired a short burst into a fallen agent feebly trying to crawl to safety. The agent screamed as slugs tore into his back and head. Crampton recoiled in horror, turned redder than ever and rose to his feet, roaring, "Our people are being slaughtered! Close in! Close in!"

"Don't do it!" Bolan countered, but the assistant director ignored him and barreled toward the cabins. The agents on the perimeter were also on the move. Unless Bolan acted, and quickly, a lot more were needlessly going to die. His fingers a blur, he fed a high-explosive grenade into the grenade launcher.

"What are you doing?" Downing asked.

Bolan had no time to explain. Angling the M-16 skyward, he gauged the trajectory and fired. He couldn't hope to hit the cabins from where he was, but he could, and did, land the grenade right on top of the beat-up old pickup in the parking lot. The blast was loud and fiery, but even louder was the explosion when the gas tank went up. The force blew the pickup into the air, flipping it onto its shattered roof.

The soldier's ploy had the desired effect. The FBI agents halted in their tracks, including Crampton. Overtaking him, Bolan grabbed him by the arm and practically threw him to the ground, then hunkered. "Not another step! Call off your agents, or you'll have to answer to your director for your failure to obey a direct order."

The threat was as effective as the grenade. Crampton calmed down immediately and blurted, "Sorry.

I've never been involved in anything like this before. Hell, I've never had to fire my gun in the line of duty.''

Few agents ever did, but Bolan had to wonder why in God's name Washington sent him instead of someone with more field experience.

Almost as if the AD had read Bolan's mind, Crampton said, ''The director thought it would be a feather in my cap to handle an operation like this.''

Now Bolan understood. He had met Crampton's type before. Peacocks with badges. All they cared about was advancing their careers. Thankfully, there weren't all that many, since they had a habit of making the lives of earnest, dedicated agents miserable. ''Have your people stand down. I'm going on.''

Without waiting for the command to be carried out, Bolan pivoted and stalked toward the lodge. He had only gone a few yards when the grass beside him rustled. He knew who it was without looking. ''What do you think you're doing?''

''You're big on following orders. So am I,'' Downing said. ''And my orders are to stick to you like glue.''

''Your devotion to duty is duly noted. Now get back there with the rest.''

''No can do, Mr. Belasko.''

Bolan stopped and turned. The iron set of her jaw told him it was pointless to argue. Either he slugged her and left her there unconscious, or he made the best of a situation that should never have developed in the first place. He was going to have a long talk with Brognola when he got back.

''Tell me what to do and I'll do it. I won't get in your way. I promise.''

"You could be killed, Agent."

"I knew when I signed on that the risk of dying in the line of duty came with the job. So quit nitpicking. Sir."

"Do what I do, then." Bolan had delayed too long already. "And keep your head down. We don't want that cute button nose of yours shot off."

Downing blinked.

"On me," Bolan directed her, and was off through the high grass, beelining toward a cabin several doors to the west of those occupied by the terrorists. There were twelve cabins in all, staggered in a long row and separated by small islands of shrubberies and trees. A stone walk threaded among them and over to the office, to the east.

Suddenly the door to cabin number four opened and the lone terrorist dashed toward cabin three, the one his friends were in. Pivoting from side to side, he sprayed lead indiscriminately.

"Drop him." Snapping up the M-16, Bolan fired. Downing's shots echoed his own.

The terrorist was flung to the stone walk. He tried to push himself up, cried out in Arabic and collapsed.

Roars of fury erupted from cabin number three. SMGs opened up, firing into the tall grass, but Bolan and Downing were no longer in the same spot. The Executioner had led her to the left, and they were only twenty yards from cabin number seven. The grass ended well short of it.

Slowing so Downing could come up beside him, Bolan said, "When I give the word, run like hell." Four more strides and he barked, "Now." They hurtled from cover with a dozen yards to go. At least one of the terrorists spotted them. Bursts of 9 mm lead were unleashed in their direction, but they reached the cabin unscathed.

Without delay Bolan moved around to the northwest corner. From there he had a clear line of sight at the west side of cabin number three. The window had been busted out but he didn't see anyone. "I'm going to work my way closer," he informed Downing. "I want you to cover that window."

"Are you sure this isn't an excuse to ditch me?"

"You're a qualified marksman, remember?" Bolan rebutted. The range wasn't all that great, sixty yards, but the window was narrow and the terrorist would be in shadow. It would take some fine shooting.

"They won't lay a slug on you," Downing vowed.

Bolan ducked in among some shrubs and on past them to cabin number six. Staying close to the rear wall, he sidled to the corner and on into the next strip of vegetation. Cabin number five wasn't in a direct line with number six, but to the south about ten yards. He had to cross another open space to reach it, and glanced back to ensure Downing was doing what she was supposed to do. Then he flew toward cabin six like a linebacker out to tackle it.

A terrorist filled the window, a submachine gun firm against his hip. In the blink of an eye Downing's M-4 chattered. Dark splotches marked the gunner's face and he staggered back, his SMG firing into the floor.

Bolan gained the safety of cabin number five and gave Downing a thumbs-up for a job well done. Moving to the front, he sidestepped to the corner.

The next cabin, number five, was the one the lone terrorist had occupied. His body still lay in the path.

A shout suddenly went up from Crampton, but the

rattle of automatic fire from cabin three drowned it out. Or was it cabin three? Bolan debated as the firing continued. It seemed to be moving away from him. It stopped for a second, and Downing yelled, "Belasko! One of them is making a break for it!"

Before the words were out of her mouth, Bolan spotted a stocky terrorist in full flight to the southeast. He had a Skorpion, and he was raking the grass and the trees with the intent of punching through the federal cordon. But he couldn't keep them pinned down forever, and he knew it. His right hand disappeared under his jacket and reappeared clutching a grenade. Jerking the pin, he slowed and cocked his arm. He was close enough to the agents to catch seven or eight within the blast radius.

Bolan fired more out of reflex than conscious thought. He aimed at the man's right shoulder and arm, his slugs shearing through sinew and bone just as the terrorist started to throw.

The grenade fell from fingers gone numb or limp, right at the man's feet, and bleating in dismay, he dropped his subgun and grabbed the grenade with his other hand. In the same motion he flipped it toward the Feds, but it was only a foot or so from his outstretched fingers when it detonated. Half the man's face and a sizable chunk of his chest were blown off. Yet despite that, the body took another couple of steps before keeling over.

Bolan ran between a couple of pines to cabin five and along the front to where he had an unobstructed view of the cabin containing the last Al-Jabbar gunner. The door was wide open, and from within came a singsong voice in prayer. He started toward it but the prayer ended and a swarthy face appeared in the doorway. Only for a moment, though.

Backpedaling, Bolan centered the M-16's sights on the entrance. As soon as the terrorist stepped through, he would fire.

Another moment, and a long, dusky-hued object protruded from one of the shattered windows. The thickness of a man's arm, it was capped by a cylindrical cone.

Bolan instantly knew what it was, a Russian-made RPG-7 missile launcher. It swung toward him, and he did the only thing he could do. He spun and ran. He hoped to reach the far side of cabin five before the terrorist fired, but he wasn't quite there when he heard a telltale whoosh. The HEAT missile struck the corner where he had just been standing, and the force of the explosion pitched him to his hands and knees.

Covering his head, Bolan pressed his forehead to the ground as pieces of wall and roof pelted him and the surrounding area. Most of the debris was small and only stung, but a few pieces were large enough to leave bruises and welts. A chunk of wood the size of a watermelon missed his ear by inches.

A cloud of dust and smoke rose. Holding his breath, Bolan wheeled and flung himself around the corner toward cabin three. He had to reach it before the terrorist reloaded. With a range of close to five hundred yards, the RPG-7 could reach any of the Feds along the perimeter. The missile packed the explosive power of five grenades rolled into one and would exact a costly toll.

Groping through the cloud, Bolan nearly tripped over the body of a SWAT member. He stepped over it, groped right, groped left, and suddenly the doorway was straight ahead. Sprinting across the jamb, he saw the terrorist feeding another missile into the launcher.

The fanatic was caught flat-footed but made a stab for an Uzi on the floor at his feet.

Bolan emptied his magazine. When the last of the shells had clattered to the floor, he slapped a new magazine in and went outside.

Downing ran up to him, worry on her face. "For a second there, when he fired that missile at you I thought you were history."

"You did good nailing the one in the window," Bolan complimented her. "One day that dream of yours will come true."

Crampton and a knot of agents were hurrying from the field. Now that the crisis was over, the AD was in full operational mode and dispensing orders as if he were a four-star general. "Havelson, get the vehicles up here ASAP. Ziegler, I want this whole area taped off. Stinson, get cracking on the fingerprints. Caldwell, I want all these cabins gone over with a fine-tooth comb. We might find a clue as to where the rest of this bunch went."

Bolan slung his M-16 and moved toward the parking lot. His presence was no longer required. If the FBI learned anything important, they were under orders to relay it up the chain of command to Brognola. He unclipped his cell phone.

"Mr. Belasko, a word with you if I might?" Crampton placed a hand on the warrior's shoulder. "I would take it as a personal favor if you wouldn't mention my little lapse a while ago to anyone higher up. If you get my drift."

"Never again," Bolan muttered.

"Pardon?"

"Nothing." Bolan shrugged off the hand, turned on the phone and tapped the number for his ride home. Grimaldi had promised to stay nearby and be ready for a swift liftoff. "Get me out of here," was all Bolan said.

"You will, won't you? Keep quiet, I mean?" Crompton pressed. "I'd hate for it to reflect adversely on my career."

"I'll do what's best."

"Thank you!" Crampton declared, and pumped Bolan's hand in gratitude. "In return, you can count on me for a glowing account of your performance in my report to the director. I'm a firm believer in spreading the credit around so everyone benefits." Beaming happily, he waltzed toward his agents.

Bolan shook his head. The AD had misunderstood. In this case what was best was to let Brognola know it would be a bleak day for America if Assistant Director Crampton ever rose a notch higher in the Bureau hierarchy.

A gleaming Cobra blazed out of the sun. It hovered for all of two seconds over the parking lot, then touched down as lightly as a feather. The canopy rose, revealing the grinning features of Jack Grimaldi. "You rang, boss?"

Bolan glanced over his shoulder. Agents were swarming over the cabins like bees over a hive. In front of cabin three, staring at her reflection in a broken pane of glass, was Agent Downing. She was touching a finger to the tip of her nose.

THE RIDE TO Philadelphia was much too long to suit Aban Abbas. Every minute wasted was another minute the American authorities had to track them down, and he couldn't bear the thought of being thwarted. Not after all he and his brothers had gone through. Not after the cost to Al-Jabbar in money and men, and the loss of their headquarters in Somalia.

Sefu was driving the SUV, Aban beside him. In the back seat were Rakin and Sharif. Jamilah followed in the sedan along with Barakah, Yasin and Hosef.

Abbas had left the rest of his followers at the lodge to get ready for the assault on Washington, D.C. Every weapon had to be cleaned and reloaded, every piece of ordnance inspected. He tried to raise their contact, Mukhtar, on his cell phone again, but there was no answer.

"Relax, big brother," Sefu said. "He is not expecting us for another ninety minutes yet. He could be anywhere." Sefu nudged him. "I can't believe we are together again. You have no idea how much I have missed you."

Abbas smiled. His younger sibling had always looked up to him. "I have missed you, too."

"When this is over I hope we will have some time to ourselves. I would like to hear about Mother and our brothers and sisters. I miss them. I miss our native land, our native people."

"Then you will be pleased to learn that when this is over, you are to return with us," Abbas announced.

Sefu was so stunned he inadvertently let up on the gas. The speedometer dropped from sixty-five to forty-five, and only the honking of the horn in Jamilah's sedan snapped him out of it. Accelerating again, he said breathlessly, "Do you mean it? Honestly and truly mean it?"

"After we destroy the National Security Agency, we will be the most wanted men on the planet," Abbas predicted. "The Americans and their allies will stop at nothing to ferret us out. We must recall all our brothers and go deep into hiding."

Rakin made a sound somewhere between a snort and snicker. "I do not like the idea of cowering from our enemies."

Abbas shifted. "It is common sense, nothing more. Remember Afghanistan? Would you have us suffer the same fate as the Taliban?"

"You overestimate these Americans," Rakin asserted. "They are not the gods of technology they pretend to be."

"And you underestimate them if you think they will leave any stone unturned in their search for us." Abbas had never liked having his decisions questioned. He particularly didn't like being challenged in front of his younger brother. But he swallowed his pride for the time being since he had need of the renegade Saudi's deep purse. "Have more faith in me, my friend. When the time is ripe we will renew our war on the Great Satan. Until then, we will rely on you for much of our sustenance, and will be forever in your debt."

Rakin wasn't pacified. "I did not join your organization to serve as its treasury. I do not mind funding Al-Jabbar as long as my money is put to use destroying those who would strip Muslims of their rightful religion."

"How can you find fault with our leader?" Sharik came to Abbas's defense. "Look at all the great work he has accomplished. The destruction of the Echelon site, the many assassinations. And now he is about to do what no others have ever done. To strike at the very heart of the Great Satan in so spectacular a manner, the whole world will marvel.''

"Speaking of which,'' Rakin said, ''we have yet to learn exactly how we are to achieve our mission. It is not as if we can walk into NSA headquarters unchallenged. There are bound to be a multitude of guards, security cameras and more.''

Abbas glanced out the rear window at Jamilah before answering. ''In terrorism, as in any endeavor, the simplest approach is the best. I have done my research, as always. Yes, the NSA buildings are extremely well protected. But did you know that they, like the FBI and the CIA, allow visitors inside? Not into sensitive areas, to be sure. But politicians, journalists, even schoolchildren are given limited run of certain floors.''

"Is that how you plan to get us in?'' Rakin sneered. "Posing as journalists? We would not get ten meters in the door.''

"Do not insult my intelligence like that ever again,'' Abbas said sternly. "I intend to exploit another flaw in their security. One ideally suited for what I have in mind.'' It would also, if all went well, solve the other little problem he had. Although the thought of disposing of Jamilah troubled him deeply. It wasn't her fault he couldn't control his baser urges.

Abbas stared out the window. It wasn't too late to reconsider. Maybe the others wouldn't think less of him if they learned of his dalliance. For a moment he wavered. But only a moment. He couldn't bear to have the image he had worked so hard to achieve tarnished. He could not bear to have his followers think he was too weak-willed to resist the needs he had criticized in others. He was their leader, their teacher, their master. He should be above carnal temptations.

A tiny voice at the back of Abbas's mind objected. It urged that the step he was contemplating was too drastic. He should banish Jamilah from Al-Jabbar, not kill her. Yet that was bound to incite talk behind his back. The others might suspect and might think less of him, even as Sharik now did.

Abbas steeled himself. He had to be true to his original purpose. Later, once the deed was done, he would ask God for forgiveness and get on with his life. And pray he was never tempted again.

Traffic was heavy but they made good time. They had left the Huntsman's Lodge at 4:00 a.m. in order to arrive in Philadelphia by nine, and pulled into Mukhtar's driveway forty minutes early. His house was in an older neighborhood, set back from the street amid towering maple trees.

Stretching, Abbas moved past a van to a concrete walk. The yard was freshly mowed, a flower garden flourishing. From a bronze post on the front porch hung a small American flag.

"Is this Mukhtar one of us or one of them?" Rakin groused. "We should cut this accursed thing into pieces."

"Mukhtar is blending in, as he was instructed," Abbas said, and rang the doorbell.

In a few seconds the door opened. Mukhtar was in his late sixties, much too old for the front ranks of the Holy War. But he was invaluable in other respects and as devoted to the cause as the rest of them. "Would you care for some refreshment, great one?" he offered. "I have some prepared."

"I would rather see the Eye of God first," Abbas said.

"Of course, of course," Mukhtar responded. "I

had the men who delivered it place the crate in the basement. Follow me.''

"Were there any problems?" Abbas inquired as they filed down a hallway.

"None at all, great one. The crate cleared customs without a hitch. The express delivery must have cost you a fortune for something that size.''

Sefu stepped up close. "What is this Eye of God? Why have I never heard of it?''

"You will see shortly,'' Abbas answered. At the end of the hall was a doorway and a flight of steps leading down. The terrorist leader had been able to contain his excitement so far, but now, as he reached the bottom and Mukhtar switched on the light, he saw the crate and an electric bolt shot through his body. "Open it.''

Sharik, Jebel, Barakah and Yasin sprang to obey. Using a crowbar and a large screwdriver supplied by Mukhtar, they soon had the top off and were piling the packing material to one side. When they saw the four large Etruscan-style vases, they looked at one another in bewilderment.

"Lift them out,'' Abbas directed. "One will be heavier than the others. Place that one before me.''

Everyone crowded around. The vase was waist high, twice as broad at the bottom as at the top, and exquisitely detailed.

Abbas tapped it a few times. Only an expert could tell it wasn't a real Etruscan vase. And thanks to the special alloy shielding, not even an X-ray machine could detect the false bottom and the cavity underneath. "Break it open. But do so carefully.''

It was the work of moments for the four men to reduce the vase to so many broken segments, revealing an oval object about the size of a soccer ball wrapped in heavy padding.

Motioning for the others to move back, Abbas squatted and removed the padding himself. And there it was, in all its gleaming majesty. He placed his hands on the cool metal and said softly, "The Eye of God."

"What is it, Aban?" Sefu asked. "Surely we can't destroy NSA headquarters with something so small?"

"Surely we can," Abbas declared. "What you are looking at is one of the world's first tactical cobalt bombs."

CHAPTER TWENTY

Rumors, rumors and more rumors. They poured into the intelligence community every day, from every country on every continent. Separating the chaff from the legitimate kernels was an ongoing chore. Most turned out to be false, the product of hearsay or misinformation. A few, a precious few, turned out to be genuine and more than made up for the many false leads.

This latest bit of intel had Hal Brongola worried. Swiveling back and forth in his chair at Stony Man Farm, he reread the report from Interpol that was relayed to him less than an hour ago. A major illicit arms dealer had been arrested the day before, a Libyan operating out of Crete, with strong ties to many Arab countries. As part of a plea bargain, he had agreed to spill some juicy tidbits. The juiciest was his claim to have brokered a deal between a terrorist organization and Iraq for a newly developed cobalt nuke.

The organization was Al-Jabbar.

Brognola had been inclined to dismiss it at first. Everyone knew Iraq had been trying to go nuclear for decades now, and the best intel suggested they had gotten nowhere. Nor had there ever been so much as a whisper they were working on a cobalt bomb. "Dirty nukes," the devices were called, because cobalt bombs spewed radioactive particles into the atmosphere that stayed radioactive far longer than those from other types of nuclear bombs, and consequently contaminated a much wider area. He shuddered to think what would happen if one ever fell into the hands of fanatics like Al-Jabbar. They would have no qualms about using it.

But did they have one? Brognola doubted it until a second message from Interpol showed up mere minutes ago. The arms dealer had provided more details. Apparently he had dealt with Aban Abbas personally, and had learned Abbas planned to have the device shipped quickly to the United States so it would be waiting when he and his followers got there.

That last made Brognola sit up and rethink his outlook. How else could the arms dealer have known Al-Jabbar was coming to America unless he had really talked to someone belonging to Al-Jabbar? And that bit about Abbas wanting the bomb to be waiting for them when they arrived was exactly what Abbas *would* want.

Brognola had hoped the FBI raid would net them all the terrorists in one fell swoop, but only four had been accounted for. Seven or eight remained at large. And although the President had authorized the greatest manhunt in the history of North America, it took time to put the wheels of law enforcement into motion—time Brognola was afraid they didn't have.

Every agency at the federal, state and local level was being asked to go all out on this one, to expend every resource. The stakes had been high when it was thought Al-Jabbar had conventional explosives. Now that they might have a cobalt bomb, the stakes were astronomical.

As if all that weren't enough, there was an added dimension to consider. According to the arms merchant, the cobalt nuke wasn't a full-size version but one no bigger than a basketball, a little bundle of thermonuclear horror that could be stashed anywhere and programmed to go off when the terrorists were miles away. There wasn't a fanatic anywhere who wouldn't give their eyeteeth to get hold of it.

At least Brognola had a few new angles to work on. First and foremost, every shipping company was being checked. If Abbas had sent the nuke to America through a legitimate carrier, there would be a record of it somewhere. Smart of Abbas, Brognola thought, to go that route, rather than have it smuggled in. Customs inspectors weren't quite as diligent about inspecting the shipments of major carriers.

A light rap on the door brought the big Fed's musing to an end, and he turned his chair. "Feel free."

Barbara Price had that look she wore when she had good news to import. "We haven't heard about the fingerprints or from the lab boys yet, but the phone company has come through with a list of all the phone calls to and from the Huntsman's Lodge since Sefu Abbas checked in under an assumed name."

"And?" Brognola said hopefully.

"There weren't all that many. Only seventeen, in fact. Except for three, they were all local calls. Most likely made by the owner, Carl Lester, whose body was found stuffed in a closet in the office."

Brognola knew that tone. He sat up, his elbows on the desk. "The other three?"

"Were all placed to the same number in Philadelphia. To a Mr. Jonas Periwinkle. Age, sixty-eight. A retired machinist. He resides at 137 Thorndyke, in northwest Philly. He's lived there for thirty-seven years. No criminal record that I could find. Not so much as a parking ticket in all that time.''

"Thirty-seven years?" Brognola repeated. "Doesn't sound like your typical sleeper, does he?" Most had been in-country for a much shorter span, on average from five to ten years. Then there was the name. Usually sleepers chose names like "Smith" and "Brown," common, ordinary names to better suit the image they wanted to give of being common, ordinary Americans. "Periwinkle" was about as unordinary as a name could get.

"He didn't fit the profile, no," Price said. "Then I did some digging. It seems Mr. Periwinkle emigrated to the U.S. from Libya and changed his name. Over there he was known as Mukhtar al-Samussi."

"A lot of foreign nationals change their names," Brognola mentioned. Still, the simple fact the terrorists had called this Periwinkle—or al-Samussi—so many times was a red flag meriting investigation. "Where are Striker and Jack about now?"

"Somewhere over southern Pennsylvania or northern New Jersey, depending on how long it took them to refuel.''

"Have them divert. Tell Jack to land at Willow Grove Naval Air Station. I'll call and arrange special clearance. And give Striker Periwinkle's address."

"You want him to go in alone?"

"After the fiasco in the Catskills, you bet I do.'' Brognola almost forgot the most important item of all, and called Price's name as she was going out the door. She poked her head in.

"Yes?"

"Fill Striker in on the intel about the cobalt bomb. Advise him from this point on all the stops are out. I want Al-Jabbar taken down, and I mean hard."

THE EXECUTIONER cruised around the block twice in the rented car that had been waiting for him at Willow Grove Naval Air Station, courtesy of Hal Brognola. He had changed into his civvies and his trench coat and was armed with the Beretta 93-R and the Desert Eagle. In the back seat was his duffel.

The neighborhood lay quiet under the midday sun. Most of the homes were Gothic style and well-maintained. He pulled to the curb in front of 137 Thorndyke and got out, making sure to lock the doors. Tall trees shaded him as he walked up a curved drive, past a van parked in front of the garage.

An old man was puttering in a flower garden and quietly humming. Bolan had seen him from the street. One hand under his jacket, he stood close to the corner of the garage so no one inside the house could fire on him and said, "Mr. Periwinkle? I'd like a word with you."

Periwinkle looked up. He didn't seem the slightest bit surprised to find a stranger almost on his doorstep. "Yes, young man? How can I be of service?"

"Where are they?"

"To whom do you refer?" Perwinkle's English was excellent. "I don't have the foggiest notion what you're talking about."

"The men who were here earlier," Bolan bluffed. "Playing games will get you nowhere. If you don't tell me, you'll tell the federal agents when they take you into custody."

"Is it illegal to grow flowers now?" Periwinkle joked. Setting down his trowel, he rose and brushed off his pants. "There must be some mistake. Come inside. I'll treat you to a cup of coffee and we can sort this out."

Bolan wanted to go in anyway to check the house over. Drawing the Beretta, he held it under his jacket. "Lead the way," he said, watching the windows closely.

Periwinkle moved stiffly. "These old legs of mine aren't what they used to be. Half an hour of gardening and I can barely walk. It's true what everyone says. Old age really is a bear."

"Do they say that in Libya, too, Mukhtar al-Samussi?"

"There's a similar saying, yes. But how in the world did you know my old name and where I'm from?" Periwinkle wistfully smiled. "I haven't thought about my early years in ages. It brings back some fond memories. And a lot of bad ones. Times were tough back then, young man. I wanted a new, better life for myself, so I scrimped and saved until I had enough money for passage to America. Never regretted my decision, either." He opened the front door and gestured for Bolan to go in ahead of him.

"After you."

"You can have a seat if you'd like," Periwinkle said, jabbing a thumb at the living room. "It won't take me but a few minutes."

Bolan kept on following. An air of total stillness gripped the house, persuading him they were the only ones there. But he didn't relax his guard. "What is Al-Jabbar up to, Mukhtar?"

"Who?"

"We know they've contacted you. Tell us what they're up to and the Feds will go a lot easier on you."

"Sonny, if I had any idea what you were talking about, I'd gladly do as you've requested. But for the life of me, I've never heard of any Al-whatsis."

They entered the kitchen, which was a mess. Dirty plates and saucers were heaped high in the sink, and used coffee cups had been left on the counter. An open loaf of bread was on the table, along with a butter dish and several butter knives.

"I had a bunch of my bowling buddies over this morning," Periwinkle said, stepping to a coffeemaker. "Still got half a pot left. Or would you rather I make a fresh one?"

"Sit down at the table so we can talk," Bolan directed him, but the old man ignored him.

Periwinkle switched on the machine and opened a cupboard. "I don't know about you, but I can never get enough. Guess I'm a caffeine addict." He took down two cups. "The only other addiction I have is to vanilla fudge."

Bolan let the man prattle. Lowering the Beretta to his side, he waited for what was sure to come.

"At my age caffeine and sweets give you a little extra energy," Periwinkle was saying as he slowly opened a drawer. "And I can use all the energy I can get." He paused. "We'll each need spoons for the cream and sugar."

Bolan leveled his pistol.

For someone his age, Periwinkle could move fast when he had to. His hand swept out of the drawer clutching a ten-inch steak knife, and whirling, he raised it overhead and sprang. But he had only taken a couple of steps when he saw the Beretta, and stopped as abruptly as if he had run into an unseen wall.

"Drop it or die."

For a moment it appeared the old man would choose suicide. He elevated the knife another inch or two and took a step, then faltered. Licking his thin lips, he stared at the Beretta's muzzle and said softly, "I like living."

"The knife," Bolan reiterated.

It hit the floor with the ring of steel on tile, and Periwinkle shuffled to the table and sank into a chair. Covering his face, he groaned.

The soldier unclipped his cell phone. A car full of federal agents and a cleanup crew consisting of Brognola's own people were awaiting word five blocks away.

Periwinkle looked up, his eyes brimming with tears. "I did it for the money more than anything. Before Al-Jabbar I worked for some others. They paid extremely well."

"All I care about is where Abbas went from here."

"You've got to understand. I didn't know what was in that crate. I swear I didn't. When he told us what it was, I couldn't believe my ears. I mean, guns and plastic explosives I could understand. But a thermonuclear device?" Periwinkle began to cry.

Bolan went over and squatted in front of him. "It's true, then? Bin Abbas got his hands on a cobalt bomb?"

The old man nodded, his cheeks glistening. Coughing to clear his throat, he said, "Dinky little thing. You'd never guess to look at it. I asked him how powerful it was, and he said it has a blast radius of about a half mile."

More than enough to destroy the heart of a major city, Bolan reflected. Strategically placed, it could wipe out the White House and Congress.

"I never guessed he'd go this far or I'd never have wanted any part of it," Periwinkle rambled on. "I don't want to go down in history as being party to the worst terrorist act in the history of the world." He broke into deep, racking sobs. "What have I done?"

Bolan gripped his arm. "Snap out of it and tell me where they've gone."

Sniffling, Periwinkle got a grip on himself enough to say, "I'll tell everything I know for complete and total immunity. Otherwise you can forget it. At my age, I wouldn't last a year behind bars."

"I'm not the person to talk to."

"Then you'd better get on that phone with whoever is. Because I'm the only one who can help you stop Abbas." Periwinkle wiped a sleeve across his face. "And you don't have forever."

Bolan phoned Brognola's office at the Farm and was mildly surprised when Barbara Price answered. "Where's Hal? It's urgent."

"Aaron needed to talk to him about a glitch with one of the Crays. He should be back shortly."

"I need him right away." Bolan explained why, and she set down the phone and hurried off.

He glanced at a clock on the wall above the stove. It was one-thirty. "How much time *do* we have?"

"I wish I knew. Abbas is playing this one pretty close to the vest."

"You must have some idea."

"All I can tell you is that he plans to set the bomb, then catch a freighter out of Baltimore. But whether that's tonight or tomorrow, I couldn't say."

"It doesn't sound like you know anything worth immunity."

"I know the target he's picked, and how he plans to go about sneaking the bomb in," Periwinkle said. "That should count for something." He wiped at his face again. "And I know something else. All those people who died at the World Trade Center will be a drop in the bucket compared to how many will die this time."

THE SUV AND SEDAN were traveling north out of Philadelphia on Interstate 95, and Sefu was relating how he had killed the owner of the Huntsman's Lodge and outfoxed the FBI.

Aban Abbas had the radio tuned to an all news station, as was his habit. When mention was made of a special bulletin concerning a clash with terrorists, he barked, "Quiet!" and turned up the volume.

"WNEX news has learned that earlier toady agents of the Federal Bureau of Investigation engaged as yet unidentified terrorists in a gun battle at a secluded hunting lodge in the Catskill Mountains in New York. Details are sketchy at this point, but it is known several agents lost their lives and several more were airlifted to a New York-area hospital in critical condition—"

"No!" Rakin cried. "What of Muzaffer and the rest?"

"WNEX has also learned at least three terrorists were slain and a fourth might have been airlifted to the same hospital and is now under guard. The FBI has called a news conference in an hour, and WNEX will have more information as it becomes available.''

The station resumed a rundown of sports scores from the night before. Abbas turned down the volume and glanced sharply at Sefu. ''So you outfoxed the FBI, did you?'' Placing his hands on the dash, he bowed his head. ''But the blame is not entirely yours. I should never have left them behind.''

''What now, great one?'' Sharik asked. ''Do we call off this holy mission?''

''Never!'' Abbas was incensed by the suggestion. ''We owe it to ourselves as well as our fallen brothers to see it through to the end.'' He pointed at a sign ahead. ''Sefu, take the next exit and get on the interstate heading south. We must reach a town near our target no later than five-thirty.'' From a pocket he took a map, unfolded it and showed his brother where they were in relation to where they had to go.

''We can make it in time,'' Sefu promised.

Originally, Abbas had planned to place the cobalt bomb in close proximity to the NSA's headquarters early next morning, then race to Baltimore and be on a freighter leaving at noon. But if the news report was right and one of his followers had been taken prisoner, the man might talk. It was well known in terrorist circles that Americans used drugs and torture to loosen tongues that wouldn't loosen otherwise. The Americans denied it, naturally, but it was just another of their many lies.

Muzaffer and the others at the lodge hadn't known about the cobalt bomb, but they did know the target, which was why Abbas now felt he had to push up the timetable. But based on the information Mukhtar supplied, only one window of opportunity existed. Any other time would incite suspicion.

As the two vehicles sped south, Abbas mulled over what to do. It became clear a diversion was called for. The only thing was, whoever took part stood little hope of making it out alive. He glanced at Sharik, then out the rear window at Jamilah, and all the pieces fell into place.

Little was said the rest of the ride. Occasionally one of the others would glance at the bomb, nestled in a blanket between Sharik and Rakin, but they kept their thoughts to themselves.

The National Security Agency was headquartered at Fort George C. Meade in Maryland. Located some eighteen miles southwest of Baltimore, the fort covered more than fourteen thousand acres and was the command site for various Army units. Security, needless to say, was tight.

From the outset, Abbas knew he faced two problems. First, how to get onto the base unnoticed. Second, finding a suitable spot to plant the bomb. Although it could be hidden anywhere within the fort's boundaries and it would still destroy the NSA when it detonated, for personal as well as practical reasons Abbas wanted to secret the device as close as possible to NSA headquarters.

Vehicles, though, weren't allowed past a certain point.

With one exception.

It was no secret the National Security Agency employed enough people to make the Fortune 500 list.

The majority worked at two monolithic buildings within a quarter mile of each other. Exact numbers were hard to come by, but Abbas had seen an article that mentioned as many as seven thousand people worked in each.

That many people generated a lot of paperwork, and a lot of trash. Tons daily. Much of it was classified and was disposed of by NSA personnel either by shredding or burning.

The rest was hauled away by a private contractor.

Mukhtar al-Sumussi had spent several days last week watching the comings and goings at Fort Meade from a park near the north entrance. Abbas had instructed him to be on the lookout for utility and service vehicles that entered the base daily, and the giant orange sanitation trucks, with the company name painted on them in big, bold letters, were hard to miss. Or to lose when Mukhtar shadowed them.

At exactly 5:37 p.m., the SUV and the sedan pulled up in front of Premier Sanitation, Incorporated, in Severn, Maryland, after making a circuit of the block. A single-story brick building housed the company offices. Behind it was a parking lot for the trucks, ringed by a seven-foot-high chain-link fence. A gate at the rear of the lot hung open.

"Everyone out." Abbas slid from the SUV and beckoned to Jamilah and the others. Only a few pedestrians were abroad, and there was no traffic to speak of. "Jamilah, Rakin and I will go in the front. The rest of you are to go around back and in through the gate. Kill everyone, but do it discreetly and hide the bodies. We will meet by the trucks."

Abbas approached the double glass doors bearing the company logo. His jacket concealed a Turkish-made 9 mm Kirrikale, one of a case supplied by the smugglers in Kildana. His had a stubby custom sound suppressor attached.

A petite secretary in a small reception area greeted them with a friendly smile. "Good afternoon, and welcome to Premier Sanitation. How may I help you?"

"Is anyone in?" Smiling suavely, Abbas nodded at two doors behind her. One that read William Petersen, President.

"Mr. Petersen is," the secretary said, "but as a general rule you can't see him without an appointment."

"I can." Drawing his pistol, Abbas shot her.

Jamilah caught the woman as she slumped and quietly eased her to the floor, while Rakin locked the door and pulled the blinds.

William Petersen was a portly man in his late forties. He was picking his teeth with a silver toothpick when Abbas entered and quickly dropped his hand to his lap, embarrassed to be caught in the act. "Who are you?" he demanded, flustered. "And how did you get past Dierdre?"

"Like this," Abbas told him.

A bullet through the left eye ended Petersen's teeth-picking days, and Rakin hauled the body to a closet and rolled it inside.

Abbas led them to the other door, which opened onto a long, narrow hall.

The first room they came to was empty but in the next, which had a coffee machine, a pop machine and a machine full of candy bars along one wall, sat three men in orange coveralls with Premier Sanitation printed on the back. They were drinking coffee and talking, and stopped in amazement when Jamilah walked in.

"Whoa, baby! Talk about a hottie," the youngest teased. "Am I ever glad you came into my life."

"I doubt that," Jamilah said sweetly, and shot all three dead with three perfectly placed shots through the head.

At the end of the hall was another door that led onto a platform. Five orange trucks were backed up against it, with a parking space for a sixth.

Jebel was out by the gate, looking as nervous as a kitten in a room full of dogs. Barakah, Yasin, Malik and Sefu saw Abbas and climbed stairs to the platform.

"There's not a soul back here, brother," Sefu reported.

"The rest of the workers have gone home," Jamilah guessed.

Abbas walked to the edge and nodded at the empty slot. "Not quite. One truck has yet to arrive. Sefu, stay out here with Jebel and Malik. When the last driver shows up, dispose of him, then join the rest of us in the owner's office."

While in there, Abbas had noticed a large wall map. Studying it, he discovered it covered Severn, parts of Glen Burnie, Southgate and Odenton, and Fort Meade. The daily routes had been highlighted in erasable marker with a different color for each truck. Pickup times were also noted.

Jamilah was beside him. "The next pickup at the NSA is not until eight o'clock tomorrow morning."

"I know."

"Can we afford to wait that long?"

"No. As soon as the missing truck arrives, we will put the last phase into operation." Abbas sat on the desk and laughed.

Jamalah's delicate eyebrows pinched together. "I don't see the humor."

"Don't you?" Abbas laughed harder. "We are about to attack the National Security Agency in garbage trucks. If that isn't humorous, I don't know what is."

CHAPTER TWENTY-ONE

The Cobra streaked over the Maryland countryside at its top speed of close to 150 miles an hour. A casual onlooker might compare it to a giant locust winging in for the kill, and that was exactly what it was.

Perched in the front of the cockpit in the seat normally filled by the co-pilot-gunner, the Executioner watched another town flash by under them. Kids stopped what they were doing to gawk in awe. Some adults waved. All were blissfully unaware the Grim Reaper was poised to wipe out tens of thousands of them unless a band of hate-filled fanatics was stopped before it was too late.

"Almost there, Sarge," Jack Grimaldi announced. "Too bad these babies don't come with CD systems. We could crank up 'Flight of the Valkyrie' and do this in style."

"A joke at a time like this?"

"Who's joking? Didn't you ever see *Apocalypse Now*? That scene where the choppers go roaring in with Wagner blaring is the greatest in movie history."

"You could always hum it," Bolan said dryly.

"A joke, at a time like this?" Grimaldi mimicked him. "And from you, no less. Now I know the world is coming to an end."

Despite himself, Bolan grinned. His friend was only trying to loosen him up. To go into combat too tense was almost as bad a mistake as not taking it seriously enough. His helmet headset crackled again, but not with Grimaldi's voice. The pilot was patching Brognola through.

"Striker? What's your ETA?"

"Any moment now. What's the latest at your end?"

"I've cleared you with the military and the FAA. You are cleared to enter any and all restricted airspace and won't have an F-16 breathing down your neck. I've also talked to the commander at Fort Meade and he's put the base on red alert. They're doubling the gate guards. No one will get in without an ID check and a vehicle search."

"That will help," Bolan said. But it was well to remember a little thing like that wouldn't stop someone as determined and resourceful as Aban Abbas. "What about the National Security Agency?"

"I've spoken to the NSA chief, and they're evacuating all nonessential personnel from their buildings. Since we don't want a panic on our hands, the word's being spread that the buildings need to be checked for possible anthrax contamination." The big Fed sighed. "If only we knew exactly how much time we have."

Bolan understood. It would take a good hour or more to evacuate that many people.

"One other thing. We still can't get through to Premier Sanitation. We keep getting their answering machine. They close at six, so it might mean nothing."

By Bolan's watch it was ten minutes past seven. He could have been there a lot sooner but Mukhtar al-Samussi had refused to reveal details of Abbas's plan until he had the immunity agreement in writing. Brognola had to call a federal attorney in Philadelphia, wasting more valuable time. The Libyan got his wish, but he wasn't getting off as free as he hoped. For while the agreement granted him immunity from prosecution, it didn't protect him from having his citizenship revoked and being deported to Libya on the next ship out.

"This should be Severn below us," Grimaldi announced.

The Cobra was flying so low and so fast, to Bolan every town and suburb looked pretty much the same. His friend had the benefit of being linked to the most sophisticated GPS equipment in the world at Stony Man, and seconds later Grimaldi brought them in directly over Premier Sanitation and hovered.

Three orange sanitation trucks were parked adjacent to a platform at the rear. A gate in the fence was shut and secured with a padlock. All the blinds in the windows had been drawn, and no one was moving about.

Grimaldi swung the copter around and Bolan plainly saw a Closed sign on the front door.

"Looks normal enough, doesn't it?"

That it did, Bolan agreed. "Maybe we beat them here." In which case he could arrange a suitable surprise. "Is there space enough around back for you to set down?"

"Need you ask?"

The Cobra lifted over the building and out over the lot. From their new angle Bolan could see into the cabs of the trucks. All were empty. "I want you to drop me off, then go back up and wait. While I'm inside, contact Hal and ask him if he can find out exactly how many trucks the company owns."

"You think some are missing?"

"Could be," Bolan said. The three vacant spaces bothered him.

"Hold on to your stomach," Grimaldi advised him.

The Cobra dropped like a rock but landed so gently there was barely a sensation of setting down. The instant the canopy was open, Bolan removed his helmet, slung the MP-5 over his shoulder, slid out and dropped. Darting to the nearest truck, he waited until Grimaldi had taken the bird up before bounding up the steps.

All seemed peaceful enough. Bolan glided to the back door and tried the knob. It was locked, as it should be. Stepping back, he triggered a burst into the wood around the lock, then planted his foot where it would do the most good.

The door slammed inward, revealing a darkened hallway. All the lights in the building were off, and it was as quiet as a tomb.

Bolan warily advanced. The owner might have a fit about the door, but time was of the essence. Brognola could always apologize and offer to reimburse him.

Something—a sense of movement—brought the soldier to a stop. Crouching, he strained his senses to their limit, but nothing out of the ordinary registered. As silent as a specter, he crept to a doorway. It was a break room filled with food machines, a long table and chairs. Nothing seemed out of place, and he started to move on when he spied dark splotches near a chair. Drops of liquid of some kind. Spilled pop, he thought, but it wouldn't hurt to see.

As Bolan stepped into the doorway, a shadow detached itself from the side of a candy bar machine. He flung himself into the hall a microsecond ahead of hammering autofire. Simultaneously, another shadow appeared at the end of the hall and cut loose. The rounds missed by a whisker.

Bolan returned fire, and the gunner down the hall disappeared. He flattened as the one in the break room fired through the wall, trying to catch him with a lucky shot. After that, silence descended.

The hallway was too exposed. Past the break room, on the left, was another doorway. If Bolan could reach it, he would be in a perfect position to keep an eye on the break room doorway and the end of the hall without showing himself. Suiting the thought to deed, he levered upright. The terrorist in the break room belatedly woke up and hastily fired, stitching the wall in his wake.

Ducking into the room, Bolan squatted. He ejected the MP-5's magazine even though it was only a third empty and replaced it with a full one. A grenade would come in handy, but he had left them in his duffel in the chopper.

"American! You hear me?"

Bolan shifted toward the front of the building. The terrorist's English was atrocious, the words barely understandable.

"We know you! You demon, eh?"

Bolan had no idea what the man meant.

"Greece! Turkey! Somalia! Yes?"

His cheek to the MP-5, Bolan wished the guy would show himself.

"Great one know come! We wait! We kill!"

Focused on the end of the hall, Bolan almost missed spotting a figure flick across the break room doorway. He pivoted, thinking the guy up front was trying to draw his attention so the other one could nail him.

"Barakah, Yasin, kill demon! Barakah promise!"

Now Bolan knew their names. It was careless, just as it was careless of Barakah to yell and give his position away. The man was either an idiot or he was up to something. And since everything Al-Jabbar did had the cunning hand of Aban Abbas behind it, idiocy was ruled out.

Minute followed slow minute, but neither of the terrorists made a move. Bolan began to wonder if they were deliberately trying to delay him, to keep him there so he couldn't go after the others. But that presupposed Abbas expected him to show up, which seemed a bit far-fetched.

"Demon! You there?"

Bolan unfurled to his full height. If they expected him to play by their rules, they had another think coming.

Barakah shouted in Arabic and the man in the break room, Yasin, responded.

Now Bolan had a good idea where they both were. Palming the Desert Eagle, he tossed it well past the break-room door. The big pistol smacked the floor with a loud crack and slid several feet.

Yasin did exactly as the soldier wanted; he peered around the jamb to see what had made the noise.

The laser sight's red dot was a quarter-inch above the terrorist's right ear when Bolan stroked the MP-5. A short burst, only four rounds, yet it chewed Yasin's skull apart like termites chewing through wood pulp. Yasin's knees caved and he folded like a broken accordion.

Barakah called out in alarm in Arabic, and after a minute did so again but in English. "Demon! My friend dead?"

Bolan glued his gaze on the end of the hall, his

finger wrapped around the trigger. All he needed was a glimpse. Just a glimpse.

"Yasin! Yasin!" Barakah cried, then growled like an angry beast.

"Demon! You hear me? You kill friend. Now Barakah kill, too, eh?"

Bolan heard a sound he couldn't quite place. A shaft of sunlight pierced the hallway. Then, somewhere outside, a woman screamed and was silenced by the chatter of an SMG. Comprehension dawned. The blood in Bolan's veins became ice. He sped down the hall, fearing what he would find when he reached the street. He was flying across a reception area when the SMG chattered a second time, but not so near.

Only a few yards from the entrance a middle-aged woman was sprawled in a spreading scarlet pool, the grocery bag she had been carrying as riddled as she was.

Farther down the sidewalk were two teenagers, a boy and a girl, the girl thrashing in the throes of impending death.

At the far corner on the right was Barakah. He smiled a cruel smile and ran up the next street, his SMG spitting a lethal refrain every few seconds.

The fanatic was gunning down every civilian in sight. Bolan raced toward the corner as more screams and panicked shouts filled the air. By the time he got there the terrorist was nowhere to be seen, but he had left seven bodies as a testimonial to his thirst for vengeance. From around the next corner on the left came more autofire, the screech of brakes and a resounding crash, then what sounded like a child screeching in terror. A screech terminated by Barakah's SMG.

Bolan's blood was no longer ice. It was molten fire.

He came to the next corner and beheld more grisly slaughter, five bodies and a car that had crashed into the front of a jewelry store. He also saw Barakah fly around yet another corner at the end of the block. The bastard was a two-legged antelope.

Sirens wailed in the distance.

His legs churning, Bolan desperately sought to overtake the fiend. To his rear came the whoosh of rotor blades, and the Cobra dipped low and hovered. Grimaldi tapped his headset, then gestured as if asking what he should do. Bolan waved him on, signaling to show the direction Barakah had gone. Nodding, Grimaldi arced over the intervening buildings.

It only took the soldier a few seconds to round the next intersection. The Cobra was hovering midway down the block, next to the neon facade to a bowling alley. Grimaldi pointed at the glass doors. Shrieks and yells erupted inside amid the dull bark of Barakah's damnable weapon.

Bolan was reaching for one of the handles when a heavyset woman stumbled out, nearly knocking him over. Her eyes were wide in shock, her flowery blouse spattered with blood that did not appear to be hers.

"He's killing them!" she shrilled. "He's killing everybody!"

A lump of raw anger formed in Bolan's throat. He pounded up a carpeted walkway and saw people fearfully huddled under tables and behind racks of bowling balls, anywhere they could find a place to hide. Bodies were all over the place. Lying near the counter, next to a row of video games, littering the alleys. Nine, ten, eleven, he couldn't count them all.

An exit door on the other side of the building crashed open, disgorging Barakah. Bolan gave chase, and in his eagerness to end the carnage he almost committed a cardinal blunder. He almost burst outside without stopping to look.

The exit door opened onto a parking lot. Barakah was between two cars in the second aisle, waiting, and when the soldier leaned out, the killer drilled the doorway from top to bottom. Stinging shards pelted Bolan's cheek and arm as he jerked back. The instant the firing stopped, he tore on through, bent low behind a car so the terrorist couldn't see him. He heard the patter of feet, then the high-pitched whine of a turboshaft engine and an oath in Arabic.

Bolan peered over the trunk.

Barakah was fifty feet down the next aisle, glaring skyward, his escape barred by the Cobra. It faced him nose-on, the GE M-197 three-barrel 20 mm cannon pointed at him like an accusing finger.

Grimaldi was glaring back, and never, in all the years Bolan had known him, had he ever seen the look on Grimaldi's face that he saw now. It was the look of the avenging angel of death. He knew it, and so did Barakah, but that didn't keep the terrorist from snapping an FBP submachine gun to his shoulder and trying to bring the chopper down. He got off only a few rounds that banged harmlessly off the war bird's armor.

Now it was Grimaldi's turn. With a rate of fire of up to three thousand rounds a minute, the M-197 could turn a tank into a sieve. What it could do to mere flesh and bone had to be seen to be believed. Barakah twitched and danced like a puppet with its strings severed, but the dance was short-lived. His body began to break apart. Blast after blast chopped him to bits as Grimaldi fired...and fired.

In the sudden silence that followed, Bolan rose slowly. There was barely enough left of the terrorist to fill a garbage bag, and the asphalt around him looked as if it had been mangled by a thousand jackhammers.

Wails and sobs drifted out of the bowling alley. People needed help, and needed it badly. Bolan was skilled at rendering first aid, but if he stuck around, many thousands more were going to need help no one could render. Catching Grimaldi's attention, he indicated an open area where the chopper could land. The lanky pilot nodded, and in under a minute and a half they were airborne again.

"Head for Fort Meade," Bolan ordered.

"Sorry I got carried away," Grimaldi apologized as he banked. "All those bodies in the streets—"

"Have you heard from Hal about the trucks?"

"He says the company owns six."

"Then three are missing." Bolan slid the MP-5 between his legs. "Any word from the base?"

"At last report no one has tried to crash the gates. The evacuation of NSA personnel is underway, but it's going slowly. Bumper to bumper, is how Hal described it." Grimaldi gained altitude to avoid some phone lines. "Why three trucks, you reckon? The old pea in the shell game?"

"That would be my guess." Bolan had played it as a kid. A pea was placed under one of three walnut or pistachio shells. Then the shells were slid back and forth and around and around, changing places constantly to confuse the person who had to guess which shell hid the pea. Abbas was playing a variation, using sanitation trucks, instead of shells, and a thermonuclear device, instead of a pea.

"Hal also said to tell you the military police are out in force, and the civilian police in Laurel and other surrounding towns are establishing a cordon on all roads leading into the base." Grimaldi dropped the nose and put the aerial pedal to the metal. "Between you, me and the goalpost, buddy, I don't see how in hell these bozos are going to get that bomb anywhere near the NSA. Those garbage trucks will stick out like my aunt Harriet's big ears."

His friend had a quirky point. Bolan couldn't see how Abbas hoped to do it, either. And that troubled him. The terrorist leader was a lot of things, but stupid wasn't one of them. "Take us higher."

"One bird's-eye view, coming up." Grimaldi angled the Cobra upward, leveling off at fifteen hundred feet.

Bolan leaned forward for a better view. They were fast approaching Fort Meade's perimeter, a high fence stretching as far as the eye could see to the southeast and the northwest. Exactly how big the base was became disturbingly apparent. To make matters worse, some of it was forested, with trees growing close to the fence at several points.

"There's no way the MPs can prevent a breach," Grimaldi stated, summing up Bolan's thoughts.

"Patch into their communications net. If something happens, I want to know the second they do."

In a few seconds Bolan's helmet buzzed and a voice with a Southern drawl declared, "This is Charley Tango Two. Sir, we could use a few more bodies at Gate B to speed things along. We've got vehicles backed up both ways from here to forever."

"Negative, Charley Tango Two. We don't have

personnel to spare. You've got to get by on your own, Sergeant.''

''How close are we to that gate?'' Bolan asked.

''I can have you there in two shakes of our tail rotor.''

It was exactly as the MP had described. Traffic was backed up both ways for more than half a mile, inbound traffic because every vehicle had to be stopped and searched, outbound traffic because of the thousands of National Security Agency employees being sent home.

''Well, we can rule out the terrorists getting in that way,'' Grimaldi commented.

''Follow the fence,'' Bolan told him. It would be simple for Abbas to crash through with the stolen sanitation trucks. They were the next best thing to tanks. Once those huge mechanical monsters gained enough speed, they were virtually unstoppable.

''Maybe they'll wait until it's dark. That's what I'd do.''

Tactically, that made sense. But Bolan wouldn't put it past Abbas to do the unexpected and send the trucks in while it was still light. All that congestion was bound to delay the MPs' response time.

''Just got word from the big guy.'' Grimaldi cut into the base chatter. ''The Army is sending up some choppers of their own. It'll be a few minutes yet, though, before they're in the air.''

The more, the better, Bolan thought.

''There's also word the Air Force has scrambled a pair of F-16s. ETA in twenty-two minutes.''

A thick tract of trees bordered a section of fence just ahead. The fence itself bordered a lush park complete with bike trails, a playground and a baseball field with a game in progress. A canopy of maples, oaks and willows hid much of the rest.

Bolan peered intently through the foliage but saw nothing unusual. He shifted to focus on the next section, then stiffened. For a brief instant he thought he'd glimpsed a patch of orange near the park entrance. "Take us lower and back over that park."

"Do we root for the home team or the away team?"

Bolan scanned the area where he had seen the orange, but all he saw now was a young woman on a bike. She had on a red windbreaker, and he wondered if that was what he had seen.

"Sarge! There!"

It came hurtling out of the trees doing over fifty miles an hour, an orange behemoth that had jumped the curb and was making a beeline for the fence. The driver didn't care that the baseball diamond was in his way. Some of the kids saw or heard it and scrambled for safety, yelling to warn their friends. But for others there was no escape. Several youngsters who had been watching the game were scattered like tenpins. The boy on first base turned directly into the truck's grille and disappeared underneath.

"Those murdering bastards!"

The Cobra streaked toward the diamond but the pilot didn't dare fire, not with so many kids so close. Bolan grimaced as a coach was reduced to pulp by the truck's giant wheels. The outfielders had scattered, but a group of girls were at the edge of left field, transfixed by the horror. Bolan saw the truck swerve a few degrees, directly toward them, and his forefinger involuntarily curled around the MP-5's trigger.

"God, no," Grimaldi breathed.

At almost the last moment the girls parted and ran,

screaming their lungs out. The truck roared past, into more trees, and was only twenty-five yards from the fence.

"Can you take them out?" Bolan urged.

"I can sure as hell try."

Again the Cobra dipped, swooping toward the truck like a hawk toward prey. Tree limbs dissolved into splinters as the cannon ripped them to bits, but the truck never slowed, never changed course. It hit the fence dead-on and flattened a thirty-foot section like it was so much paper. Beyond were more trees, and a road.

Grimaldi banked for another strafing run.

At the same moment Bolan's headset blared. Reports were coming in from military police on the west perimeter. Another sanitation truck had broken through, and the MPs were in pursuit.

The chopper went into a dive. Grimaldi brought it in so low, Bolan clearly saw the terrorist in the cab. It was a young man of twenty or so with dark curly hair, smiling serenely to himself as if he were out for a Sunday ride instead of engaged in a heinous act of murder and destruction.

Thunderous death chugged from the M-197 and clods of dirt erupted like volcanoes, pockmarking the earth in a straight line directly into the truck. Jagged holes blossomed in the cab, but it rumbled on without swerving or slowing.

"If at first you don't succeed…" Grimaldi said, taking the war bird into a tight loop few pilots were skillful enough to duplicate.

Bolan put a hand to his helmet. Over the base channel came the clipped voice of an officer dispatching MPs to the east fence. A third garbage truck had busted through, and there were reports of people being deliberately run over. Abbas was sending his followers in from different directions to add to the confusion and make it that much harder for security to stop them.

"Where the hell are those Army copters?" Grimaldi complained. "We could sure use them right about now."

They could use a miracle, the soldier mused. For not only did they have to stop the three trucks, they had to find and disarm the bomb before it was programmed to go off. And that was when it hit him. Abbas wouldn't risk having the bomb neutralized. Odds were, it would be detonated manually when the truck it was in was close enough to the NSA.

Which meant they only had minutes before Fort George C. Meade was turned into a radioactive wasteland.

CHAPTER TWENTY-TWO

The Executioner looked up. Five hundred yards distant, across the tops of stately maples, reared the twin buildings that served as headquarters for the National Security Agency.

Below them the battered sanitation truck was approaching an intersection. So was a compact car. Two women were in the front seat, talking. They made no attempt to slow down, since they had the right of way. But the stop sign meant nothing to the terrorist. Too late, the driver of the compact slammed on the brakes. It slewed into the intersection and was struck broadside.

The truck shuddered, bounced and barreled on, leaving a twisted pile of metal and crushed remains.

"Get in front of him, Jack!" Bolan urged.

Grimaldi was already doing just that. A burst of speed carried them shy of the trees, where he swung the chopper around with dizzying speed. The young terrorist leaned over the steering wheel to peer up at them but didn't try to veer aside. "Come to Papa," Grimaldi grated between clenched teeth.

The whole copter vibrated to the blasts of the M-197 as a barrage of 20 mm rounds bored into the hood, into the windshield, into the driver. Grimaldi yipped for joy as the terrorist's body thrashed and danced.

Leaving the road, the truck plowed across a field and partway up a grassy knoll. The tires on the passenger side rose off the ground and gravity took over. In slow motion, the truck canted onto its side and slid toward the bottom, gouging deep ruts in the soil.

"Get me down there," Bolan said. Gray tendrils curled from the engine. A hand appeared in the driver's open window but sank back again. In his mind's eye Bolan imagined the terrorist arming the bomb. They might have mere seconds left.

Hardly had the Cobra landed than Bolan had the canopy open and was racing to the knoll. Again the hand appeared, smeared red, but again the terrorist couldn't pull himself out. Clambering up, Bolan slid along the frame until he could see down into the cab.

The young terrorist had slumped against the dash and was struggling for breath. A pair of holes in his chest, bubbling blood, hinted he wasn't long for this world.

Covering him, Bolan looked for sign of the bomb. "Where is it?" he snapped. "Do you have it or does someone else?"

The young man raised his head. He said something in Arabic, limply moved his hand in a circle, spit out, "Poof!" and grinned.

Bolan didn't know what the cobalt device looked like, but he was sure he would recognize a bomb when he saw one, and it wasn't in the cab. He went to hop down, then saw the terrorist prying at a pistol. "Thanks for nothing," Bolan said, and shot him through the forehead.

Grimaldi hadn't left the chopper. He was on the

radio with base security, reporting the location of the upended truck, when Bolan climbed in. "They've got a jeep full of MPs on the way," he stated after clicking off.

"What about the other two trucks?"

"Still converging on the NSA. The one to the west has been shot to hell but just won't stop. The one east of us is in heavy traffic, and the Army is reluctant to cut loose for fear of adding to the death toll."

Bolan strapped himself in. "Get us there."

Chaos had been unleashed on Fort Meade. Sirens and car horns blared, and the flashing lights of military police and emergency vehicles dappled the roadways. Columns of smoke curled from a dozen spots. When the Cobra vectored in, Bolan saw the smoke came from a long line of crushed and crumpled vehicles.

Off toward the NSA a fireball burst into bloom. A gas tank, Bolan suspected, as Grimaldi tilted the copter on its rotors and zoomed in.

Another sanitation truck was weaving in and out of the bumper-to-bumper traffic. With reckless abandon, the driver rammed into vehicle after vehicle. Some flipped over. Others were smashed aside like so many bumper cars.

MPs were trying to stop it, but they were handicapped by the snarl and by fleeing drivers who abandoned their cars and fled on foot.

"I can't fire into that," Grimaldi said.

In a frantic bid to stop the destruction, a military policeman in a jeep whipped it into the truck's path, then braked. Jumping out, he adopted a two-handed stance and popped rounds at the cab.

Gaining speed, the sanitation truck slammed into the jeep like a great orange rhino into a smaller rival. The

MP tried to leap to safety, but the jeep rolled over him as if he were no more than a stick. In all likelihood he was mercifully unconscious when the garbage truck drove over him a second later.

Grimaldi swore, declaring, "God, I hated to see that."

No more so than Bolan. "Use a TOW." The Cobra was armed with four tube-launched, optically launched, wire-guided antitank missiles. Designed with fins that snapped out once the missile cleared the tube, they had a range of over four thousand yards and a flight speed in excess of six hundred miles an hour.

"You want me to fire into all those people?"

"Jack, if that's the truck with the cobalt bomb..." Bolan left the statement unfinished. There was no need to elaborate.

Grimaldi's thin lips pinched together. "Say when. And hope to heaven I haven't lost my knack."

A junction had appeared, crammed with vehicles. Too many for even the sanitation truck to batter aside without backing up a few times. Bolan figured the driver would go around instead. On one side were a lot of parked cars and a concrete abutment that would stop a panzer. On the other, though, between the jammed cars and several buildings, was a long, narrow open space that would let the terrorist gain a little on his pursuers. "There." Bolan pointed.

Grimaldi winged wide for a better angle.

Autofire from two jeeps was pelting the truck, the bright glint of ricochets sparkling like fire emeralds. But none of the shots came near the cab. One of the jeeps fell behind when it had to brake for a pedestrian who blundered in front of it. The other narrowed the gap but then had to swerve to avoid a car trying to escape the jam. That left the garbage truck all by its lonesome.

Bolan's every nerve was on edge. If the TOW missed, in ten more blocks the truck would reach the NSA. The terrorist might take it into his head to trigger the nuke any time now.

Then came the moment of truth. The truck reached the intersection, and rather than smash on through, the driver did exactly as Bolan hoped and swerved to the left.

Not a heartbeat later one of the Cobra's launch tubes disgorged a missile. Lightning with fins, it flew almost too fast for the eye to follow, the blazing thrust of its exhaust a burning ember against the backdrop of sky and ground. It struck the truck's container dead center. The explosion lifted the rear end and punched it sideways, sending the truck careening in a flaming skid.

The driver's door was flung open and the terrorist bailed out. Landing on his shoulder, he did an acrobatic flip into a crouch. Not until then did Bolan realize it wasn't a "he" at all, but the same raven-haired woman he had seen on the tanker. She had an SMG in her right hand, a rolled up blanket under her left arm.

"See that?" Grimaldi hollered in excitement. "It must be the nuke."

The sanitation truck, now an inferno on only two wheels, crashed into a building, taking out most of the front wall. Fire, smoke and dust mushroomed outward.

"Find a spot to land," Bolan commanded.

One of the jeeps had caught up and MPs were spilling out both sides but they were drilled before their combat boots touched the ground. Four good men died in half as many seconds.

The female terrorist darted into the smoke, but Bolan saw her reappear as the Cobra was descending. By the time he climbed down, she had ducked into a three-story building midway along the block. He sprinted over.

The door opened onto a paneled corridor awash in fluorescent light. A middle-aged man in a beige suit was in a fetal position on the floor, clutching his abdomen and groaning. Blood seeped from between his outspread fingers. On seeing Bolan, he recoiled in fear and pleaded, "Please don't shoot me!"

Careful not to take his eyes off the corridor, the soldier sank onto one knee. "I'm after the woman who did this to you. Where is she?"

"She ran off," the man said, his face contorted in agony. "All I did was step from my office to see what all the racket was, and she barged in and shot me. Why? What did I ever do to her?" His chin sagged to his chest. "I feel so woozy, so strange—"

The man slumped onto his stomach, his eyes rolling in their sockets.

Fully aware that at any moment he might be obliterated, Bolan moved swiftly from room to room. In one of the offices two women were cowering under their desks. He asked if they had seen the terrorist and they whispered she had gone on down the hall.

At the bottom of a flight of stairs Bolan paused and cocked his head. The sound of footsteps drifted down. He was at the first landing when a door banged open and shut, and for a second the blare of car horns and the shriek of sirens was crystal clear. It told him exactly where she had gone.

The roof exit had a bar, not a doorknob. Bolan pushed as gently as possible to minimize the noise, but he need not have worried. An SMG was chattering close by. Inching the door far enough open to slip out, he spied his quarry. She was on her knees by the roof cresting, her back to him, firing down into the street. Beside her was the bundled blanket.

Bolan took precise aim. Somehow she sensed him, because she suddenly sprang to her left and whirled, whipping up a Skorpion. Bolan fired a millisecond before she did, his rounds ripping her from thigh to shoulder. The few shots she got off bit into the roof. Staggering, she lost her grip on the SMG and fell onto her side.

Hate-filled eyes fixed on Bolan as he walked to the blanket. He gingerly unraveled it and frowned when he discovered nothing was in it.

The woman laughed. She was quite lovely, but now her creamy complexion was marred by dirt and grime, her disheveled hair caked with dust. "I had you fooled, demon," she said in flawless English.

Bolan kicked the Skorpion out of her reach. "Is it in the third truck?"

"Do you honestly think I would tell you?" She laughed again, then coughed, and scarlet drops dribbled from a corner of her mouth. "Soon you will die, you and many more. I will look down on you in hell from paradise and savor your eternal suffering."

"All those innocent people you killed," Bolan said.

"There are no innocents in this world. Only those who think they are," the woman responded. "You are tainted, demon, you and all your kind, with the mark of Satan, our manifest foe."

Bolan wasn't about to debate dogma with a fanatic. He frisked her for weapons, found a pistol and a dagger and sent them skittering across the roof. "Someone will be along to get you to a hospital if you live long enough." He had to get to the Cobra and began to back away.

"You cannot stop us, demon," the woman said, smiling rapturously. "We are God's soldiers, and none can stand before Him."

To the west several Army copters were performing strafing runs. Apaches, from the look of them, their chain guns blazing. Bolan pointed and told her, "The last truck will never reach the NSA. Al-Jabbar has failed."

The woman's rosy lips creased in a mocking grin. "You think you are so smart. But our leader is smarter than all of you combined. Soon enough, you will find that out for yourself. As the flesh burns from your body and your bones are reduced to dust, remember, demon, that I, Jamilah, said it would be so."

One of the Apaches let fly with a rocket, and a fireball mushroomed high into the sky. For a moment Bolan took his eyes off the woman to watch it, and when he looked back again, she was on her feet, swaying unsteadily. Thinking she was going for her weapons, he covered her, warning, "Don't try it."

Jamilah steadied herself and squared her slender shoulders. "You are a formidable foe, demon. Truly, Satan is strong in you. But God is stronger in me. And to Him I commit my soul."

Before Bolan had any inkling what she was up to, she wheeled, and with surprising speed and vigor, leaped to the rim. Balanced on the brink, she glanced at him and smiled one last time. "Death to the Great Satan! All glory to God and His children everywhere!" Then she jumped.

Bolan ran to the lip and peered over just as she hit

the sidewalk. She almost landed on top of a woman with a small child, and both screamed in horror.

Racing down the stairs, the soldier jogged to the Cobra. There was no need to check Jamilah for signs of life. She couldn't have survived the trauma.

Grimaldi had the latest news. "The Army copters blew the snot out of the third truck. MPs are on the scene, and they just radioed in there's no sign of the cobalt bomb anywhere." He nodded at the lifeless husk across the street. "Did she have it?"

"No."

"Then where the hell is it?"

Bolan wished he knew. "Take us up again. I'd like to see what's left of the last truck for myself." There wasn't much. The rocket had turned the container into twisted scrap and split the cab like a melon. Amazingly, although the driver died in the blast, his body was still intact and had been dragged from the burning wreckage. Bolan had Grimaldi descend for a closer look and recognized the Palestinian he had chased halfway across the Mediterranean.

An officer was on the scene, a major directing soldiers in a search of nearby trees and high weeds.

"Do you think they'll find it?" Grimaldi asked.

No, Bolan didn't. Trying to reason out the puzzle, he had his friend climb to five hundred feet and level off. Three trucks, three dead members of Al-Jabbar, but no bomb. It was possible the device had been destroyed by one of the missiles. It was also possible it hadn't been in the trucks to begin with.

Bolan thought back to the shell game he played as a boy. Sometimes the pea hadn't been under any of them. Sometimes the person moving the shells palmed the pea to trick the players. "We've been snookered."

"I didn't quite catch that."

"The bomb was never in the trucks. They were decoys to draw us off." Bolan sat up. Jamilah had been right about one thing. Abbas was as cunning as they came. And as ruthless. He had sacrificed her and the other two in order to keep base security occupied while he or someone else snuck the bomb in right under the military's nose. "Head for the National Security Agency."

"What are we looking for?"

"We'll know it when we see it." Or so Bolan hoped. It might be too much to expect Abbas to still be using the stolen vehicles, but the terrorists had been on the go ever since and might not have had the time to steal new ones.

"Why do I feel like someone just pulled the pin on a grenade and dropped it under my seat?" Grimaldi remarked.

Traffic was bumper-to-bumper clear into the parking lots that surrounded the NSA. A lot of people had tired of sitting there and climbed out to stretch their legs or talk. Heavily armed security was posted at the entrances and exits. More were on the roofs with sniper rifles.

"The terrorists would have to be invisible to sneak in there."

"They don't need to. The bomb has a blast radius of half a mile." Bolan twisted to scan adjoining parking areas. Abbas wouldn't be foolish enough to try to get any closer to the NSA than was absolutely necessary. But there were so many parking spaces, so many cars. Spotting him would be like finding that elusive needle in a haystack. If he was there at all.

"Take us as low as you can go without hitting anything, and circle."

"Too bad we don't have a Geiger counter," Grimaldi mentioned. "That puppy is bound to give off enough radiation to register."

Bolan shifted toward the other side of the chopper, scouring row after row. It occurred to him that Abbas would want to plant the bomb out of eyesight of the security teams at the NSA. "Hop over that small building on the left," he suggested.

On the other side was another parking lot. Bolan scoured it from end to end and was about to tell his friend to try a lot to the north when he noticed a Dumpster garbage bin in the building's shadow.

Parked beside it were the SUV and the sedan.

"Take us back to the other side and land," Bolan said, opening his duffel.

"What's up? Did you see something?"

Bolan told him. "As soon as I'm out, dust off and inform the base commander. Have him throw a cordon around the area, but warn him not to move in or it might provoke the terrorists into making martyrs of themselves."

"And what am I supposed to do while you're playing cat and mouse? Twiddle my rudders?"

"No matter what, don't let the SUV or the sedan leave."

"Consider it done."

Bolan retrieved a pair of grenades, slapped a magazine into the MP-5 and again went through the routine of climbing out. He rushed to the nearest corner and around to the rear. A cautious peek assured him the two vehicles were still there. He also spotted three men on the near side of the garbage bin, crouched around a gleaming metallic object about the size of a football. "Bingo," he said under his breath.

One of the men was the other terrorist from Thenas. The other two looked enough alike to be brothers and had to be Aban and Sefu Abbas. The older of the pair was pressing buttons on the bomb's control pad. Programming it, Bolan realized.

The fate of untold thousands was in the warrior's hands. He took a bead on Aban Abbas, then saw him go rigid. A jeep full of MPs was conducting a sweep of the parking lot. There hadn't been time for the base commander to issue orders for everyone to stay away, so it was mere coincidence they had happened by just as the trio were arming the device.

The MPs cruised past the trash bin, oblivious to the fact it hid the ones they were after. Aban Abbas and the others stood and turned to watch the jeep depart.

Bolan sped across a grassy strip and was almost on top of them before they heard him. All three whirled, the terrorist from Thenas unlimbering a subgun from under his jacket. A burst from the MP-5 chopped him down.

"Don't move!" Bolan growled at the brothers. He would just as soon shoot them, but they might be of use.

Sefu jerked his hands in the air but Aban merely glared and said, "So. Face-to-face with the elusive demon at last."

"Have you programmed it?" Bolan demanded, bobbing his chin at the gleaming cobalt nightmare.

"What is that quaint American expression?" Aban smirked. "It is for us to know and you to find out."

"Back up and keep your hands where I can see them." Bolan had to get a look at the control pad.

Aban and Sefu swapped glances, and Aban nodded. Both obeyed, but Aban did so reluctantly. "You can't disarm it," he declared. "Not unless you know the code. And I'm the only one who does."

A rectangular digital timer at the center of the pad read 0:00:00. Bolan had stopped them in time. "No need to disarm a bomb that hasn't been armed yet." He returned the terrorist leader's smirk. "It's over, Abbas."

"Is it?" Aban said, and suddenly barked commands in Arabic.

Two things happened at once. The downed terrorist sat up, sluggishly bringing the HK-53 into play, while Sefu screeched like a banshee and sprang.

Bolan took out the most immediate threat first. Three rounds through the "dead" terrorist's cheek disposed of him for good. The Executioner swiveled to do the same to Sefu Abbas, but the younger brother was faster than he appeared. A double-edged knife struck the MP-5, swatting the barrel aside, and Sefu clamped one hand on Bolan's throat and hiked the knife for a fatal thrust.

Wrenching loose, Bolan slammed the SMG into Sefu's face, knocking him back. He leveled the MP-5 but saw Aban Abbas dive toward the cobalt bomb, an arm outstretched, one finger stabbing at a red button. The purpose of that button was plain. Spinning, Bolan kicked Abbas in the head a microsecond before the button could be pushed, tumbling the older brother into the grass.

Then Sefu was on him. Grabbing the MP-5, he slashed at Bolan's throat. The soldier jumped back, sparing his jugular, but Sefu held on to the SMG and stabbed low at his groin. Sidestepping, Bolan let go of

he MP-5 and slammed a palm-heel strike against
Sefu's nose that reduced it to grisly pulp and rocked
he man on his heels.

Aban was up and lunging at the bomb.

Whirling, Bolan got hold of a wrist and a forearm
and flipped him head over heels. He raised his foot to
stomp on Aban's head but Sefu closed in again, cut-
ing and hacking, trying to force him back so Aban
could reach the bomb. The soldier gripped the younger
brother's wrist, snapped the arm as straight as a board
and drove his knee into the elbow.

Sefu shrieked in torment.

Before Bolan could capitalize, there was Aban, try-
ng for the bomb one more time, a crazed glint in his
eyes, his finger spiking at the red button. Bolan tackled
him and they rolled five or six feet. Aban rose first,
swinging. A right cross clipped the Executioner's chin.
A left caught him across the cheek.

Blocking another right, Bolan connected with a
solid uppercut that flattened the mastermind. He raised
his right hand for a killing stroke, only to have it
seized by Sefu.

"I've got him, brother!" the younger Abbas cried.

The soldier couldn't keep the older brother from the
bomb indefinitely. He had to end it quickly. Arcing
his left knee into Sefu's groin, he doubled him over,
which freed him to leap at Aban, who fought back
with a ferocity born of obsession.

Both of Abbas's hands wrapped around Bolan's
throat, but he didn't resist. The terrorist squeezed,
seeking to strangle him, but still the soldier didn't try
to break free. For in the meantime, he had drawn the
Beretta, and now, jamming the muzzle against Aban's
sternum, he squeezed off four swift shots.

Sefu screamed as his brother fell. He had the knife in his other hand now, and he hurled himself forward in berserk rage.

At point-blank range Bolan fire twice into the younger brother's face. Sefu catapulted against the trash bin, tried to right himself and sprawled in a heap.

Sinking down next to the bomb, Bolan checked the display. It still read 0:00:00. Catastrophe had been averted. He holstered the Beretta and leaned back, breathing deep.

Grimaldi dashed around the corner holding a pistol. He stared at the bodies, then lowered the side arm and cracked, ''So this is what you do when my back is turned? You sit around loafing?''

The Executioner grinned. It felt good to be alive.

James Axler
Öutlanders®

SEA OF
PLAGUE

The loyalties that united the Cerberus warriors have become undone, as a bizarre messenger from the future provides a look into encroaching horror and death. Kane and his band have one option: fix two fatal fault lines in the time continuum—and rewrite history before it happens. But first they must restore power to the barons who dare to defy the greater evil: the mysterious new Imperator. Then they must wage war in the jungles of India, where the deadly, beautiful Scorpia Prime and her horrifying bio-weapon are about to drown the world in a sea of plague....

In the Outlands, the shocking truth is humanity's last hope.

DEATH LANDS®

Damnation Road Show

*Available in June 2003
at your favorite retail outlet.*

Eerie remnants of preDark times linger a century after the
nuclear blowout. But a traveling road show gives new
meaning to the word *chilling*. Ryan and his warrior group
have witnessed this carny's handiwork in the ruins and
victims of unsuspecting villes. Even facing tremendous odds
does nothing to deter the companions from challenging this
wandering death merchant and an army of circus freaks. And
no one is aware that a steel-eyed monster from the past is
preparing a private act that would give Ryan star billing....

James Axler
Outlanders®

TALON AND FANG

Kane finds himself thrown twenty-five years into a parallel future, a world where the mysterious Imperator has seemingly restored civilization to America. In this alternate reality, only Kane and Grant have survived, and the spilled blood has left them estranged. Yet Kane is certain that somewhere in time lies a different path to tomorrow's reality—and his obsession may give humanity their last chance to battle past and future as a sinister madman controls the secret heart of the world.

In the Outlands, the shocking truth is humanity's last hope.

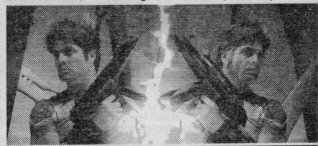

Or order your copy now by sending your name, address, zip or postal code, along with a check or money order (please do not send cash) for $6.50 for each book ordered ($7.99 in Canada), plus 75¢ postage and handling ($1.00 in Canada), payable to Gold Eagle Books, to:

In the U.S.	In Canada
Gold Eagle Books	Gold Eagle Books
3010 Walden Avenue	P.O. Box 636
P.O. Box 9077	Fort Erie, Ontario
Buffalo, NY 14269-9077	L2A 5X3

Please specify book title with your order.
Canadian residents add applicable federal and provincial taxes.

GOUT25

THE Destroyer®

WOLF'S BANE

A wild child of the bayous, Leon Grosvenor is a two-legged freak show of shaggy hair and talons with an insatiable hunger for raw flesh. His unique abilities as a bona fide loup-garou have earned him gainful employment as a contract killer for Cajun mafia boss Armand "Big Crawdaddy" Fortier. Remo's not buying this werewolf business, but when he gets a glimpse of good ol' Leon's wet work—well, he's still not a believer, but he *is* certain that Leon needs to be put out of everybody's misery. And damn soon.

Available in July 2003 at your favorite retail outlet.